A TASTE OF VENGEANCE

A SAM ABEL NOVEL

CLARKE MAYER

First Published by ROGUE STORIES LLC in 2023.

ISBN: 979-8-9856289-4-4

Cover Design by J Caleb Design

Editing by JD Book Services

To Risa, who always read my work and listened to my ideas. Her red pen is ferocious but fair. All storytellers should be lucky enough to have a friend like her.

1

———

Father Jan Lukas had been waiting at the mist-carpeted train platform in Bern for longer than usual. The locomotive that had delivered him chugged far off in the distance, wheezing like an exasperated animal as it traveled along the rail. Every soft tick of his watch was another paranoia-inducing second passing by. The Bern blackout was in full effect, which left the platform in the mediocre light of a half-moon.

There were only several other people on the platform: one disheveled boy selling papers heralding another day's outcome of the war, a young woman tending to a cooing baby, and a dirt-stained drunkard muttering to himself absentmindedly. It wasn't like the driver to be late, and this gave Lukas cause for concern. He considered finding a room for the night, then boarding the morning train to return home; however, his faith in his work convinced him to abandon this idea.

The train he'd arrived in was delayed by several hours

—bombing raid, or at least, the threat of one. They seemed endless. He usually accounted for them in his schedule, but the earlier warning had delayed the train particularly long.

He was several miles outside of Stuttgart when he heard the sirens wailing. The train halted soon after. The alert woke an otherwise slumbering city to muffled and echoing horns of warning along the German countryside. The night was black as ink, and though no fighters or bombers appeared, the train lingered anyway. When the signal was triggered, all of the train's interior lights were turned off, leaving the carriage engrossed by the stillness of the late hours and the soft whispers of speculation from the passengers about when the train might move again. Even if no bombers were nearby, there was always the risk that the tracks ahead could be out, which would be another setback entirely. Luckily, that had not been the case, so after roughly three hours of waiting, the locomotive started up again and continued its journey to the Swiss border. Lukas was thankful they had not been forced to switch trains, which was always a nuisance, and one that was particularly unsettling for a man smuggling state secrets.

The trip went as well for Lukas as it could have. Even his survey by the border guards had been uneventful, perhaps because the night-shift soldiers were less sharp. Even though being caught would mean certain death, he held little fear. He'd reconciled his own mortality long ago, but could not part with the information stitched into the soles of his shoes. Neither could the men he was going to see.

So now he stood on the platform checking his watch once more. He was going on a whole ten whole minutes of waiting. It felt like it had been an hour. Idle men are suspicious. The longer they linger, the more interest in their activities grows.

Night trips were traditionally safer, but they were not free from danger entirely. Battle broke out when the men behind the lines *said* it did, not because it might be inconvenient for travelers. It didn't matter if it was in the countryside or a sleepy train platform, no place was free from action.

He dropped his head, let his eyes close, then said softly to himself, "Lord, I thank thee for a safe arrival. Through your grace I live to see another day. With your blessing I might live to see another. Your presence is my shield, and your word my sword, and with both I swear to defend your kingdom. Should you will it, I shall receive you, for the power and the glory are yours, for ever and ever, amen."

Lukas was a stag-like man. He was trim and astute, with sharp piercing eyes and a nimble spirit. He'd always been skilled at not drawing attention to himself if possible, though he was also quick to flee if he did.

The drunk strewn across the sidewalk hiccuped, the evening's booze rising up into his throat to haunt him as he turned over and cozied up against a cement wall. Luckily for him the night was agreeable—it was chilly for a summer night, but pleasant all the same. Dimly lit by the lamp casting a conical amber glow over the center of the sidewalk, the boy selling papers fished in his pocket for a cigarette. *A little young to be smoking*, Lukas thought, but with bombs falling daily, who was he to chastise?

Why is a boy out selling newspapers in the middle of the night? he wondered. *Who does he expect to buy them? The drunk? The woman with the baby?* Certainly not Lukas. He considered inquiring about the boy's presence during the devil's hour, but thought better than making conversation with anyone he didn't have to. In fact, he had no words for anyone in Bern other than his handler or his adjutants. The less people aware of his presence in Bern, the better.

The handler was an American by the name of Combe, and he was preceded by two men initially referred to as "The New York Boys." Lukas had been questioned relentlessly, felt out over the course of six or so months to deduce whether he was a worthy ally, before he'd even met Combe himself. The priest proved his value when he delivered, and *kept* delivering. In short order he started working with the American in Peenemünde.

Traveling under the guise of priesthood didn't raise flags typically, but *everyone* was suspect on the Führer's watch, even the woman with the chortling newborn and the drunk seated against the cement wall. One might suggest that a Catholic priest was just as suspect as any of the other undesirables imprisoned, but a man of the faith doesn't scream "enemy," even if he was on the list—especially if the priest could provide a passport necessary to justify his travels. He'd flipped his faith like a chameleon to suit any scenario he found himself in: today a Catholic, tomorrow a Lutheran. They'd come for *all* of them eventually, because no creature of divination usurped the Führer's law. The proverbial sun was setting, but it hadn't faded entirely.

It helped that he possessed an amiable disposition, as might be expected of those delivering the Lord's word. A never-ending smile stretched across thin lips—though it had wavered outside of his parish in the last several years. Anyone willing to hear the word of God was met by his rosy cheeks. The emerald eyes were disarming as well, and though he'd dedicated his servitude to Christ, in another life where he was free to pursue women, he'd probably have cleaned up. As it was, in his church the women had taken a liking to him, gathering to hear his sermons even on days when there was no service. "Just came to light a candle, Father," they'd say, though they'd always seemed to forget to actually do it once they'd gotten talking. They claimed it was because his proclaiming of the message was so powerful, especially during war time when it had been needed most, but the men had alerted him to the truth. "Don't be näive, Father," one had joked. "You listen when we don't, and you're easy on the eyes, see?"

That had been quite some time ago. He didn't deliver the message like he once had—to pews teeming with people. Those days had ceased, specifically after his place of worship had been devastated so badly it was structurally unsound. A blast through the side wall during the exchange of power brought on by the *Anschluss* had torn open a hole larger than most homes. Now his message was confined to beer halls and basements, locations of safety from both bullets and Nazis; it was still vibrant as ever to anyone who'd listen, albeit with less volume. He didn't know whether the days of old would return. There was a time when it was safe for the parishioners to walk to the house of worship, a time when he could preach freely and safely. He dreamt the day would come again—with his involvement it *might*. That was why he was standing there in the middle of the night, waiting anxiously on the train platform in Bern for a car that still hadn't arrived.

The boy locked eyes with him briefly, tucked the paper in his hand back into a satchel wrapped over his shoulder, then inhaled from the cigarette. His eyes lit up, small orange circles reflecting in the wolf-like irises of a night creature, then he stepped off the sidewalk, out of the pooling light, and into the shadows of the blacked-out street. Perhaps out of curiosity, Lukas let his gaze follow the stringy kid as he faded into darkness, but promptly noticed him duck his head into the passenger-side window of a parked car for a moment. He exchanged words with the passenger, flicked his cigarette casually into the night air, then stomped on it before disappearing completely.

A car engine rattled to life, then two headlights flared before the car began to crawl forward. Once it came into focus, Lukas saw it approach his position. His nerves fired in unison, a tingling sensation that sent his heart rate rocketing and weakened his knees. As the car approached, the headlights illuminating Lukas as if singling him out, he took ragged breaths. To flee would be unwise—they'd already spotted him, friend or foe, and the best choice was to act naturally.

He was, after all, in neutral territory, as neutral as a territory could be as of late, but that didn't mean that he couldn't be picked off without incident—especially in a city of spies. The enemy and the ally occupied the same shadows in Bern; sometimes it could be difficult to decipher who was who. He was just a priest on a curb, waiting for a ride and enjoying the cool night air. Why should anyone suspect of him of wrong-doing?

The car jerked sharply, hugging the curb, then

stopped in front of him. The passenger cracked the window, just enough that Lukas could hear his voice say, "Dangerous for a man to be out this late at night." His dialect was Swiss-German with a tinge of native Italian.

Staring back at him through the dark passenger seat was the most vocal of The New York Boys, a stringy fellow known as Louie. Briefly, his profile was illuminated by the light of the driver's cigarette. A small cloud of smoke poured from the seam of the open window.

Lukas wrenched the rear passenger-side door open and slumped into the bench seat. He was hugged by the plump leather as the driver, known as Phil, eyed him through the rearview mirror. Even though the two of them had met many times before, Phil's eyes were inquisitive, darting and untrusting. He never spoke as much as his co-conspirator. Louie half-turned and presented Lukas a cigarette, but the priest waved it off. The car lurched forward and away from the curb, and they were swallowed in quiet and darkness.

The city was sleeping. A car with three men traveling in the dead of night was suspect, but neither Louie or Phil showed any fear. Lukas himself relaxed further, happy to be free of the train platform. Regardless of whether they were uniformed, *Abwehr* and *SS* officers in plain clothes still prowled the neighborhood, just as their American and British enemies did. Within the Swiss borders no man was sovereign if you asked him the right questions.

They traveled through the inner city for some time, as was customary, first passing over a small bridge that crossed the Aare, then turning what some might consider unnecessarily down small side streets—even doubling back several times and passing the same monuments. This was an effort to lose a tail or spot one if it existed. There were so few cars on the road that night one might think it was easy to spot someone following them, but Lukas, and the men escorting him, were smart enough to know some spotters stuck to the foot paths. It was safe to assume that anyone standing on a street corner and watching their movements was dangerous.

The car finally arrived at a cobblestone path, bouncing and rattling over the stones before coming to a halt in a medieval section of the city. Flanking the driver's side was a three-story building of stone and arched windows. It featured no name on its façade, just a lone wooden door on the street level and another nearby embedded in a high wall and covered by the branches of a tree. The only guiding illumination was the falloff from the car's headlights.

Lukas exited the vehicle without a word, leaving the two New York Boys smoking up front. He proceeded, but not before checking over each of his shoulders, through the door and into a dark courtyard. At his approach, mice scattered toward the weak points in the walls. The rear door of the building, a fire exit, was open. Lukas climbed the narrow steps to the third floor, feeling his way through the dark corridor until he arrived at the apartment he sought.

On the wooden door, a shaft of moonlight illumi-nated the words "Ansel Combe, Special Assistant to the American Minister" etched into a gold plate. Lukas produced the code: knock once, wait, knock again, wait, then knock twice. A series of locks and latches were undone from behind the door, then the figure of the scholarly Ansel Combe appeared silhouetted by candlelight.

"You're late," Combe said, ushering Lukas through the threshold and quickly sealing the door behind him.

"Maybe you can convince the allies to hold off on their campaigns," Lukas grumbled.

Combe was a plump man, well-groomed and professorial. He'd fit superbly lecturing from a podium in a university hall. A white-collared shirt peeked above an olive-green cashmere sweater, a greying beard dangling over both. A pair of spectacles rested gently on the bridge of his nose.

Lukas didn't always meet Combe. Sometimes the priest would hand his materials off to Louie and Phil and be on his way. Tonight, it seemed, Combe was available.

Combe directed a hand toward a wooden chair opposite his own. The room stank of pipe and cigarette smoke. The seat Lukas took was still warm—he wasn't the only source who'd come to visit the American this night. Lukas read the man's expression. He looked extra wary tonight.

"How are you?" Combe asked. The handler always started with a temperature check.

"Tired of waiting," Lukas snapped. "What more do you need? How many more photographs must one take before action is taken? You're wasting time. Do you understand the value of what I'm bringing you?" Realizing that he'd unintentionally raised his voice, Lukas forced himself to calm down. He was shooting off from the mouth like an automatic weapon.

"I don't call the action plan," Combe said, clearly trying to disarm his asset. "I just contribute." Unlike

Lukas, Combe remained calm and steadfast. "And I very much recognize the value of your material, as do my superiors."

"You go and tell your bosses something for me, yes? You tell them every day wasted is another where I grow more impatient. I can only be patient for so long."

"I don't know that threats will yield the results you're looking for," Combe warned. "We're all working very hard—"

"Not *all* of you," Lukas interjected.

Combe grimaced, then lit a cigarette. Lukas had learned that keeping agents and operators happy was the most difficult part of Combe's job. One might think handling and transporting material from an enemy-surrounded territory was the most challenging aspect, but he'd explained to Lukas that managing personalities had commanded most of the handler's patience. Worse still was when assets threatened their allegiance. In this world, loyalty changed at the drop of a hat.

"I'll see what we can do," Combe reassured Lukas, then rose from his chair and ambled to the kitchenette. He retrieved a filet knife from a drawer and handed it to the priest. Lukas frowned, then removed both of his shoes. He poked the knife into the sole of the first of the pair, needled at the fabric inside with the tip, slashing here and slicing there until he'd finally removed the sole completely. From the dismembered shoe Lukas produced several lengths of photographic negative film. Combe grabbed one of the rolls and held it up to the light. Within one of the cells was a spear-like shape of a rocket.

2

───────

A torrid breeze rattled the pine needles that decorated Peenemünde's shores. Like a musical instrument, the displacement of the flora had a symphonic quality, something divine and foreboding as if the weather was being conducted by Beethoven himself. The sensation was uncanny, prickling the hairs on Lothar Eichler's neck in the same way cold air might, yet the weather around Usedom was anything but cold. Something was stirring on the beach-front forest of the scientific community—Eichler was sure of it.

And shouldn't he be? Had he been crying wolf when he warned his superiors of the low-level security present at Flussrand? Certainly not. The military base had suffered a sabotage unlike any since the war had begun, and among its casualties was the dreaded tank *Erdschlag*, pet project of the hawkish Eichler himself.

The once project manager had made clear that Germany was at risk, raising the red flag as much as one could up the party ladder. No one listened. When he asked for more men, no one listened. When he requested the support of the *SS* his pleas fell on deaf ears. Eichler even tried to open lines of communication to the *Reichsführer* himself.

The tank had been destroyed by a saboteur, and all Eichler had been able to do was wonder why no one had come to his aid. Why had the regime risked the safety of a massive project, specifically one of such a great financial drain? Standing on the sun-drenched shores of Peenemünde, he finally understood. Resources and attention had been diverted *here*, to the quiet forest nestled at the bottom of the Baltic Sea. Here, where no one assumed any activity at all took place. To prying eyes, only vacationers looking for sun and sand were visible—innocent citizens partaking in leisure, perhaps to escape the bombed-out husks of their cities.

That was anything but the case. Upon closer inspection, the secrets of the *Wermacht* facility revealed themselves to anyone looking hard enough. Wedged in between stacks of pines were launching pads, and tucked inside the walls of factories were rocket prototypes. One in particular, the A-4 project, was hidden particularly well. There was still plenty of tinkering to be done, and not enough men to do it, but it was not far from being perfected—not far at all. Some more adjustments, and then Speer's plan to roll the weapons off assembly lines ten and twenty at a time would come to fruition. And who had been tasked to protect the island and its interests? Lothar Eichler, of course.

Some men fail upwards. In fact, Lothar Eichler believed most, if not all, of his superiors had. It seemed that to earn the attention of the Führer one might need just commit a blunder and blame other parties. Lothar

Eichler, some might say, was one of those people. Somehow, perhaps because of his ability to deflect blame and come out of sticky situations shining, he had only continued on his path of upward mobility. He hadn't dodged a bullet—he'd successfully negotiated the attack of an armada. Yet unlike his cohorts, he lacked the political and military background which favored rung-climbers to reach the heights of the Führer's inner circle.

Despite his failures, Eichler had parlayed his interrogation at *Prinz-Albrecht-Straße* into a warning regarding gross negligence within the secret-keeping of coveted weapons projects. Though the blame for the destruction of Flussrand had initially landed at Eichler's feet, he'd swayed his inquisitors' opinions. He had a paper trail of issued warnings and requests, and proof that his petitions to his superiors had gone unheard. So, when the axe fell regarding the damaged tank, it landed on no one in particular. Instead, an effort was made to ensure the same mistakes did not befall the site at Peenemünde; part of the solution was Eichler, now owner of the coveted title *Sicherheitskapitän*.

The wind tickled the flaps of his long coat as the sun rose along the eastern sands. Infinite beach stretched north and south. On the horizon, he saw a plane sputter through a jagged bit of cloud. *A British sortie?* As a second plane came into focus, he recognized the form of the two Messerschmitt 109 aircraft. *Wilde Sau*, Eichler thought. *Patrol fighters, no cause for concern.*

There were compromises at the site, the most glaring of which was Peenemünde's lack of heavy artillery and air defense systems. "To turn the site into a military stronghold would only raise its profile," was what his superiors had claimed, and to that he agreed. If one wanted to scream "strike here" to an enemy fighter, then all they needed to do was display air defense weaponry. On the contrary, a site that did not present as well-defended didn't really present as anything at all. Because of that, air defenses at the site were minimal. For all intents and purposes, a quick fly-by of Peenemünde would suggest nothing out of the ordinary. And so it was decided that the facility would hide in plain sight; its defenses would be sealed lips and subtlety.

Did the newly dubbed *Sicherheitskapitän* rely on some extrasensory prowess to perceive threats before they arrived as if gifted some extraordinary ability? Who could know? More likely, logic prompted him to be skeptical. The comfort of Peenemünde's inhabitants, their aloofness to the battle being waged in other directions, the high value of secrets and the risk of trading them were what made Eichler so uneasy. After all, it had been under his nose that his very own secretary, the defector Sigrid Lang, had fooled him and sold his project out to the Allies.

Another point that bothered Eichler, and what others failed to lose sleep over, was the question, "What happened to Udo Ramm?"

"Dead," most had replied.

"Figured out and put in front of a firing squad," others had said.

"Plane crashed over the Atlantic," some had guessed, but Eichler suspected all of the conjecture to be untrue. Eichler, fearful of more sabotage, postulated that Ramm had defected.

Security was tight, and getting into Peenemünde was a multi-step process that required *much* more than credentials. Just finding one's way into a restricted area was difficult, because most Peenemünders within departments knew of each other. And yet, despite the fences, the obscurity of the location, the newly added presence of Himmler's *SS*, the hush-hush protocol surrounding the facilities' activities, and the ability to deploy at least *some* anti-aircraft defenses, the hairs on Eichler's neck stood at attention much in the same way they did during the end-of-life period at Flussrand. Something stirred; it was in the disquietude of the air.

For those other than Eichler, mornings at Peenemünde were a time of leisure and activity. Most residents enjoyed the opportunity for a quick dip in the ocean before shuffling off to their respective departments. Some were lucky enough to have homes not far from the shoreline. Many of those afforded the luxury were primaries or heads of their designated departments. It wasn't uncommon to spot an engineer working on his backstroke as the sun rose over the ocean, then taking notes at a launch pad by the early afternoon.

A pudgy man—stripped down to his underwear—placed a swimming cap over his head, then waved to Eichler as he submerged his toes in the approaching tide. Eichler nodded before fixing his attention toward the horizon. He considered the early morning a time of great vulnerability; it was a perfect time for the enemy to strike, especially bombers and fighters. Most of the workers and families were still half in dream state, and fighters could navigate by the morning light.

Despite his lack of good sleep, Eichler's complexion was healthy. The sun and saltwater had done wonders for him, as well as perhaps just the general air of camaraderie and community surrounding the facility. Long gone was the company of grunts and soldiers. It had been replaced by the candid smiles of women and children scattered among the men who called Peenemünde home. To be awarded a post at Peenemünde was a luxury, and one that required great scrutiny into the past of a potential recruit. After a preliminary examination, the *SS* would do their own due diligence, and if one passed, they would be asked to come to Peenemünde. No one learned any details about the site until they actually arrived, and even then they knew little of what it had to offer. In fact, most Germans didn't even know Peenemünde existed.

Satisfied as he could be that no threats were looming, at least not *visibly*, Eichler folded his hands neatly behind his back and set off into the forest. Peenemünde's eastern side was abundant in pines. The trees added camouflage and kept the island obscured, but also gave the location a strange beauty where beach and forest coexisted. The temperatures were moderate and favorable, and the air fresh and warm. The quiet was enjoyable as well. The air space had been relatively restricted, patrolled only by *Luftwaffe* aircraft at Göring's disposal. The air strip on the northern tip of the island was controlled by the air branch, at times working in concert with the Peenemünde operation, even if it had primarily been a *Wermacht*-controlled endeavor.

The greedy hands of the *SS* had reached for the operation recently too, under the guise of protection, but more truthfully with the notion of providing labor resources. Eichler had disliked this new approach, not only because the treatment of the prisoners was quite hideous, but also because it was a great safety risk. Sabotage, he argued, was, "a serious cause for concern" if prison labor was to be used.

But the requirements of the A-4 project outweighed the fear of subterfuge. Demands from the military, *Reichsminister* Speer, and even, rumor had it, the Führer himself, had slammed the project into high-gear, and thus the need for bodies—both skilled and unskilled—meant that whatever resource could be dedicated to the project would. This major ramping up of people moving in and around Peenemünde had only made Eichler's work more difficult. He feared the colored-badge system wasn't enough to maintain security measures. The absence of a proper military force made matters worse, because a major attack on the facility did not just risk the physical components, but also the information contained in the brains of the men working there.

And what information there was! Eichler felt privileged to be among them. Inside the structures dotting the island, men tinkered and toyed with the components of the rocket, sometimes through the night, and often through the weekend. That did not mean employees were abused—far from it. To work at Peenemünde was to be treated with an air of respect and a degree of pampering. There was a soul in the air at the site, an awareness that the engineering being done there was for a greater purpose. This spirit had often been instilled by chief of the project Werner Von Braun—even if many working on the project had never glimpsed a prototype. Often men relegated to smaller departments to manufacture something simple knew little if anything about what it would be used for—but they knew it was something *wondrous*.

Most had heard the test firings when they did happen. Some who looked up to the skies had seen the fiery tail of the weapon with their own eyes, but few had been lucky enough to get close to the launch pad and see it up close. Eichler, having secured credentials few could, was privy to the weapon, and had even seen a prototype in action twice.

The first launch he'd witnessed was promising: the rocket had flared, punched upward toward the sky, and raged against a large gathering of clouds. After some time, the wreckage had been retrieved from the Baltic by the salvage crew via boat. The reason for the collection of spent resources was two-fold: certain parts could be repaired and reused, and information about weaknesses collected.

One particularly frustrating problem for the scientists at Peenemünde had been keeping the rocket's fuselage cool after launch. Eichler had witnessed this problem himself when he'd personally been invited. He'd been awarded the privilege in the interest of safety. He had argued he should be made aware of the nature of tests so they wouldn't be confused with attacks. The degree of respect one must garner to see a launch was great, and Eichler reveled in his success. Like many Peenemünders, he subscribed wholeheartedly to the work being done there, as well as the ideologies that went along with it. First and foremost, unquestioning loyalty was a requirement for those who graced the site's gates.

For quite some time, the project had been only a fanciful dream. It was a machine of the imagination, privately funded by the good graces of those who shared in the pioneering goals of space travel, and designed by civilian men with the audacity to push against the sky. A large number of men at the facility had come directly from the *Raketenflugplatz*, the prototypical collection of engineers and ideologues.

"Let these silly men play with their toys," many had said. But the spirit of engineering was mighty in the Fatherland. Soon enough the weapon that had been relegated to the ideas of science-fiction stories had become very real, and very *promising*.

"Help build the spaceship!" Eichler often heard chummy scientists say with a chortle. Theirs was a bond that had been started far before their time at Peenemünde, and their goals had not changed, regardless of whether their paths and the *Wermacht's* didn't directly align. The engineers, scientists, builders, and tinkerers at Peenemünde were inexorably controlled and monitored by the highest levels of the regime. The days of scraping together resources and begging for funding at the *Raketenflugplatz* were long gone.

With the influx of resources and manpower, so too came the bureaucracy of management. Bitter embattlements over who actually governed Peenemünde ensued. The *SS* wanted to lay claim, as did the *Luftwaffe*, but current control fell into the hands of the *Wermacht*, liaising with Werner von Braun to ensure the project saw completion. This infighting only made Eichler's job more difficult, but challenge was rife for all who called Peenemünde home. Reliability was key before the assembly lines started turning the rockets out, and the pressure to present a finalized model weighed heavily on its many residents.

After the brisk dawn walk, Eichler arrived near his residence, House 1, a large dormitory-style building hosting mainly bachelors. Men with families and unique skills were awarded larger accommodations. At Peenemünde, rewards coincided with ability. A man who could handle a wrench would live just fine—perhaps outside the gates, but in good accommodations nonetheless—whereas a man who understood the finer physics of ballistics and could *apply* them would live inside the compound and among his coworkers. But just because one was living in the lap of luxury did not mean they were free of the watchful eyes of security.

No one in Peenemünde was free from scrutiny. In fact, civilians and military personnel of all levels were encouraged to report on each other's behavior. This atmosphere created a sense of accountability, and also discouraged the sharing of information. Eichler thought that had slowed the project considerably, though it also contributed to its safety. Rarely were materials ever gathered or constructed in one place, and the same could be said for the storage of documents. To Eichler, Peenemünde was the exact opposite of Flussrand.

Eichler was reminded of that as he passed the main entrance. Beside the door was a large poster draped down the exterior wall. In stark, narrow lettering, the words "What you see, what you hear, when you leave, leave it here," stared back at its reader. Some might perceive it as a reminder, though many understood it better as a *threat*.

Eichler changed his clothing in his quarters and traded his civilian garb for his official costume: long black coat, boots, a collared shirt, and the badge that signified he was responsible for important security measures. The badge was gold, featured the eagle perched on the *swastika*, and bore the number 124 above that. Forgetting one's badge was unacceptable— the small articles of privilege denoted who could go where and when. There were few, if any, exceptions to such rules. Once dressed, he resumed the journey to his routine breakfast in the officer's mess hall.

Despite the pressures of strict security in and around Peenemünde—some maintained that *staying* in was more difficult than *getting* in—obedience and accountability reigned supreme. All were required to sign documents and swear oaths. Eichler's dedication to the project had come in another, more rare form, when he'd been required to sign a document to witness the test of the rocket officially—a *Verpflichtserklärung*, a formal obligation and declaration of commitment.

None who graced Peenemünde were absolved of signing that document, and furthermore all were held to the same degree of accountability, from the man who pushed the broom, to the lab coat studying liquid oxygen.

Ensuring the security of Peenemünde took up most of Eichler's day. He left no stone unturned when he traveled around the facility. Often he did so without the aid of a vehicle. He believed the world revealed itself to those who traveled on foot.

When night finally arrived, off-duty officers gathered at a picnic area. Several men rose from their seats and stood at attention after witnessing Eichler's entrance— his heavy boots always drew attention. He saluted them half-heartedly, then waved them to ease. Far from the front line, and out of plain sight, those at work enjoyed the luxuries of a distant war. Seated at the long tables were men clad in VkN uniforms: *Versuchskommando Nord*. They were among the lucky recruits, pulled from frontline military units for their special technical or engineering backgrounds. The warm chatter among them suggested Peenemünde was a far better place to rest one's head than the Russian front—some had been plucked directly from it. The formation of the VkN represented another all-hands-on-deck element driving the completion of the rocket forward.

Eichler poured himself a coffee, bummed a cigarette from a guard who patrolled one of the checkpoint gates, then cozied up on a bench overlooking the shore. A group of children gripped sparklers in one hand and the fingers of a parent in the other while they marched in line formation toward a fire. Another agreeable night. Those were abundant at Peenemünde.

The *Sicherheitskapitän* held no nostalgia for the forests of the *Schwarzwald*, especially during the cold months. He'd loathed it then, and he loathed it now. Peenemünde was a paradise, a hidden village of great builders and soldiers, women and children, pioneers and world-changers. To live on the island was to be in the company of both safety and greatness. The price paid to ensure utopia was high, but all present subscribed to it.

Though Eichler's transfer to the facility might have seemed a step downward from project manager, he saw in his recruitment an opportunity to prove himself once more. His management of the construction of the mighty tank *Erdschlag* had proved his value as an overseer. The work at Peenemünde was dissimilar in every way, embedded and injected with secrets in its identity —and closely held by all.

The light from the fire bathing Eichler's skin dimmed; blocking the illumination was a young, panting soldier in uniform. When his eyes finally found Eichler, he saluted and scurried over.

"*Sicherheitskapitän*," he said breathlessly. "I'm sorry to interrupt you."

"Let's have it, Herr Vogel," Eichler replied warmly to his adjutant.

"Sir," Vogel said, and side-stepped to reveal the silhouetted figure of Aksel Falke, feared spy-hunter of the *Reich*. He was more commonly known as *Der Fänger*, but few had the privilege of calling him that in his presence. He was easily recognized by the patch that covered one eye. The other that still functioned was piercing and seemed to look directly through men. As the amber eye gazed upon Eichler, he felt its searing investigation.

3

―――――

Across the Atlantic in Washington D.C., the sun was only just beginning to set on the brick façade of The Yard. The SSD-employed were still hard at work. Several women behind a large switchboard packed away in a glorified closet on the first floor fielded calls from across the globe. The board was a patchwork of glowing lights and wires. If humans hadn't been present in such abundance, a family of rats could make a nice home of the room. The operation would rival a small phone company's demand. While many chattered eagerly with operators and contacts on the other ends, there was one woman in particular who said nothing, but produced a face of bewilderment.

"Come again?" she said through the mouthpiece, wondering if perhaps she'd received a call in error. All that followed was a series of meaningless taps over the earpiece. She hung up, then after a brief moment, a light on the switchboard flickered.

"Dispatch," she answered. The clicking began again.

She cupped her hand over the mouthpiece, signaled Blanche Bencel—a mother goose of sorts who even bobbed when she walked—over to her station, then ripped a piece of paper from a pad and scribbled in sloppy strokes on the sheet. The action drew the attention of the other women around her, her frantic writing uncharacteristic and cause for concern. The scratching of lead against paper was deafening amidst the silence as the rest of the women held their calls and gawked like the rest of a flock. The switchboard flickered with unanswered calls. Beside it, curious women craned their necks to see what was happening.

Blanche arrived with a clipboard gripped tightly in her arm. Her long plaid skirt waved with each step. She was approaching sixty, yet had more fire in her veins than three of the twenty-somethings combined.

Blanche snatched the phone from the girl and listened intently as she chewed on the length of her own pencil. After a moment, the clicks registered as code. She deciphered it with the pad and pencil, then tapped several buttons on the switchboard before removing and fastening one of the wires into place.

The switchboard glittered vibrantly; every face in the room was still locked on to Blanche's as she tucked the gnawed pencil behind her ear.

"Back to work," she barked, feeling all eyes upon her. The ladies did as commanded, refocusing their attention on their own calls after partaking in a shameful moment of gossip. Soon the din of a phone patchwork resumed.

Upstairs on the fourth floor, Iris—or the "secretary supreme," as the girls below were fond of calling her— looked over the top of her glasses at the ringing phone.

She removed the phone from its cradle, inquired as to who was calling, then deciphered the clicks herself. Once finished, she promptly switched the line over to be received in the office beside her. As per usual, the door was closed. It was not only to ensure the privacy of the spy chief fielding calls behind it, but also because the odor of pipe smoke was pungent enough to nauseate even the strongest of stomachs.

The call interrupted Hank Brandt's daily routine of spit-shining the many glittering badges affixed to his coat. He reached for the chirping telephone—the brown one that *rarely* rang—before resuming his customary pipe-smoking. A man in constant motion, he rose from the desk and paced as he greeted the caller.

"Hank," the man on the line said.

Brandt, immediately recognizing the British voice as one belonging to a man codenamed "Matchbox", checked his watch. "A little late for you over there, isn't it?"

However, the Brit quickly cut to the chase, saying "You know that thing you've been working on?" The voice was old, but seasoned. It invoked the same riddle-like statements Brandt often employed. "In the Baltic?

"Go ahead."

"It's happening," Matchbox said. "Very soon."

"Are you saying what I think you're saying?" Brandt asked.

"It's being seriously considered at the highest levels."

"Aren't *you* the highest level?"

"Even I have a master, Hank."

Brandt, now stopping at the window overlooking the Potomac and ceasing his insatiable appetite for motion, asked, "Our people, or yours?"

There was a short pause, perhaps even a sigh on the other end of the line before Matchbox said, "Ours. Let's keep that under lock and key, yes? This is just a call from one chap to another."

Brandt immediately felt the change in the dynamic. "When?" Brandt asked. There was another long pause, as if Matchbox was feeling out how to proceed before he actually did.

"Can't be sure, I'm afraid," Matchbox said. "It's in late planning stages: weather conditions, mapping, sorties—the usual. It's all being finalized. Your people *were* cut in, of course, but they declined." There was a hint of backtracking in Matchbox's tone. "I'm sure you knew that."

He didn't. In fact, this was all news to Hank Brandt. He hid his shame before replying, "Of course. I was waiting to know if we were going to throw our hat in *officially*."

"I'm of the impression yours will be continuing on with manufacturing targets."

"So I'm told," Hank lied once again. "So why the call?"

"Well," Matchbox replied with a soft sigh. "The information sharing has left something to be desired. We've prepared our own sorties, so we're quite confident in our way, but I'm wondering if I can't chew the ear of the great Hank Brandt a moment before we make our final assessment—get you to throw in your two cents, so-to-speak. Off the record, naturally."

Brandt stewed for a moment. If a bombing raid was on the horizon, his man on the inside, Roger Fowler, would need to evacuate immediately, which was no easy feat for a man operating behind German lines.

Despite his concern, the spy master's intel was starting to pay off, and to Navy and Army higher-ups, no less. Whether information had been shared across the pond or not, the results were now looking fruitful. It was a rewarding experience, not just because Brandt had been funneling war secrets of good value sourced by his field workers into the branches of the armed forces, but because it was helping him build relationships—many of which had suffered prior to the vetting of his tradecraft. It was rare he got so much as a thank you, but that didn't matter; Brandt had decided to play the long game, to build his outfit up with the most precious of weapons: information.

After a long pause, Matchbox said, "Anyway, hip hip for you, and all that. Don't tell the suits back in D.C.— my boys wouldn't like me dancing with another girl at the ball."

"When the time comes, be sure to fill me in, would you? They don't tell me everything here."

"Shame," Matchbox replied. "I would have thought the man who told all would be granted the same privilege."

Brandt spent the next half hour dispensing all of the information he could about the mysterious Peenemünde Army Research Center to Matchbox. To do so was unorthodox, but Brandt trusted Matchbox. Most of the good intelligence he could easily recall from memory: security procedures, geography, officials of note, and even defenses. The RAF had gathered much of their own information, as Matchbox had proved; most came from two Polish janitors who'd developed a vendetta against their captors, and some was from inconspicuous sorties. But it was no match for the detailed deliveries Brandt received from the Bern Station, made possible by American insert Roger Fowler and his courier, the Austrian priest Father Jan Lukas.

When he was finished dispensing information to Matchbox, Brandt left the seclusion of his office and snapped his fingers at Iris. "Got a pencil?" he asked. In no time at all she had one in hand. "Follow me," he instructed her, and the two made haste to the radio room on the third floor.

The investigation of The Yard settled as the war raged forward. The FBI had ceased snooping around Brandt's outfit—if only temporarily—and now he was free again to navigate the dark pits of Europe. For a moment, earlier in the summer of '42, he'd wondered whether his operation would buckle under the pressure of bad press. It wasn't long before Brandt figured out that journalists, like any good assets, could be bought off too.

Brandt's identity was no longer as shrouded in mystery as it had been during the formation of his coveted SSD. Still a private citizen, he was awarded luxuries in war time unavailable to those registered in the armed forces or holding positions of rank. Hank Brandt often found himself operating outside the bureaucratic stronghold the rest of the armed forces were accustomed to. He was rarely subjected to congressional oversight—for better or for worse. Brandt was responsible for impressing only a few *very* powerful people. Luckily, he did that well.

Brandt took a seat by a radio panel and spread the paper across a small desk while an operator stood by awaiting instructions. To the average person, what

Brandt began to dictate to Iris was complete gibberish, but to those with special credentials, it was a dire warning. The code couldn't have been deciphered by anyone who wasn't privy to the methodology of communication with the spy chief. Brandt and Iris had their own special system to relay messages without saying them outright, the same way any field operator did if they needed to send or receive communications.

Brandt used his own key in particular, and it changed often. On the 1st of every month, he and Iris convened to deduce what the key would be for the next thirty or so days, and this would be relayed to a man in the field—in this case specifically, the Bern Head of Station Ansel Combe. Brandt reached into his breast pocket and pulled out a small card, a cheat-sheet of sorts. The spymaster would never dare carry it behind enemy lines, but in the safety of SSD headquarters, there would be plenty of time to destroy it if the situation arose. Should an operator need to relay a message of importance to him, or he to them, Iris functioned as the intermediary for D.C. and beyond. It certainly wasn't the easiest way of communicating sensitive information, but it was the *safest*.

Iris presented the mess of letters to Brandt. To the lowly radio operator who would read the note, it meant nothing. Even he was unaware of what the message stated if deconstructed.

Brandt, for once, set his pipe aside and gripped the pencil as he studied the letters. They didn't look like much of anything upon simple inspection, but Brandt had the card with the key to makes sense of it all resting beside the paper.

It took some patience. Even for those with great

concentration, it could be difficult to decipher the code. The key listed each letter of the alphabet in linear order in one column, and the corresponding replacement in the next. It read as follows from the left to right column, "ABCDEFGHIJKLMNOPQRSTUVWXYZ," and beside that, "ZPFQCRNUODTMEHBLKA-WGVXSYIJ."

The men and women on the third floor of The Yard might deserve a pay raise, he thought briefly. He already found the process taxing, and he rarely did it himself. On top of that, the cyphers coming in from foreign operators were much more complex.

The tip of his pencil alternated between the column and the paper in front of him as he scratched the corresponding letters to the message. Initially, the code letters written were "ZAABSUCZQ WGZGOBH, VANCHG." He went on moving down the list, his pencil gliding faster as he developed the cadence of the pattern. When he finished, he leaned back in the seat and inserted the pipe into his mouth. His face was grave, and the burn marks that always creased uncomfortably on his face made the man look pained.

On the paper before him, Brandt had penciled, "ARROWHEAD STATION, URGENT." He nodded to Iris, and she gave the okay to the radio operator to send the message off. Brandt had lost track of the frequency in which the priest showed up to deliver Fowler's intelligence to Combe. Combe would know better. Brandt could only hope that he would catch his Head of Station at just the right time, and that the message could be relayed as quickly as possible.

4

———

*C*rack. The bullet-like glove came swift and forceful, sending Sam Abel stumbling backward into the three rubber-band-like ropes at his rear. Had they not been there, he would have landed flat on his back, but they sprung the spy forward and ready to spar again. Disoriented, he raised his two gloves once more, this time sure to keep his left forward to shield his face.

The old Irishman hit hard—and with little effort. There was a poetry to his style that Sam hadn't yet figured out. The old man had one tiny little tuft of white hair clinging to the top of his head that resembled a cotton ball, and it bobbed lazily whenever he moved. His two dull-grey eyes never broke with his opponent's. The man was sinewy, all speed and little muscle, and had varicose veins that snaked throughout his still-nimble legs and arms. None of his weaknesses made him any less dangerous. His name was Patty Sheehan, but his trainees knew him as "Shiner."

"How many times've I told ya to cover your face?" Shiner asked. His native Irish crept through—there was something of home still left in him. His own dukes up, his feet dancing like mad around the ring, he moved toward Sam once more. "You're all cigarettes and spit, Abel."

Sam moved forward to meet him, his lungs heaving through exasperated breaths as he prepared to clash with the old scrapper once more. Sam felt out the distance with his left glove while trying to ignore Shiner's taunts.

"I've seen your type," Shiner said dismissively. "Got ya figured out." He was smiling a toothy grin. Several of his teeth were missing, likely a snapshot of the errors of his old fighting days. The rest were yellowed and stained, perhaps from coffee or cigarettes—or both—or maybe just a lack of proper dental care; Sam wasn't sure. If the old man *did* smoke, his lungs showed no signs of decay. "Ya've got the guts, but no style—no *finesse*."

Sam swung a predictable right hook, slow and easy to read, and Shiner dodged it as quickly as if he wasn't a day over eighteen. Shiner followed with an open-gloved warning shot from his left hand. It wasn't a powerful strike, just a feeler tap to let Sam know that he'd *got him*.

Shiner fought southpaw, and Sam, for all the times they'd sparred, still found the fighting style difficult to combat. Shiner mocked him again: "Perhaps another cigarette, then?" It irked Sam to no end that the geriatric assassin was able to hold conversation during sparring matches while Sam struggled to keep his hands up.

Sam jabbed with his right again, this time mustering up a bit more force in the punch. Shiner always instructed him to never hold back, regardless if the

Irishman didn't do the same. Shiner extended a guarded arm to block the fist as if batting away an annoying fly. "The shoulder's still weak, Abel," Shiner said. "If I can see it, so can your enemy."

It was true. Sam still felt a handicap in his right arm, the remnants of a knife wound from Udo Ramm. The injury had healed, albeit slowly, but Sam was sure his arm would never return to its full strength. He was thankful the fighting was only for training purposes and not a career goal. If he was good at his job, he wouldn't need to fight. The spy would never have had a chance at a title.

Outside the only window present, a stray dog foraged through the trash cans lining the dark back alley of a D.C. side street. Shiner's gym was an old basement textile shop with a leaky ceiling and the musk of years-old mold. The old man insisted on training at five in the morning—and that wasn't the expected arrival time, it was ass in the ring. This rule was instituted by Shiner not only because it "created discipline," but also because less people would see Sam and him train. Sam was still, after all, living in the shadows. Shiner was privy to that. Hank Brandt had called in a favor, and Shiner hadn't said another word about it.

Many SSD operators came through the rusty iron doors of the gym away from daylight hours, ordered to do so by Brandt in preparation for field work. If men were going to go behind enemy lines, they needed to at least know how to throw a decent punch and protect themselves if necessary—maybe even get the shit kicked out of them once or twice. Shiner also made any poor bastard trainee run—not on *his* time, of course. If they didn't run, he *knew*, and that was particularly painful for the smokers, of which there were many. The penalty for a lack of extracurricular exercise was a good battering from the old man during training.

Shiner continued to dance around Sam, noodling him with an extended arm every so often to entice him into action. "Come on, Abel," Shiner said. "If this were a real match ya'd have the crowd boo'in and the organizers cussin'." Shiner threw a jab that slapped Sam in the nose, and though it hurt, it was another warning-style shot to get him worked up. "You've got the stamina, I see it in ya, and I know you're still smokin' like a chimney. You've got somethin' else in ya, you *do*— somethin' not a lot of guys have. *Heart*, maybe. Balls. But you're still sloppy."

Sam started with his own footwork, hopping on his toes and circling Shiner to look for his chance. "In my profession, we prefer to be quiet when we work," Sam said, struggling to get the words out.

"Horseshit!" Shiner retorted. "You boys can scoot around like rats all ya like, but when the fight's on, there ain't no amount of darkness that can cover your ass. Ya've got to learn to *take* a man, and take him good, but ya gotta do it smartly." Sam debated whether "smartly" was even a word, or if Shiner was just making another one up again. The trainer was apt to use "Shinerisms," as Sam had called them. They were malaprops, but Shiner's way.

"I seem to do alright," Sam argued.

"That's not what I've heard," Shiner said with a chuckle, throwing several punches in succession. He sent out a left, right, left, all of which connected with Sam, disorienting him. A second later, he said, "I heard ya got your ass handed to ya in Germany, and then in New York, and I've handed it to ya myself on several occasions, and ya know that's the truth."

Sam's eyes flared, and he darted toward Shiner before cranking his right arm back and throwing it toward the Irishman, but Shiner diverted the attack and sent Sam tumbling over his own feet and toward the opposite end of the ring. Shiner toyed with him again: "The fight's over here, Abel. You should join in."

"How about we take off the gloves," Sam said, wiping the sweat from his brow. It was a statement made in jest—the defeat was getting to him. He'd made improvements fighting Shiner, he was sure of it, but the old man had never let slip that the spy was making progress. Never once did he say "better" or "looking good" or "that's it!" Sam was beginning to think the old man just liked to screw with his head, as if he had no *real* trainees of his own and toying with Brandt's recruits was just some twisted way of getting his kicks.

"Alright," Shiner said with another crooked grin. "I'll oblige." Shiner tossed away his gloves, and Sam did so too, throwing the pair out of the ring and against the leaking walls of the musty room.

Dull morning light cut a beam through the dust-filled ring. It took on a cool glow that was starting to overpower the few dim bulbs hanging from the ceiling —that meant their sparring was almost done for the day. But today, before the session was over, two men would spar with bare knuckles before they called it quits.

Shiner raised both fists, his old, battered knuckles seemingly all bone and weathered skin. How they hadn't cracked under the stress of repeated blows, Sam wasn't sure. If the old man hit him, even *tested* him, the punch was going to hurt. But the spy was using bare knuckles now too. If he got one good shot on Shiner, perhaps he'd shut him up for the morning, maybe take another of his teeth too.

Sam moved quickly now, his feet doing fancy work back and forth just as Shiner had instructed him over the past several weeks. "As many distractions as you can muster," the old man had said when they'd started training earlier in the month. "Make sure he's looking at several things, not just one. Footwork is important. Make like you're going this way, then go that."

Sam loathed the training. Fisticuffs during operations was rarely called for, though he'd endured it when it happened. He relied on *not* being seen, rather than creating scenes. Still, the training had given him a little more confidence. He might not *always* have his trusty knife.

"There ya are," Shiner said, circling Sam. Was that a compliment? The man moved naturally, as if fighting had been inserted into his blood at birth and was as normal a function as breathing. Shiner always seemed to know what Sam was going to do before he was going to do it. "Ya've got to know where the fight is going to be, not where it *is*. Ya can't just haul off and start sluggin' a man when you've got the fire in ya—you've got to let him beat himself."

Sam understood the idea. He'd often said to himself the key to a man's next move is in his eyes, not in his action, yet Sam still had a hard time cracking Shiner's code. The trainer was uncanny in his ways, and Sam never seemed able to get a read on him. Sam had barely ever landed a punch on Shiner's torso since they'd been meeting. The lack of victory drove Sam mad.

"Don't blame me if I mess up that pretty face, Abel," Shiner said. His eyes were gleeful and teasing. "You're the one who asked to lose the gloves."

"You don't have many teeth left," Sam said.

"Don't I know it," Shiner replied, and the two men moved closer, nearly knuckle to knuckle. Sam threw the first punch, and it was a fade right-left, which fooled the Irishman, but still didn't connect.

"Well, alright," Shiner said wide-eyed. "That's somethin' new." Sam could see he'd surprised Shiner, and it gave him the extra boost he needed to move once more. "A tip," Shiner began, "ya let your opponent do most of the work. Do better at dodgin', and duckin', and he's tired before you are. There you'll find your opportunity. Let him make his moves, and you sit waitin'. When he thinks he's got ya, that's when ya make your move." Shiner hooked with his left with half-force, connecting with Sam's cheek and knocking his head sideways. *That* one hurt. It was all knuckle, and had Shiner actually put some strength into it, it might have knocked Sam out cold. "That one's gonna leave a mark."

Sam attacked clumsily, trying to jab at Shiner. He was frustrated, and he wanted to knock Shiner one good just to show the old man he could take him. But Shiner was spry, and despite Sam's efforts, he failed miserably. Sam, frustrated, tried an uppercut when he got in close, but that was foolish—the swing was slow and uneven, and Shiner took the opportunity to pat Sam on the nose with a fist and then knock him to the ground with the opposite hand.

A second after Sam hit the ground, he looked up,

and briefly thought he saw *two* Shiners. Even the attack made him feel as if he'd been hit by two men, rather than one. The base of his skull had struck the floor hard, and there was a buzzing vibration encompassing his face. After a moment, the multiple Shiners merged into one singular vision. Shiner extended his hand, and Sam took it, allowing the trainer to lift him up.

But just as Sam was back on his feet, he went in for another attack on Shiner with a right hook. The elderly fighter saw it coming a mile away—they were back at it. Now seething, Sam finally took the old man's words to heart and let his trainer keep leading. Shiner was really going at him now, throwing fists in rapid succession and with few breaks.

But when Shiner had extended his right arm just a little too far, put that extra force in it that offset his balance in the smallest way, Sam quickly recognized the error. Sam threw a left hook in the brief window of opportunity. And as if some type of miracle had occurred, he finally struck Shiner and sent him crumbling to the floor.

Shiner frowned. Sam, pleased with himself for making up for so much lost time with one good effort, reached a hand out to help his trainer up. Just as Shiner took hold of his trainee's grip, he delivered a sweeping kick to Sam's knee that sent the spy tumbling backward to the floor once more.

This time, no one reached a hand out for assistance. "You're gonna need to do better than that, Abel," Shiner said as Sam stood on two weak legs. A scowl on his face suggested he was of half a mind to start right up again.

"Sweeping a man's leg isn't part of the rules," Sam

said while wiping at his nose—his hand came away with a red smear.

"There ain't no rules, Abel," Shiner replied sternly. "Not doin' what you're doin'. In the ring, no one is your friend, and outside of it, the same is true. When you're out there, there ain't no ring, no referee, no score cards. *All's* fair—ya'd best remember that."

Sam scoffed. He didn't need to be told that.

"You've got a lot of anger in you," Shiner stated. "I can see it behind your eyes; you're a man unresolved."

Sam hopped out of the ring and pulled a cigarette from his trousers. He lit it, inhaling the smoke and allowing the sweat to cool his body as he took a seat on a dingy wooden bench. Shiner sat down next to him, wrapping a towel around the back of his neck. The old man had barely broken a sweat.

"A few less of those would do," Shiner said as he motioned toward the cigarette.

"Tell me about it," Sam replied through an exhale. A guttural cough followed as he cleared a clump of mucus from his throat.

Outside of the ring, Sam harbored far less resentment for the old man. There was a scrap to him that the spy respected. What his story was, or where he'd come from, Sam had no idea, but he suspected the man had seen his fair share of trouble—inside the ring and out. *Cat would have liked him*, Sam thought, *and he her.*

Several months had gone by and still there'd been no word as to her whereabouts. Brandt had screwed up with that one, regardless of the value of her skillset. Sitting there with Shiner, Sam wondered just how the hell Brandt had found any of these people, himself included. The spymaster had known a lot about a lot, and knowing things was his skillset.

A knock echoed through the gym from the door above. Shiner stood, his joints cracking and popping as he rose. He grumbled in response, then said to Sam, "Now get the hell out of my gym. I've got real fighters coming in."

5

E ven for Lothar Eichler, a man twice now entrusted with security of Germany's most precious weapons projects, the presence of the mythic Aksel Falke was unnerving. Falke—who'd fought during the first war and still brandished the eye patch that evidenced his worst injury—struck fear through his viperish persona. His lone, fierce, and some said supernatural eye was cause for most men's consternation in his presence.

Falke had requested they speak somewhere private. Eichler provided refuge in his office, which was housed inside a concrete, blast-proof barracks on the southern end of the island just inside the main gate. Inside, Eichler directed Falke to take a seat, but the spy-hunter said he'd preferred to stand. Eichler wondered if it was yet another of his famous intimidation tactics.

Eichler, a full six inches taller than Falke, towered over him when both stood apart from each other. One might think that gave him the upper hand, but he was reminded of his place when he felt a trickle of sweat drip down his cheek. Falke's silver, swept-back hair gave him an appearance as if he'd been designed for speed, but he was an aging man now, thin and sallow in the cheeks and greying in his complexion. His appearance was in direct contrast with his actual behavior; he was as spry and energetic as any man half his age.

"*Sicherheitskapitän* Eichler," Falke said, his voice stinging with vibrato from too many smoked cigarettes. "I'm very thankful for your time in the late hour. Surely you have enough to manage without cutting time out of your busy schedule to accommodate me."

"I have all the time you need, Herr Falke," Eichler said clumsily. For a moment, perhaps because it had been at the forefront of his mind, Eichler almost called him *Herr Fänger*—the unofficial, if earned, title had traveled in circles regarding the man. His exploits were the stuff of legend. On several occasions after the disaster at Flussrand, and when the question of whether the saboteur might still be in Germany had come up, many in German High Command had suggested tasking *Der Fänger* with hunting the culprit down himself.

"Nevertheless," Falke began, "I will make this quick. I am aware that free time at this facility is rare and of great value, and I don't wish to cause you any more stress than you already have. You are in charge of all perimeter security at Peenemúnde, if my information is correct."

"I am, Herr Falke," Eichler replied. It was probably unnecessary for Eichler to use the man's title, but something about the yellow eye and its penetrative gaze caused Eichler to suspend his common sense and preserve an air of respect. Falke did not hold rank or title above Eichler at Peenemünde. In fact, Falke held *no* official or military title. He was ex-military—now a civilian —tasked with carrying out the orders of any who requested his expertise, albeit with great power granted to him by those willing to give it.

"And you are aware that roughly a mile due west, an American taking up residence on a farm was captured only recently?"

Eichler wondered whether that was a trick question. He'd heard rumors, which were rare at Peenemünde. But not everyone at Peenemünde was *supposed* to know, and he didn't want to suggest he had been discussing information he was not entitled to. Furthermore, he was concerned that the presence of an enemy so close was a poor reflection on his own ability to protect the facility. Torn between how to answer, Eichler chose to acknowledge the truth. "I have heard gossip," he lied. "Which I might add I will soon rectify."

"His apprehension was kept quiet for security reasons," Falke said. "I wouldn't expect you to know something I myself tried to conceal."

"Has his capture proved valuable?" Eichler asked.

"I'm afraid not," Falke said. "But that is no fault of ours. He was an SSD man, we know that much. Hank Brandt's people—familiar?"

"I can't say that I am."

"Nasty old man…" Falke said. His face narrowed in the way one's does when they'd tasted lemon. "Runs amok, no accountability, gets fed endless resources by the US government to fund a private militia of spies and saboteurs, many disenfranchised and defectors." Falke drew his fingers down the side of his cheek. "Horrible burn scar across the face."

"I wasn't aware," Eichler said.

"I was. It's how I caught Fowler in the first place."

"Who?"

"The American in question," Falke replied.

"Herr Falke, If I may be of any assistance—"

"In fact you may," Falke started without letting Eichler continue his obligatory offer. "I'm required elsewhere, and because of that I can't possibly continue my investigation into the network this individual may or may not have been a part of. I'll need someone to maintain the post in my absence. I'm sure that your area of responsibility is already under considerable demand, but I'm wondering if you might be able to continue the work I started here. This does not absolve you of your duty to the facility, you understand. It is, however, an investigation of great importance and one that I can only entrust to someone whom I believe capable of managing it in my stead."

Eichler, forever in pursuit of another rung up the party ladder, happily obliged. "I would be honored, Herr Falke."

"Good," Falke said. For a moment, the amber eye inspected Eichler. He had heard the rumors about the "all-seeing eye" as so many had gossiped, and how the man seemed to possess uncanny skill despite the disability. He seemed to be surveying Eichler, gauging whether he truly was capable of handling the responsibility. "I expect the man's absence will raise alarms for the Allies and yield more information about their activities."

"Should arrests be made?" Eichler asked.

"On the contrary," Falke said. "The offenders should be allowed to function as they normally might."

"I'm sorry, Herr Falke," Eichler said. "Forgive my

confusion, but why should they not be apprehended as soon as they're discovered?"

Falke retrieved a cigarette from his coat, tapped it against the back of his hand to pack the tobacco, then pressed it to his lips and lit it. His eye flared in the flame, giving it a wild, animalistic glow. Eichler wondered if it reflected light in the night like a predator, and how it had taken on its yellow aesthetic in the first place. "Do you hunt, Herr Eichler?"

Eichler, disappointed he couldn't find common ground, said he did not.

Falke drew from the cigarette. "The most efficient type of hunting is to set a trap. Any man can handle a rifle, though even that can prove challenging for the inept, but few can track and trap. I vastly prefer the latter. I find that to catch a good prey requires patience and skill, rather than brute force. Weapons run out of bullets. Traps can be reset and tried until the prey is caught off guard. When the prey eludes the trap, you may resort to a different technique to capture it. Or," he said with a pause, the fierce amber eye glowing in stark contrast to the one obscured behind the patch, "you follow it to see if it leads you to the nest."

Eichler nodded. He was beginning to understand.

"The prey thinks it's won, and so it'll behave freely. It reveals its greatest weaknesses, and *that* is when one strikes." Falke exhaled smoke from his mouth, and Eichler dutifully provided an ash tray for his convenience. "You have men at your disposal, yes?"

"Many squads," Eichler replied.

"Good," Falke said. "Inform them of the new requirements of their job, and see to it they are acutely aware of the location. I will provide you more detailed coordinates shortly, as well as any relevant information."

"Should I be concerned that this operation has been compromised?" Eichler asked. His greatest fear was that Peenemünde would meet the same fate as Flussrand.

"I can't suggest there is yet cause for concern," Falke replied. "But I cannot say this facility is as secret as some imagine it to be. Should the American have been more forthright, I could have provided you with a more concrete answer. He was not, but we should not panic. That order comes directly from the *Reichsführer* himself. He is incredibly concerned that if we were to alert everyone, the project might be sidetracked or moved and therefore might lead to great inconvenience. For now, I've suggested we closely monitor the situation. Do you have any cause for concern?"

"Not currently," Eichler said. "We have seen what we imagine to be British sorties, but I believe the facility is unassuming enough that the Allies have not become wise to the project."

"That's good to hear," Falke said. "I'm told that the work being done here is of unique importance." There was curiosity in Falke's delivery, but Eichler did not take the bait. Far be it from him to start discussing the rocket program, even to someone as well-regarded as Falke.

"Will you be requiring reports?" Eichler asked.

"Please," Falke said. "I should expect that any movement on the property will be cause for investigation by your team personally. Furthermore, if any person of interest is discovered, I want that information relayed to me in a timely manner. Under no circumstances are you to alert a suspect to your presence. That same discretion should apply to your superiors. We want him, or her, to believe they are operating freely, and therefore will not change their behavior in any way."

"You can rest assured," Eichler replied.

"I can't rest until the threat is absolved," Falke said through a tuft of smoke. "Nor should you. Not only is the *Reich* at risk with every spy inserted behind our borders, but so too is this installation. I'm told great strides are being made here, is that correct?"

"Indeed," Eichler said, once again avoiding any elaboration on the subject.

"What, more specifically, is being done here to further the cause of the *Reich*, if I may ask?"

Eichler hesitated. *Does Falke know the purpose of this facility?* Certainly a man of such important stature was privy to these types of state secrets, especially a man who traded and acted on secrets himself. Still, Eichler decided not to budge. "I'm sorry, Herr Falke. I'm not at liberty to discuss operations—a rule for all Peenemünders, you see."

Falke grinned. "A trick question, Herr Eichler. I am well aware of the procedures and oaths sworn here." Falke extinguished his cigarette in the glass tray. "You'll do just fine. Very well, then, I will entrust you with surveillance for the time that I am gone. I expect you'll carry out this request delicately—absolute discretion."

"You can be sure, Herr Falke." *He's no different*, Eichler thought, *no different than the rest of the schemers trying to get a leg up past the others.*

"Good evening, Herr Eichler."

"Good evening to you as well." With that, Falke turned on his heel and saw himself out—but not before Eichler was hit with a thunderbolt of inspiration. *This agreement that had just been forged*, Eichler thought, *should not flow in only one direction. After all, who was doing who the favor?* Just as Falke grabbed for the door handle, Eichler said: "Herr Falke." Falke turned to face him, his lone eye still shining and luminescent in the shadowy vestibule. "I might wonder if I could trouble *you* for a unique favor."

6

———

Parched winds shook the massive pines adorning the shoreline at Peenemünde. Their needles shielded Father Jan Lukas from enemy sight. Even for a mid-August night, the climate was uncharacteristically hot at Usedom, and had been that way for some days. He lingered there in the convenience of camouflage, several hefty branches prickling at him as he watched for life on the farm. A squad of *Wermacht* troops had been active nearby only moments earlier, and he waited for the sound of their truck's motor to wane before he dared step foot on the property.

Two weeks had passed since he'd last arrived at the farm. He'd lost count of how many times he'd made "the run," as he called it. He was better able to gauge his time of occupation, which by his calendar had been roughly nine months of back and forth between the small farm and his handlers in Bern—*too long*, by his estimation. Tonight it would all come to an end. Combe had given him his final task: signal the American to return home.

What bothered him was that he still knew nothing of what this message accomplished.

As he watched for activity, he seethed with frustration. For nine months the Americans failed to act. For nine months he'd continued to risk the neck protected only by a flimsy clerical collar. For nine months information he'd been transporting had failed to be utilized in any meaningful way. He had never anticipated that this intelligence gathering would not yield a result to his liking.

"Politics," they'd said when the priest had demanded results. "These things are delicate."

Lukas thought it was all irrelevant. Had the Japanese considered politics when they'd attacked Pearl Harbor? Had the Führer contemplated how delicate the *Anschluss* might be? He grimaced briefly, recognizing these ideas were the foolish ramblings of a man with growing impatience. *Of course they had*, Lukas reconciled, but he was becoming more flustered by the day. If the Americans wouldn't act, then he would soon rethink his position and along with it his allegiances. This dreaded place should have been razed immediately after he'd provided confirmation of its strengths and weaknesses.

There were other offers for his services, but he'd been an American loyalist. Did these nuggets of intelligence go to the highest bidder? On the contrary—if one thought Lukas was acting for money of rewards they'd be sorely mistaken. Unless, of course, one considered the destruction of the Army Research Center at Peenemünde a reward, in which case Lukas was all-too-happy to divulge what he knew to anyone willing to listen—or, more preferably, to *act*.

On the northern horizon, where one could see the

Baltic Sea through shimmering ripples of water reflecting a waxing moon, a U-boat was rising up from the water. It was yet another reminder of how dangerous this undertaking was. Any other man of lesser character and courage wouldn't dare go to the lengths the priest had to sabotage his enemies. Lukas was no ordinary man, and also one insane enough to think that he never acted alone. He had God on his side, so he felt security in this spiritual team of two he had manifested.

Did the Nazis have God on their side? How could they when they had burned down *His* church? But through destruction there was also rebirth, and though Lukas could still feel the flames from his collapsed home and the screams of his terrorized parishioners, he had emerged from the rubble a new man: one dedicated to defeating the enemies not only of his people but also of God Himself.

Did he have a spiritual calling? Was he anointed in some majestic way befitting the great men he'd heard about in ancient texts? Called up to a mountain? Crowned in some way to lead the armies of his savior in the pursuit of a right, just, and fair world? Only if one considered the *SS* guards marching through Vienna to be some exalted sign, and Lukas was sure it wasn't. No, he was an ordinary man who'd undertaken an extraordinary responsibility.

The wind surged up again, each of the needles of the pines whispering against each other. *Pines make a peculiar noise when they are rattled in just the right way*, he thought. There was something distinguished about the sound, a magisterial characteristic that separated them from the identity of the other foliage. *Perhaps that is why they survive the winter*, he considered. They, like he believed of himself, had been awarded some unique favorability among God's creatures. They'd received an ability to withstand the harshness of their environment even if nature itself sought to destroy them in some vicious cyclical way.

Had his luck been any different? Why had he survived the attacks on his community, and now found himself among these resilient pines? Was it perhaps a sign from the creator himself? Who could ever be sure? He *was* mysterious in his workings, and now Lukas, just like the king of kings, had acquired and perfected a bit of the mysterious himself.

An owl above his position let off a hoot as if to warn Lukas. Did the creatures of the night alert each other of predation, or when it was safe to travel? Lukas took that as his sign to move forward. He had to go out into the flat land of the farm where he'd no longer have the safety of tree cover to protect him from prying eyes. He'd done it so many times before, but the arid gusts of air funneling through the tree line urged caution. Something, call it intuition, call it divine providence, was tickling the hairs on his neck as if to say, "Not all is correct."

Armed with only his spiritual shield, he crept through the foliage and out into the open night air. Ahead, the farmhouse in which his co-conspirator resided was dark. That was uncharacteristic. On nights in which Lukas was scheduled to retrieve a package, the singular light in the forest-facing window was to be left on as a signal that all was well and the priest should proceed as usual. Curious, Lukas trudged through moist, uncut grass, the dew glistening from the moon's light and carving out a path toward his target. It was taller than usual, which was another indicator something was amiss.

The wheat field that flanked the eastern side of the farmhouse was healthy and strong. Much still remained, though one might consider it late in the season for a lingering crop—especially for a country so in need of food for its troops. Lukas did not question the abundance, because it was essential to the operation. Embedded in the soil of this farm were the secrets of its neighbor. This was darkly poetic; the enemy's secrets were being traded within its most valuable resources by foreign men hiding within its borders.

Navigating the farm, even in the dark, was not something Lukas found difficult. He'd been doing it for so long that he'd quickly picked up his conspirator's pattern, and so knew how to find the bounty without wasting time. Tonight he would reverse the pattern, signaling exfiltration through coded text. Even though the farm was not often home to troop activity, the land was so close to the Peenemünde facility that just to be in its vicinity was dangerous. A stone's throw from his position the farm met the shoreline, and from there a thin inlet separated it from the high fences of the closely guarded island.

If the sky was clear, some nights he could even see the lights from its many buildings, though more often than not it was obscured by the tall pines on its borders. There was an air of discretion about the place. To anyone who gave a damn, it was clear there was more going on behind those fences than anyone cared to discuss.

Reaching the wheat field, Lukas darted down an alley that had been cut through the crops. He followed the trail deeper into obscurity with a sigh of relief. Now, at least, he had found some cover again. He was always careful to be inconspicuous. If he was caught, he had no excuse he could use other than claiming to be out for a night stroll. Why he'd never thought of a better excuse, he couldn't be sure, but he'd made it this far, and never had his handlers questioned his cover or activities so long as he delivered on his end.

He passed another cutout where a path led back toward the farmhouse. It was here, he remembered, that he had retrieved his goods the first time he'd ever made the run. In a discreetly staked mound of soil was a small box containing developed rolls of film. Often, the smell of dirt would linger in his fingernails for days after a successful run from Peenemünde to Bern.

The heart of a man deep within enemy territory is a brave but fragile one. Thus, when the air-raid sirens over the military research facility sounded, his chest thumped. The blaring horn seemed to permeate every crack and crevice of the farm, and though most might take it as a warning, Father Jan Lukas used it as an opportunity to move more quickly. It was a common occurrence, and never in these parts did bombing follow. The shuffling sound of his feet against soil now dampened, he strode toward the coordinates where he knew his drop lay.

The siren was short lived—only one short burst to signal danger before it subsided completely. The sounds of waves struggling against the westerly winds in the north remained. The half-moon worked both for and against him, concealing his activity while also providing the bare minimum of detail.

Arriving at the end of an alley of tall wheat while the

wind bent each stalk under its passing, he paused briefly to catch his breath. Though he might still be a young man by normal standards, the stress put his body under tremendous pressure even the healthiest of men would find daunting. An intersection north where two pathways met glowed as if ordained by the moon and formed a distorted crucifix. Lukas looked for signs like these. In this case it was only coincidence. The light touched the designated spot for the next cycle of deposit and retrieval.

But upon inspection of the site, Lukas was met only with disappointment. There, where the soil should have been marked, was only regular dirt. Lukas fell to his knees, checked his compass to confirm the mistake was not his own, then deflated. The hot breeze whipped through the pathway once more, shaking the stalks of wheat and playing shadows across the soil.

In the distance, the rattle of a diesel motor traveled from south to north along the waterline. Was the car on *this* side of the water, or the Peenemünde side? Lukas couldn't be sure. With his eyes closed, he mumbled a quick prayer to himself and placed his hands on the small plot of dirt where a noticeable mound should have been.

When his eyes opened, he dug feverishly, dirt flying behind him in great spurts as if a dog had rediscovered a lost treat. A lack of tools meant Lukas had to work hard to unearth the drop. His nails were caked with dirt and sweat began to run down the corners of his scalp. His fingers ached, but he put all his effort into the dig, praying—quite literally—that his conspirator had done his job but imperfectly.

How Lukas managed to unearth a foot of dirt in

such a small amount of time was beyond him, but men in dire need and a state of desperation are capable of great things. He'd proven that to himself on so many occasions since the rape of his homeland. To his disgust, the pit was empty. Lukas leaned back on his haunches and flicked the dirt from his fingers. Heaving in exasperation, he let out a sigh before searching around himself once more to see if his ally might have changed his routine. Nothing.

It is difficult to imagine the sense of defeat a man who has navigated the land of his enemies feels when his value is tested. Does he pack it in and return to his handlers to report his findings, or does he—of his own accord and certainly against protocol—continue to investigate in order to acquire more information? A man who values his safety might call it quits, but Father Jan Lukas' calling was of such a high nature that safety was the furthest thing from his mind. So, his attentions turned to the darkened farmhouse—the first sign that something was amiss.

He hadn't met the man in the farmhouse—an American—since their first rendezvous in Bern. Lukas had never learned his name. It was unnecessary, and perhaps had kept both men safer should the worst-case scenario arise. His code name was "the farmer." In truth, the man was an expert photographer, but used his ability to farm as his cover to reside so close to such a precious Nazi secret. Though Lukas did not possess the expertise to engage in such methods of evidence gathering, he did have what his American friends referred to as "guts." In that lay merit that couldn't be taught.

Guts were what was required to do what he planned to do next, but after wavering for a moment on whether he should proceed with his investigation or leave his own coded message and flee, he resolved that to go back to Bern without more information would be a great failure. With this thought in mind, Lukas deposited a small canvas sack with a coded message and re-filled the hole before dusting himself off. He rose to his feet, then set off toward the black house in search of the farmer.

Beyond the small shack the farmer called home, the larger house was dark as well. Lukas planned to steer clear of it, for housed inside were German citizens unaware of what was *really* taking place on their property. To Lukas' surprise, he found that house full of inactivity as well. By his watch, it was still too early, even for early-rising farmers, to be retired for the night. Lukas had observed the patterns of behavior on the plot of land for nearly a year now, and everything about the current aesthetics suggested something had *changed*.

Upon closer inspection of the small shack Lukas saw that the secondary signal, smoke rising from the chimney to confirm a clear coast, was also missing. If the priest had been unsure whether there was a problem earlier, no doubt remained. He ducked low beneath the tall wheat stalks and made his way toward the shack, then paused briefly, waiting for a sign to suggest that procedures had temporarily been aborted and his concerns were unwarranted. Perhaps the farmer had suffered a small hiccup and was laying low. Lukas wondered if he should take all these signs as a signal to stay away. This thought was quickly dismissed when he saw the front door of the shack had been broken off completely. Inside, only an empty home remained.

7

A healthy moon did wonders not only for heroes of the night creeping through dangerous territory, but also for the enemies watching their actions. Its light, coupled with the powerful pair of *Wehrmacht*-issued binoculars, can reveal the activities of saboteurs even the cover of darkness can't conceal. Across the Krösliner See, behind the high fences of the Nazi's best-kept-secret, a squad of men watched intently as a shadowy figure navigated the location of what had been, but was no longer, the Allies' best-kept-secret. The reasons for that man's presence in this once-occupied farmhouse had piqued the curiosity of the research facility's security forces, specifically *Sicherheitskapitän* Lothar Eichler.

He adjusted the lenses of his binoculars as the man in the distance blurred in and out of focus. Behind Eichler a small squad of well-armed men waited patiently for his next command. Though they remained quiet, their activities were well-concealed by the arid winds characteristic of the Baltic in its warm months.

All of the men present had heard the rumors of the *Ami* enemy that had been apprehended where this shadowy figured now stood.

Little was known to Eichler about the captured man. One could guess as to the nature of his surveillance; deep in these forests of tall pine a unique weapons project had been undergoing vigorous testing. For the first time Eichler wondered if the prisoner was still alive —Falke hadn't said as much. Though one might celebrate the death of an enemy spy, the inability to discover what he knows, or *knew*, could still be considered a failure.

Any normal soldier would seize the opportunity to arrest the intruder on sight, especially since no law protected him and no jury existed to contest his capture, but Lothar Eichler was not so quick to leap. Falke had made clear spies were to be tracked, tagged, and investigated.

Eichler began to understand Falke's methodology. *Capturing spies gets us spies, but* tracking *spies gets us spy networks.*

Eichler did have some trouble with this logic. As *Sicherheitskapitän* of the Peenemünde Army Research Center, every threat was one to be quickly neutralized. As it was, this man was unaided and alone. Unfortunately, Eichler dared not sacrifice his position. Perhaps Falke was right. Perhaps it *was* more important to stay the course.

A radio straight to Eichler a few hours ago had warned of a suspicious-looking man traveling through the western farmland. Regardless of what people really knew about the outcome of the American spy's capture,

Eichler had made the vacancy of the farm well-known to his aides.

The foliage beside Eichler shifted. He sneered at one of his men, annoyed that they were not moving quietly. They'd been waiting here for quite some time, obscured by tree cover and watching. They were becoming restless.

"Apologies, Herr Eichler," a scrawny man in uniform said shamefully. Eichler didn't let his disappointment with this team go unnoticed. Most of the men appointed to his greater security unit had been pulled from small stints on the frontlines. They weren't hardened or battle-tested, and they'd been living the high life in the quiet beach community as the war of two fronts grew closer to home. Had there not been so much infighting amidst the greater ranks of High Command, he might have requested the presence of the *SS* in addition to these men.

Eichler monitored the suspicious man from afar as he trekked across the property. There was a body of water between them. Was he even a cause for concern? It was difficult to tell. Anything was possible, even the chance that this man had just fled a city under attack. Many tried retreating to the safer countryside. Maybe he was rummaging through the belongings of displaced persons in search of goods. Some had begun their exoduses from the great cities, many homeless and poor. Innocent people wandered near the secret facility all the time, and most—if not all—did not give cause for concern. It was Eichler, though, who often determined the threat level of those encroaching on the facility. He'd learned his lesson on multiple occasions that no one could be *assumed* to be trustworthy until they'd proven it. After all, this man was already ringing alarms just by standing where he was.

"Should we proceed, Herr Eichler?" another of the men asked.

"No," Eichler replied, his attention on the binoculars unwavering. "We will continue to watch."

"What more proof do we need? This man has no business occupying a home that doesn't belong to him."

"Be that as it may, we want to him to believe he's not being monitored. Let him behave as he might normally, and then he might take us back to the nest where the eggs lie."

One of the soldiers lit up a cigarette, which Eichler immediately told him to extinguish. The group was a young, untrained bunch. Eichler detested having such green assets at his disposal.

"Who is scheduled for the upcoming rotation?" Eichler asked as he let the binoculars fall to his chest. Two of the men raised their hands. "Follow this man and report his movements. Do not lose sight of him, but ensure that he is unaware of your presence. Others will be sent to relieve you in short order." Eichler was answered in the form of an exasperated sigh by one of the men. This act sent the security captain into a furious rage that saw him seize the soldier by both of his lapels and draw the man's slim body up to meet his own. "Would you like for me to turn you over to the authorities for insubordination and see to it you wind up driving a pickaxe like the others who complain about their postings?"

"No, *Sicherheitskapitän*," the soldier replied through a defeated squeak.

Eichler released the soldier from his grasp. "Then see

to it that you don't lose sight of this man and report back immediately with his movements." He could tell his face had grown red. All the blood had flowed to it, and it took every ounce of his strength not to backhand the soldier and truly put him in his place.

If he could leave his own post, Eichler would have followed the man himself, but protocol dictated that to take leave of Peenemünde—even if it meant protecting the facility—would have to be approved up the ladder. If the order came from the security captain himself, then reasoning behind the action could be justified, but men and women did not come and go freely from Peenemünde. Since this unit already resided on the outskirts, they were free to move about the region with impunity. Eichler could not abandon his area of responsibility, even if it meant he could capture the mystery man with his own hands and present Aksel Falke a trophy.

Eichler handed the binoculars back to the soldier he'd taken them from, then gave further instructions: "Two of you will remain here and report movements and coordinate with the others. I want to know where he goes, who he speaks with. Obtain a detailed description—height, weight, ethnicity, and any distinguishing features. If he gets into a vehicle, record information about its driver. If he retreats into an eatery, remain outside and survey him until he is finished. If he purchases a train ticket, find out its destination and what time it is due to leave. Under no circumstances are you to approach him. Are there any questions?"

The team replied that there were not, the others surely wary of Eichler's retaliation. Their job was one in which there was a lot of time to hurry up and wait. Now it was time to actually act on orders, and they were all-too-willing to make good on their oaths. Perhaps they could tell by Eichler's severity that he strongly suspected there was more to that man than met the eye.

Surely Falke would want to know this information, so Eichler set off post-haste to inform him of what had taken place. Though Falke no longer remained at the facility, Eichler had been given special commands that usurped even those from Major General Dornberger. Eichler now found himself answering to two Gods, one instrumental in discovering the hidden agent of espionage behind the fatherland's borders, and the other tasked with completing the rocket project housed at Peenemünde.

Was this mystery man in contact with the *Ami*, and if so, what was his role in the operation? To follow this lead could produce a great catch, and if the net was big enough, perhaps a big fish. Eichler recalled Falke's words: "When the prey eludes the trap, you may resort to different techniques to capture it. Or, you follow it to see if it leads you to the nest." Eichler felt as if he could see Falke's amber eye watching him this very moment.

8

On the outskirts on the nation's capital, there was a prohibition-era watering hole hidden beneath a shoe repair shop. It was accessible only to those who could present a password at the sub-street basement steel door. Walk past it without the sun shining directly on the narrow corridor to reveal its entryway and one would miss its cavern-like entrance. It had no name—at least, not anywhere on its façade. One could leave the White House and take 14th Street northwest and cross over on to 13th Street in Columbia Heights and be there on foot in short time. Those who frequented it recognized its location from the stray cats that congregated near the front door. Most would assume it was food that drew them, but Sam swore the animals were also being supplemented with beer.

And why wouldn't one come to that conclusion? Wasn't it the same reason men were drawn there at the devil's hour? Wasn't that the same reason Sam stood at the steel door at that very moment rapping on the eye hole?

When the steel eye piece slid sideways, two bushy eyebrows first appeared in the slot, then two inquisitive, bloodshot eyes followed. They scanned Sam for only the amount of time it took to recognize his face, then the metal slide shot back and closed both viewers off from the world beyond. Any other solicitor would have been subject to questioning, but the man who barred access to any ordinary person knew Sam quite well, and with haste, the shrieking door opened.

The man—who looked as though he weighed twice as much as Sam and had the weathered skin of a longshoreman—clapped the spy on the back with a meaty hand before returning to the bar area and tending to his ale. Only in a place like this would the patrons double as security. The foremost smell of the interior was that of wet wood and mold, and it was only barely tolerable, because it was quickly replaced by the stench of beer and whiskey. Several other patrons were scattered about, all blue-collar and tired looking. Behind the bar, the ticket to drinks was present in the form of a bearded man who nodded briefly to Sam as he swirled a rag around the inside of a glass mug. A haze of smoke hung in the air like the fog on the Scottish moors. Muffled radio chatter came from the corner of the room, but no one could elaborate on what the voice was saying.

The bartender didn't ask Sam what he wanted, because he already knew, and in quick time a tumbler of scotch slid across the bar and in front of his face, spilling a splash on to the bar when it finally halted. Sam placed several coins onto the bar, because a man on the run didn't ever leave a tab—he paid all his debts immediately in case he needed a quick getaway. Sam shot the scotch back in one quick throw and the tumbler was once again on the bar and refilled almost before the glass settled. The first drink was for getting *right*, the second was for sipping.

Sam liked the place, because everyone around him looked as if they were all clinging to their own secrets. Of course, none that he knew of were SSD-employed, and unlikely spies, but every face looked questionable nonetheless. That made him comfortable. Perhaps it was because few if any men wanted to discuss much at all. He'd never run into anyone he knew in the place, not that he knew *that* many faces in America. He liked it that way. It was one place he was confident no one cared to know much of anything about him other than what he was drinking and if perhaps he could buy an extra one for them.

He was hungry, but he'd have to wait until he got home. The bar only served potatoes—any way one liked them, but potatoes strictly. If one asked for fries, they were sliced and baked. Chips, and they were thinly sliced and baked. Mashed, and they were whipped and served, but there was no gravy in sight. Of course, potatoes were just fine for many of the patrons. They were the perfect company for a gurgling, booze-filled stomach.

Everything about the basement bar still *felt* illegal. Two rifles hung in an "X" under a deer head and looked ready to be grabbed should the G-men have come knocking years ago. A loaded pistol was within reach of the bartender under the bar—Sam only knew that because he'd caught sight of it once when sitting at the far side. Strange people who never ordered a drink would materialize from the back door to the kitchen only to exit through the front and never be seen again. Sam wasn't sure who owned the place, but he knew it wasn't the bartender because there was a silhouette that danced in the back of the kitchen every so often.

A knock came at the door after he'd gotten halfway through his second drink. The slide of the eye panel on the steel door screeched through the otherwise enjoyable quiet as Sam produced a cigarette. He could already feel the brew easing his muscles. The after-effects of Shiner's pummeling often required some relief. He heard the door open and close behind him, and the air in the room shifted as he lit the smoke.

In the reflection of the glass lining the wall behind the bar he could see the rest of the patrons craning their necks much in the same way they did when he'd entered, but they went on staring. Someone sat in the seat next to him before he could even turn to look, which already perturbed him—there were plenty of perfectly good seats that weren't within his breathing space. A set of thick, red fingers slammed some coins down on the bar; Sam could sense by the look on the bartender's face that he wasn't thrilled with the newly arrived customer.

"Mind if I ask what's good here?" the voice asked, and Sam recognized the smug tone of confidence as his own cigarette smoke wafted in the man's wake. Sam could smell the musk of a man who'd already been drinking. Staring back at him in a wrinkled suit was the crocodilian Bruce Whelan, FBI agent extraordinaire and notable frenemy. The bartender looked to Sam for next moves, but Sam nodded to signal that the man sitting beside him was okay, even if that was a lie.

Sam lowered his head toward the bar and smirked. "How'd you get in?"

"The big guy over there didn't like the look of me," Whelan grumbled while shooting a thumb over his shoulder to point to the sea-hardened security man. He dropped his voice. "But he didn't like the look of my credentials when I waved them in his face either. *Shouldn't* you be asking how I found you?"

"You followed me," Sam replied with indifference. "The question I really should ask is for how long?"

"Oh, long enough," Whelan said with a knowing smile. He threw back some of his scotch, finishing half of the glass without so much as a wince. "Let's walk and talk."

"I can talk right here."

"But I can't." Whelan took inventory of the staring faces around the bar. "Now, I could arrest you right where you stand. I'd have no problem doing that on legal grounds," Whelan said in a soft voice. Side-eyes glared from all around the room as he surveyed the threats. Suddenly the uninterested had become very interested. "They don't like guys like me here. I get it. They've been here before my kind ever existed. So, I'm assuming that if I was to break out a pair of cuffs, flash my credentials, and make a scene of it, I might expect some trouble."

"I can't give you any guarantees," Sam said.

"I expected as much," Whelan replied as he returned to his drink.

"Besides," Sam said as he nursed his own drink. "What charge do you have on me?"

"Oh!" Whelan purred in the manner of two old

friends having good conversation. He waved a dismissive hand. "I'm sure I can find something."

Sam was sure Whelan could. Despite their temporary alliance, it was seemingly business as usual with Whelan. Only a year earlier, the two men had been ready to tear each other's eyes out until they'd found some modicum of common ground in the form of one Udo Ramm, Nazi infiltrator.

"How's your boss?" Whelan asked, abruptly changing the topic.

"Go ask him."

"Can't," Whelan replied. He shrugged with confusion. "He's never here in the states."

"Shame," Sam said, feigning defeat. "And yours?"

Whelan didn't answer the question. Instead, he massaged the drink glass in his hand. "How about that walk?"

"I'd like to finish my drink," Sam replied.

"Not necessary." Whelan grabbed his drink and emptied it into a flask he retrieved from his breast pocket. Then he grabbed Sam's glass and emptied that in there too. "Now we've got road sodas."

"Isn't that illegal?" Sam asked facetiously.

"What isn't?"

Meridian Hill Park was quiet. It was the perfect place for two men of the shadows to stroll and confer without the risk of eavesdropping. Sam couldn't be sure that Whelan didn't have listeners on standby, but then again Whelan couldn't be sure Sam wasn't being watched, so both seemed to resolve silently that they were free to speak in the open air—a gentleman's compromise by two ungentlemanly men. The only people listening were drunks, and the likelihood that any wino would remember what he'd heard tonight was low.

A light mist danced in the night air, swirling in gusts and making a wet dew of the grass. They stuck to the paved path, walking at an even pace but in no rush whatsoever to get anywhere. They'd already made half of a loop around the park before anyone said anything of substance—Whelan was the first to speak.

"One of these times it's not going to be me who catches you," Whelan proclaimed, likely in the best attempt at offering an olive branch he could muster up. "As it was, I had to pull two hungry newbies off you before they beat me to you."

"Still following us?"

"We never stopped."

"How'd *they* have fared against the bar patrons?" Sam asked.

Whelan chuckled. "Not so well. Both are as scrawny as you." Whelan lit a cigarette, and Sam followed suit. In the darkness, they were just two silhouettes dancing through the night air, two burning cherries alighting their figures every time they took a pull from their cigarettes. The two men were rounding the corner as the sound of running water grew stronger. In the distance, the park fountain was in full flow.

"I'm doing you a favor here, Sam," Whelan warned. His tone had changed. Even in the darkness, Sam could make out the concern on his face. "Maybe he won't tell you, so *I* will. You're in deep, and should the right circumstances find you, *no one* will be able to dig you out."

"And you?" Sam asks.

"I've got protections: official employment, cushions, *citizenship*."

"So do I," Sam argued casually.

Whelan grimaced.

They'd neared the fountain, and their pitch was growing louder in proportion to the cascading water.

Whelan frowned. "Don't kid yourself. It would make a hell of a headline: **Feds Nab German Defector in Secret Employ Stateside**." Whelan cast his hand outward as if displaying the newspaper title. "**Hank Brandt to blame?**" Sam didn't take the bait. "Yeah," Whelan said as if in warning. "Just like that."

"Didn't you make the same pitch to me last year?" Sam asked. "I remember the headline being a bit more punchy."

Whelan stopped in his tracks. "You joke, but you won't be laughing when they've got you on the stand as a war criminal. You can always come to me, you know?"

Sam scoffed. "If I did, my boss would have my head before yours does."

Whelan and Sam were nearly shouting as they competed with the sound of rushing water coming from the fountain.

"Why are we here, Bruce?" Sam asked.

Whelan took one quick search of the park before he spoke. "Whatever he's got going on over there…" Whelan paused again, leaned in, and dropped his voice. "It's going to blow up in his face."

"How do you know?"

"Because, as I've tried to tell you so many times before, this is *our* jurisdiction."

"So?"

Whelan sighed deeply, then took a nice healthy pull of his cigarette. After a lengthy exhale, he shook his head from side to side. With the fountain flowing, he was free to speak openly. "What do you want me to tell you, Sam? That the organization is a bunch of ruffians and hoodlums prancing around in Europe under the guise of resistance fighters? That you've been subverted—no… *injected*, with a plague of people who have no common cause or goal? I mean, you're swimming with every conflicting ideology that can take a dollar and hold a gun." Whelan, recognizing his excitement, dropped his voice and stepped forward to get close to Sam. "Your boss has got commies and sympathizers embedded deep inside the organization and he doesn't even know it. Brandt's running a bunch of expats with no account-ability and no shame." Whelan glowered for a moment, then said, "No offense."

"Didn't take any," Sam said, letting the comment roll off.

"You know what I mean," Whelan assured Sam. "Now, I don't know why you're still here in DC, and I'm sure I don't *want* to know." Whelan turned and paced for a moment as he searched for his next thought. "I'm doing you a favor here, Sam, because I think you're only half an asshole—and I'd know."

Sam burned through the cherry on the end of his cigarette as he let Whelan go off. Once the man had finally paused, Sam offered a thank you. He meant it. Had Whelan been a full asshole they wouldn't even be having this conversation and Sam would probably be in a cell.

"You're a tool, Sam, that's all I'm saying," Whelan said. "A tool to grab from the box that's just the perfect one for the job, and damn if it breaks while you're doing it. You just grab another one."

"Are you offering me a job?"

"You know I can't do that," Whelan replied sheepishly.

"Then why tell me all this?"

Whelan mulled over the question. Perhaps he was searching for a good answer himself. "The whole thing *will* come crashing down—where will you be when it does?"

Sam offered no answer.

"You'd better be careful, my friend," Whelan said. "If you don't watch your ass, you and your whole operation are going to walk right into shit." He let the thought sink for a moment before he continued, "If you haven't already."

Sam nodded. He took Whelan's meaning. They resumed walking, distancing themselves from the fountain and continuing along a dark corridor populated by infrequent trees. "Well," Sam said. "You called this meeting. I'm sure you didn't haul me out here and away from my drink just to tell me you're worried about me."

"Speaking of which," Whelan said as he took the flask from his pocket. He shot the scotch back, then handed it off to Sam, who did the same.

"Well?" Sam asked.

"Some fellas lurking around your parts. What do they call it?" Sam watched Whelan contemplate the name he'd heard and forgot.

"The Yard," Sam said.

"That one. Some undesirables on your roster—American-Italians," Whelan said. "Used to be on my turf. New York. Heard they've been running around with you and yours. I was wondering if they're still here, or *over there*. Know anything about that?"

Sam had heard of the recruitment of mafiosos within the ranks of the SSD, but who was he to judge? Loyal to Brandt to the end, yet wanting to throw Whelan a bone, he replied, "Can neither confirm nor deny."

Whelan smiled as he took the flask back. "When a weak link breaks, the whole chain collapses, Sam." He broke off from the spy and tossed away his cigarette, leaving Sam exposed under a sodium lamp.

9

Lukas completed another treacherous trip from the enemy's side to Bern—this time without any intelligence. No threat of a bombing raid arose, and The New York Boys retrieved him without incident. Seated in the rear bench of the sedan, Lukas finally gained a moment of respite. His lack of product during transit gave him nothing to fear, yet his failure to investigate the farm further weighed heavy on him. The New York Boys were silent as usual as the car lurched forward.

"I want to see him," Lukas stated firmly through the haze of cigarette smoke. Louie and Phil quickly eyed each other. Who would speak first? Who was even in charge? Lukas was never sure. He always sensed a team element between the two men.

Louie spoke up. "Not tonight."

"Damn it, I want to see him!" Lukas barked. "And if you won't take me to see him, then pull the car over and let me free."

"He's unavailable. Anything you can say to him, you can say to us."

"Fine," Lukas said, leaning forward to make sure they heard good and clear. "Your man's gone. Do you hear me? Absent. Which means I won't be going back until a new plan has been formed." In his rage, his well-spoken English receded and gave way to the accent of his mother tongue. "If that's not good enough, then I'll take my information elsewhere, somewhere it will be utilized. I'm tired of waiting, and now your operation is as good as dead—maybe your asset too."

The New York Boys let this news linger for a moment as the car bounced along dark cobblestone streets. Lukas wasn't always brought to meet Combe. Sometimes information was passed through Louie for later debrief. Never had the priest behaved in such a manner, and the tension of disaster hung heavy in the air.

Lukas held all the cards. Ask a native in Switzerland what the most valuable commodity was and they may say gold or chocolate. Ask a German and they might say the discreet banking. Ask an American and they'd answer: information.

Through the rearview, Phil eyed Lukas. The priest caught a glimpse of his expression as they passed the glow of an oil lamp. There was concern in his eyes, maybe confusion. Whatever it was, it apparently had its intended effect, because once more Louie and Phil caught each other's gaze for a nonverbal plan of action before Phil nodded to proceed.

The car halted outside a small house Lukas had never been to. Louie left without saying a word, entered through the front door, and picked up a phone. Lukas could see Louie's actions through the silhouette of a window illuminated by a small desk lamp. There was a short exchange between him and the person on the other end, then Louie hustled down the front steps and leapt back into the car. They were off again.

This time, the car passed Combe's building swiftly. Lukas watched the location come and go while Louie rummaged through a dashboard compartment. Impatient, the priest asked, "What's it going to be?"

Louie turned and displayed a flinty gaze as he handed Lukas a black cloth. He wagged a finger toward the priest's eyes without a word of direction. "If that's what you want, that's what you'll get. New rules."

Lukas grabbed the cloth, examined it briefly, then looked back up to Louie hesitantly. Another car passed, its headlights briefly falling onto Louie's face and highlighting a do-it-or-don't gaze. Louie looked tired, perhaps as tired as Lukas felt himself. He sensed Lukas' apprehension. Phil clocked Lukas again through the dark rearview. His own eyes were bloodshot, reddened where they should be white. The effect only disheartened Lukas further—these two men had always carried with them an air of the unsavory. A man whose ear is grabbed by criminals and confessors to unload their sins knows their lot and can sense them a mile away.

But they'd been working together for some time now, had managed the exchanges swimmingly—everything was still above board. Lukas unraveled the black cloth, the stitching of which allowed little light to travel through it, then placed it over his eyes and tied it loosely behind his head. The car accelerated forcefully.

Faint light permeated the blindfold. Lukas felt as if he were floating in an abyss, the black void of space graced by the diffused glows of intermittent stars and celestial bodies. He was still traveling forward, swaying casually with the movements of the car when it stopped or turned, but he'd lost a sense of his geographical location after a short time. The minuscule illumination provided by streetlights waned over time.

The car left the city limits, of that Lukas was sure. The sensation of pavement and cobblestone gave way to the soft scratch of tires over dirt. After the last series of turns, the car headed straight for several minutes. *Traveling out to the country*, Lukas thought. It wasn't long before his stomach rose up into his chest—a sudden change in elevation.

His palms were clammy, but his hearing was acute. Fearful men have exceptional senses. A match flicked against a box, and then came the smell of sulfur. A waft of cigarette smoke followed—not that it bothered Lukas. He had never been one for smoking, but his parishioners certainly were. In fact, the burning stench reminded him of the candle-lighting ceremonies in the church, and he'd dared say the act provided some comfort as the two men chauffeured him to who-knows-where.

In Lukas' eyes, Christ the savior traveled in the seat beside him. Lukas unbuttoned the top notch on his coat, revealing his clerical collar, then spoke softly, lowering his head to address only himself, "Lord, the sword of your word is heavy, the shield often times cumbersome, but I know you deliver the strength to carry both."

"What'sat?" Louie asked.

"A prayer," Lukas replied.

"Mm," Louie mumbled. "Gonna need a lot of those."

"Catholic?" Lukas asked.

"Protestant," Louie replied through the muffled exhalation of cigarette smoke. "Both the same if ya ask me—you got the guy with the thorny crown, and so do I."

"All on the same team, so to speak," Lukas said as if only to convince himself. "We could use all the teammates we can get."

"Straight ahead," Louie said, though Lukas knew the man wasn't talking to him. For the first time, he sensed there was a hierarchy to this duo.

Now they were climbing a steeper incline than before, rising up the side of a mountain via a series of switchbacks as they traveled higher. Lukas hadn't been able to see much since he'd applied the blindfold, and now the matte-black nothingness only seemed to grow deeper. The priest could just barely make out the blurred illumination of the headlights paving the way up the mountain.

The temperature fell inside the vehicle, probably because of the higher elevation. Lukas might not have noticed something like that had his senses not been heightened. Now the car was being jostled, and his body was being hurled from side to side as the chassis squeaked and groaned over every minor bump on the unpaved road. *Just where the hell are they taking me?* Lukas wondered. He was thankful he hadn't said the words out loud. He wasn't one for evoking the dreaded underworld, but the unease was starting to get to him—and as far as he knew, not even God Almighty could hear the inner thoughts of a man's mind.

With each minute that passed, fear welled inside of him. But he'd asked for it. Prior rendezvous had been very calculated and planned. Had friend turned enemy since the priest had announced himself as useless? Had they camouflaged themselves as friends to whisk him away for punishment? If this was the way he was going to die, he was disappointed. He always imagined his final moments might have some degree of ceremony, of majesty, of accomplishment. And what had he accomplished thus far? Nothing—a few rail lines damaged, a munitions factory turned into a crater, and an *SS* battalion captured. Well, that was *something*.

I've had a good go at it, Lukas thought to himself. His attitude had taken a fatalistic turn. *Done some good work, spread the word far and wide—even threw my hat into the war effort where it counted. Should this be it, then my time hasn't been a waste.* He wondered if he really believed it, or if he was lying to himself to convince himself he believed it. *Christ tests like that, doesn't he?* He dismissed the idea of defeat in short time. *This can't be the end. There's much more to do—so much more.*

The car halted suddenly, though continued idling. Only the purr of the car's motor was audible. Neither Louie nor Phil said a word. Lukas resisted the urge to remove the blindfold, even though he thought they'd probably arrived where they were meant to be. The motor ceased. Insects of the night took over the theatrics.

"Blindfold stays on," Louie said, then Lukas heard the screech as the man opened the car door. There was the soft patter of footsteps against gravel before someone opened the rear-passenger-side door. The cool night air engulfed the interior of the car. A firm grip closed around Lukas' wrist, and he was guided out of the vehicle. "Don't worry, Father. I've got you. Come on"

The respectful use of Lukas' title finally put him in a state of ease. He'd been in the company of friends, he resolved, or else they'd likely have made short work of him. They could have just gunned him down on the street.

He was ushered forward. A deciduous smell gathered in his nose, and grass crunched beneath his feet. He recognized the timbre of mountain winds. A court of insects chirped, first vibrantly, then hesitantly, as the two men continued down the path. Even the critters of the late hours knew when discretion was advised. Lukas' handler wasn't forceful with him, simply directing him forward with a loose grip around the priest's bicep. "Watch your step here," he warned, and Lukas slowed momentarily before lifting a foot to feel for the small step before him. A moment later his feet found cement, and then the man released his grip and said, "Hold on."

A gate opened, he pulled Lukas through, then he shut it behind him with a soft *clang*. The surface changed again: slate stone. The echo that returned with each step suggested a courtyard of high walls. Wood was burning—Lukas could smell the charred scent.

"Sorry about the blindfold," his escort said. "I don't make the rules."

"Understandable," Lukas agreed.

Louie opened a door, led Lukas in, then said, "You can lose the blindfold now." Out in the wilderness, the kid had lost some of the Swiss-Germanic flair of his accent. When speaking English, he was a full-blooded New York Italian.

As Lukas undid the knot of the blindfold, the door closed behind him. He turned, but the man in the passenger seat had vanished. He was left alone in the entryway of a cozy home, a wood fire dancing vibrantly in a stone fireplace at the edge of the living room. Out of the front window, he could still see the idle car. Louie lingered outside, puffing on a cigarette and talking casually to the driver.

"Father," a voice sounded from the large staircase. Each old, weak wooden board creaked under the approaching footsteps. The collegiate Combe extended a welcoming hand, and Father Jan Lukas took it once the man had arrived at the base. "How are you?" Lukas, still anxious, could only produce an unconvincing nod. "I trust my men treated you alright?" He eyed the blindfold still clutched in Lukas' hand and motioned to it. "Precaution—just in case. My protection, as well as yours. You could understand why your status has been elevated." Combe retrieved a cigarette from a tin. "Mind if I smoke?"

Lukas shook his head. He feared that the more time he spent with these men, the more at risk he was of picking up the habit. Did cigarette smoking come with the territory? Lord knew his nerves could use the release.

"You?" Combe asked, but Lukas declined. Combe waved him forward, then turned to the living area.

The room was cozy and lived-in. Two long auburn couches with worn arm rests faced each other. Maroon curtains obscured tall windows. The carpeting was littered with black scorch marks, likely where rogue pieces of wood from the fireplace had singed it. In the stone setting, the wood crackled and popped. Combe motioned for Lukas to sit on the couch, then tossed another log onto the fire.

Combe took a seat as well, inhaled from the cigarette, and studied Lukas as the priest removed his coat. Once settled, he revealed his clerical collar fully, then clasped his hands firmly on his lap as if eternally in a state of prayer. There was a brief pause while the two stared at each other.

"So, you wanted me. I'm here," Combe said. "Would you be so kind as to elaborate on recent events?"

"Why are we meeting here?" Lukas asked.

"Let's just say this is a place of more discretion," Combe replied.

Lukas spent the next few minutes filling Combe in about what he knew and didn't. Combe remained astute and quiet. Only his facial expressions changed during the story, ranging from the occasional frown or eyes that arched in surprise. When Lukas finished, there followed another long period of silence and frowning from Combe while the noisy fire filled in for the absence of conversation.

"That's all very troubling," Combe finally said after a long moment of silence. Even for a man as good at listening as Lukas was, he found Combe's disquiet unnerving.

"This has taken too long," Lukas said.

"I'm afraid these things don't always revolve around our own schedules."

"Then whose?"

Combe couldn't provide an answer.

"I'm very willing to part with particular knowledge, Mr. Combe," Lukas said. There was a wariness to his tone. "Provided that knowledge isn't wasted or undervalued."

Combe nodded, his gaze wandering to the tip of his cigarette. He sat forward, addressing Lukas once more. "I'm not the execution man—I'm the *info* man."

"Then perhaps I should be speaking with him," Lukas suggested.

"Only *I* talk to him," Combe said sternly. He tapped his cigarette into a small tray on a side table, then crossed his legs and leaned back into his seat. "But he listens."

"Let me be clear, Mr. Combe," Lukas began, "you are not the only party willing to receive the information I'm offering. I have friends in the east, friends like you, who would willingly act where you haven't. If you or your friends are not willing to use what I give you to make great change, then I won't hesitate to see that a party more deserving of it is the recipient. I've risked life and limb for far too long without seeing any results for my efforts. I've asked nothing in return."

"I seem to have a ledger that reports the receipt of currency," Combe said. "Swiss, Austrian, and German."

Lukas wagged his head. "You misunderstand me. This is not a fiscal reward—this is an insurance policy. I need money to pay off those who wish to report on resistance activities, and there are many who would sell their friends out for a franc. Poor people are desperate. I need the money to ensure their musings don't fall on secret police ears. For every man that suspects devious actions, a small sum is needed to guarantee his lips stay sealed. I've even paid out of the church's purse, and Lord knows I'll pay for that later."

Combe nodded. He seemed to be stuck in a perpetual state of thought.

"So I'm asking you very kindly," Lukas said, "Before you lose me as an asset entirely, and perhaps any hold you have over this operation, to either prove to me that a result is forthcoming, or introduce me to someone that can."

Combe mulled over the demand for a moment. "Why are you doing this?" Combe asked. "Forgive me for being inquisitive, but I'm curious about motives. I know only as much as my men tell me."

"When bombs fall on men, Mr. Combe," Lukas said, "men die and other men fill their place. The war rages on. When bombs fall on factories, the war will be shortened. Every munitions factory destroyed, every weapon that can't be placed in the field, is one less day of war and one fewer dead child. It is one day closer to an end."

Combe, ever playing the babysitting handler, asked, "Do you need anything?"

"I need a result."

"I'll see what can be done," Combe replied. A log became displaced, falling into the pit of embers. The fire roared, sending shimmering flakes of flame rising up into the dark chimney.

10

There was a phone on Hank Brandt's desk—if one could see through the haze of pipe smoke clouding the spy chief's office—that seldom rang. It was not red, though some might argue the color would have been more fitting of its unique purpose, but an unremarkable brown. It was not to be confused with the phone that sat next to it, which *often* rang, and was also of an unremarkable coloration, specifically black. So when the brown phone chimed, its song sent the burn-scarred man into a frenzy that saw him leap from his chair in such an uncontrollable fashion that the embers from his pipe were sent scattering along the documents on his desk, nearly burning precious intel in the chaos.

If someone had been watching, though those chances were slim, they might wonder why he had reacted in such a way—everyone except Iris, whose calls were almost always funneled through on the black phone. But even Iris didn't have access to the brown phone, and was educated in its sensitivity—she was not permitted to answer it should it ring during Brandt's absence. She was gone for the evening, which saved Brandt the embarrassment of fumbling his way to remove the phone from its cradle.

In the tungsten glow of the desk lamp, the dim pool of light reflected up at Brandt's grimace as he placed the phone to his ear. Why had he expressed such agony in the process of answering the call? Because few people had access to the number, and if someone was on the other end of the line, the reason was because there was an emergency only Brandt himself could be made aware of and address. Bracing himself for information that was far more likely to be bad than good—*good* information traveled through the normal communication channels— Brandt clutched the pipe stem between his teeth and placed the phone to his ear.

"Dispatch," Brandt said calmly, enforcing protocol. The line of communication was disguised as one in the business of sending taxis out to patrons. The brainy administrative branch at The Yard all agreed it was a good justification as to why anyone would be ready and willing to answer such a late night telephone call if one was received in error.

"Wonderful night for a trip, wouldn't you agree?" It was Combe.

"That would depend on where one would like to go," Brandt replied.

"Indeed," Combe said. "It's a long trip, I'm afraid—a trip very far east. Do you think you can manage that?"

"We can send someone," Brandt replied. "Might take some time, though, I'm afraid."

"Actually, I was quite hoping it might be you *yourself*," Combe said. Static crackled along the line, which suggested the connection was poor, or perhaps distant. "A have a very particular client in need of assistance, and the sensitive nature of said client's activities require a very discreet type of help."

Brandt stared into a cloud of smoke that swirled from his lips before he spoke. "Very difficult. The weather is just absolutely terrible out there—very dangerous to be out and about in this type of storm. How's it by you?"

"Absolutely terrible here as well," Combe replied. "In fact, we're about ready to pack it up and go home if it doesn't break."

"No," Brandt said abruptly. "It'll clear. You're to stay put." Brandt checked his watch. Even with all the tools and assets at his disposal, a last-minute trip to meet Combe would require absolute discretion, heavy lifting, a little bit of luck, and a lot of lies. It would be a treacherous journey, and that had nothing to do with the euphemisms regarding weather that both men had been using. It would require a trip across battle-scarred Europe, and the airspace was no safe place for a man who held in his head some of the most high-value secrets known to any person inside or outside America. The request of his physical presence by a subordinate could only mean that one of his operators had run into some type of snafu: an operation had been jeopardized.

"I'm happy to do that," Combe said. "I'm afraid, though, that one of our friends is going to need some convincing—perhaps a little coaxing and a pat on the back."

"Elaborate," Brandt said.

"Our friend," Combe began, "you know, the *religious* one. Well, he's had a bit of a crisis of faith."

"So help him to see the light," Brandt replied. "That's *your* job."

"I'm all too happy to do so," Combe said, "although I seem to have lost my way too. The Lord is testing us. The farm isn't yielding the crop it once was. In fact, it's not yielding anything at all, and well, that's just causing everyone quite a bit of concern."

With that Brandt shuddered. Had his man on the inside been compromised? He removed the pipe from his mouth, something he rarely did; normally he clutched it like a newborn with a pacifier. "Are you saying what I think you're saying?" Brandt asked against his better judgement. His mother had always given him the sage advice to not ask questions if he wasn't going to like the answers.

"I believe I am," Combe said. "In fact, it seems that the whole farm has shut down for the season. Strange, considering the harvest isn't over, wouldn't you agree? I find it hard to believe that a farm with such a healthy yield would suddenly close up shop unannounced, and so does the man of faith."

"Is he there with you now?" Brandt asked.

"He's in hand," Combe responded. "He is completely out of sorts, and I think he needs a push in the right direction before he loses faith completely."

"What about our man in the Ministry?" Brandt asked. "Has he received word of exit?"

"Nothing."

"I'm on my way," Brandt said. "Normal procedures."

"We'll be waiting."

Before Brandt could even hear the full statement, he had already slammed the phone back down on the receiver and was tapping the bowl of his pipe against the ash tray on the desk in a flurry of sparks.

He collected the papers on his desk, themselves top secret, and secured them in a safe. Iris would see to it that they were sorted in the morning. Oddly enough, the secretary was privy to many state secrets which she really shouldn't have been, but he knew she could be trusted not to disclose any of them. Though more people knew about their activities than Brandt would care to admit, the trysts the two of them had shared over the last year had confirmed her ability to remain tight-lipped. He'd learned that the hard way. Even spy chiefs are prone to error.

Brandt dug several passports out of his desk, a package of tobacco, and a briefcase with battered seams from beside his desk. He pulled a brown overcoat from the hanger beside the door without a glance back at his office before he shut and locked the door behind him. The top floor of The Yard was quiet, which was expected; he was the only one besides Iris who ever occupied it. Below, on the second and third, the activities of SSD employees were in high gear.

There was no such thing as day or night at the SSD, just as in war. There was only now and later, and now was the right time to act, whereas later would indeed be too late. Several of his subordinates called out to him, but his pace was too brisk to stop. At any other time he would have gladly paused to consider the questions or concerns of his worker bees, but the matter at hand was too delicate.

Was Hank Brandt acting irrationally? He didn't think so. When one of the most important intel-gathering operations deployed inside Nazi Germany was at risk of going belly-up, a spy chief needed to insert himself into the fray to see that its momentum wasn't halted. If a spy operation's value was determined by its currency, then losing the Peenemünde operation would be like draining a savings account. Worse still, Brandt knew for sure that his was not the only operation on the island, and though other "friends" had their fingers in the pot, he was hoping to be the one to remove the honey before the bears came sniffing.

But it was not Brandt who had discovered the gold-like honey that functioned as such valuable currency. He was on the receiving end, sure, but he did not get his hands dirty. For that task, he employed domestic and foreign operators alike—the latter being his favorite kind—to be his eyes and ears across the globe. There was an inherent danger that came with the occupation, not unlike being a front-line trooper, but unique in its own way. Every so often he and his operators were reminded of that risk.

Did that mean he should throw the baby out with the bathwater and assume that his man in Peenemünde was a lost cause? Normally that would be the case, because Hank Brandt was not in the business of sending in rescue teams for compromised actors. In this partic-ular scenario, he felt an unwavering need for an answer, not just because closure and finality were important in this line of work, but because the intel in this operation was evolving daily.

He wanted to curse his own superiors for not acting sooner. Had they heeded his advice and bombed the ever-loving hell out of the island, perhaps his man on the inside would be home. The absence of communica-tion did not necessarily mean that his operator was dead;

on the contrary, he could be very much alive and housed in a POW camp, but that only gave Brandt more pause for concern. Captured men were at risk of talking, and every moment that ticked by was another in which an asset's resolve was tested.

Who was this mystery operator that had failed to communicate with his liaison? His name was Roger Fowler, and his greatest two strengths were photography and discretion, making him a wonderful addition to the SSD. He was also fluent in German, but that did not mean that he would be able to talk his way out of a bad situation. Couldn't Brandt just wait two weeks until the next drop cycle occurred, send the priest back in, and see if this had all just been some misunderstanding— some operational choice that Fowler had made of his own accord? Not according to Ansel Combe. Brandt needed to leave now, at the soonest available opportunity, because what else is having your own military-grade aircraft good for if not to fly it across the Atlantic in the middle of the night?

A flood of possibilities accompanied Brandt on his brisk exit from The Yard. The first was the information he'd heard about the RAF raid and its looming approach. The second was whether Fowler was alive, and if so, had he talked? The third, and one that was particularly gruesome in theory, was whether Fowler had the potential to spoil this forthcoming attack. And the fourth, worst of all, was what had led to Fowler's capture, since so few people knew of his activities. This final scenario haunted Brandt, because it could have meant that someone in SSD had spoken to—or they themselves were—the enemy.

But before he left he would have to collect another

operator, a foreigner-turned-domestic tool he could count on. Brandt himself would not be inserted behind enemy lines—that would be far too great a risk, even if he was famous for the occasional frontline charge with America's infantry. Besides, though he possessed the military training to carry himself in enemy territory, he was growing old. He would need to send someone in to act as his proxy, and though he'd never said it aloud, he'd considered this operator his personal favorite.

So before he arrived at the car that would take him to an airfield that never slept, he made a stop to use a secure telephone. Not far away in the pits of D.C., his favorite operator was on call for delicate situations like the one present. At this hour, his asset was probably training with a friend; the man was not a spy like Brandt, but a fighter nonetheless, and when he wasn't lending his expertise to young up and comers in search of glory in the ring, he was imparting his knowledge to operators Brandt suggested might get their hands the most dirty. Brandt was thankful he'd had the foresight to cultivate this relationship, because the man he was about call upon was going to take a trip to Germany, and the likelihood that he would have to use those dangerous hands was very, very strong.

11

———

A car at The Yard waited on standby to take Sam to Washington National. He still had the glaze of sweat from an early-evening Shiner session on his skin. There was "no time to stop anywhere," he'd been instructed by the man who'd ushered him to the plane. "Not even for cigarettes." Sam found that detail *particularly* painful. The sun began to set during the trip, painting the city in a rusty-orange hue, and Sam arrived on a private strip annexed from the rest of the airport. Sam thanked the driver for the car, and approached the plane with nothing but the clothes on his back, a half pack of cigarettes, and the watch he'd been gifted by the long-dead Sigrid Lang.

Against the twilight-painted DC skyline, the silhouette of a cargo aircraft stood as foreboding as a raven—a Gooney Bird, the name the troops had affectionately given the widely used C-47. It was an easy craft to recognize: the nose was always pointing proudly up into the air ahead as if ready to meet its challenger with dignity. Beside its landing gear, two men in military fatigues were performing their last-minute checks. The plane's propellers sent dust flying around the tarmac, so Sam clutched the lapels of his coat tightly. Next to the tail of the plane and painted in the dim red of the emergency landing lights stood Hank Brandt. His long, brown, multi-pocketed coat flapped in the breeze theatrically as he stared back at Sam from the plane's steps. Then, as if right on cue, his face glowed in the soft amber hue of the flame from his his pipe.

Was Sam ready? As ready as one could be when they had no idea where they were going. This was the case most of the time, because despite the fact that news of success traveled quickly once operations were completed and shelved, pending ones were discussed by few people. Only those privy to need-to-know information could connect dots before operations were launched, and even Sam was kept out of the loop until he had met the man with the burn-scarred face for intel.

He'd didn't even get a chance to take care of his "leaving for a while" rituals. Normally, he'd ensure all appliances were off, check the taps, and leave markers so he'd know if anyone had been in his apartment while he'd been gone. He assumed his apartment was being watched by SSD men—not that he had confirmation. He often wondered if the spy chief employed spies to spy on his own spies. If so, they'd watch his apartment. With so many men on the payroll, the idea that there were informants watching informants wasn't preposterous.

As the sun dipped behind a swath of clouds traveling northeast, the sky erupted in a bright-red-glow. The tarmac was wet with the residue of an afternoon rain, and Sam, now a skilled photographer, recognized that these majestic sunsets often came on the tail end of a passing storm. An almost full moon hung low in the east. The delivery car sped off immediately, then Sam and Brandt stood there for a brief moment in stillness.

"*Hast du dein travel bag?*" Brandt said like a red-blooded American. His dialect was *atrocious*. It was a rhetorical question.

Sam inhaled from the cigarette, then exhaled softly as if processing the brief jolt that always came with a last-minute assignment. They were the types that had minimal planning, suboptimal intel, and fly-by-the-seat-of-your-pants tactics—in short, everything dangerous Sam was good at.

He snuck one last look at the sky before climbing the steps of the plane and taking his seat inside. Behind him, Brandt followed and sealed the door shut and the sound of the propellers became muffled. The spy chief signaled the pilot to proceed with takeoff, then took the seat across from Sam. The personnel around the plane waved it off for departure after the door had been shut. The propellers kicked into high gear and the bird jolted before beginning to circle around the runway for takeoff.

"It'll be some time before we get to Station 105—Chelveston," Brandt said.

"Chelveston?" Sam asked. "That's an RAF runway." The words rolled off Sam's tongue with an air of arrogance. He wondered if Brandt sensed his skepticism.

"Not right now," Brandt replied. "The 305th's set up shop."

"That the group that's been hitting all the magnesium and aluminum works?"

"Among others," Brandt replied. "Our boys seem to think the name of the game is precision. That hasn't been jiving so well with our friends across the pond."

"Scorched earth or bust," Sam replied. "Any targets set on tungsten shops?"

Brandt chuckled with a toothy grin. It was Sam who'd foiled the plans of the Nazi infiltrator Udo Ramm during his effort to source American tungsten. An outpouring of smoke left Brandt's wheezing throat.

"Be straight with me, Brandt," Sam said. The chief ceased smiling. Sam didn't speak with insubordination generally, but unlike many of the other operatives, Sam had a seniority with the old man uncharacteristic of his other relationships. "Where are we going?"

"*Back*," Brandt replied simply. Sam needed no more evidence that the vague word was code for "Germany." Sam's eyes wandered. Could Brandt sense Sam's reluctance? It was hard to tell. "You know the rules, Sam."

It wasn't often that Brandt hung Sam's unique predicament over his head. When he did, it was to remind Sam that he was the one indebted, not Brandt. Had Whelan planted the seeds of insecurity within the spy? Sam had quite liked keeping both feet on American soil, but who better to operate in the *Reich* than a man who'd come from deep within it?

"Rules bend until they break," Sam said.

"I was an attorney. I know a thing or two about rules, or what are *perceived* as the rules. Let me tell you something about the rules in the courtroom: they only apply in so far as the way a man mounts his case, and furthermore, what his client is willing to get as a result."

Sam remained unconvinced. Brandt clutched his

pipe between his teeth, then tipped his head toward Sam before saying, "Need I remind you how I found you?"

"Alright, then," Sam said, taking inventory of Brandt's shadowy, scarred visage. The spy chief was more out of sorts than usual. "That bad, huh?"

"I always pegged you as an optimist, Abel," Brandt said.

"I am," Sam replied. "But if you're standing here to scoop me up *in person*, I know it's not good."

"That's a glass half empty," Brandt replied.

"Some people think the glass is half empty, some think it's full. The way I see it, we can all just agree the glass contains liquid."

The plane finally reached its cruising altitude. Sam noted it had been retrofitted to become Brandt's flying office. Seats faced each other, ready to entertain meetings; there were filing cabinets against the fuselage; and there were several other people accompanying Brandt and seated in the tail section whom Sam did not know.

A small lamp fixture hung from above the closed plane window, casting both of the men in a ghoulish, shadow-soaked orange. As if Pavlovian, Sam lit up a cigarette and Brandt packed a pipe. Once both men had gotten their fix of tobacco, Brandt said, "So." He lingered on the word for a moment, turning the pipe stem over in his fingers. "Got a bit of a problem over there."

"Where?"

"Peenemünde."

Sam thought on the word for a second. He had a vivid recall of things like that, a sharp memory. "Ramm," Sam simply replied. He wasn't sure if he said it out loud to answer Brandt, or if it was to convince himself.

Brandt nodded. "And?"

"Rockets."

Brandt nodded. When he did, the burn scars covering the side of his face creased into even darker shadows. He said, "You keep it up, you're going to have my job one day."

"Wouldn't dream of it," Sam said as he exhaled smoke.

Brandt smiled once more, but then the smile quickly subsided and the old man's face grew stoic and stern. Sam even thought he noticed the man sit up straighter. Had the boss been treating the spy more like a friend and less like a subordinate? Brandt's mouth opened, and he said, "Sam, what I'm about to tell you cannot leave this plane. Is that understood?"

"I thought that was a given," Sam replied.

"Sam," Brandt said like a disciplinary father.

Sam nodded, then said, "Understood."

Brandt took a deep breath, folded the pipe into one of his hands, and clasped both hands together on his lap. The old man had *actually* stopped smoking his pipe for once. It was in that moment Sam realized how different the man had begun to look.

His complexion had grown grayer. Much of the color had left his checks, and a little pouch was showing over his belt buckle. His teeth had yellowed further and the blood vessels in his nose had begun to break, forming small red cobwebs on his nostrils. Large dark bags under his eyes evidenced his lack of sleep. Despite his slightly unkempt look, he still bore the various pins of valor on his jacket.

Brandt said, "The Ramm operation yielded valuable material."

"What can I say?" Sam said. "It's a habit."

Brandt grimaced. It had been Sam's intel that had made Brandt privy to the rocket manufacturing facility on Germany's northeast coast. Ramm had sacrificed that intel upon capture and Brandt had been trying to grind the man for information ever since. Sam hadn't heard a damn thing about the place ever since he'd delivered the German up, but he'd at least figured out *where* it was.

"Our friends across the pond have done the legwork," Brandt said. "And it's going to come to a head."

"When?"

"I don't know."

Sam sensed the shame in his voice. For once, a plan had been concocted and sent into motion and Brandt knew nothing about it other than that it would take place.

"We've had a hiccup," Brandt said. "A man on the inside is at risk, and furthermore, could put the whole operation on glass legs. I need someone inside to source information."

"Why don't you just tell your man to flee?" Sam asked. "Why go in there and rendezvous with him?"

"That's where it gets complicated," Brandt replied. "We don't know *what* happened to him. He could have gotten cold feet, lost his marbles, been blown—we don't even know if he's alive. All of those are possibilities."

Sam inhaled deeply from the cigarette, then slowed the smoke to curl from his lip in a snake-like climb as he thought about what a mission like that would entail.

Brandt said, "We have a very tiny window, and

within that, an even smaller window—a frame within a frame."

"I'll say," Sam replied.

"If he is alive…" Brandt said before pausing. He cut the thought off and regathered his phrasing. "If he's already…"

Sam's faces contorted briefly with confusion. The plan seemed so rushed, so slapdash. It wasn't at all like the type of operation the spy chief normally executed.

Brandt finally found the words: "We need to know that what's coming hasn't been compromised."

"And what is coming?" Sam asked.

"That's beyond even my pay grade," Brandt said. "The whiff of Peenemünde has been lingering for some time now. Most people wrote it off as disinformation, fear-mongering, even. No one believed that there was a secret rocket factory sitting at the tip of a beach island. I tried to stress its importance on many occasions. We've passed intel back and forth, but it wasn't until they did their own recon that they took the threat seriously. They've flown so many sorties over the damn place the scouts can navigate by eye."

"And the intel's good?" Sam asked.

"It's better than good," Brandt replied. "They've got manufacturing facilities, housing, factories, research and development centers—launching pads." When the last word left Brandt's mouth his face became grave and stiffened. The chief sat back into his seat, obscuring his face in shadow even more than it already had been. "That's from our own source."

Sam leaned forward, his left eyebrow growing into a high, suspicious arch, and said with confidence, "*They* don't know you had a man inside."

"Some things are better left unsaid," Brandt replied. "They don't know that *I* know." Sam weighed the man's words for a moment—the great game had split. "And don't you think they're not at it themselves, inserting their own informants in our outfit. Once they started to run with this one everything got real hush-hush—for tea-drinkers exclusively. Sure, they might have requested assistance, but that was after the fact, and in my opinion, the lazy option." The burned man inhaled from his pipe, and the black spheres of his eyes flared enigmatically. "They're going to run their ops, and we're going to run ours."

Sam could take the hint. This mission was a true solo act. Forget that in the past the assistance of the Allies had been reliable and dependable; there was no doubt the Soviets were one step ahead of the game, and perhaps the British as well. The free-sharing age of information for mutual aid was coming to a close.

"I need to know, Sam," Brandt pleaded. It was rare the spy chief displayed vulnerability. "I need to know we haven't blown the whole thing."

"Understood." Sam switched gears. "What about that other thing?" Sam asked, referring to his search for Lothar Eichler.

Brandt scowled, then shifted in his seat. "When are you going to drop it, Sam? There's nothing more you could have done. It's been over a year. We don't run vendetta operations. Is this becoming a problem?"

"No problem at all," Sam asked, but he didn't relent. "So, that's a no?"

"I'm afraid I don't know any more than you do," Brandt said.

Sam could tell the chief was growing annoyed. He

could also sense he wasn't being truthful. He had always known he was in the business of lies. His presence within SSD was one of such a hush-hush nature that he rarely thought he was told everything. Or anything. Today, he was *sure* Brandt wasn't telling him everything. Men were lost in the field all the time. If an operation or man was blown, it was scrapped. What made this one so special? And why did Brandt seem to squirm at the mention of Sam's question?

"If you don't mind," Brandt began, "I haven't slept in days, and we've some long flights to Bern." He slouched into the seat and closed his eyes. The plane continued to climb. Soon all Sam could see from the window was the cascading blue turmoil of the Atlantic.

Sam was aware of the Bern operation, the main funnel for German and Axis defectors to meet Brandt's brain, the collegiate Ansel Combe, for a vetting process before being employed or utilized in any meaningful way. Sam had only encountered Combe once, and considered him a good addition to the operation—not just because he knew Combe was smart, but because he added an air of legitimacy to Brandt's outfit when the spy chief got a little too reckless.

Where Brandt leapt, Combe tip-toed, and now that the Americans had entered the war in full force, the need for subterfuge within the *Reich* itself had grown even greater. Not all problems could be solved with a bullet, and Combe preached that aggressively. On several occasions, Sam had been made privy to the professor-like Bern liaison's methodology, and much of it included sowing the seeds of disarray from the inside via deflated Germans themselves. Particularly valuable were the many who'd become disgruntled with the Führer's war, especially as the battlefront grew closer to the fringes of the fatherland, and there was a strong need for men with a conscience to make themselves available and do what American soldiers could not. Combe existed as the top of the food chain for vetting these individuals.

"Everyone wants something," Combe had explained when lecturing operators about agent-running. "Whether it be money, freedom, or *revenge*."

Sam wondered if blackmail was somewhere on that list. It had been how he had been recruited. Sam held no resentment regarding that. In fact, he might argue he and Brandt had grown to be friends since they'd started working together—as much as two men could be who knew a great deal of each other's secrets. Sam had his own dirt on Brandt, not that he'd ever hang it over the man's head. In truth, it was Sam who'd quelled the hunger of FBI agents to smear Brandt's name.

The plane stopped at multiple locations for refueling. Sam didn't ask what they were. He was sure at one point they'd been in Canada, and also Greenland or Iceland. He took every opportunity to sleep when they were in the air.

On one leg of the trip, the spy woke to a foggy glass window as the plane descended. He finally felt refreshed. The plane had come into some choppy air as it circled a large "X" that formed an airfield. Tributaries and staging areas surrounded the runway. It was an impressive location, and Sam could see an abundance of B-17 bombers parked along its perimeter. The amount of airpower at the field was enough to turn a city into a wasteland.

When the plane touched down, Sam saw guide

lights on the runway cutting through the thick mist hanging in the air. He pressed his face against the window, and upon further inspection he saw uniformed men holding flashlights. The atmosphere was so thick with moisturized air that he could barely see any of the area not immediately hugging the runway. The propellers of the plane slowed when the plane halted, and Sam witnessed a large group of airmen crowded around a hangar nearby.

How anyone could depart for a mission in conditions like these was beyond Sam, but he was well aware the Allies had been carrying out attacks with growing frequency. Though Sam couldn't fly a plane himself, he was keen enough to know the European countryside was unforgiving to fighters and bombers alike in less-than-desirable flying conditions. The plane turned down one of the carved-out paths, then came to a stop among a group of bombers parked in a long line. Men had gathered to load explosives into the bellies of the aircraft as Sam and Brandt switched planes.

While they moved from one plane to the next, Brandt retrieved an attaché case from an unnamed man. Brandt never spoke about it, and Sam didn't ask. It was another item to add to the list of things Brandt wasn't telling him.

12

The safe house was perched on a mountain overlooking the sleeping city of Bern. It was a quaint, dark home flanked on all sides by high concrete walls draped in healthy ivy. It resembled many of the other homes carved into the slope. If one was looking closely, they might recognize a flickering golden glow in the sole window of its second floor, a signal at the late hour that the residents were still awake. It was far enough from the Swiss city that the clandestine conversations of its occupants need not be whispered.

Sam and Brandt had used forged documents proclaiming their titles as American diplomats to hide their arrival into Switzerland from the records. Brandt made Sam shave and put on a blazer to sell the idea. Their passage through border security was quiet and uneventful—that was because the men who had handled their transfer were on SSD payroll and rewarded to look the other way. There were few ways to pass through the Swiss redoubt for spies, and even for a man like Brandt who possessed all the resources one could need, it was still a dangerous process.

The home was nondescript in comparison to its neighboring houses. That was the very reason the house had been chosen. Behind its walls, little men spoke about a big world: men from all walks of life, some trustworthy, many not.

Men who'd been called upon to pass through its rear door usually came offering secrets, and if they'd been brought to the home, their secrets justified their entry. They were only invited in the case of having something to offer; the vigorous vetting process ensued far before they could ever grace the home, and what they brought was of exceptional value. Rarely did those secrets come without a price tag—safety, security, and money were among many of the reciprocal offerings sought. To enter the house came with inherent risks. Just because a man was called upon to pay a visit did not mean he'd ever learn the names of the men inside—at least, not their *real* names.

And tonight, like many nights, the home harbored what some may consider the unsavory. On the first floor existed an expatriate seeking solace in the arms of a once-neutral country, and sitting across from him a saboteur from within. There were two men behind the second-floor window, and both were American. One had resided there indefinitely, and the other had paid a special trip to visit him for a rare—and quite dangerous—but important face-to-face meeting. The nature of the mission at hand required the utmost secrecy, and the common methods of communication like cables and diplomatic bags relaying information were out of the question. The secrets discussed that night remained only in the minds of the men wise to them, both of whom sat with grim expressions beside a crackling fire.

Brandt stared in silence at Ansel Combe. The room was grand, though cozy. Wood paneling kept it warm and inviting, yet the conversation at hand was anything but.

Brandt caught a glimpse of his own reflection in the dark window. The burn marks decorating his face always looked particularly menacing in the glow of flames, as if the foe that had scarred them so many years before continued to mock him. In the deep creases where Brandt's skin had been punished by fire, large valleys of shadow were formed.

Combe had deep creases in his forehead too, but his originated from a state of perpetual thought, and a perplexed, stumped looked about his face. He sighed deeply in frustration as if trying to crack some algebraic equation, then rose to his feet and threw another log on the fire. It erupted in a display of sparks and flickering embers that floated up the chimney. Brandt winced, then the fire settled again. Combe paced around the room in wide circles, and Brandt packed his pipe with tobacco in anticipation for even the smallest thought.

Combe gazed toward infinity as he took soft, contemplative steps around the room. He paused for a moment and stared out the window, tucking his hands behind his back and clasping them together at the wrists. Outside and beyond, the Bern countryside sat idly in darkness. Visible in the healthy moon were the homes of its citizens, most of whom were now deep in dreams. Night was always the safer time to start scrutinizing documents and hammering out the details. During the day, the risk of inquisition was just too great.

Discretion was of the utmost importance if the Swiss station was to be maintained, and if you asked Brandt, he'd tell you exactly how important that was.

Brandt lit his pipe, then said, "Don't stand so close to the window."

Combe, now shrouded in the vibrant orange glow of the healthy fire, turned again and continued his tour of the room. His face remained fixed on the floor below as he took each step. He was deep in thought, and Brandt was letting him have at it. After he'd finished the perimeter, he stopped in front of the fire and turned to Brandt. He remained there in silhouette, a grim figure who was anything but eager to agree the chief had to act on this newly acquired information.

Brandt's coveted operation had finally blown up in his face. For nearly two years now the unorthodox man had gotten free rein over his activities, and had run virtually unchecked. He had a sizable slush fund with which to operate, and nearly limitless resources. His unsanctioned operation had vastly expanded his reach as American boots marched closer toward Europe. That same off-leash dog operating style had provided results, results that many of the people in charge of the war had begun to notice. Where once skeptics had been wary of his bold choices, they now sought to benefit from his expertise, and more importantly, resources.

They'd laughed at him when he suggested old methodologies of eavesdropping. They'd scoffed when he recommended turning and training enemy captives. They'd hissed when he suggested putting Americans in enemy uniforms. That was against the Geneva Convention, they'd said, and Brandt had responded, "And so is nearly everything the Nazis have been up to." There comes a time to fight fire with fire, and Brandt knew the nature of fire all too well. In the right hands, fire was a tool, but in the wrong hands, a dangerous and unwieldy flirt with nature.

When he'd suggested sending men inside to eavesdrop on high-profile conversations, they'd told him it was a foolish child's game, a high-budget hide-and-seek. They were wrong. When he'd suggested unleashing skilled saboteurs into the enemy's theatre, they'd told him it was useless. He'd been assured on numerous occasions "the only thing that is going to win the war is sheer might and an abundance of troops." Sure, many men would die, but they'd do so honorably. They'd fight for their country until they spilled their last drop of blood and become immortalized as heroes.

Brandt saw only an evolving war. No longer did bullets need to fly across country lines until the men who'd suffered the least losses were able to claim victory. That was the old way of doing things, the foolish way of doing things—*uncultured*, so to speak. Brandt liked to view the war as a patchwork in which the man sewing with the most delicate needle and thread would wind up with the winning pattern, not the man who hastily constructed his linen in an effort to make cheap, quick fabrics.

When he'd told them that it was our own borders that needed securing—not from artillery or bullets or U-boats, not from the *Luftwaffe* or *kamikaze* fighters, but from men in plain-clothes depositing secrets in brief-cases and handing them off to other unassuming men to be transferred in plain sight—the top brass had cackled and guffawed. They were wrong. Brandt had proved that at nearly every turn.

Slowly but surely, they'd seen it. Not just men with glittering brass and colorful patchworks sewn into their uniforms, but the real decision makers. The men who wielded pens in Washington and pored over maps in war rooms—it was these people Brandt had so desperately wanted to convince. And they'd paid attention. Not immediately, but *eventually*.

Now the chickens were coming home to roost, and Brandt found himself navigating a mission not of his own design, but one he might have thought up himself had they not beaten him to it. The problem was, he'd shot himself in the foot in the process. He'd played with fire and gotten burned. Again.

Combe continued to pace, now in smaller circles that didn't place him so close to the only window in the room, and massaged his thick beard. He always did that before he'd get *the* idea. Brandt had seen him do it many times. Brandt took a pull from his pipe in anticipation.

"We have to assume the worst," Combe said finally.

"Describe the worst," Brandt replied.

Combe sighed. "He's been caught."

"We don't know that for sure."

"We don't know *anything*." Combe's eyes narrowed and he bit down on his lip; now he was really going at the beard in long, rapid strokes. "How could this have happened? Everything was above board—his papers, his workbook. He might as well have been who he said he was. Now this—it's suicide."

"But we've got to try," Brandt said. He exhaled the smoke from his pipe in a long plume while his words lingered. "Because if we don't, we could jeopardize this whole thing. My work—*yours*."

"I just don't see it," Combe said. "The level of risk is

unfathomable, and the chances of success even more so. You could compromise our asset—then what?"

"Not if we line every piece on the board up in our favor," Brandt replied. "Besides, what good is having men with bigger balls than the other guy if we don't let 'em swing now and then?" Brandt shifted in his seat. He was becoming restless, evidenced by his frequent checking of his watch. It was currently three in the morning, Bern time. Brandt sighed, then said, "You're not supposed to tell me how hard something is going to be to do, but to tell me how it *can* be done. I know it's insane, damnit, but we're at a crossroads here."

"What about our friends across the pond?" Combe asked, still focused on warnings rather than solutions.

"That's my problem to worry about," Brandt said. He pointed his pipe toward the man with fierce jabs to illustrate his frustration when he said, "And they should have thought about that before they stopped sharing. I handed over valuable intel—good, *solid* leads." He harrumphed. "All they did was scoff. I've been a good, honest player in the game, and then I find out they're already ten steps ahead. Well let me tell you something," Brandt said, now wielding the pipe like a fencer. His voice had become loud and ferocious, a man who'd been questioned and was now asserting his superiority. "We've got our own plans, too. And we'll execute them as we see fit."

"Quiet down," Combe said to Brandt. "You're yelling." It was insubordination, of course, but Brandt thought nothing of it. Combe was allowed the defiant privileges awarded to good operatives. Switzerland was a hotbed for shadowy activity, both friend and enemy, and they'd maintained the Bern location as a reliable asset for far too long to lose it to something so foolish as carelessness.

Brandt wasn't sure if he was angrier that the British had begun keeping their own secrets, or that the man in front of him hadn't come up with a feasible plan when Brandt had expected he would. He inhaled from his pipe once more, calmed himself, then reduced his volume to a more appropriate level. He said, "I'm sorry. It was hard enough getting in a room with you to hash this out, and I'm just disappointed at the idea of leaving with nothing." When Brandt said it, he knew it wasn't true. It was the turn of his allies toward secret keeping that was really angering him. It was preposterous to assume that the Allies would share *everything*. Hell, the Soviets had been carrying on like that since the beginning, but Brandt felt as if the walls were closing in and he was at risk of being crushed.

"These things need time, Hank," Combe said. "Planning, intel, coordination. You know that better than most. What happened to the man who waited patiently for the long con to pay off?"

"We don't have *time*. We need to know if we've ruined this."

Combe, ever the thinker, scowled at Brandt. "It's not about him—this is about the facility."

"Of course it's about him," Brandt said. "*And* the raid." There was the honesty, even if it came late. "If something's changed, if I've bungled this—I have to know. We need to warn them. One man is something, but a whole fleet..." Brandt didn't even finish the thought. "A trap, Ansel—that's what I'm worried about."

"You think he talked?" Combe asked. "We both know he didn't."

"How can you be so sure?"

"I just am," Combe replied.

"Bullshit. You don't know, and neither do I."

Combe reached into his pants pocket, retrieved a cigarette, then lit it as his brow furrowed. He thought harder, exhaling smoke. "Then we send Lukas back in."

"No," Brandt said. "It can't be him. We send Sam."

"But he's blown, Hank," Combe pleaded. "You know it, and I know it. His face might as well be plastered on the walls, and you want to send him *there*? Why don't you just have him knock on the front gate?"

"We can't assume that Lukas isn't either," Brandt said. "How do we know he's not in the same boat?"

"At least he's not off and whining about some damn girl," Combe barked. He was shouting now too, like Brandt had been. "At least the priest has taken a vow of chastity."

"That's low, Ansel."

"No, sleeping with an asset is low. *Two* is a downright punishable offense."

"Lukas can't do this," Brandt argued. "Come *on*, Ansel. What's he going to do, hold confession until someone breaks and talks about the American? I get it. He's your man. You created him, worked on him, spent the time."

Combe grunted. Brandt could understand his frustration. Combe's own cherished agent wasn't equipped, and Combe seemed to know it. All that time cultivating the perfect relationship, and along came Brandt with his mercenary. But they were on the same team, and the clock was ticking, so Brandt knew Combe would acquiesce.

"It was my man who found out in the first place," Combe said.

Brandt, sensing the spinning wheels of a useless argument, decided to plead with the future, rather than the past. "We've got to know, Ansel," Brandt said. "If we've lost the wrong man, we could lose *a lot* of men."

"Then we send them both," Combe said. "Maximize our chances."

Brandt thought about it. To lose two more operators on top of a third was a big ask—not to mention three times the amount of scrutiny should it go public. However, it had to be done.

"Fowler was good, damn it," Combe snapped. "I should know. I put him in there."

"Then you owe it to him to make sure it wasn't in vain." Brandt: one, Combe: zero. "So let's hammer out just how the hell we're going to get them in there."

13

———

What do a priest and a rogue operator have in common that they may discuss when left alone? Very little, actually. Did they carry on with conversation? No. The room was silent, and the crackle of fire filled in the awkward gaps of silence for them. Beyond the window, the nightly blackout had extinguished activity in the city beyond.

Though Sam didn't look at the priest directly, he could feel the man's eyes upon him. He wondered, perhaps, if the clerical man was judging him—not that he cared. They had not yet been formally introduced. When he and Brandt had arrived, Combe had quickly whisked the chief off to the second floor for a private conversation away from both sets of ears.

How is he involved? Sam wondered. He could easily deduce the Teutonic features, and so he assumed that the man was, like the spy himself, of the enemy territory. *He has defected*, Sam resolved, *like me*. Because he sat in the same room as Sam, he must have been trustworthy to both Brandt and Combe. Still, Sam had no inkling of him other than his religious affiliations. He was not part of any briefing, nor had Sam heard of him or the operation in passing.

When Sam worked up the nerve to make eye contact, his suspicions were assuaged. Perhaps Sam lived in a perpetual state of untrustworthiness, because his notions that the man had been staring at him were totally inaccurate. In reality, the man was looking down at his clasped hands, murmuring under his breath in such a soft tone that Sam could't hear anything he'd been saying. It didn't take a top-notch operator to figure out that the man was praying. Regardless of this sanctimonious action, Sam could sense the impatience in him. Was it the fidgeting fingers? Was it the rapidly twitching lids covering the eyes?

An introduction would have been nice, even if it had just been a first name. Sam didn't dare to discuss any operational matters with him, so there was no motivation for small talk on the spy's end. There was only two men sitting in a room waiting on their two superiors.

Above, the throes of heated debate echoed through the wooden floorboards. Brandt and Combe were going at it, whatever *it* was. Sam wasn't surprised. From what little he knew, a very precious operation was in great jeopardy. Whatever the context of the operation was, Sam knew the priest had some dog in the fight, otherwise he wouldn't have been sitting here now. The question was: what was Sam's role?

"Jan," Lukas finally said after the silence had gone on just a bit too long. "Jan Lukas. That's my name. And yours?" He spoke in German; his instincts about Sam, too, were on point.

"Sam," the spy replied. He harbored no hesitation using the name. It wasn't Sam's real name. Though one would say the name the same in any language, Sam naturally spat the three-letter word out with a German tongue.

"From America?" Lukas asked in English.

"Today," Sam replied. Lukas understood him. Sam wondered if Lukas was also a man of no nation—men who spoke many languages sometimes were.

Sam lit up a smoke. Small talk was not one of his strengths, and he didn't know Lukas well enough yet to share operational details with him, even if Lukas himself probably knew more than Sam.

Before Lukas could speak again, the men upstairs had finished their conversation and descended to meet their operators. Brandt looked more haggard than Sam had ever seen him, and Combe looked as if he'd been up grading papers into the early hours of the morning. The fire was dying, so Combe took the opportunity to tend to it as Brandt found a seat. The spy chief sighed so heavily when he slumped into the chair one might have thought he'd been pricked and deflated.

Brandt packed his pipe, then with absolute irreverence, choked out the obligatory introduction: "Sam, Father Jan Lukas. Father Jan Lukas, Sam Abel."

"We've gotten that far," Sam replied.

"Good," Brandt said. Wasting no time, he sucked on his pipe and went into operational mode. "Then let's get right down to it. We've got a man missing on the inside —a very important man, spearheading a very important operation. We've reason to believe he's been compromised. Dead or alive, a great plan is now at risk." Brandt's eyes darted to Combe as if searching for support. "We've agreed that both of you should head back in to source any information you can, then get the hell out."

Sam looked to Lukas, noted the clerical collar, then turned back to Brandt—he knew there was an air of confusion evident on his face. Lukas, oddly, did the same. It was as if both men had sized each other up briefly, determined they didn't like what they had seen, but decided to hold their tongues before any could present their case.

"Respectfully," Sam began, "I'd prefer to operate alone."

Lukas scoffed. "I'd say the same."

"No," Brandt snapped. "I'll be straight with both of you." Brandt directed the pipe stem toward Lukas, then said, "He knows the lay of the land. He's been there and is familiar with the territory. That being said, we don't know that he hasn't been been compromised as well."

"Then why send him at all?" Sam asked.

"Do you know Peenemünde?" Combe cut in. He didn't even wait for Sam to answer before saying, "I didn't think so."

"He's a *priest*," Sam snapped. He turned to Lukas. "I mean no offense."

Lukas scowled.

"He's been in far longer than you," Combe rebutted. "Back and forth, no less." Combe paused briefly as if restraining himself, but then he just let his true feelings rip anyway. "Truthfully, I don't even want you in there —with your grimace, and your cigarettes, and your bullshit. I'd rather have him and *only* him."

"We need an insurance policy," Brandt added before Combe could continue on with his tirade. "We split you up on arrival, and that gives us double the chances of determining where we stand."

"Has he even been trained?" Sam asked.

Lukas now became his own advocate. "Trained? In what? I've been providing top-level material for almost a year now, and you've just arrived. We've been here all along. Where were you?"

"Listen, *Father*," Sam said condescendingly, "I've seen more than—"

"Quiet," Brandt commanded. They hadn't even left the comfort of the Bern safe house and already the foundation was showing its cracks.

"There's a chance you're blown too, Sam, and you know it," Combe argued. "They know your face and you've made far too much noise. You're not subtle—you're a disaster." Brandt motioned to calm Combe down, but the professorial man was enraged. "This man is a far better operator than you'll ever be. We don't need a mercenary, we need a prayer."

"So, two blown men," Lukas said with an exasperated sigh. "What a plan."

"We don't know what we don't know," Brandt reasoned. "So it's decided. You go in—*both* of you."

No one spoke. Only the crackling fire was holding conversation, and it didn't have much to say at all. Sam and Lukas looked like two children who'd been put in their place by their parents. Combe didn't like that either of the men had felt they had any say in the matter. Brandt played too fast and loose with Sam, and Combe had said as much, but perhaps that was what they needed now more than ever.

Whelan's words echoed in Sam's mind. *You're just a tool, Sam.* He certainly felt like one now. Sending blown men in only meant they were disposable. To discover the fate of one man, two of value were needed, but those two themselves were also at risk.

"A proper briefing would be a good start," Sam said. Brandt assured Sam it would come the next morning—tonight, they would rest.

14

There was another safe house in the Americans' possession tucked beneath the snow-capped peaks of the Silberhorn and situated on the edge of the Thunersee. If there were such a thing as paradise, Sam thought the view ought to be close. Sunlight sparkled along the water and struck the eastern edge of the mountain range, making the peaks appear blade-like against the sky. Deep in the forest and flanked by only several other houses of similar architecture was a large chalet with curtains in the form of high concrete walls. Another ivy-coated gate barred entrance to what seemed the only break in the structure.

As Sam's car approached, the gate opened for the car and swung around a dirt horseshoe. Beside the car was a fountain of ivory angels splashing in what should have been water if the pump was working. Instead, they were frozen in awkward positions that didn't dictate their actions properly without the aid of the liquid. Large bushes pressed tightly against the front of the house obscured the first-floor windows almost completely. Above on the second floor, large double windows were covered by drapes. To add to the discreet nature of the building, it seemed the windows had been tinted.

Sam was dropped off by two men Combe kept calling "The New York Boys." He wondered if they were the men Whelan had been referring to. They certainly seemed to fit the part. The passenger, who'd said his name was Louie, tipped his hat in the rearview as Sam exited the car.

Sam lit up a smoke and approached the door, glancing back at the horns once more and wishing he'd had a camera. The door was of deep, black, heavy steel, nothing like its native architecture. It bore no handle, but simply a lock. Sam searched for a buzzer, or a knocker, or anything he could use to announce his presence, but he soon found he didn't need to.

The deadbolt securing the door made a heavy *clack*, then Sam pushed on the door with several fingers. The door opened, and he stepped into a shadowy vestibule leading to a hallway and a staircase. The spy stepped forward and was surprised to find that the windows had bars on the *inside*. He hadn't even seen them through the dark glass. *Of course*, Sam thought. *You don't want it to look suspicious, but you do want it to be escape-proof.* The bars had been retrofitted into the windows' construction.

The living room, which flanked the left side of the vestibule, was neat and tidy. A small radio on a couch-side table sounded with the chatter of a morning news program in German, though Sam found it difficult to hear what was actually being said as the signal faded in and out. The mountains were screwing with the signal's strength. He smelled coffee and the dew of morning.

Sam leaned through the doorway, which revealed a kitchen behind the living area, and noticed a man stirring a cup of coffee. His back was turned to Sam, but Sam quickly noticed the pistol holstered on his hip. He wore a cheap brown tweed suit, which had no other markings or insignias that specified the nature of his job. When the wooden floor creaked under Sam's step, the man turned as he sipped his coffee, then nodded to Sam.

"Shut the door," he said after the slurp. "And lock it." Sam did so.

Sam's attention then turned to the staircase as someone moved swiftly down it. Another man, also armed, and also wearing a cheap tweed suit, greeted Sam in the vestibule. He said, "You armed?"

"No," Sam replied. "Should I be?"

"No," the man said. He reached his hand for Sam to take it, then said, "McCormick." Sam shook the man's hand, though he did not provide his own name, then McCormick said, "If you were, I would have requested you check your firearm." McCormick pulled out a set of keys from his pocket, unlocked a small drawer beside him, then slid the drawer open and instructed Sam to empty his pockets. Sam deposited his falsified Bern identification and a small knife into the drawer. He then displayed his cigarettes and matches. McCormick said, "The cigarettes are okay, but be careful you don't burn the place down." Sam signaled his understanding with a nod, then McCormick said, "He's upstairs."

Sam proceeded up the stairs, the walls of which were decorated with oil paintings of Swiss life: children in *lederhosen* chasing fireflies, a mighty twelve-point buck standing triumphant against a waterfall, and a photo-real rendition of the Swiss Alps. Sam reached the top of the staircase; there were several bedrooms, as well as a bathroom. From the farthest room, which faced the back of the property, came the classical serenade of a violin hissing off a dirty wax record.

The door was slightly ajar. Shadows played around the foot of the open doorway where the sun had cast its light against a moving figure. The sound of clinking grew louder, as if someone had been setting a table in preparation for breakfast. Soon, Sam could hear the figure behind the doorway humming along with the violin. It was a man's voice, and judging by the jovial nature in which he joined in with the violin, he seemed quite content.

Sam pushed the doorway open, and the man, who hadn't been facing the spy initially, turned the left side of his face slightly. Sam recognized the vertical scar that reached nearly the entirety of the man's face right away, even *if* it was still cast in soft shadow. Udo Ramm.

A thin smile crept up the side of the cheek, then Ramm turned to face Sam fully and the grin grew larger. The tip of his right lip met the new scar Sam had given him a year earlier, and unlike the one the Nazi had gotten when he was younger and studying in university, this one was horizontal—and *still* healing.

"Good morning, Mr. Abel," Ramm said with the notorious German purr. "I hope you've brought an appetite."

Ramm had set up quite a spread. The room was overwhelmingly characterized by sketches and art. He had used his time in captivity to produce drawings of much of the information he was privy to, and the smell of graphite hung heavy in the air. Easels had been set up wherever there was free space. In addition to renderings of rockets and rocket-based equipment, there were numerous iterations of the Swiss Alps in oil on canvas.

The table displayed various fruits, pastries, sliced meats, cheeses, and toast that had been browned lightly and smeared with jam. In addition, all the accompaniments one might expect when sitting for a meal had been placed on the table in a setting for two. Ramm said, "They don't allow me use of the stove or oven save for very special occasions." He presented a small aluminum pot, then asked, "Coffee?"

The whole environment threw Sam for a loop. The Nazi the spy had successfully defeated—and captured— seemed to be living quite comfortably. Though the second-floor bedroom also featured barred windows, it was otherwise quite warm and welcoming. Soft light from the rising sun filtered through the windows and birds sitting on the sills chirped eagerly. Behind the window was a courtyard of pavers and finely kept grass. Sam guessed by the content of the paintings that the captive was granted access to it from time to time for a bit of fresh air—it had a fine view of the valley and the mountain redoubt. Because high walls flanked the three sides of the courtyard, Sam didn't expect the man could escape even if he tried. Still, it was tidy and cozy, and felt more like Ramm had been placed under protective custody rather than imprisonment for war crimes.

"Please," Ramm said with warm welcome. "Sit." Sam hesitated for a moment. Ramm seemed to notice the spy lingering in the doorway, then said, "Mr. Abel, we have much to discuss, and according to your superiors, *very* little time with which to do it." Ramm poured coffee into both cups, then pulled Sam's seat out from the table and gestured a hand toward it. Ramm sat eagerly in his own seat, pulled his chair in, then went to work filling his plate with fruit.

Sam took the seat, grabbed a cigarette from his pack, then struck a match. Ramm said, "I'd prefer you don't smoke." Sam lit the cigarette, waved the match to extinguish it, then took a nice, long, disregarding drag before tossing the dead match on to a plate. After that, he got comfortable in his chair. As far as Sam was concerned, Ramm wasn't in a position to have preferences.

"Have you been busy, Mr. Abel?" Ramm asked.

"More than you, I imagine."

"Quite the contrary," Ramm replied. "My schedule is quite full." Ramm deposited cream into his coffee, then offered some to Sam. Sam shook his head; he didn't even entertain the coffee in front of him as he stared at the viciously scarred man.

Why? Sam wondered. *Why had the man flipped so easily? Why had he crossed the fence and what did he gain?* He thought it better to just come right out with it, and said to Ramm, "So much for loyalty."

Ramm smiled, then stirred the cream into his coffee. "That's not so."

"Oh?" Sam asked.

Ramm sighed, then sipped from his coffee as he mulled over his answer. Ramm said, "Mr. Abel, I'm a…" he appeared to consider his words carefully, "a *pragmatist*, I believe that's the word? I see an opportunity and I take it."

"No, you're just hedging your bets," Sam replied.

"I'm not familiar with the vernacular," Ram said. Though the man's English had been quite impressive, perhaps some American lingo had been lost on him. "I think you take my meaning." Ramm placed his coffee cup down on the table, then shifted in his seat to a more comfortable, conversational position and crossed his legs. "I'm well aware of when I've lost, and so too when I win."

Sam eyed some of the renderings. "Are those the revenge weapons?" He thought for a moment about the way Ramm had referred to them. "The *Vergeltungswaffen*?"

"*Vengeance* is a far better word. It translates more appropriately. Though I'm not fond of it myself." Ramm looked on at his work admiringly. "They are more accurately the tools of pioneers."

Sam scoffed. He took another drag of his cigarette, and this time was sure to exhale his used smoke unceremoniously toward Ramm. "*Pioneers?*" Sam asked.

"Indeed," Ramm replied. "Don't let the use of the rocket fool you. *Heer* and *Luftwaffe* usages will tell one story, but the men crammed into those workshops will tell you another."

"And what story is that?" Sam asked.

"One of an exploratory compass," Ramm replied. "And many of the men on that island know the same narrative—they're just not currently on your team." Sam's eyes narrowed. Ramm asked, "Have I lost you? Let me say it more simply: if the weapons were successful, that would mean we'd been provided more resources and funding. With more resources and funding, we would have built better machines. Better machines change the world." Ramm leaned forward. "The men and women who work at Peenemünde, they're *idealists*. They don't wake in the morning with thoughts of how they're going to maximize death. No, they're pondering the landscape of exploration." Ramm leaned back into his chair again. "I think I'm talking too much. You're here to learn, Mr. Abel, and I'm not so sure that your commander would appreciate me telling you all the details that don't pertain to your specific mission. Not to mention, from what I've gathered, you're very short on time."

Ramm rose from his seat, turned toward a desk resting under the window that overlooked the courtyard, then retrieved several large rolls of paper that had been secured with bands from the drawer. "I've become quite the artist in my spare time. With so little to do, one might consider taking a hobby." Ramm removed the bands from the rolls, then spread them across a long desk that flanked the window. "Come," Ramm said.

Sam tamped the cigarette down into the ashtray with a soft hiss, then grabbed the coffee cup from the table and sipped from it as he approached the desk. He could use the stimulant—the time changes and travel were messing with his schedule. Ramm took several small trinkets from the desk, one a clock, another a heavy crystal chalice, and used them to pin the large documents down at each of its corners.

"Peenemünde," Ramm said, and waved his hand over the large map. Sam remembered the German saying the word a year earlier when they'd had their first run-in. The word had no meaning when the man had first spoken it to Sam, but some due diligence had revealed that it was an island, a large finger on the northern side of Germany stretching into the Baltic and flanked by a small inlet—the Peene River—that separated it from the mainland. It was roughly one hundred miles east of the rough edge of Denmark. It was also seventy or eighty miles north of Berlin, and probably a good hundred or so from Hamburg. It was an unassuming plot of land, decorated mostly by pine-covered beaches. That was about all Sam had gathered with a preliminary bit of research.

Now that the spy had a map in front of him—drawn by a man more familiar with its details than could be found in a text—a new picture was painted. The image was one of an operational layout, at least with regards to the many man-made structures that had been constructed on the island. The first bit of geography Sam noticed was the airfield to the northwest. It was a large, circular piece of land that took up nearly half of the tip. Sam's primary interest, though, was all of the bits decorating the eastern beach side of the area that hugged the Baltic.

Ramm had labeled points of interest in German and English. From the northeast tip, Sam worked his way down as he read through many of the labels: Ordnance Test Area, Experimental Works, Housing, Work Camp. There was also a liquid fuel production center on the western side of the map alongside the Peene. Nestled between the work camp and the residential housing was both Old Town Karlshagen and a military camp. Below the work camp was a town called Trassenheide. The entire area was only roughly two miles according to the key Ramm had written.

Sam also noticed the test stands and launching sites. It was from those locations that the men hidden beneath the dense pines were testing rockets. Small tributaries leading from each of the points of interest were, Sam now saw, roads that led across to the western side of the map. Sam studied the map momentarily as if to deposit it into a memory bank.

"This is crude," Ramm said. "Perhaps if you could elaborate more on your mission, I could be more specific." Sam didn't take the bait. Ramm was fishing, and Sam was smart enough to know that, but the information in this scenario only flowed in one direction—from Ramm to him.

"Heavily guarded?" Sam asked.

"Very much so," Ramm replied. "However, where it derives its strength it also reveals a weakness."

"How so?" Sam asked.

"Peenemünde is under lock and key, but because it demands the need for minimal attention, it doesn't have the type of defensive response one might expect. Foot patrol? Sure. High fencing and monitoring? Absolutely. Proper anti-aircraft and invasion preparedness? I'm afraid not."

"Why the hell would your people keep something so valuable so vulnerable?" Sam asked.

"For the same reason you'd never heard of it in the first place," Ramm responded. "Peenemünde has been right there for everyone to see—a gorgeous beach community nestled on the coast—and yet no one noticed."

"How do you get in?" Sam asked.

"You don't."

"Impossible," Sam replied.

"Then difficult."

Sam frowned as he examined the map. "Air defenses?"

"Göring will keep the *Luftwaffe* on standby to answer any threat that may arise, but the airfield at

Peenemünde is not prepared for an air battle. The night fighters travel in boxes."

"Boxes?" Sam asked.

"Control sectors of grouped radar and searchlights," Ramm said. "They're quick to respond, but not necessarily with adequate firepower. It serves as an efficient warning system, but not one suited for proper defense. It's all part of the effort to divert attention away from Peenemünde."

"Doesn't look like it worked," Sam said. A thin smile crept up the side of the spy's cheek.

"Through no fault of my own," Ramm replied. "I was relieved to find that the British had already been well aware of the location. It seems my recklessness with the information you procured from me did not contribute to this upcoming result, whatever that may be."

"Good time to jump ship," Sam said.

"Was it ever." Ramm glanced down at the map, then said, "A shame the innocent won't be afforded the same luxury."

"What do you mean?" Sam asked.

Ramm pointed to the housing estate on the west side of the map. "Whatever they're planning, Mr. Abel, I'm sure will be devastating. Peenemünde isn't a military base—it's a community. There's women and children, husbands and wives… " Ramm paused before turning to the spy, conviction in his eyes. "Families."

Sam sat on the statement for a moment. What was being planned that he wasn't aware of? With every piece of information he received from Brandt or Ramm, he felt like he was learning *less*. Brandt had told the spy that the mission was strictly need-to-know information, and it seemed to Sam he didn't know much at all. Ramm was trying to drive the sympathy home, but Sam was undeterred.

"Mixed in with what I'm sure are high-ranking men, scientists, *Heer*, *Luftwaffe…* " Sam said. "Should I keep going?"

"You'd be correct," Ramm replied. "Many of the best and brightest are currently on the island. Some are military men who happen to be good with a hammer, and some are good at calculating numbers."

"And the rocket?" Sam asked. "Is it live?"

"Yes," Ramm responded. "And as terrifying as you might imagine it to be."

"How do they test them?" Sam asked. "Shoot them off into the Baltic?"

"Precisely. These docks here," Ramm pointed to the shoreline, "are where the recovery vessels are launched. Valuable information is gathered from the wreckage, whether it be a success or failure."

"Have they got good results?"

"Acceptable."

Sam's eyes drifted to another sketch on an easel in the corner of the room. Ramm was a skilled artist; the sketch of the rocket looked as if had been done by a machine, rather than human hands. Ramm had shaded the rocket in quarters, one section of the weapon white, and another black, then below that an alternating pattern. He'd even done a sketch which showed a maintenance tower hugging the rocket's side where crews could work on the machine. The entirety of the mechanism must have been as tall as ten men—maybe more.

"The *Aggregat 4*," Ramm said.

"How does it work?"

"Liquid propellent." Ramm stepped over to the design Sam was scrutinizing and stood with his chin lifted in wide-eyed admiration. "The fuel uses a mixture of ethanol and water to generate thrust. Coupled with an aerodynamic frame, gyroscopes for guidance, and rudders for better control. An amatol warhead fixed in the nose detonates the payload upon impact."

"And the range?" Sam asked.

"Roughly two hundred miles—on a good day," Ramm replied. "Launched vertically, the machine can reach over one hundred miles in height. It travels anywhere between twenty-five hundred and five thousand kilometers per hour depending on the conditions of the launch."

Damn, Sam thought to himself. The spy had never seen a weapon quite like it. At that speed, there was no stopping a projectile like that. The weapon could deliver its attack before anyone was even aware of its presence. Even the massive tank *Erdschlag*, which he'd single-handedly destroyed, didn't frighten him as much as the weapon sketched on the paper. *Erdschlag* was cumbersome and slow moving; the rocket was fast and undetectable.

"Ground-based radio guidance systems have been implemented for better configuration and communication," Ramm added.

"What about radio interference?"

"Sometimes the rockets are guided in a rudimentary way: a simple fuel cut-off."

"How many are there?" Sam asked.

"Enough."

"Do better."

"Production was temporarily halted in an effort to

work kinks out. The machine wasn't operating flawlessly. The plan was to reach operational consistency, then the assembly lines would be able to produce thousands within a year's time—if they haven't already."

"Thousands," Sam said with a grim growl. The words left his lips somewhere in between a statement of fear and a question.

"And Peenemünde isn't the only home for production."

"Do *they* know that?" Sam asked, referring to his superiors.

Ramm turned to Sam, then said, "I've held nothing back, Mr. Abel. I have no reason to. We've come to an agreement, your friends and I, and so in exchange I've made any relevant information readily available. I am here to verify further findings."

Sam took interest in several more of Ramm's drawings. The captive had sketched anything he could from memory: engines, fuselages, launch pads, and even the assembly line in the factory where the weapons would be pieced together.

"We are not monsters, Mr. Abel," Ramm said. "We just happen to belong to a very specific region on an imaginary map with lines that separate us from you. Most of the men on that beach have the same dream: to push the envelope and redirect the exploratory compass —but weapons bring money, and money brings results."

Sam surveyed the room. Ramm had made it his own —the defector had clearly filled his free time sketching non-weapon imagery, like flowers, landscapes, and even sketches of Berlin with shading a well-trained artist might envy.

"Who else is there?" Sam asked. "Top guys—*names.*"

Ramm displayed a devious, guilt-ridden smirk, then said, "I don't believe that's part of the brief I was instructed to give you. Though I can assure you, there are *many* sought-after men who often grace the grounds at Peenemünde."

Could it be? Sam wondered. He wanted to know, wanted to ask Ramm straight out, but he knew the German wouldn't give him an answer. Despite Ramm's instruction to aid the spy, he was toying with him. Sam didn't want to tip his cards. Ramm saying nothing said *everything*.

"Strange, isn't it?" Ramm asked. His eyes were fixed on Sam's and full of intrigue.

"What?"

"How we've found ourselves on the same team, of course."

Sam shuddered at the thought. Earlier in the year he had been the only thing stopping the mad German infiltrator from falling from the top of a Manhattan skyscraper. If Brandt hadn't wanted Ramm alive, Sam might have just let him meet his death. The spy had marked the good side of his face with a knife and lived to tell the tale. Now, here he was being educated about the enemy *by* the enemy. How long this agreement would last, Sam had no clue, but the fact that he was being sent to the fatherland again made him suspect that he and Ramm were not the last of the Germans to cross the fence in favor of more promising opportunities.

"Sometimes we are given unique opportunities," Ramm said. "I took mine when it came. Didn't you?"

Sam eyed Ramm's scars. "You're an ugly man."

"We're all ugly, all of us men," Ramm said.

15

Aksel Falke peered over the tip of an arrow. His hands steady, the amber eye fixed on the target ahead of him, he held the bow with a focused grace only a man of great patience could possess. Fifty yards away and camouflaged in a shroud of tree cover was the pointed crown of a stag. Much like its hunter, only one eye was visible in the deer's profile. *The crown is fitting*, Falke thought. It was a mighty animal, easily five hundred pounds. Also like the hunter watching it, the deer was well-equipped. Its tines were firm and sharp, rivaling the arrow currently pointed directly at them.

Falke, waiting for the right moment to strike, watched intently as the red deer lingered. The forest possessed a mystical aura in the radiance of a rising sun. Gnats danced around the deer's head like fairies in a fantasy tale. The deer's head descended, and for a moment it vanished completely, but Falke didn't stir. It was visible again when it rose to chew on whatever greens it had discovered. It was unaware of Falke in waiting.

No fauna had taken note of Falke's presence, at least not in any meaningful way. Birds chattered and the general soft chorus of a forest layered the large ocean of trees. He'd blended in discreetly, perched between two dead, mossy stumps and crouched on one knee. His bent leg was starting to go numb from the uncomfortable position, but he dared not shift even the slightest bit. His arms were burning, one extended on the edge of the bow and the other pulled back and ready to unleash the arrow. Holding this position was a great test.

The stag's ear twitched, suggesting something had piqued its attention. Falke still hadn't moved. It was something else—the crack of a branch, the shift a small rodent, or perhaps the rattle of leaves against the breeze. Then the animal turned toward Falke, stared directly at him, but failed to recognize the hunter and went on chewing. After some time, the animal stepped out from the natural plant barrier, and Falke saw it in all its majesty. It was broad and muscled, each soft foot striking the earth with unintentional recklessness. Unaware of its predator, it behaved in a manner befitting of prey with a false sense of security.

Now Falke drew the arrow more tightly; the time was coming for it to soar. The stag paused again, its head waving left and right, sniffing at the air. Over the top of the arrow, Falke's probing eye focused in on the animal, directing the tip of the weapon along the broad side of the deer and taking aim for its vitals. Something in the forest stirred, and the deer took note—its head was at attention, the crown pointed high and proud.

Falke, sensing his prey could escape at any moment,

wasted no time releasing the arrow. It tore through the trees with a whisper-like sizzle… and missed the deer completely. Falke rose to his feet as the animal sprinted forward. It leapt in great strides, its body arching as it bounded around the roots of the mighty trees decorating the forest.

Falke readied another arrow, drew it quickly, and took aim for the fleeing stag. He was following its path, watching the animal as it separated the distance between them. Falke's eye narrowed, the stag coming into focus as he followed its movements. It was fast, and soon it would be out of range. He found his moment, and fired another arrow—and this one missed too. The deer darted left, switching course completely. Falke readied another arrow, a grin of success crossing his thin lips.

The stag leapt into a trap and was surrounded by a net that sent it crashing to the forest floor. He'd never intended to strike it with an arrow in the first place.

Once the stag had been captured, Falke shouldered his weapon and lit himself a cigarette. No longer rushed, he savored it as the deer struggled in the trap. The animal stood no chance of breaking free.

The forest behind Falke shifted, and he spun around and took aim at the source of the noise. There, a *Heer* soldier stood frozen, Falke's arrow pointed directly at his chest. Falke held the position for a moment while the smoldering cigarette dangled from his lips. The soldier raised both hands, his expression one of a kid looking death in the face as he stood stiff and panting. Falke dropped his weapon. He was thankful the private hadn't ruined his hunt.

"I'm sorry, Herr Falke," the soldier said, sounding

exhausted. "I've been searching for you. I ran as fast as I could."

"Relax," Falke told him. "There's no reason to rush." The soldier seemed to notice the struggling stag ahead, then returned his gaze to the smoking Falke.

"A call," the soldier choked out. "For you—from the field. Urgent."

"Are you strong, son?" Falke asked the fearful soldier.

"I'd like to think I am, Herr Falke."

"Good," Falke replied. "Rally up a man or two and bring that animal home."

The soldier gulped as the animal writhed. "But it's… still alive, sir."

"Then kill it," Falke replied as he brushed past the soldier and left a trail of smoke in his wake.

Falke took the call in the forward military barracks. Without even asking who it was, he simply said, "Go ahead."

"Herr Falke," the voice on the other end of the line spoke. "We're here. Outside of the city in the hills."

"And what have you found?" Falke asked. "Discretion, mind you."

"He's met with a man in a home on the mountain," the voice on the line said. "An American."

"Continue to monitor him," Falke said. It seemed Lothar Eichler had proven quite useful in short time.

"There's more," the voice replied. "Two others have come, one in particular I think you would be interested in hearing about."

Falke, intrigued, took a seat beside the phone and nursed his cigarette. Behind him, a group of soldiers tending to clerical work looked on in silence, their attention fixed on the one-eyed man. "Go on."

"The man from America, the one with the burn scars," the man replied. Falke's eye grew wide, the dark pupil now almost fully obscuring the normal yellow tinge. "He just arrived, and has another man with him in tow."

"And they've met with the other one? The one from the farm?" Falke asked, his interest growing by the second.

"One big happy family," the man replied. "All holed up inside the home."

"Are you *sure* it's him?" Falke asked. "The man from America, the recruiter? It is definitely him?"

"One couldn't mistake this face," the man replied. "It is him."

Falke leaned back into the chair, ran a hand across the silver wave of hair, and smoothed it as he contemplated the weight of this discovery—the famed Hank Brandt, spy chief of the American Allies, was off US soil and in his team's sights. Such a catch was worthy of pause. To blunder it would be a great failure, and to execute good out of it would be a trophy unlike any other. Falke's name would be paraded in the streets. He'd go in the history texts. Songs would be written in his honor.

"And security?" Falke asked.

"Non-existent," the man on the phone replied. "Two drivers, but they don't linger at the location."

"What about the man he arrived with?" Falke asked.

"Him we don't know," the man on the line replied. "But he has also made contact with the priest."

"And you're sure you haven't been spotted?" Falke

asked quickly. "No one has followed you? No one is aware of your presence?"

"We passed through the border unquestioned," he replied. "Had them strike us from the records, as well. For all intents and purposes, we're not even here."

Falke massaged the stubble of his unshaven chin, then tucked a bony finger under the patch where the missing eye was and itched feverishly at it. Beside him in the room, the others watched his every move. He scowled at them, which sent them scurrying to resume their activities.

"Watch closely," Falke said. "Don't act yet. Continue to report on their movements. If the priest leaves, you alert me immediately. Stay with the burn-scarred man. He is now the priority."

Falke tapped the cigarette into an ashtray, then rose to see two young men dragging the net containing the dead deer from the tree line and toward the camp. The day suddenly felt very young as the sun cut wide beams of light into the room. If things continued to go his way, he might not end the day with one magnificent trophy, but two.

"Wait," the man said before Falke could hang up. "You're never going to believe this…"

16

———

The Resources Branch of the Bern operation was known to few SSD officials. Housed in a deep forest chalet dubbed *Edelweiss,* it was comprised of only two operators: one a bearded man of American descent and built like a bull, and the other a scrawny German man whose bug eyes seemed almost comically large when viewed through his spectacles. In Swiss country the American was known only as Gale, and the German simply Hugo—the former was an SSD insert and Combe's loyal and reliable Resources overseer in Bern, and the latter as a defector reliable when it came to identifying German tradition, custom, and presentation. Hugo's expertise vetting and verifying field material was uniquely valued; he was a former journalist for the *Völkischer Beobachter* and possessed an uncanny recollection for detail.

Their home also featured the high walls so favored by the SSD, and were worthy of the privilege considering the high-risk contents that frequented the property. It was here that infiltration matter was harbored, transported, manufactured, scrutinized, and cultivated. Gale, despite his mighty stature, was rather tender in his ways. One might assume the little old German, Hugo, with his slender fingers and bookish appearance, was the one who tended to delicate documents. But it was the hulking American who tended to those types of details. Gale took great care with tasks like forging a travel visa or passport, and Hugo was there to authenticate and inspect their worthiness.

It had been Gale, this gentle giant with hairy, bear-like arms, who created all the relevant materials for the now-missing Roger Fowler, including his workbook and credentials. To work in the fascist economy required that a man's information was true and incontrovertible. So when Gale heard about the red alert, he was rather distraught that perhaps he or Hugo had failed to send Fowler off with solid documentation.

Combe, ever the handler, assured the hulking man that this was unlikely. Hugo agreed this was true. He stood by his work and also had plenty of reference materials to make sure it was undeniable: copies of various German birth certificates, identification cards, passports, party-specific documentation, and several large photo books of party dress and *Wermacht* uniforms for reference. Of course, rarely did he or Gale make a uniform from scratch when a real one would do, and they were the proud owners of nearly every variation of Nazi government or military outfit and wardrobe—though none were stored at *Edelweiss*.

The home was given its name for the aforementioned flower discovered on its property when it was initially inspected by Brandt and Combe. Rarely had the flower been seen in the vicinity since, unless of course one was apt to go climbing in the nearby mountains. Hugo seldom left the protection of the residence, but on several occasions Gale had ventured off for fresh air and arrived bearing another rare flower to place in a small glass of water in the home's dining room. He liked to think that as long as a fresh flower lived on the property the safe house was protected.

And so when the letter came through—deftly handed off to Gale in the city at a meat stall by one of The New York Boys—about Roger Fowler's predicament and the needs for "next steps," the brawny American and the insect-like German set about gathering the items on the list. All items requested were attainable, though some were more difficult to obtain than others. Though it may have been hard to believe, the easiest items to procure were the *Versuchskommando Nord Standarten-führer*—or VkN Standard Leader—uniforms and accessories. Gale, with the assistance of Hugo, sewed the intricate oak leaf lapels himself; he was so proud of his work he thought it looked better than the real thing. Hugo implored him to degrade his work to some extent, if only because he believed they looked *too* good.

This cover costume had been decided upon at Ramm's urging. Wearing the uniform would help to ensure Sam and Lukas would have good reason to travel freely should any inquire about their movements. The VkN was a very specially constructed group of troops, valuable and unique to places like Peenemünde because officers and the enlisted were apt to have technical or engineering degrees.

Authenticating documents for the uniform were not

hard to recreate either, though there had been some debate among Hugo and Gale regarding why Combe had asked for such high-ranking material. Hugo thought it much more inconspicuous to make someone inserted behind enemy lines an *SS* Storm Leader, or even a Storm Unit Leader at best. Here, the ranks were diluted and spread more broadly, which presented less chance for problems if an operator's identity was in question. The VkN was a much more specific branch, and the concern was that hiding behind it could lead to more scrutiny. Hugo had briefly voiced his concerns, but he went along with the request anyway. Operationally, Gale and Hugo were told very little about the need for the materials, or where their usage might be applied. This was just good compartmentalization. Far be it from Combe to distrust either Gale or Hugo, but the sharing of details was of such a strict nature that neither man at *Edelweiss* knew much about the application they didn't *need* to know.

Harder to find were standard-issue firearms. Often the items on these lists that one might think most easy to find were the most difficult. There were hidden caches all over the countryside for tools at Resources' disposal, but they didn't contain *everything*. The VkN suits themselves had been unearthed from a false grave with a coffin containing a myriad of Nazi party uniforms cleanly pressed and preserved for an occasion like this. Also hidden in the coffin were phony medals and regalia —though they looked and felt like the real thing. The security badges were forged from photos Roger Fowler had provided. Once dug up, the grave was emptied and moved to discourage grave-robbers from attempting to pillage the contents of the coffins. One might not think this a risk, but it had happened once during the course of Combe's year in Bern.

When Gale and Hugo were satisfied everything on the list had been procured, they sent up the signal to Combe. This signal was done in the form of burning smoke through the chimney on the back corner of the house only used for this reason, rather than the main one in the living area. Where this smoke could be seen from, neither Hugo nor Gale knew, but it could be easily recognized by Combe from the view of his second-floor window beyond the valley. Also requested was a tin of cigarettes and a forged statement—by Hugo's natural German hand—from the *Reichsführer* that any man presenting the documentation may pass freely at the behest of Himmler himself. This was a document Hugo and Gale were particularly proud of. They also acquired five hundred *Reichsmarks* and Swiss *Francs*. The final items requested by Combe were two L-pills, or potassium cyanide capsules. They were some of the few items that actually *were* stored at *Edelweiss*.

It was decided amongst Brandt, Combe, Lukas, and Sam, that Lukas was the best bet for the retrieval of all of the items Resources Branch had procured. Brandt couldn't be caught out in the open in Bern without raising attention, and Combe had been embedded too long to risk exposure. Sam was unfamiliar with Bern country and was immediately vetoed as well. That left The New York Boys as an available option, but their priority now was security and so were also scrapped as potential assets for retrieval. Lukas had experience, and could be counted on to be discreet. He understood the geography of the city, So Combe spent a few hours training him in the art of tactful handoffs.

Lukas set off from the home on the hill on a bicycle. The trip was a leisurely, downward journey along the mountain switchbacks. The cool morning air was a welcome change for Lukas, who'd been holed up in the house for some time now and was starting to get a little bit of cabin fever. In fact, they *all* were.

Combe and Lukas had played nearly a hundred card games while Sam smoked endless cigarettes and Brandt stared stoically out of the second-floor window. Meals were sparse and uneventful, and mostly consisted of silent grunts and mumbles of disappointment because they were limited to cheeses, sausages, and breads. They were all in agreement that none should go outside the home unless operationally necessary, and so far it had only been Lukas who'd been given the opportunity to leave. Sam often paced around the garden when he smoked cigarettes, and Brandt was definitely nipping at a flask he didn't hide well but also never offered to share.

Lukas would not be making the return trip home via the bicycle, for even a man in the greatest shape of his life would find the uphill route a difficult climb. He planned to abandon the bicycle in a side street near a butcher shop, then drape it with a sign stating that it was free for the taking. Even spies have hearts.

He had been instructed to pass by a chocolatier's shop at approximately nine in the morning where Louie would be purchasing a large chocolate basket. Lukas would then redirect himself to go acquire a cup of coffee in a nearby coffee stall. He would drink his coffee for one hour, walk along the river for another, then enter into the front of a hotel right in the center of the city. To lose any tails that he might have, he was then to enter into the hotel lobby's first-floor lavatory, which, because it was situated so far from the fire exit, had its own exit into the back of the hotel that adjoined with a street opposite the entry point.

There, he would be reacquired by Phil, albeit in a different car than Lukas had ever seen him in before, this time disguised as a ski-resort shuttle. A small exchange would be made about the nearby skiing options, a price negotiated for the travel—all of it was of course pre-written—and then Lukas would climb into the back of the car beside an obnoxiously large basket of obviously very expensive chocolates.

It all went off without a hitch. The return trip was silent if uneventful. The priest was becoming a better operator with every trip completed.

When Lukas arrived once again at the safe house with a chocolate basket in his hand that weighed far more than any bunch of candies had any right to, he triggered the attention of his three allies. A moment of levity was brought on when Sam, dying for something other than the dwindling mediocre rations, tore the cellophane and gold bow from the basket and went immediately for several of the caramel-filled chocolates. Brandt followed suit, grunting in pleasure as he stuffed several in his mouth; sensing the joy it brought, Combe and Lukas partook as well. It was only after nearly all of the chocolates had been devoured and the table was a mess of crinkled wrappers that the padding between the chocolate and the basket was removed and the true nature of the gift revealed.

Under the wadding of unnecessary papers that made the chocolate basket feel far more ritzy than it truly was, rested a plastic package. Combe opened the package, spilled out its contents carefully, and then spread the requested items across the table. Brandt swatted at the discarded wrappers, clearing a place so all could be scrutinized.

Lukas agreed that the uniforms looked good—flawless, even—and was curious how such a good replica had come about, but neither Brandt nor Combe elaborated. Still, the vote of confidence from the man constantly lurking around the enemy lifted everyone's spirits. The travel documentation was also scrutinized by everyone but Brandt, who didn't speak German. Sam made a comment about wishing he'd had such incredible resources during his last outing in Pforzheim, but quickly dropped the subject since operationally it wouldn't be appropriate to discuss it in front of Lukas. This notion was seconded by stern looks from both Combe and Brandt, and Combe quickly changed the subject to propose a vote for which chocolate had been the best from the batch. All agreed it was the dark chocolate squares filled with caramel.

After the uniforms hung for a couple hours, Sam ironed them to work out any creases. Combe also did a trick with the teabags to stain up the credentials and make them appear a little more war-ridden, though he was careful to not go too far. Due to the immediate nature of the operation, Combe hadn't requested that Gale or Hugo do it, wanting to expedite the process.

Now, with the resources procured, the players in place, and the operation discussed, the four men spent the evening very much chatty in contrast to the previous two nights. In the next twenty-four hours the two operators would be reinserted—with any luck, they'd find some answers. Brandt finally shared his whiskey, though he hadn't brought enough to get any man drunk. Perhaps it just took the edge off of what was a tense several days. That night, after everyone had retired, Brandt watched all the planes that populated the Swiss sky above from a crack in the curtains on the second-floor window.

17

"Herr Eichler," a voice boomed from the security captain's doorway. Vogel stood at the open door and was curiously at attention. Rarely was Eichler interrupted in such an egregious manner—someone had arrived. "Representatives from the *Reichsführer's* Office," Vogel announced.

Eichler quickly corrected his posture, performed a party salute, then secured his hands to his sides upon recognition of the *SS* man addressing him. No wonder his own team hadn't held the line—they'd been usurped. The man in the black coat—his skull-and-cross-bones insignia grinning in contorted terror—removed his cap promptly after entering.

"Herr Eichler," the man said. Eichler's stone-like stiffness never wavered. "It was very clearly stated that this was to be given to you directly—no exceptions." Eichler eased.

A small bead of sweat ran down the *SS* man's temple,

falling gradually to his cheek and confirming he'd made an exhausting trek to deliver the information. This morning at Peenemünde was already sweltering. Labeled on the front of the tightly strapped folder were the two bold words, *Geheime Reichssache*: "Super-Top-Secret Reich business." Below the intimidating lettering, a further statement was printed: "Misuse is punishable in accordance with the conditions of this law, provided that no other conditions of punishment come into question."

Eichler's eyes flared. "Thank you," he said to the *SS* man, who saluted the security captain before he set off. Eichler's fingers grazed the front of the folder softly, sensing the supreme secrecy of its contents.

The folder in his hand was not of Peenemünde. Important information—procedures, technical drawings, protocols, most of which he wasn't privy to anyway—never traveled like this. He'd liked that about Peenemünde. It was unlikely a map, data, or a sketch could fall into the wrong hands—unlike the fiasco that had happened with his former secretary Sigrid Lang. Furthermore, this was direct from the head office.

Eichler raced through his morning security checks. It was rare that anything out of the ordinary presented itself—the byproduct of a tightly run ship—and as usual, all security personnel had accounted for their respective stations during radio calls. Now all that lay in sight were the calm azure skies of another favorable day on the Usedom Peninsula. His physical inspections could wait till lunch. The document resting on his desk was battling more vigorously for his attention.

Back in his office, Eichler lit a cigarette as he untied the string clasps securing the document. He dug inside like a child tearing candy from a wrapper, no regard for the packaging and intensely focused on the goodies. In his hand were several sheets of paper, the foremost bearing the official credentials of *SS* letterhead.

At the top, in stern Gothic font, the documented was headed by the title "*Reichssicherheitshauptamt,*" and below that, aligned left, the address of origin: *Prinz-Albrecht-Straße 8, Berlin.* Farther down, many characters followed, consisting of seemingly random letters and numbers. Eichler knew them to be a log of the information shared, used before and after to catalogue its contents. In the top-right corner, the note had been stamped with the date, and another red stamp below that read "*Geheime Reichsache,*" another reminder that the letter resting in Eichler's hands was a state secret.

The letter began, in earnest, Sicherheitskapitän *Eichler, Regarding your inquiry to Herr Falke about the events occurring at Flussrand, March, 1942, a further investigation has been reopened based on re-examination of the information.*

It is my request that you confirm or deny the likelihood of the suspect's involvement with said events. A photograph has been provided. Due to the sensitive nature of this individual and his history, your prompt reply should be addressed directly to me. It is strictly forbidden to return information to any authority other than myself, Abwehr or otherwise. Should we find that the suspected party is in fact who we believe him to be, a further investigation may proceed, of which you are likely to be called on as witness. I trust that your reply will be timely and thorough.

At the bottom of the document, the final typed words read "*Heil Hitler!*" and had been signed, "*Der Reichsführer-SS*, H. Himmler, August 13, 1943."

A letter from the Reichsführer himself. Few would be

called upon by the man, and most did well to avoid him completely. Eichler had clawed through his investigation unscathed, a humiliating and debilitating process consisting of reiterating the story and details multiple times while his own loyalty was questioned repeatedly. He was relieved to find that was all he was forced to endure—many who graced the building at *Prinz-Albrecht-Straße* could not call themselves so lucky. He heard rumors of what went on behind the closed doors there: bone-chilling and skin-crawling anecdotes of "information gathering."

Eichler paused for a moment before he turned the page over, pulling on the crackling cigarette as he read through the letter a second time. He knew what he might find. *Was it better to be proven right, or to never know the truth and live in blissful ignorance?* Eichler thought the former.

He turned the document over, and there, clipped to the top of the page and staring back at him, was the face of a broken man. His cheeks were puffy and swollen, the eyes thin slits from continued abuse. Blood had crusted around the mouth, presented as only shadow in the black-and-white photo. And yet, despite the obscured features of the battered face staring back at him, Eichler recognized him *immediately.*

The lines on Eichler's jaw became sharp edges, his breaths ragged and stifled. A clamminess developed almost instantly in his skin, the type of dampness present in men before they suffered cardiac failures. In his hand, the cigarette burned unattended, its host caught in a vacuum of focus. For a moment, he just stared at the image. It was *him*, yes, the man in Flussrand who'd destroyed Eichler's precious *Erdschlag* and seized his moment of glory. What would Herr Eichler have become had it not been for the man staring back at him? *Kommandant der Geheimprojekte? Rüstungminister?* He would never know. Perhaps it *was* the smattering of injuries present on the man's face that made him recognize him so easily, the saboteur, the *spion*. Eichler's own men had roughed the man up before he'd escaped, and there was a resemblance: what had been done then, and what he saw now—a man tortured.

Even the hair was right—the deep black color, the subtle waves at the tips, the shine reflected in the camera's flash. What Eichler recognized most, though, were the hard-bitten eyes. Even near death, there was a smarminess present in the expression. No, that wasn't it… it was a *callousness*, the eyes of the uncaring. That twisted bravery that suggested the man would die with integrity.

Though cuffed and nude, the man showed no fear in his expression. He'd been well aware the photo had been taken, had been ready to produce the macabre smirk that said, "Go ahead. Take your picture," with his head tilted and displaying a penetrating side-eye of contempt. *It's you*, Eichler thought contemptuously. *You who've slipped through my fingers, you who've derailed so much, you to whom I'd give so much for an opportunity for vengeance. What would I give? So much.*

Eichler stared at the photo intensely for several more minutes, now transfixed and meditative. He'd been transported, ushered with his thoughts to Flussrand, isolated in its mighty forests and reliving the events of the night *Erdschlag* had burned. There was fire, a raging inferno that had turned the mighty tank into a blackened steel husk. The saboteur, tied to the chair in the musty supply room and unwilling to break, taunted him with the same eyes then and now. He thought of the dead girl, Sigrid Lang, her body contorted in the road and depleted of all blood. He remembered her translucent and cool skin, and her mouth moving like a beached fish's. He heard her gasping for air, uttering the same word over and over again in breathy whispers, "Sam… Sam… Sam."

It was *him*.

Eichler wanted to phone *Prinz-Albrecht-Straße* immediately, to relay the message that the man in the photo was indeed the one they'd sought, but before he could his attention turned to the details below the photo. The name listed was not the one Sigrid had said, but another, "Stein, Dieter. His height was noted: 6'1". Eichler noticed another tab beneath the picture— another photo, clipped to it, featured Herr Stein, this time in totally different light. He was young, handsome, and unblemished. The spy Eichler had met was a man, and the one staring back at him unscathed in the photograph was still a boy. His torso was still lanky and unable to fill the *Wermacht* clothing it occupied. This photo had been taken face forward, an official record of the individual.

Official documentation began again, this time coming straight from the *Abwehr*, Central Division. It constructed a detailed, if inconsistent, dossier on the individual. Aliases: none. Parents: Stein, Karl, and Stein, neé Schumer, Trudel - deceased. Birthplace of origin: Berlin for Trudel, America for Karl. Divison: *Abwehr*, I-Ht, G, H West.

One of our own, Eichler muttered to himself. *We're being eaten from the inside out.* The revelation was earth-shattering. Here before him sat the dossier on one of the most-wanted individuals to set foot on German soil, even if only by Eichler, and he had been one of their own the whole time. The text continued: *The report that follows, conducted by members of IIC-2, verified by Kühn, Hanz, states information gathered on the individual, alias, "Stein, Dieter," and his subsequent activities during his time recruited as an* Abwehr *operative. The individual in question was recruited from the civilian sector, completed basic* Heer *training, and then further trained with H West. He is adept in, but not limited to, the following skills: infiltration, sabotage, information gathering, and combat. Due diligence was performed, as is required, regarding the individual's background, and no reason for doubt arose beyond the inability to speak with the individual's family members, who records indicate were deceased upon his recruitment.*

Further investigations of the individual led to questionable ties, including to Buch, Aaron, a rabbi wanted by the Einsatzgruppen *intelligence authorities.*

Stein is believed to have escaped from capture, January 1941, before transport to Pforzheim for further interrogation. His destination was unknown, and no further information had been gathered about his defection or immigration to another country. No confirmation of the individual's presence in the homeland has been made, and it is assumed he escaped the border and is currently still hiding. A complete investigation discovered the individual in question provided false documentation regarding his place of birth, lineage, and name. Upon confirmation that the individual's documentation proved false, Stein was apprehended by the SS officers and temporarily imprisoned before escaping.

The individual should be considered dangerous. He possesses extensive military training as well as an understanding of the techniques and tactics used by I-Ht, G, and H West. Individual showed high aptitude before enrollment, and thusly was a prime candidate for selection. Whether the individual has assumed another identity is still in question. If discovered, the appropriate authorities should be notified immediately for apprehension. Stein possessed state secrets, and is therefore considered a threat should he reintegrate in some way. Authorities should assume he has defected to a foreign enemy, and therefore has compromised information of value.

Eichler flipped the page to the next where the text continued. "Addendum" had been printed in bold lettering on the top of the page, and the ink was much more fresh and recently typed. It read, *Whether the individual in question was involved in the events preceding the destruction of Flussrand is still in question. Reports from survivors of the incident who produced firsthand intelligence seem to coincide with both description and ability. It should be noted that the defector, Lang, Sigrid, is assumed to have had contact with the individual. All departments working at or with individuals at Flussrand should consider their information and intelligence compromised henceforth. The activities of Stein, likely operating under a different identity after penetrating the border, are consistent with the capabilities discussed in the aforementioned report, but no confirmation has been made. Further investigation is underway to determine whether the individual in question has reintegrated, and if so which power he is representing. Stein possesses unique abilities that would suggest him fully capable of carrying out the attack on*

Flussrand, and it should be noted that after an attempt to salvage documentation from the facility, inspection discovered a plethora of missing documents. The defector had been providing sketches and copies of said documents, which might lead one to assume that everything was compromised. The defector, Lang, Sigrid, assistant to Eichler, Lothar—now Sicherheitskapitän *Eichler - Peenemünde—was killed on site trying to escape with the individual in question. Though she was unable to survive long enough for interrogation, the enemy is believed to have left with information concerning more than just the data regarding* Erdschlag *itself, but more importantly,* Wermacht *movements, assembly line instructions, schematics, and crucial rail layouts.*

Certain findings postulate Stein to be affiliated with, or a member of, the Schwarze Kapella, *though further investigation did not corroborate that thesis. Several captives of the group were questioned extensively, but no information collected led investigators to believe Stein was indeed a member. Further investigation was suggested. Representatives from Section III suggest Stein may have penetrated Brandenbergers to relay information into enemy hands on several occasions, though this is merely conjecture. No further information regarding Stein's presence has been discovered. Any further inquiries should be directed toward the undersigned.*

Below the findings, the letter bore the signature of Hans Oster, Deputy Chief of the *Abwehr*.

Eichler turned the page back over, pulled inexorably again toward the photo. *Stein, Dieter*, Eichler thought, and then referred once more to the words of the dead girl: "Sam… Sam… Sam." *What was the connection?* Had she been conflating the words with some other reference? He remembered the investigation sharply; he didn't recall anyone within the defector's sphere named Sam—not a family member, not a friend, or a lover—and the lengths at which her life had been turned over had been exhaustive.

The saboteur had been using a different name, Eichler theorized, and that name was Sam. *Sam what?* He couldn't know, and wondered if he'd ever get the chance. Did it even matter? God help the man if he attempted to return to the fatherland, and furthermore, if he crossed paths with Eichler again.

A long, unnatural length of ash hung from the cigarette between Eichler's fingers. He tapped it in the tray, and the burnt paper and tobacco broke apart like a rotted carcass.

He heard the sounds of a disorganized, shambling march outside the building. Eichler rose from his seat and surveyed the arrival of the group from the window. Habit had forced him to take note of all who traveled around Peenemünde. He was privileged to have access to many locations and tried his best to remember faces when he could. It was impossible to remember all who traveled through the peninsula, especially since the arrival of the *SS* and their labor workers.

The sluggish ambling of men gave away their identities in short time: prisoners from the work camps recruited for tasks to expedite the completion of the rocket. At their front, an *SS* officer clutching a rifle led them down a path that turned toward one of the assembly halls. There were roughly thirty or forty men marching, each with their heads hanging low under the weight of oppression. Beside the group, and with one eye fixed on his prisoners, another officer monitored their movements; to the rear of the group was another officer to keep them in line.

This was a rather frail-looking group, and likely one that wouldn't be required to do the type of physical labor others were forced to. These were prisoners who'd been awarded the privilege, if that was what one could call it, of working inside the factories, assembling small parts or overseeing manufacturing of fine mechanics. They were Poles, mostly, some Jews and some not. Some were French prisoners captured during the invasion.

Eichler had seethed when putting them to work behind the fence was mandated—not because he harbored any feelings of ethically minded guilt, but because he thought their presence within the perimeter was a great risk. The idea of recruiting the enemy into the ranks, whether they possessed technical or mechanical ability or not, was unwise, but that was what had been demanded. Far be it from Eichler to suggest otherwise. With the influx of prisoner labor came the arrival of Himmler's SS. Eichler did not like that they'd tread on his territory. Protesting this idea was not in his best interests—he was lucky the cards had fallen where they had and considered his input on the subject out of line. The SS was just another organization vying for control of the project; every branch was in line for glory, employing whatever means necessary to taste it.

"Help build the spaceship!" Did the pioneering ideology apply to the grey-faced men dragging their feet toward the factories? One couldn't imagine. "Sabotage the spaceship!" was a much more apt slogan. Never mind the strict measures taken to ensure project secrecy —*anyone* was capable of sabotage. Eichler had learned that lesson the hard way.

A strange sight it was to behold, indeed. Beside the shambling group, a group of giddy, well-dressed girls trekked toward their own respective positions of employment a stone's throw from the enemy. They often worked in the same sectors. The integration of slave labor into this paradise seemed to turn no heads, nor did it cause any feelings of dismay for the citizens working so hard to see the completion of the weapons. All labor at Peenemünde was one in the same, striving toward one goal: finish the *Vergeltungswaffe*. The vengeance weapons.

The rally cries were effective. General Dornberger often gathered Peenemünders together to lift their spirits. His speeches reminded the residents of the importance of the work being done on the island and also of the risks of such a venture. He'd reminded them of the importance of sealed lips, not just through stringent guidelines, but also via the threat of being carted off to Buchenwald or Dachau should they fail to keep them shut. Encouraging those involved with the rocket to report on each other's activities kept everyone on their toes. Thus, despite Eichler's fears of whispers among friend or enemy, the project had been safe thus far.

It was *selbstverständlich*, "understood," that one didn't talk about the work being done outside their respective departments. Once, a subordinate of Eichler's had asked nonchalantly if the rocket was truly a site to behold, and Eichler had dismissed the comment completely, reprimanded the soldier, then threatened to strip him of his credentials and report him. The soldier never made the mistake again. In fact, he refrained from saying another word to Eichler unless prompted. To be a member of a secret society, one had to ensure the society retained its secrets.

Eichler picked up the phone on his desk. When the operator responded, he requested a direct line to *SS* headquarters in Berlin. Once the call was transferred, he requested the ear of the top of the pyramid, "By order of the *Reichsführer* himself."

18

———

The high walls of the Bern safe house courtyard were the perfect cover for a spy in a foreign country looking for fresh air. Brandt had not slept over the course of the evening. The clock had just struck three o'clock, the witching hour, when the moon finally dipped beyond one of the large trees covering the corner end of the property. It cast long shadows on the property, so when the muted silhouette of a figure approached the spy chief, he rose to his feet and quickly took a defensive posture.

Brandt was unarmed, but he was put at ease when he recognized the flash of a white clerical collar. Brandt's clenched fists relaxed, and he took his seat again on the stone bench at the corner of the garden.

"May I?" Lukas asked.

Brandt nodded. Then, sensing an incoming conversation, he packed his pipe. Like Sam, it was as if smoking came as naturally as breathing for Brandt. The danger of the operations they conducted seemed moot when in reality they were signing their death warrants hourly. For a moment Lukas fixed his attention on the mountains in the distance. Even in the summer, their snowy caps were stark and bright against the dark evening sky. A grouping of stars hung above the cloudless peaks.

"Where'd you learn to speak English?" Brandt asked.

"The same place I've learned much of what I know," Lukas replied. "Scripture."

The sky above seemed to hypnotize both men. Wind sweeping across the Silberhorn swirled in great tufts, causing the trees on its slope to bend and throb. In the valley, all the sounds of a haunting evening seemed to collect in one deep pool.

"I guess I owe you a debt of gratitude," Brandt said. The burning pipe tobacco lit his face briefly in the dark courtyard. "Consider it repaid."

Lukas, clearly confused, turned to the spy chief as if to request elaboration.

"I'm going to tell you some information," Brandt said. "Top secret, ultra classified. Are you willing to keep it confidential?"

"I am," Lukas said. "Secret-keeping is one of my fortés, as you might imagine."

Brandt grunted. "You're owed it. Combe's told me a lot about your information gathering. You're a brave man."

"I'm not brave," Lukas replied. "I'm just doing what any man might do."

"If any man did it, we wouldn't be having this conversation. In fact, I'd be back in America with my feet up on a chair and a glass of cognac in my hand—

and enjoying good American tobacco, for that matter. And you, well, you'd be wherever it is you'd be."

"Vienna," Lukas replied.

Brandt nodded. "So since you held a gun to your handler's head, and dragged me thousands of miles over here to get your way, you should know that you're going to get it." Lukas perked up. "Some time soon—and don't ask me when—the Royal Air Force is going to raise hell on that tiny little island."

"How soon?"

"What did I just say?" Brandt scowled. "Operationally, I haven't been included in the planning stages. My intel—" Brandt paused and turned his burn-scarred face to Lukas. "*Your* intel, was instrumental in that planning."

Brandt watched Lukas clutch a rosary as he delivered the information. The priest closed his eyes, mumbled something softly to himself, then tucked the necklace back under his coat. Brandt didn't see the purpose. He'd seen millions of men pray and have their requests go unanswered.

"Just know that this will be the last time," Brandt said.

"My work isn't done," Lukas said.

"But *ours* is." Brandt looked the priest dead in the eyes. "We're done."

"Why are we done, Mr. Brandt?"

"Because I don't like being threatened—that doesn't play. You want to hang other *treffs* over my head as your bargaining chip? That's no way to maintain a relationship. You're loyal to us or you aren't loyal at all. You got what you wanted, and so did we, and that's the end. You need to keep what I just told you between us, do you understand? No one else can know. Especially him." Brandt shot his chin forward toward the house. He wasn't referring to Combe, but Sam. "As it stands I don't know what our missing man has or has not said, and putting you two back in there is a huge risk, but it's one I need to take."

"Why *can't* he know?"

"It's a matter of safety," Brandt replied. "Of mucking it up further. A man can't reveal what he doesn't know, can he?"

"I suppose not."

"And worse still," Brandt began. He sighed, pausing for a brief moment, before he continued. Why was he giving up so much? Was the clerical garb of Lukas one that forced confession, even for a man so secretive as Brandt? He went on anyway. "There's a man there—a man Sam would very much like to see dead."

Brandt stared out to the sky. A cluster of clouds shifted past their position and once again yielded to an infinite expanse of stars. "Have you ever seen it—the rocket, I mean—with your own eyes?"

Lukas shook his head. "Only what was present in the photo negatives."

"Hm," Brandt mumbled through the pipe stem.

"They say it can travel into space," Lukas said. "Perhaps even touch God."

"Then why don't you ask him for help?"

"I have," Lukas retorted. "I suppose that's why *I'm* sitting here with you."

"Can I ask you a question?"

"Anything," Lukas said encouragingly.

"What kind of God lets all this happen?" Brandt waved his pipe outward to signal the greater war abroad.

"If he's got so much to offer and so much to say, then what the hell is this all about?"

"I'm afraid I don't have those answers," Lukas said, distraught. "But I imagine that even in the midst of evil men like *those*, he created ones like us, yes?"

"Sounds like a cop out if you ask me," Brandt said. Lukas sighed. "But what the hell do I know?"

Another brief silence passed. Both men continued to stare at mountain ranges punching into the night sky as if they'd find the answers there. Brandt felt small. Below these big mountains, little men made large plans.

"Do you pray?" Lukas asked.

"No," Brandt replied.

"Perhaps you should tonight."

"For whom?" Brandt asked. "You?"

"Perhaps," Lukas said. "And those pilots."

Brandt ashed his pipe on the stone bench before tossing it into his coat pocket. A German Catholic himself, now surrounded on all sides by the enemy, he could use all the prayers he could get. Lukas grabbed hold of the spy chief's extended hand, then closed his eyes once more. Brandt followed suit.

19

How do two spies travel across the Swiss border and across nearly the length of the fatherland without being caught? Much in the same way Peenemünde derives its security: by hiding in plain sight. Wearing the skins of VkN officers was not a fool-proof method, though, so further cover was needed. Should someone suspect their authenticity and inquire further about both men's activities, their story could easily be shot down and the mission blown. The border was a particular debate of much frustration between the four parties.

For the first time ever, Sam was included on the planning side of the operation. As European natives, both he and Lukas had invaluable input—especially the priest, since he had spent the most time recently behind enemy lines. While waiting for the materials procured by Gale and Hugo, Combe thought further about good cover for the infiltrators. On the second floor, he toiled over reports from different sources, mostly by candlelight, until he discovered something that felt just right. Intelligence gathering suggested that trade between the Swiss and Germans was still very much active, and one of the most coveted goods traveling amidst those deals was in fact the perfect foil: fuel.

The rail lines were out of the question. All parties agreed on this. For the first leg of the journey—and until they'd at least cleared the vicinity of Berlin—Sam and Lukas would pose as couriers tasked with delivering the oh-so-precious petrol directly to Peenemünde itself. A hasty request for any relevant documentation was put in again to Gale and Hugo and provided in short time. Brandt was impressed. The spy chief inquired about the feasibility of sending Hugo himself in, but the old man was weak, feeble, and far more compromised than Sam. In fact, Hugo had a well-known target on his head, and excursions for the ex-journalist far from *Edelweiss* were few and far between.

But how does a spy network with limited resources and funds purchase such sought-after gasoline in such short time? An American film studio called Supreme Pictures—run by one of Brandt's old attorney contacts —with assets inside Bern was willing and able to provide Swiss currency to the chief. Also helpful was that Peenemünde had very high demand for fuel for the rocket tests—Ramm had confirmed that.

With this plan, all parties were confident they could march right up to the front gate at Peenemünde without much difficulty. Of course, the ruse would end far before both parties arrived at the research center. It was determined that once the spies were clear of Berlin, they would sleep a night, gather their intel the next, then make the return trip back to Bern.

Sam was confident he could talk his way through any checkpoint, and Lukas was as well. They were both German natives, and bore the Teutonic features that would hopefully provide extra camouflage. Hell, Lukas had been traveling in and out of the country for some time now, but that was always alone, and journeying with Sam was a variable he hadn't yet been met with. They had all the supporting documentation necessary to travel by order of the Research Center at Peenemünde. Ramm was instrumental there as well, since he knew exactly what that documentation should look and sound like. He gave them detailed information about supply order request forms, and even helped perfect Major Heigl's signature, since he'd be the final stop for VkN activities. Ramm himself had helped forge it. Where resistance might be met, they always had the letter from the *Reichsführer* to fall back on. This was the get-out-of-jail-free-card that gave everyone a modicum of ease.

The final element required for the trip was a truck, or as Lukas kept calling it, a "lorry." That gave everyone a good chuckle, though no one could say why. That had not been easy to procure either, but Louie managed to cut a deal with a mechanic in Zürich who was sympathetic to the cause. The mechanic had been a low-level informant along the border, and had come into possession of several beat-up German military transport vehicles—stolen, of course—that had been on their way to Italy to halt the incoming Americans. They'd been abandoned at a depot when the Americans infiltrated Sicily; more importantly, they bore German tags that helped add cover.

Additional reserves of diesel fuel were provided to the team as well since the prospects of tanking up during the trip were both slim and too conspicuous. An absence of fuel had been a notable blight on the German war effort, but an abundance of the chemical in transit by VkN officers wouldn't seem suspect. If Sam and Lukas could manage it, they'd make one straight shot to the outskirts of Berlin before resting. The plan was a rushed one, though it was anything but sloppy. The heads of the four men together seemingly formed one great brain under pressure, and few variables were left to chance.

The idea of parachuting in was floated, but Lukas and Sam lacked the training. The prospect of two spies with broken legs and tangled parachutes was quickly dismissed. Also considered was infiltration by boat from the Baltic, but the sea was still very heavily controlled by German U-boats, so that plan was dismissed as well. The return trip would be made in the same way. Sam and Lukas would rely on their cover as supply couriers with another order request that had been as masterfully forged as the first.

At first a route along the Rhine was discussed, but that was vetoed by Combe as potentially dangerous. It was too close to occupied France. Sam was also thankful it had been cancelled, because it was so close to Karls-ruhe and Pforzheim—terrible memories. A trip through Lichtenstein and Austria, then by way of Prague and Poland was also floated, but a heavy *SS* presence in the Polish territory was a significant fear for the operators, and there was too great a potential for Sam's cover to be blown. Finally, as Occam's Razor dictated, it was agreed that the shortest distance between two points was a straight line; considering the war did not take place within the heart of the fatherland, all agreed the route should be as straight a shot as possible.

The spies would hug the Bodensee, travel north past Stuttgart, bear east—avoiding Nürnberg as best they could—stay west of Dresden, and finally make their way north to Peenemünde. What good was the *Reichsautobahn* the Führer had boasted about if it couldn't be used to traverse the country quickly? Even without stopping, the trip was likely to take sixteen to twenty hours by Hugo's estimations.

There was one variable that could not be ruled out, or planned for, and that was the risk of an air attack from an Allied fighter. To die by the hands of the Allies, or have the mission blown as a result, was a macabre thought for everyone. However, it couldn't be avoided.

There were no sentimental goodbyes when the two spies left Bern. There were handshakes and "godspeeds" all around, but the tension in the air was thicker than the fog cascading down the slopes of the Alps. Brandt and Combe stayed put—there was no reason they should be seen in the company of these two men. Brandt was scheduled to depart back to America by way of a short stop at Chelveston. The priest and the saboteur were escorted by Louie and Phil in the middle of the night, arrived in Zürich to retrieve the truck before the sun even rose, and were crossing the border in short time. Their travel papers were all in order and the truck was dispatched by border officials without any fuss. None of the inspectors raised an eyebrow, though they did check the truck briefly and were satisfied when the cab revealed exactly what the transport list stated: two hundred gallons of fuel heading for Peenemünde, Germany. They were just two innocent drivers making their way to the north of the fatherland to deliver goods.

Far be it from men with all necessary travel documentation—even if forged—to raise unwanted interests.

Once the border had been cleared, Operation God Finger had commenced in earnest. God Finger because the priest had done the dirty work with his hands; God Finger because Brandt the chief was taking an active part in the mission; and God Finger because the rocket resembled one to rival God's own. Now all the two men needed were the fingers of God to shepherd them there and back safely.

The first section of the journey through Baden-Würtemburg was uneventful. They'd cleared four hours of driving at a good clip before the country had even woken. Most of the scenery was lush and mountainous, and despite a series of small villages that kept both men on their toes when they passed by them, they hadn't seen much in the way of resistance. They had passed a *Wermacht* checkpoint of curious infantry officers, as well as a pop-up barracks, but had quickly been waved on.

They had been held up in traffic behind a line of trucks heading northwest—France, perhaps. Sam had thought it wise to slip in right at the back of the line to quell suspicion. This worked until the trucks broke off near Stuttgart. Sam, who'd managed the driving thus far, maintained a north-eastern bearing. At several locations they were forced to take smaller, ill-maintained roads where the primary options had seen the effects of bombing raids. At one point, they had to turn around completely, the road ahead so crater-filled and inaccessible that to attempt to navigate it would likely ruin the plan completely. Allied raids had made the troops work for their trips, and some roads had been completely destroyed to deter tanks.

When they neared Nürnberg, a driving rain halted their journey. The weather came so swift and fast that the windshield wipers were rendered useless and the two men found themselves lodged in a ditch and stuck in nearly a foot of mud. Without an option and lacking manpower, it was Lukas who came up with the idea to pry open one of the boxes storing the fuel bladders and use the lid for traction against the tire. Once dislodged from the mud pit, the lid was so destroyed and splintered that both men agreed it was better to dispose of one of the crates completely. Anyone looking for treasure might stumble upon a canister of gasoline ditched behind a tree root somewhere west of Leipzig.

Other than those that bore directional significance, few words were spoken between the two men. Perhaps it was fear, perhaps concentration, or maybe they just hadn't found anything in common yet, but a ride which could have otherwise been dominated by small talk and the anecdotal histories of two very unique men was populated by uneasy silence. One curious characteristic about their rare exchanges was that both men spoke in German. It had been some time since Sam had spoken the language, but it came so naturally that he hadn't even realized he'd been doing it until Lukas finally broke into an Austrian lilt during the mud incident.

When they finally started seeing the signs for Hanover, Lukas took over driving duties. He was far more confident behind the wheel than Sam. Though Sam fancied himself the better driver, Lukas was more familiar with the *Reich*. Whereas Sam's grip of the wheel was white-knuckled, Lukas handled it gracefully.

Halfway between Hamburg and Berlin, wedged in the low-lying gap of no man's land equidistant from both great cities, Lukas and Sam shared their first formal planning conversation regarding when to make their final stop. They'd been traveling straight through, no breaks other than to relieve themselves, and the sun was falling in the west. The trip had become more quiet now that they'd cleared the highlands. Lukas mentioned a marshy land near Neubrandenburg that he had once taken cover in himself, and proclaimed the value in its unfriendliness to tanks, vehicles, and troops.

Sam, unfamiliar with the area, put up little debate to the suggestion. They would need to sleep the night before their investigation began in earnest, and they'd been performing now without adequate rest ever since they'd arrived in Bern. To push through now would be unwise. Neither man felt sharp any longer. They set up a makeshift camp behind a patch of trees off the path leading into the village.

Unbeknownst to Lukas, Sam had smuggled a flask— a parting gift from Brandt. He propped the doors of the truck open and hopped up on to the tailgate before taking a swig, then offered it to Lukas as he dragged the back of his hand across his mouth. Lukas obliged, then joined Sam aboard the truck bed.

For a moment they sat in silence. Sam took note of just how full the moon was. He could easily see his hands in front of him as he grabbed a cigarette from his breast pocket. The moon was still waxing—probably only one evening off from the end of the cycle. Tomorrow it would be full. Lukas handed the flask back to Sam after another helping.

"Priests drink?" Sam asked.

"*Tonight* they do," Lukas replied. Sam helped himself again, then capped the flask and pocketed it.

They weren't here to party, they were here to gather information.

Lukas looked to Sam. "Did you know him? The farmer?"

"In passing," Sam replied. "The same way you might know anyone else you've worked around. I never met him properly, if that's what you mean. Had you?"

"Once," Lukas said. His eyes drifted toward the moon. "Just to establish the relationship, the *routine*. It was his idea—the burial cache pattern, I mean. He was brave."

Sam savored a puff of the cigarette. "You speak about him as if he's already gone."

"My friend," Lukas said, "it is *very* unlikely that he is still alive."

"What convinces you?"

"It is Peenemünde," Lukas replied. "Even the trees have ears." Lukas paused for a moment. "I never learned his name. Come to think of it, I still don't know it."

"Fowler," Sam said. "Roger Fowler—that was his name."

"Are you sure I'm supposed to know that?"

"Does it really matter?"

"That's not optimistic," Lukas said admonishingly.

"You said it was unlikely he's alive yourself."

"One can maintain hope."

"If we're here, there's probably not much to be optimistic about." He could see he'd deflated Lukas, so he course-corrected: "There's a chance, I suppose."

"Chance. Fate. *Que sera, sera*," Lukas said.

"How many languages do you speak?" Sam asked.

Lukas smirked. "As many as are needed."

"For?" Sam asked.

"For the same reason I imagine you're here, my friend," Lukas replied.

"Which is?"

"Justice," Lukas said in English. The priest grew contemplative as his gaze remained fixed on the moon. He started in English again: "To see to it that the *Reich* falls as quickly and efficiently as possible."

"Define efficient."

"Less bloodshed," Lukas said. "At least for those undeserving. And punishment for those who are."

"Sounds more like revenge," Sam said.

"Perhaps," Lukas said. Sam thought maybe the priest was feeling the buzz from the whiskey. Maybe Sam was too. It was rare his conversations lasted more than was necessary. "But then again, what is revenge but adequately delivered justice for the wronged party? Revenge is only justice in-so-far as the slighted party determines it to be. Revenge is compromise."

"How's that?"

"Because justice suggests a compromise between the offended and offending parties," Lukas said. "Really, it's a compromise within the self of the offended party— they must compromise a part of themselves and reconcile to deliver justice. If a man's brother has been murdered, he may kill the murderer, but he also must rectify that he becomes a murderer himself. That is revenge."

"Do they teach that in the book?" Sam asked.

"Not in so many words," Lukas said. "But my own judgement shall come some day and I'm prepared to answer for my actions, justified or otherwise." A proudness erupted in his tone and Sam noticed his chest rise in confidence. "As I am sure you are." Lukas turned to

Sam. His eyes grew hopeful, pleading. It almost seemed as if he wished Sam himself were his temporary judge. "Am I right? Is that why you are here? Is that what we have in common? You speak both tongues—*Muttersprache und Amerikaner*. You are German, yes?"

"Among other things," Sam replied, forever cryptic.

"But you came from America…" Lukas said with confusion. "With Brandt. So you are American?"

Sam didn't give a straight answer. Instead he just nodded, and Lukas took his meaning. "And you fled?" Lukas asked. "As I did?"

"For a time," Sam said. He wondered if Lukas was encouraging him to begin a confession, but he offered little. "But now I'm back."

"For revenge?" Lukas asked.

"I'm not sure what it is," Sam replied. "I just know it when I see it."

"A dangerous man," Lukas said. "That's you, Sam Abel. I know them when I see them. The kinds I wouldn't cross."

"And why's that?" Sam asked, curious.

"Because men like you have a way of drawing trouble," Lukas said. "A kind of inevitability—and a grave one, perhaps, for those who've wronged you."

"And what about you?" Sam asked. "Are you a dangerous man?"

"That's yet to be seen," Lukas replied.

They took two-hour shifts sleeping; Lukas prayed during his waking hours, Sam chain-smoked. Intermittently throughout the night, air raid sirens screamed in the distance. The Allies weren't sleeping at all.

20

Lukas' familiarity with Peenemünde was, operationally, an absolute necessity. Should Sam have attempted the trip alone, he'd have been in a world of trouble. Lukas was privy to all lesser-used roads, which helped the duo to avoid checkpoints and more major thoroughfares. The presence of soldiers and *Wermacht* activity increased greatly as they progressed through the Mecklenburg lowlands and traveled northwest. Though the team was still far from any active war zone, there were frequent reminders that they were still in a military state. True to character, both Sam—who'd taken over driving again—and Lukas saluted all military members and civilians they encountered. After another long stretch of driving, they'd arrived in Griefswald by late day, which had been designated the final destination before they were officially in range of the farm.

Lukas, no longer in need of the map, folded it into tiny squares as Sam hooked the truck around a dirt bend. They were getting close to their target. Along either side of the truck were extensive patches of farmland, but every so often the Baltic would wink through the trees to the north. The smell of saltwater was beginning to creep into the cabin of the truck. Above, the sun was unleashing a great yawn in the form of bright light illuminating a cloudless sky.

Ahead, a barrier came into focus down a long stretch of narrow path. The road was closed. A sign signaled that entry was forbidden. Sam halted the rattling truck and turned to Lukas for further instructions, but he had none. The priest massaged the point of his chin with his thumb and forefinger, his mouth curled slightly open in quiet thought. Staring back at them was a hastily built wooden gate blocking access to the road beyond. Moving it was out of the question—it was outfitted with razor wire.

Lukas instructed Sam to head southwest for some time, imagining that they would take a parallel route to their destination. To their dismay, after traveling several more kilometers along what they suspected to be a minor detour, they were met with yet another roadblock, this one more demoralizing than the last. Had they been on foot, navigating these inconveniences would be of no consequence, and a debate ensued briefly regarding whether to abandon the truck altogether. Agreeing that it added greatly to their overall cover, they proceeded yet again to a detour that took them indirectly to Griefswald by way of a northern path.

They found themselves on another dirt road, the stench of ocean life both fresh and decaying permeating the shell of the truck. They entered a different part of the fatherland completely, one that Sam had never experienced—a seafaring community. The pathway was encompassed by large pines on either side, creating a tunnel-like atmosphere as they approached their destination. Further road closures thwarted their journey, and the feeling that they were being funneled toward a particular route became clearer with every passing kilometer.

Ahead, a clearing in the trees gave view to the town proper. Smoke rose from a chimney in the distance. They passed several farmers carting goods by horse and traveling in the opposite direction. Another closure forced them to turn east once more. A smattering of trees at the corner of the road obscured what was hiding behind their camouflage.

Sam stopped the truck. Ahead, tall fencing had been erected at each edge of the road and stretched deep into the forests beyond. A gate barred entry to the road, and beside it on the north side was a kiosk of freshly assembled wood with radio antennas on its roof and telephone lines draped along its exterior. They were close enough to the outpost that to turn around would only draw the type of attention neither man sought. In the kiosk, and obscured by the dim glass of afternoon light, a silhouette seemed to take notice of the approaching truck. Sam forged on.

When the two infiltrators arrived at the gate, a boom arm dropped in front of the truck's hood. From the security box, the shadowy figure stared curiously at the two men in the vehicle. His lips moved, and there was a phone resting between his shoulder and ear. To the right of the truck, a grizzled *SS* officer stared on, a machine gun slung over his shoulder and a cigarette smoldering in his mouth. Even in the punishing heat, he wore his signature attire, clothed in a charcoal-colored black uniform that did those required to wear it on a hot day no favors. He kept a good twenty steps between himself and the car.

Nothing about the scenario should have signaled danger. These men were doing their jobs: assume everyone is suspicious and be unusually curious. For the Nazi that had nothing to hide, it was just another step in the delivery process; for two infiltrators, it was a nightmare.

The *SS* man in the booth hung up the phone. He picked up a pistol from the table beside him and deposited it into his holster before setting off through the door. As he rounded the corner, he signaled for Sam to roll down his window. Sam did. Hot air rushed into the cab, and with it the stinging odor of the ocean.

"Yours as well," the officer said while motioning to Lukas. Lukas did as asked.

"Good afternoon," Sam said to the officer, who'd now arrived at the driver's-side window. "Sweltering today."

"Shut the automobile off, please," the officer said. Uninterested in small talk, he immediately cut in with: "Identification."

Sam and Lukas both retrieved their identification documents and handed them over to the man at Sam's window; as he took them, his eyes studied both men in the truck. Lukas took quick inventory of the other man on his side, who was now suddenly very close and seemingly curious about the details of the truck's exterior. Uninterested in Lukas as his partner did the investigating, he set off at an un-rushed pace around the backside of the truck.

Lukas feigned inconvenience, Sam exhaustion.

Nothing should suggest this trip was out of the ordinary. They were two men tired from running supplies back and forth, that was it. The inquisitive officer studied both sets of identification for a moment, alternating between the two faces before him as he did. From the trees, insects wailed against the heat.

Sam and Lukas were sweating—thankfully, a welcome breeze rushed through the cab of the truck a moment later. Who wouldn't be sweating? It was hot as blazes. Even the scrutinizing *SS* man swiped the sweat from his brow as he studied the two documents.

"Destination?" the *SS* man asked.

Sam, ever quick on his feet, replied, "Confidential… " he paused, looked at the badge on the man's breast, then added, "Herr Schöbel."

Schöbel, now intrigued, said, "Well, you must be going somewhere?"

"Indeed," Sam replied. "But I'm under strict instruction not to divulge the information. It's all here in this paperwork, you see?" Sam produced the letter from Major Heigl that, by proxy of the German Air Ministry and Army Research Branch, had tasked these two petty clerks with retrieving and delivering fuel.

Schöbel took those documents too and, now with more curiosity, began to read their instructions. Sam thought this letter was proof enough to end the inspection. To produce the letter from the *Reichsführer* too soon might be poor execution. They were lowly delivery men, and only that.

Sam searched both wing mirrors—he'd lost sight of the other officer, who he assumed disappeared behind the truck. Now Lukas was sweating something fierce. Sam also felt a thin trickle of sweat sliding in what seemed to be slow motion down the vein on his neck. Beyond the driver's window, Herr Schöbel was doing every bit of due diligence one might expect from an *SS* man tasked with guarding the greater Usedom area. He took another pat at his head, wiping away the sweat around his cap. The sun broke through a patch of clouds, causing all parties to squint as the rays beat down on them. After a few more moments, Sam caught sight of the other guard signaling to his partner in the driver's wing mirror. Schöbel recognized his request, then lifted his head to Sam. "Open the rear gate, please."

Shit. This was taking too long. Sam should have produced the get-out-of-jail-free letter from the get go. An inspection should never have been allowed. The longer they lingered, the longer the opportunity for questions from the guards, and more questions only ever led to more chances for inconsistency.

Sam, with no choice but to oblige the officer, said, "I've the key right here, Herr Schöbel. Allow me to step out and open it for you."

Schöbel nodded, then said, "You step out too," to Lukas.

Now it was clear why there had been so many road-blocks set up. This post was designated as a funnel point. If anyone was coming in or out from this direction, they needed to pass through Herr Schöbel and his ilk. And Lukas had not known about it. Was this a new security protocol, or a response in the wake of Roger Fowler's possible capture? Before Sam could debate these possibilities, he was jamming the key into the lock.

Lukas ambled toward the rear, too. He was supposed to be acting naturally, but Sam thought something about the stolen VkN uniforms wasn't working in his favor. He didn't seem to know how to behave like a militant, something that came naturally to Sam.

Keeping a distance again from the truck, and now with his automatic rifle gripped tightly in his hands, the other officer scowled as Sam opened the truck's rear door. Schöbel placed their identification documents in his coat pocket while Sam tended to the lock—*not getting those back any time soon.* The lock popped, and Sam sent the truck's door sliding up into its hinges. Thankfully the plan had actually utilized the lies it was comprised of, because every man standing there was suddenly hit with the powerful fumes of the gas. Above, the sun continued to beat down on Sam and Lukas below, but the sweat showing on their uniforms did not originate from the heat. For the *SS* men, the black party attire revealed no sweat marks, and they were clearly hot too. It was the tension of the situation that had Sam and Lukas so anxious. Had the spies been sweating like this in cold weather, the jig would have been up long ago.

Schöbel popped the lid on one of the crates, checked its contents, then compared it against what was listed on the delivery manifest. Sam was growing impatient. *It's gasoline. The manifest says we're hauling gasoline. What more do you need to know?* Plenty, apparently, because Schöbel next wanted to know what the intended use of the gasoline was.

"Above my rank, I'm afraid, Herr Schöbel," Sam replied. He turned to the glaring officer. "They don't tell us much other than where to drop it." The unnamed officer continued to glower at Sam. Was he the bad cop in this equation? The one who stands by silently while the man one *thought* was in charge conducts the inquisition?

Sam watched the quiet officer's eyes survey Lukas. The two men who had the least to say seemed to be signaling the loudest. Schöbel popped another crate open—still more fuel. *What was taking so long? Why had they not been satisfied? Everything was above board.*

Schöbel checked the manifest once more, then, seemingly satisfied, put the lids back on the crates containing the cans of gasoline. Sam breathed a sigh of relief—he was fairly sure Lukas did too. In addition to the tension in the prolonged search, the heat was becoming unbearable in the uniform.

"They may be unloaded here," Schöbel said as he wiped his gloves. He hopped down from the truck. "We will help you."

Sam paused. "But our manifest requests the delivery to the stated location and *only* that location, Herr Schöbel."

"Never mind that," Schöbel replied. "We're under strict new orders to receive certain supplies at this post. We'll see to it that it gets where it's going, you can be sure."

Sam grinned uneasily. "I'm afraid I'm not comfortable with that, Herr Schöbel. You see, if my superior was to find that I didn't leave these items in the custody of those specifically listed within the documents, I could suffer the penalties."

"Then your superior would have no trouble in contacting this post to learn of the change of plans."

So what is it? Sam wondered. *Does he not trust us, or is this departmental in-fighting? Are we suspect, or are we being had?* The *SS* and the *Wermacht*, forever at each other's throats—apparently even Peenemünde was not immune. Sam considered that if the officers had been in serious doubt of his and Lukas' intentions, both infiltrators would have had a bullet in their heads. *SS* men killed for far less. Schöbel had started walking back toward the post, and the other officer was still on standby with his rifle at the ready. Sam was out of options.

"Herr Schöbel," Sam said, stepping after the man in one last-ditch effort. He had to make the call and use his golden pass. Schöbel was still holding their identification. "Forgive me, but there is one more document I possess that might be of aid."

Schöbel turned, seemingly willing to hear what the final argument was, and Sam produced the *Reichsführer's* letter. Schöbel immediately recognized the source of the document. It was as if the style of the paper itself spoke volumes before anyone had even had a chance to read it. The letterhead alone commanded Schöbel's attention in such a way that had turned the tide almost immediately. As Schöbel read, Sam lit up a cigarette just to give his damn hands something to do. "*Zigaretten?*" he offered to the officer standing by. The man shook his head from side to side, still clutching his rifle. Sam motioned to Lukas, and Lukas—surprisingly—obliged. Perhaps the priest himself needed something to do with his hands. Lukas lit it clumsily, took a drag, then coughed for a moment before catching his breath.

Sam thought Lukas' choice was flawed, because the *SS* officer who hadn't let them out of his sight watched suspiciously as Lukas forced himself to smoke. When Schöbel got to the bottom of the letter, it was clear he recognized the signature, the highest of the high in the land if one didn't have a letter from the Führer himself —his eyebrows rose in high arches. He stepped forward, brandishing the letter outward for his partner to scrutinize. The silent officer let his rifle fall from his grip, hang from his shoulder, and now set his full attention on the letter before him. Sam's suspicion was confirmed: *this* was the man they'd truly needed to convince.

Lukas remained focused on the officer's eyes as they darted downward, left to right. He stopped at the bottom of the letter, took note of the *Reichsführer's* signature, then folded the document and whispered something to Schöbel. The two men spoke in hushed tones for a moment. Sam couldn't hear what was being said, and it wasn't helping his fear at all. When the two men were in agreement, Schöbel turned to Sam.

"I'll just need to call ahead," Schöbel said with a coy smile. "Above my rank, I'm afraid." He'd repeated Sam's words exactly. Schöbel set off for the security kiosk, and all three men looked on as his silhouette spoke in soft muffles with someone on the other end of the line. Time seemed to crawl as they stood there waiting. The heat was awful, the stench of fuel no less so. Schöbel fixed his attention toward the group as he engaged in a lengthy conversation with the receiver of the call.

Sam would be lying if he said he wasn't thinking of overpowering the man standing next to him and stealing his weapon. That would still leave Schöbel to contend with. Furthermore, it would set off a chain of events when their bodies were found that would trigger a manhunt. There was no reason to start out on bad footing. Still, Sam readied himself for the worst-case scenario. If it came down to it, he was going to have to perform. They weren't going to have traveled the length of Germany just to get stopped so close to their destination.

Sam's cigarette had burned down to his fingers. Beside him, the unnamed officer's gaze was still firmly affixed to both of the detained. With every passing moment, Sam became more convinced that the scenario was not going to end well; this endeavor was going to get messy before it had even begun proper.

But to his surprise, Schöbel hung the phone up and exited the kiosk with all of the two truck occupants' credentials and travel letters in his hand and a forgiving smile stretched across his face. He took a swat at a small control panel beside the kiosk and the boom arm raised. His attitude had changed completely; gone were the skeptical eyes of the *Reich's* most-feared security personnel. Schöbel handed over all the supporting documentation, then signaled to the man with the machine gun to operate the gate. He tossed the cigarette, eased his gun from his grip, thankfully, and ambled over to the gate's controls.

"Thank you, Herr Schöbel," Sam said. Lukas nodded in thanks as well, still silent.

"No, thank you for cooperating," Schöbel replied. "There's a lot of dangerous men lurking about, and security is of the utmost importance here." A curt smile followed the statement. Everything about it made Sam uneasy. He detected something sinister about the man's demeanor—this was phony friendliness. Sam chalked it up to the discrepancies between *Wermacht* divisions. It didn't matter. The gate was now open and the road ahead clear for travel. Sam and Lukas hopped into the truck and continued toward Griefswald, thankful that the team at *Edelweiss* had been such masters of forgery. They had entered Usedom.

21

A launch would be taking place at Test Stand VII in short order. Eichler had been briefed regarding its logistics earlier in the morning. He often felt like the last to know these types of things, but the late warnings were purely operational. There was no need for information to be provided any earlier than was absolutely necessary. Protocol, determined by Eichler himself, dictated that a full inventory of the perimeter would be taken several hours prior to a launch.

He started on foot at Karlshagen with Vogel, his adjutant. The migration of white-coats north toward the research and engineering facilities evidenced a busy morning. It seemed all hands were on deck as men marched with briefcases and clipboards in hand. The stress of a forthcoming launch was written on their faces. Peppered throughout the white-coats was the olive garb of military officers; at Peenemünde, they were often one in the same. There was always an air of the immediate on a launch day; bodies moved with purpose and the grave expressions of men hoping for success. Children marched on brigade—oblivious to the events unfolding around them—and parents to their respective factories. The general air of a beautiful and eventful day was in full swing at Peenemünde. Every so often, Messerchmitts soared in twos above, and U-boats could be seen poking out of the water in the east if one looked hard enough. Within the perimeter area, all systems were a go.

He then traveled south to Zinnowitz, where the foot patrol of the perimeter area ended. There, the *SS* had established its own checkpoints and security measures on land. Eichler worked in tandem with the *Kriegsmarine* to monitor shore activity via the U-boats patrolling the Baltic north of Poland. It was the rare case in which Himmler's *SS* and the *Heer* had a proper handshake. Eichler gathered the rest of the reports by vehicle, utilizing a truck gathered from the motor pool at Zinnowitz. The north end, specifically where Test Stand VII stood, was monitored by the *Heer* and *Luftwaffe*, and that was because few people were able to get near it. That put it out of Eichler's zone of interest, and so he proceeded west toward Trassenheide to speak with the rest of his teams.

Within the perimeter, the *SS* was also responsible for the slave labor housed—if that was what one could even call it—within the shabby wooden shacks of the makeshift work camp. At the southernmost perimeter, all had still been quiet. There had been a couple questionable travelers picked up near the Lagoon at Szcezin while fishing that the *SS* had quickly learned were civilians who'd wandered a bit too far up the peninsula. They were redirected to fish elsewhere.

The sun was harsh in the late day as Eichler traveled along the low-lying lands north of the Achterwasser. In fact, he wagered it was the hottest day he'd experienced at Usedom. Some fast-moving clouds traveling northwest had provided brief bits of respite, but they were few and far between. Any time he'd stepped out of his truck to source a report from his crews he was met with unforgiving winds that were anything but relieving. He wondered why High Command hadn't canceled the launch altogether. As far as he knew, the test was still scheduled.

He continued west toward Wolgast. One might question why Lothar Eichler felt it necessary to make all these trips himself when a phone or radio call would do just fine, but he was a thorough individual who demanded to see that his teams were always prepared and at the ready, rather than passively waiting the day away. Had he had his way prior to the sabotage of Flussrand, perhaps the saboteur would never have had the opportunity to set foot within the facility. Much of Eichler's motivation was predicated on his prior failures, and he was determined not to make the same mistake again—especially at the coveted Peenemünde. On a launch day especially, he felt a great need to confirm inactivity with his own eyes.

With the launch preparations ending in the early evening, and the test set to begin immediately following confirmation of all systems, Eichler maneuvered to his final area of responsibility. At Wolgast, he arrived to convene with another of his clusters of troops, and it was here that he was met with a report that was exceptionally out of the ordinary—he knew it would dramatically change the course of his day. It began with a call at the barracks, specifically addressed to him, and he answered in the office behind a closed door. Rarely did people speak freely at Peenemünde, and Eichler had relieved the officer on duty of his post to receive the communication.

"Herr Eichler," a voice said when he placed the phone to his ear. Eichler recognized the voice of Herr Schöbel, *SS* Officer on patrol near Griefswald.

"Herr Schöbel," Eichler replied.

"We've had a development here," Schöbel said. "Two men, one fitting the description provided."

"Continue," Eichler said. Though conversation through phone lines at Peenemünde wasn't advisable, a border guard sharing information with the head of security about a wanted individual was necessary.

"They're traveling in VkN uniform," Schöbel said, "with credentials to match. They've a letter from the General that permits passage to deliver fuel, and when scrutinized they produced a very peculiar letter from the *Reichsführer*—forged, no doubt—instructing unobstructed passage to Peenemünde."

"Are you sure it's him?" Eichler asked.

"The description matches," Schöbel replied.

"Have you a delivery manifest?"

"I do."

Eichler barreled through the doorway, snapped his fingers at one of the secretaries sitting at the desk in the main office, and commanded she bring him a VkN delivery manifest. She provided it post-haste. He slammed the door on her face, then grabbed for a pencil from his pocket and scanned the ledger. He traveled down the list, confirmed that no such delivery had been ordered, at least not today, and double-checked *just* to ensure he wasn't being too overprotective. On a launch day, the delay of resources could have terrible repercussions, and if Eichler was the responsible party at the end of that delay, all he would be made to be was a fool, not a hero. Furthermore, if fuel was still absent or in demand, the launch would have been halted or rescheduled.

Eichler, fearful of jumping to conclusions and sounding an unnecessary alarm, asked Schöbel, "And your manifest? Have you any indication that the resources on your end were requested or scheduled for delivery?"

"Not today, Herr Eichler." Schöbel's voice was snide and suspicious. Eichler tapped the pencil against the manifest as if keeping up with a high-tempo tune. The VkN hadn't scheduled any deliveries today, nor had anyone from General Dornberger or Major Heigl's teams, and the launch team hadn't alerted him.

"Should we apprehend the individuals in question?" Schöbel asked.

"No," Eichler briskly replied. "Allow them passage."

"Pardon?" Schöbel asked, sounding confused. Neither man had supreme authority over one another. They were supposed to be working in unison, complementary teams securing the greater Usedom area through information and communication, but Eichler as *Sicherheitskapitän* had final say if someone was going to be permitted to arrive within the southern security checkpoint. Since that was where the men claimed to be heading, and because it was the only way to get a vehicle bearing those types of materials into Peenemünde itself, Eichler made an executive decision to allow passage. Falke had instructed him to, and though it went against his orders at Peenemünde, he would put his security teams on high alert. He wondered, though, why Falke hadn't alerted him that the intruder may be returning—or if he'd known at all.

"You may allow the vehicle passage, Herr Schöbel," Eichler commanded with the tone of a superior officer.

"As you wish," Schöbel replied, though there was a dismissiveness to his voice that irked Eichler. Before Eichler hung up, he requested of Schöbel all of the information he could gather about the truck and its passengers. He was provided with the make and model, as well as the names of the two VkN men in question. He quickly wrote all of the information down in a small notepad he kept on hand.

As he replaced the phone on its cradle, Eichler second-guessed his decision. He had now broken the highest security protocol in the land, inviting the enemy itself close to the supremely protected base, and done so willingly—on a launch day, no less. Falke's desperate need to discover more about these saboteurs outweighed Eichler's own concern with his failure to protect the center. Perhaps Eichler felt less concern because he knew exactly where these two suspicious men would be heading: the farm.

Just as soon as he'd hung up the phone, he made radio calls to all of his external posts with explicit instructions to source the location of these VkN men, with further instructions to monitor and not confront them.

He tore through the office with great purpose, leaving in his wake the air of immediacy that left all of the secretaries within the office speechless. As he exited, he commanded the soldiers at the western post at

Wolgast to be on high alert. Furthermore, he sent a battalion of men up the coast to the north, and then ordered men to patrol the northwest perimeter as far as Karlshagen, where his area of responsibility ended.

He alerted no one in High Command, because to do so and find himself at the wrong end of a mistake would be a *massive* blunder. Sending the alarm bells ringing on a launch day could also lead to wasted resources. Just to get the rocket to the launch stage of preparation was a great undertaking, and one that he didn't want to meddle with. Eichler was confident they could monitor and manage this one individual. The lingering question on his mind was, "Who is the accomplice?" Perhaps Falke was right: patience with the individual might yield further treasure.

He hopped into his vehicle and commanded Vogel to head north to the western perimeter. Vogel seemed to sense the unease of his superior. He asked, "Is all well, Herr Eichler?"

"He's back," Eichler replied. "The man on the farm has returned."

Eichler had made Vogel aware of Falke's requests, if only because they spent so much time together and Eichler considered him within the sphere of need-to-know information. Vogel, though predominantly Eichler's personal attendant, was also a de facto second-in-command, and could be trusted with knowledge only Eichler was supposed to be privy to.

"Are we to apprehend him this time?" Vogel asked as the truck bounced along uneven, unpaved road.

"No," Eichler replied. "We continue to perform reconnaissance."

"Forgive me, Herr Eichler," Vogel began, "but

should we not be concerned with the timing of his arrival? With a launch in sight, does it not worry you that this man is within striking distance of the facility and yet we're allowing him freedom of travel?"

"He is Falke's property," Eichler argued with the authority of a superior. "Should Falke want us to, then we will act. Right now, we are to continue with the plan as requested."

"Understood," Vogel replied as he fought with the steering wheel. They were traveling beside a large wall of pines, up the western-most path across the inlet separating the island from the farm. "I must admit," Vogel had dropped his voice to a low murmur, "I feel sympathy for the man."

"Why is that?" Eichler asked.

"To be in the sights of *Der Fänger*?" Vogel squeaked with a giddy, child-like grin. "The all-seeing eye of Aksel Falke? He's supernatural, you know? That's what is said, anyway."

Eichler only listened. He'd heard the rumors about Falke himself, the fanciful musings of gossipers apt to formulate their own tall tales about the legendary hunter of the *Reich* and his peculiar torture techniques. But how many had been true? Eichler assumed few. These were fables constructed to strike fear into his prey, and Falke probably welcomed them. Eichler wasn't convinced. *Adept? Sure. Supernatural? Unlikely.*

And yet Eichler himself wouldn't deny that Falke was deserving of his infamous persona, because he did indeed capture those he sought. Furthermore, he had that incredible aptitude to strike fear into those in his presence. How much of that was inherent in his personality, and how much came from his unique physical attribute in the form of the lone amber eye?

Eichler felt a tinge of unworthiness in the presence of even Falke's mention, but Peenemünde was *Eichler's* territory, not Falke's.

"And after what happened with the American," Vogel added eagerly. He was smitten with admiration. He noticed Eichler's scowl and seemed to think better of continuing, so he refocused on the road.

The westerly winds were picking up along the coast. At times they even shook the truck as Vogel attempted to maintain his northern course. The pines danced like spectators welcoming the men toward the finish line.

"Go on," Eichler said. "About the American."

"Forgive me, Herr Eichler," Vogel said with a squeak. "I shouldn't have been discussing matters to which I've no privilege."

"Never mind," Eichler said. He was forceful now, changed from a man listening to one directing the conversation. "You'll finish your thought. That's an order."

Vogel seemed to debate this for a moment. He shrank into the seat as Eichler stared him down. To speak as freely as he just had was a great sin at Peenemünde.

"I just meant, Herr Eichler... " Vogel said. The words still failed to come.

"Herr Vogel," Eichler boomed. "You've already failed to observe the rules in one instance, which is a punishable offense, so now I'm giving you an opportunity to redeem yourself. Kindly elaborate on the *American*."

Encouraged, even if still sheepish, Vogel did: "The

one that Herr Falke caught. I was only speaking of what befell him and how one should be so unlucky—"

"What befell him?"

"The snake," Vogel said with confusion. His demeanor suggested Eichler should have known exactly what he was speaking about. Eichler didn't.

"What snake?" Eichler asked.

"Herr Eichler," Vogel said. "Surely you heard the story?" Eichler's grimace communicated he had not. Vogel hesitated before beginning again. "Herr Falke tortured the American." Vogel frowned. "In only the way he does." Vogel's gaze became distant as he navigated the coastline. "I heard—" Vogel started, then corrected himself. "It's been said that he confined the man in one of the cement barracks with a snake. One of the Asian ones. The hooded kind."

"A cobra," Eichler presented.

"Yes," Vogel said. He mimed a "yuck," then agreed. "A cobra."

Eichler considered this in silence. The fanciful stories of Falke's exploits were always sprinkled with the untrue, but here it was coming from his own adjutant. And at Peenemünde, the stories were so protected because more often than not they *were* true. *But*, Eichler considered, *what did Falke learn that aided us in any way during this torturous episode? Nothing*, Eichler considered—that was why he was on his way to the scene of the crime to continue with this game of cat and mouse. Or, as Falke might have it, *snake* and mouse.

22

———

S am and Lukas traveled north when they reached the forests of Freest. The farm was within reach. They had encountered other troops along the way, but those groups consisted of off-duty men unwilling or unable to question their presence. There had been a couple of odd looks from troops here and there when Sam and Lukas passed through, but they'd hoped they hadn't drawn any unwanted attention in the process. The plan was to park the truck within the forest, and then Sam could set off on foot and figure out what had transpired with Roger Fowler. After that, they had planned to gather intelligence about troop and aircraft presence before they maneuvered back south to make the return trip.

The sun was getting low in the west, now casting a wide beam against the rippling waves on the Baltic. The smell of saltwater was intense, and the shade from the tall trees welcome. In the northeast, Sam was able to spot two *Luftwaffe* craft taking off and landing on what he assumed was the airfield. For Brandt, that would be a good indicator that Peenemünde was still at ease.

The two infiltrators were as near to Peenemünde as any sane men would want to get, and Sam began to see that Ramm was being truthful with his information. With the evidence of a strong military presence, Sam's suspicions about Fowler's fate were becoming more grim the closer they got. How a man had stayed embedded for so long was impressive to Sam, and it made him gain some respect for Lukas as well.

"Yes," Lukas said as he seemed to recognize the location. "It's just up there. Forgive me, I've never navigated by day." He glanced out the window toward the twinkling sea. "It's takes on a different characteristic in the light, I must say."

A small dirt road branched west and stopped before a thickly wooded path. Sam considered it as good a place to park as any. They were surrounded by dense forest on all sides and certainly out of the direct view of the military campus. Now that the sun was filtered, the forest took on a haze of dim orange. The two men hopped out of the truck and took inventory of their surroundings.

Sam retrieved the map he'd been presented by Ramm and traced his finger around the farmland. The two men were parallel to the airfield and the eastern riverbank. Between them and Peenemünde was only a length of a forest the size of a football field and a thin strip of water.

"It's quiet," Sam said as he adjusted his cap.

"Quiet can speak volumes," Lukas said.

Sam glanced northeast toward the general direction of the farm. He checked his compass, then glanced at

Sigrid's watch. They'd have to wait a while still before going to the farm.

"I should go with you," Lukas said.

"No," Sam replied. "Your face is the one that's most at risk. You stay with the truck. We can't stay together. If I don't resurface within thirty minutes of leaving, you take off. We can't both risk being caught."

"What value does that serve?" Lukas asked. "Why come all this way to obtain no information?"

"Because if something happens to me within thirty minutes, that's about all the information you're going to need to bring back."

Lukas took Sam's point. Separately, they had double the chance of returning to Bern with a shred of information: confirmation that operation God Finger was indeed fully compromised and that American activities at Peenemünde should cease—or not. Sam was just about to set off for the farm when a blast of hot air ripped through the forest, sending the trees into a frenzy that looked as if they'd begun a riot.

The deafening whine of a distant siren in the east interrupted their conversation. Sam immediately sprang into high alert. He crouched low, signaled for Lukas to do the same, and watched the horizon through the intermittent trees. All that was visible was the edge of the opposite forest where the Luftwaffe field resided.

"An air-raid siren," Lukas said.

"There's not a plane in the sky," Sam replied. "It's something else. Keep silent." Sam crept farther toward the riverbank. Lukas followed, both men hunched low and moving as stealthily as possible. As they approached the shore, the siren's cry tapered off and the sound of the Baltic warring against the riverbanks grew louder. Sam tucked himself against a large swatch of plant life and Lukas flanked his position. The siren wailed once more.

Sam quickly folded the map and inserted it back into his pocket, then grabbed his binoculars. He couldn't see anything of value from his hidden position, so he tossed them to Lukas to give the other man a chance. Lukas shook his head back and forth dismissively, then threw the binoculars back to Sam. Sam waved him forward and both men left their position and traveled forward again toward the riverbank.

A thunderous *crack* sounded from the east.

"No," Lukas said without consideration. "It's too soon!" Sam thought this mighty peculiar. There was a lingering moment of confusion with the priest, but curiosity got the better of Sam. The deep rumble of something terrifying coming from Peenemünde grew stronger.

The earth shook with the might of a titan's steps. Sam rose to his feet, his attention sharp and animalistic. An earthquake was uncharacteristic on this part of the globe—possible, but unlikely. Sam took off through the trees ahead, dashing toward the river without a word. Lukas followed with him.

"Sam!" Lukas called in a harsh whisper. The spy didn't respond. Lukas chased after him as if trying to capture a dog off a leash, regardless of the myriad of branches and leaves attempting to assault them.

Both men halted when they came to the edge of the tree line where the marshy wetlands met the river inlet. Sam huddled up to a large tree, and Lukas followed suit. Despite the excitement, both men were wise enough to remain camouflaged. Sam scanned the airfield. Perhaps a massive new warplane would be seeing flight. Sam didn't think any plane, even a massive bomber, would produce a noise like that, but with the Germans, one could never be sure.

Sam's attention turned then to the tree line on the east side of Peenemünde, where even in the early evening light a mysterious glow penetrated the trees. Considering the sun was at his back, and it never set in the east, the visual was intriguing. The rumble subsided to a distant groan, and what followed was the sound of what Sam could only imagine was a thousand fires burning at once. Sam received his first visual of the disturbance when a conical shape rose slowly above the tree line.

A thousand fires was an accurate statement; when the cylindrical body passed the tops of trees, it was followed by several fins at its base, and trailing that was a fiery cone of burning fuel in the weapon's wake. What was burnt upon ignition followed behind the machine in a massive, curling dark cloud of disintegrated chemical tail. For a moment, the two men watched in the silence of awe as the rocket rose into the sky above, pushing with all of its magnificent force against the powerful resistance of Earth's gravity. The sound traveled all the way to both men—a raging, crackling drone as if the weapon came with its own unique battle cry.

"My God," Lukas said as he formed the sign of the cross against his chest. Sam remained silent. The spy was too fixated on the display across the river to speak. The machine only gained speed as it traveled, and now it was climbing into the sky and toward the high clouds above.

It was easy to spot against the skyline; much like in the schematics and diagrams Ramm had sketched, the body of the rocket was an alternating checkerboard pattern of black-and-white rectangles. Even from where Sam stood, the weapon still seemed gargantuan. Soon the rocket began to turn slightly, causing a long, bending trail of smoke to follow like a hellish, deformed rainbow's arch. Beyond the tree line, the lingering smoke from the initial blastoff began to rise, and the woods on the eastern side of Peenemünde became more and more obscured.

As the cylindrical death machine continued up into the sky, it became a faint dart among the clouds. Though both men could still hear it traveling, once it plowed through a large bulk of cloud cover it was gone. There was quiet. Nothing stirred in the deep woods surrounding both men. It seemed that the rocket had struck fear into every animal and insect present in the forest. Sam thought even the trees themselves seemed to have frozen in shock, though it was a fantastical idea.

"That good enough proof for you?" Sam asked as his eyes remained fixed on the sky above.

"Yes," Lukas replied.

"Me too."

No further evidence was required that Peenemünde was operating as usual. A research facility on lockdown does not display its weapons so openly if it fears an attack from its enemy. Tick one box. Now all that was left for the duo was to get an answer regarding Roger Fowler. All points led to the farmhouse, but to enter the home right now would be conspicuous. They would wait until dark. The two operators set off for a cluster of dense trees at the edge of a small inlet that would keep them near the farm.

Once they'd found cover, Sam returned to the statement Lukas had made earlier: *'It's too soon!'* Something about it didn't sit right with him. For a moment he just watched Lukas' nervous, darting-around gaze. He let the priest's lack of speech do all the talking. Sam stepped forward, stalking Lukas as if he was about to pounce on him. "What do you know?"

"Nothing," Lukas said.

"You said it was *too soon*," Sam said.

"I was merely commenting—"

"Don't lie," Sam said. "I can tell if you're lying, and you *are* lying."

Lukas, now back-stepping, said, "Nothing I'm sure you don't already know."

"And what would that be?"

Lukas nearly tripped over a tree root as he continued his retreat. "About forthcoming plans."

"*What* plans?" Sam asked.

"I was told not discuss it with anyone," Lukas choked out. "You can respect that."

"Start talking," Sam said. "I don't like not knowing the facts."

Lukas backed himself right up into a tree trunk, which nearly caused him to jump out of his skin. Now Sam was right up against him, face to face, leaving him no chance of escape. "I'm not sure that I can," Lukas cried. "Operationally, that is."

"Operationally *what*?" Sam was seething. "Stop speaking in riddles."

"I wasn't suppose to tell anyone," Lukas said. "I'm sworn to protocol too, you know?"

"I don't give a shit about protocol right now," Sam warned. "You know something I should, and for some reason it was kept from me. What is it, and why?"

Lukas seemed to debate answering. "A Royal Air Force raid," Lukas said finally.

"When?" Sam barked.

"I don't know."

"Do *better*."

"Any time now," Lukas squeaked.

"How do you know?"

"Brandt."

Sam felt foolish. It wasn't like Brandt to keep things like that from him. Why hadn't he been given all the details?

"Be more specific," Sam ordered.

"I don't *know*," Lukas said. "Honestly. I just know that the events have been set in motion—that's straight from your master's mouth."

"Why didn't *I* know? Why did no one tell me?" Sam was almost yelling, not a good behavioral choice considering the circumstances.

"I was told not to," Lukas replied. "It was precautionary. I shouldn't know myself. If you were to be compromised too, there was fear that you could in turn jeopardize the mission."

"And you?" Sam argued. "You're the great secret-keeper of no fault?"

Sam could see the statement angered Lukas. His jaw clenched, his eyes narrowed, and now he moved forward to challenge Sam. "I'm more valuable an asset than you'll ever be. You're a mercenary, that's all—a glorified troublemaker. Combe said it himself: he didn't even want to send you. You're a *risk*. From what I heard, you're more compromised than me. I've put myself in great trouble just being around you. I've worked for *years* at this— years of my life back and forth, the risk of death and torture ever-present. I've sacrificed everything and then some. What have you sacrificed?" Lukas paused to allow Sam to answer, but then seemed to decide his tirade was not over, and kept going. "The man we're looking for, *he* sacrificed. Regular men, men like me, we're the ones who put the materials on the table. If you can't accept that, then you can take your scowl and turn around and go home. I'll finish here."

Sam had no rebuttal. He wondered if his anger was misplaced. It was Brandt and Combe who had most disappointed him. He always assumed that information had been withheld regarding certain operations, but it irked him anyway. Had Brandt and Combe lost faith in him, in his ability to protect sensitive information? Hadn't he endured torture at the hands of Lothar Eichler at Pforzheim? Or was the mission indeed one of such importance that even the most trusted operators couldn't be given all the details?

"Why do you know?" Sam asked. "What makes you so special?"

"I threatened to walk," Lukas replied. Sam began to pace, throttling the tension down considerably. "If your bosses weren't going to give results, then I was going to take the information to another bidder. I didn't join in this operation to play games—I came for revenge."

Sam focused his attention on the rusty hue of the horizon. The sun would fall completely soon. There was one job left to do. They didn't have to be friends—they had to survive.

"What else?" Sam asked. "What *else* don't I know?"

Sam sensed Lukas knew more—he could *feel* it. He wanted to shake the truth out of the priest, to force him to talk. Logic got the better of him. Feuding with an ally right now could only lead to more danger.

The rage of confusion welled up inside Sam. Lies, lies, and more lies. Lies about Peenemünde, lies about the RAF. There was a long moment of silence as the sun fell in the west.

"It's fate," Lukas said. His eyes were fixed in reverence along the vast ocean north.

"What is?"

"I've been back and forth here many, many times now. I've lost count. Never have I witnessed the weapon with my own eyes, what I've worked so hard to foil. And there, clear as day—as if divine—I've seen it. And now it will be destroyed. That is fate."

23

Westerly winds carried the spent fuel from the rocket across the Peene, clouding the sky in a charcoal blanket. The setting sun cut an ominous slash across the lower horizon that painted the forest in a dim tangerine sheen and seemed to point at the island itself. It was if a deity from above had drawn a sword down onto Peenemünde. To the north, boats sped across the Baltic to retrieve what could be salvaged of the launch. And all while the island was displaying its most precious of secrets, Lothar Eichler had invited those that sought subterfuge in.

Eichler skirted the riverbank as he twisted the focus ring on his binoculars. The dull, blurred mass of an undefined figure morphed into the sharp outline of a man. He'd received a radio call only minutes prior. Four of his men were already gathered near the water's edge, camouflaged in olive fatigues and clutching carbines under a cluster of pines.

Eichler had confirmed the person of interest was the

priest who'd first intrigued both Falke and him. This man was undoubtedly the liaison of the captured American spy. He was now standing back on German soil, within the perimeter of Peenemünde no less.

Eichler waved a hand behind him to signal his team to hold their position. Their eagerness was evident in this fateful second encounter. The priest, as Falke had suggested, had not altered his behavior—at least not in any way that signaled his operation had been abandoned. In fact, it seemed he was in full conversation with a still-obscured figure. Had Eichler not known better, he might have assumed the priest was talking to himself, or perhaps, praying. However, the question-and-answer format seemed to give away the presence of another party, so Eichler watched intently for their reveal.

He couldn't see properly. Still unable to get a clear picture, he instructed his men stay put, then skirted the foliage to get a better image of his targets. He crept softly, careful to conceal his body as he recognized the shape of the two figures, then grabbed for his binoculars again. Eichler turned the focus ring between the lenses.

As the other target came into focus, an ethereal sensation of recognition cascaded over Eichler. First, he felt confusion, as if what he was looking at was an illusion. He wondered, even if only superficially, if perhaps he'd never really woken up on this day and was dreaming. Had that been true, he recognized that this lucidity likely would have been at fault with the dream world, and he was sure he would have woken up. A warm breeze whipped across the river, tickling the skin on his fingers as he steadied the binoculars—that was confirmation enough that what he was seeing was real. For standing next to the priest, engaged in heated conversation, was a man Eichler had never thought he would see again.

The next wave of feeling was one of disbelief, which made his second-guessing of a dream scenario all the more powerful. Standing there was the man who had caused Lothar Eichler so much undue stress, so much strife, and so many setbacks to the plans and goals he had dreamed for himself. That, truly, was the only dream world that had been shattered, unlike this very real situation unfolding before him. He would never forget that face which had caused so much trouble for the *Reich* and had sabotaged Eichler's almighty project.

"*Sam,*" Eichler whispered softly to himself. That was the name the traitor Sigrid Lang had been mouthing until she'd taken her last breath. That was the name that had plagued Eichler since the destruction of Flussrand. That was the name, real or not, of the man standing within the vicinity of the precious Peenemünde Army Research Center. He recalled the document that had come to his attention from the *Reichsführer's* Office. "Or is it *Dieter?*"

The third sensation to plague him was the gradual warming of his skin. It could have been the temperature and the baking winds that the island so identified with this summer—or it could have been his excitement. His heart raced and his breathing became short and ragged. Moisture gathered in the pits of his arms, and his stomach churned with the sudden coursing of adrenaline through his blood. It all gripped him so intensely. Of all of the co-conspirators of this priest, all the American operators and agents sent in to undermine the regime, all the enemies of the party that could be standing there, in the flesh, ready to do more damage—it was *him*.

For some time, Eichler couldn't do anything but scrutinize Sam. He soon recognized both men were in VkN uniforms. He watched Sam, noting the features he remembered so well: the trim torso, the callous eyes. The stature, so confident and sure. He was a man without fear; Eichler could respect this. He'd remembered that characteristic being evident during his own personal investigation of Sam before the escape.

This was Sam, or Dieter, or *whatever* his name really was, the absolute bane of the security captain's existence, and had been so now for almost two years. He recalled their first scuffle on the eve of the Pearl Harbor attacks. This man who had bested Eichler not once, but twice, was standing within firing distance of any of the nearby rifles. His life could be ended with one well-placed bullet, just as the life of Sigrid Lang had ended when she'd aided his escape.

Eichler considered his next steps as he watched through the binoculars. There were many options at his disposal, but only one he had sworn to uphold: to report all activities directly to Falke. Nowhere in Falke's explicit instructions did he ever say to engage any potential enemy targets. But Eichler could not help but debate whether this was an extenuating circumstance; the thought of letting this man slip through his grasp once more was too great a burden to bear.

He could rush to a phone and call Falke, but there was no guarantee that he would get him on the line. He could call over to *Prinz-Albrecht-Straße* and demand the attention of the *Reichsführer*, but there was no guarantee he would receive the call either. He checked his watch: it was nearing the end of the day. A flaming magenta sunset was clutching the horizon line across the water. He could try to send up the ladder for General Dornberger or Major Heigl, who surely would be able to make an executive decision as to how Eichler might proceed. The problem Eichler was plagued with was that all of those procedures ran the risk of losing a visual on the spy, and perhaps losing him forever.

He wasn't thinking clearly. All that occupied his thoughts was revenge. It was as if all of his normal faculties for reasoning were completely absorbed by the immediate satisfaction of capturing the man himself, and he was acutely aware of this. What would he do if he could grip this man's throat? *I would squeeze his neck until the life left his eyes.* He wanted to pummel his face, to beat him beyond recognition.

But there were other possibilities. What accolades would be awarded the man who captured the saboteur who had caused the party such aggravation? This was someone who had once been part of—and then sought to destroy—the regime. Was there a greater trophy available short of delivering up Roosevelt or Churchill or Stalin themselves? To Eichler, there was nothing more valuable.

"Look!" he'd say to High Command. "I have found him, the man who destroyed *Erdschlag*. The man who dared face the sacred shores of Peenemünde! I have gift-wrapped him, and because there were no ribbons or bows available, instead I have used handcuffs!" He could picture himself kicking the spy's body down a red carpet and right up to the front door of *Prinz-Albrecht-Straße*.

Suddenly he was carried away as if in a dream, picturing in his head the reaction to his labor. There was applause all around by High Command, followed by pats on the back and utterances of a job well done. The Knight's Cross was pinned to his collar, presented by Göring himself. The fat old man finished presenting the award with a warm, firm handshake. He gripped Eichler's shoulder to escort him along, his signature baton in-hand, then invited him to join the exclusive club. Forget Peenemünde, that was the inner circle.

The fantasy was vanquished when he imagined the fuming Aksel Falke questioning his actions. Falke, with his all-seeing eye, condemning his approach and making clear his insubordination. Would High Command care? Did the complaints of a battle-scarred man from the old war count when Eichler had done the undoable? *Jealousy*, Eichler reasoned. The old man would be jealous, but what had he done? Would he understand the gravitas of capturing this most-hated infiltrator? It would be Eichler who had made the call, *he* who had acted without hesitation and decided that action should be taken.

Eichler mulled over his next move. Time was running out. Light was soon to fade. Should he take too long, then his targets might vanish, and without any idea where their next destination might take them, they could be gone permanently. All the resources of the *Reich* wouldn't matter if this unicorn disappeared once more through the forest. This was lightning in a bottle, a rare occurrence of circumstances unlikely to be recreated.

If he called for a superior advisor, it would waste crucial time. If he usurped Falke, he could risk insubordination. If he did nothing, well, nothing would come of this very delicate situation, and Eichler considered that he'd never forgive himself.

What pushed Eichler over the edge and gave him the strength to do what he was about to do and disobey his explicit orders and protocol? *Power* was the simplest answer. One might categorize it as glory, even respect. Because Lothar Eichler foresaw an image of himself, standing on the balcony of the high mountain retreat at Berchtesgaden, overlooking the Alps and yukking it up with the highest of the high in the Obersalzburg.

Hermann Göring was there, the *Reichsmarshall* and leader of the *Luftwaffe*, and he was asking Eichler for his input regarding air defenses around the Peenemünde facility while also commenting on how well he wore his Knight's Cross. So was Albert Speer, and he was telling Eichler that yet another tank would be produced, one that would rival even the capabilities of the long-gone *Erdschlag*. Shouldn't Eichler have input in its creation? Perhaps he could name it, Speer added. Eichler agreed. When Speer had finished singing Eichler's praises, Goebbels chimed in, and wondered whether Eichler might want more face-time in the ministry, perhaps be paraded around to rally the people when it might be needed. Finally, staring back at Eichler with a rare grin, was the Führer himself. He had one hand on the railing of the great mountain overlook and the other patting the head of Blondie, his German Shepherd. He called for Eichler to speak with him so they could perhaps discuss what his plans were for the future. Outside the picture window, the snow-capped Alps rose high into the clouded sky, mountains flanking the men Eichler thought capable of rivaling their great heights, himself among them.

Depositing his binoculars back into his pocket, he set off to rally his men. He'd made his decision: this opportunity was too great to obey the rules set forth by Aksel Falke. Lesser men than Eichler had made waves in the party by cutting the throats of their superiors, and Falke was not immune. Eichler would make his case should it be presented to a high court by Falke, and he was confident his actions would be justified. Falke was not here, and if he was the one to make the call, then he should have been present. Eichler was the security captain, and this was a great security risk. Under no circumstances could he allow this enemy operator to leave the premises. Should anyone be aware of a failure to capture this man by Eichler or his team—and within the presence of a launch demonstration, no less—the axe could fall on his head, and he'd narrowly avoided that outcome after the disaster at Flussrand.

"Check your weapons," Eichler said to his team. "We have been ordered to apprehend those two men." Ordered by whom? one may have asked, but it was irrelevant. As far as these men were concerned, Eichler was in charge, and if Eichler said to leave their posts, then that's what they would do. A spark flared within the group. These men never saw any action around Peenemünde—the *real* war was so far away—and now they would put their training to the test. Eichler commandeered a radio from within his truck and signaled to his men in the west to ready themselves.

But if Eichler was totally honest with himself, it was not just his lust for the top of the mountain that propelled him into action, but a motivation much more primal and simple: vengeance.

24

There are certain defining moments in war that were beyond even a man like Hank Brandt's control. Limitless resources do not necessarily mean that a man has limitless power, and there were people above even the spy chief that were responsible for decisions beyond his influence. In the sleepy mountains of Bern, the threat of a major Axis attack was nill, even for Americans hiding within its borders. Most of Brandt's time was spent waiting, because espionage is a long game.

The collection of information for later use can often seem fruitless. Brandt traded in secrets, and because secrets by their nature are not often shared, few people had the capacity to act on them. Every so often the stars aligned, and when they did, the timing was rarely convenient. Though Brandt had the power to obtain that coveted information and see to it that it landed in the hands of those who could make use of it, his influence regarding its usage was still questionable.

There are intricacies in global politics, even if at

times it may seem like people are deciding whether they'd like steak or fish for dinner. Sometimes, those decisions are carried out without regard for consequences. These were big-picture decisions, made by men who saw the big picture, and required little input from those not "in-the-know."

And sometimes in those moments, the hands of a man like Hank Brandt were tied, even if he was the one holding the rope in the first place. Brandt did not make calls in the way those in Washington, London, or Moscow did. He merely provided the information that made such a call worthy of considering in the first place. Often, Brandt was unaware his currency had been spent, but every so often he'd be thanked before the transaction had occurred. That evening, as the sun set on the dark, mountainous Bern suburb, a transaction had occurred, not simply of Brandt's facilitation, but collected from the efforts of many different men working toward the same goal. To say that the timing was inconvenient would have been an understatement, but major attacks both to and from the enemy often were.

So when the news reached Brandt by telephone—so urgent that he had been contacted at his hidden station —he was not at liberty to suggest alternative plans. In fact, those plans were already being carried out whether he liked it or not by forces not beyond his influence, but certainly beyond his control. Naturally, casualties occurred in these types of situations.

The news came by phone, which was the least-eventful form of delivery, but one Brandt had become accustomed to. In fact, he probably shouldn't have even heard the news in the first place, but Brandt had friends in the highest of places, and some men couldn't resist dropping a good nugget of information when the wheels had begun turning and had no way of stopping. The moments preceding profound and world-altering events in history are rarely known by most, and few are privy to the information around them before they happen. Depending on how the events shake out, that is either a gift or a curse.

Hank Brandt's phone was his lifeline, wherever he may be. The week had started with information via phone that sent the sky metaphorically falling. The call he'd just received would suggest it was now *literally* falling. And wasn't it poetic that in a military installation created quite literally to cause hell itself to fall from the sky, those manufacturing the weapons should suffer the same fate they wished upon others?

Brandt was unprepared for the call, though it was one he'd been waiting for. Iris had worked her magic to make the connection. It was the kind of call that made him gnaw at his pipe until his teeth were sore. A lot of hard work by both he and his men had been leading to this moment, and when it finally came, it had a more profound effect on him than he could ever have imagined it would.

"Hello, Hank," the man on the line said. It was Matchbox. His voice contained no emotion or excitement, but rather the restrained and calculated delivery of a British man with information to provide. Usually it was Hank Brandt delivering information.

"Evening," Hank replied.

"Not just yet here, actually." The correction was unnecessary, but military types have a knack for proper detail, and Matchbox was no exception. "Are you sitting down?"

"Should I be?" Brandt's tone was defensive. A suggestion that he was of weak physical character irked him particularly. Regardless of his own insecurity, he did take his seat beside the phone.

"That thing you've been working on," Matchbox continued, "the one on the Baltic."

Brandt, no stranger to code, provided confirmation that they were discussing the same subject with a cryptic reply of, "The space men?"

"That one," Matchbox confirmed. "It's happening."

Brandt, now at full attention, rose from his seat again. The efforts of both he and his team's work were finally coming to some sort of fruition. He began to pace as far as the tethered phone cable would let him. "When?" he asked with an air of excitement that knocked his age back to one more child-like.

"Tonight," Matchbox said. "Actually," there was a pause where Brandt had to assume Matchbox was checking his watch, "several hours from now."

"*What?*" Brandt asked. His excitement had deflated. He'd paced so far from the phone that he had almost pulled the receiver off the table completely in his clumsiness. "No, it *can't* be tonight."

"I'm afraid it is," Matchbox replied without remorse. Or had there been a hint? Who could tell? "They're on their way right now."

"Call it off," Brandt barked. He knew this was a pointless request, but he made it regardless.

"Impossible," Matchbox replied. "By last count, there's a few hundred Landcasters, a couple hundred Halifaxes, and some Sterlings for good measure. As long as the weather holds, and the advisers say it will, it's unlikely a tree ever grows there again. I just thought you should be the first to know since your team did a lot of heavy lifting on this one. Quite some timing, too, I'd say, being as it's the third anniversary of The Hardest Day. Give 'em hell, I say."

Brandt paused. He didn't gnaw the pipe. He didn't pack it with more tobacco. He only thought about who was on the inside and sent at his behest, and the danger they were currently in. Shouldn't a man like Brandt have expected that? Wasn't that risk always part of the job?

"Hank?" Matchbox called out. "Are you still there?" Another long stretch of dead air passed. "I thought you of all people would be excited. Told the brass you should be the first to know. Don't tell me I did the wrong thing by telling you. Truthfully, you *shouldn't* know. I just happened to be on the planning end. Kind of out of our hands now, you see. Just a courtesy call."

Brandt lingered for a prolonged moment while he prepared to spit it all out. For once, Brandt decided to lay all the information on the line, and for a man whose pride came from retaining his secrecy, it was a Herculean effort. "I've lost one."

The line was silent for several moments.

"On the Baltic," Brandt said.

"Your friend?" Matchbox asks. "The farmer?"

Brandt couldn't bring himself to confirm it, but his silence did. There was another long pause while Matchbox considered what Brandt had said.

"Well I'm afraid it's just too late to worry about that," Matchbox replied. Was he sympathetic? It was hard to tell. Did he care that Roger Fowler might die, if he wasn't dead already? Did he care that Peenemünde may very well be prepared for this attack, and that Bomber Command had no idea what its men had in store? Did he care, even though he didn't know, that Sam and Lukas were still there?

Brandt still didn't speak. There was no way to pull his resources out. There was no way to know if the RAF was walking into a trap because Roger Fowler had failed, no way to warn the men on the ground of what was to come. There was only chance—a chance that Sam and Lukas were in the right place, a chance that they could see the storm coming on the horizon. If not, it was now their fate to endure Hell on Earth.

"Going to be a big deal for you in DC, Hank," the man on the line reassured Brandt. "They're going to throw your name in. A lot of hard work brought home. From what I hear, the lawn is green—*very* green."

For once in his life Hank Brandt's ego did not inflate. In fact, it fizzed as if someone had punctured a balloon and let it whizz about the room before landing limp on the floor. The man who held no fear in his heart, whether it be on the battlefield or of his own insecurities, finally experienced the sinking feeling that with his victory had come a great loss. He had cultivated his top operator, guided him every which way to create what he believed to be the single best card in his deck, and now his card had been trumped by another higher, better card. All Brandt felt he could do in that moment was fold.

Still unable to speak, Brandt half-listened to Matchbox's words: "Pat yourself on the back, Hank—your people too. You helped greatly."

Brandt, without another word, slowly returned the phone to its base. For a moment he just stood there, his eyes darting around the room and looking at everything but taking in nothing. Beside him, Ansel Combe watched him in anticipation, but even he seemed to recognize that Brandt was troubled by the phone conversation.

"What is it?" Combe asked.

"The raid," Brandt replied. "It's happening tonight."

Combe, just as shocked as Brandt was, removed his glasses and rubbed at his eyes with his thumb and forefinger. As handler of this operation, he too quickly realized what was at risk, even though everything they had done this far had been working toward this outcome. Men had died to gather the information that was now being acted upon, yet now two great men didn't feel so great at all. Some might have considered them larger than life, but the lack of conversation between the two suggested just how little they felt. They were powerless. The goal they had worked toward was here in front of them. Even if they'd like to stop it, there was nothing they could do to make that happen.

The priest had gotten what he'd wanted. Whether he had ever imagined he would be in the forefront of his own plan, Brandt and Combe would likely never know. Brandt imagined Lukas had reconciled it, because he'd never have gone through the great lengths to do the work he'd done had he not.

Now, all either man could do was wait. The weather in Bern was calm, perhaps too calm. It was that same calm weather that would allow RAF Bomber Command to carry out its mission, sneaking in under the cover of night undetected. With any luck the first wave would have its desired effect: to hit the enemy in its crucial points before anyone even knew they were coming. Further waves might encounter resistance, but the reports of the men who'd done the good work at Peen-emünde—if they were still at all accurate—suggested the research center was anything but prepared.

Brandt had lied to Sam—about everything. Now the spy chief would eat his words, perhaps even choke on them. He felt nothing but loss for his operator and the danger that lay ahead. The end of the Peenemünde research facility was imminent, and maybe Sam's life. Somewhere in the forests of Northern Germany, Hansel and Gretel had neared the witch's home, and perhaps she and they would both burn in her oven.

25

———

S am spotted the truck through a clearing of trees—it had not been on the path earlier. He hadn't heard it arrive, and the two soldiers he saw were already combing the forest with rifles at the ready. He took cover, then signaled silently that Lukas should do the same. They were *Heer* men, probably privates or local patrol. He heard them talking, one giving instructions to the other and indicating they should fan out.

"*Bist du sicher, dass es hier war?*" one asked.

The other said, "*Ja, es war heir.*"

The soldiers climbed up over a small ridge, then paused. The man presumably in charge said, "*Umschauen,*" to the other. They hadn't found the truck yet; if they had, Sam and Lukas would already have been properly caught. The soldiers' activity had caught the two operators by surprise, and they'd become separated. Sam weighed rejoining his teammate, but to traverse the clearing would leave him exposed.

Sam hid behind a large cluster of trees and did his

best to track both directions of each of the men. If he'd been alone, he'd have just played it quiet and waited for the men to give up. He was presented with a larger problem: Lukas. Sam suspected Lukas was not nearly as adept at hiding. He signaled for silence to the priest, and Lukas hunkered down behind a tree trunk. Presented with few options, Sam quietly unsheathed his knife from its scabbard and flanked the soldier closest to him.

The edge of the blade glinted in the fading sunlight peeking through the forest canopy. The sun would set completely soon. The blade was polished and unused. When Sam was done, it might just need a good cleaning. Surprise would be key, but a little noise might do well to draw the troops away from Lukas if they found him. To fire his weapon—or for Lukas to—would only invite more trouble. A gunshot out here was tantamount to a five-alarm-fire alert.

Forest crunched between a pair of approaching boots. Sam could hear snapping twigs to his right growing closer with every step. Luckily the area was rife with trees, and the maze-like nature of the patch of land was only too perfect for Sam. He didn't just perform well under these conditions, he thrived in them.

Sam listened to gauge how close the soldier might be. The footsteps paused. The man was near to the spy —Sam could even smell his cigarette. He tracked the other soldier as well, who was approaching the spot Sam had left Lukas.

When the soldier began his trek once more, Sam grabbed him from behind and efficiently sliced his throat. He guided the soldier's fall to reduce potential noise. Sam hadn't even had the luxury of looking into his face before the man flopped onto the ground and turned his head upward. There was a bewildered confusion present in the eyes of men quickly disposed of. When a man meets his death in such an abrupt fashion, the brain doesn't even have time to recognize what has happened. For all intents and purposes, if Sam had to kill a man, it was the least personal—but most humane—way to do it.

The soldier clasped both of his hands around his neck as he stared up at Sam. Blood leaked between the man's fingers far quicker than he could quell the flow. He choked on the liquid, gagging and gurgling and trying, Sam thought, to call out to his partner. It was no use—his airway was flooded. One might think this a cold move, but he might have killed Sam should he have seen the spy first. Sam seized the advantage.

What was not an advantage, but still an element Sam valued, was the requirement to kill up close and personal. The spy would use a gun if he had to—some situations just called for one. Guns, however, were lazy and impersonal. Any idiot could pull a trigger, but with a knife a man had to be skilled enough to get intimate with his target. Should Sam lose his knife in a fight, he'd have to go on with his fists, and thankfully he was improving in that department because of Shiner's training.

The blood leaking from the man's throat began to coat the forest floor, forming a dark, syrupy pool. He twitched for several moments as the blood left his veins, and then he was silent. Sam checked the surrounding area—only quiet.

Now Sam was on the move. He'd have to find the other soldier. Killing these men would only bring more attention to Lukas and him—Sam knew that. Leaving them to continue their search, however, would only make maneuvering the area more difficult. Lukas was close to the western bank separating Sam and him from Peenemünde—he could see the liquid oxygen plant ahead.

Sam headed north. In little time he was parallel with the other soldier as he continued his search. The trees here were less dense, so Sam's approach was much trickier. He didn't have the luxury of the same cover he'd just had. Sam was daring, but he wasn't stupid. He tracked the man, keeping low and out of sight as he slowly closed the distance between the two of them.

A pine branch cracked under Sam's step, and the patrolling officer immediately whipped his head around. Sam tucked himself behind another tree—but the soldier had switched directions. He was heading *toward* Sam.

"Henrik?" the soldier called out.

Henrik, Sam thought. He hadn't gotten a chance to see the man's name tag.

"Henrik!" the soldier called out again. Sam reminded silent. In the wake of the launched rocket, the insects and birds had resumed their discussion. There were cover sounds all around.

Sam heard the soldier yell, "*Da drüben!*" to the partner he didn't even know was now dead, then several shots rang out through the forest. The soldier had spotted Lukas. Sam double-timed his step as he whipped in and out of patches of trees. The adrenaline was pumping through his veins now; he felt the tell-tale signs that only came with this type of situation. His heart throbbed deeply, his feet moved light and airy, and his breathing was rapid.

He heard several more shots ring out, then several more yells from the man—he still only counted one distinct voice—and followed the point of origin. The gunfire came from the east, which only led him closer to Peenemünde itself. Now he was moving with the speed of a gazelle and the spring of a cheetah's step. Something animalistic exposed itself when Sam went on the hunt, and like a ferocious predator, it was more often than not he captured or killed his prey.

Sam saw a smattering of downed trees ahead, one of which had dried out and blackened innards. A lightning strike had likely destroyed it not long ago, and where it had fallen it had pulled several others down with it, forming a large barrier in the middle of the woods— which the soldier was heading toward.

The soldier held firm before the massive tree, took aim, then unloaded bullets into the tree's side. Sam paused behind the man, readied his knife, then weaved in and out of several trees as the soldier exchanged his spent ammunition for fresh rounds. He did it quickly, leaving Sam with no opportunity for surprise. Sam couldn't see his position, but knew Lukas was a sitting duck. Somewhere in the forest, the priest was at risk of catching a bullet.

A movement in the thin sliver of light below the tree caught Sam's eye. He waited for it once more, then saw motion in the small window—he recognized a boot when it came into focus.

Sam waited until the soldier began to navigate the fallen tree. He assumed the soldier had found Lukas. The enemy had his weapon drawn to his eye, and was sweeping the forest for movement. Sam and Lukas couldn't do this much longer. Their position had been given away and their window of opportunity was dwindling.

"*Da drüben!*" the soldier yelled again, then bursts of gunfire interrupted the otherwise silent forest. The atmosphere had alternated between a natural serenity and the onslaught of mechanical terror. Sam saw Lukas tear out from behind the patch of foliage, fleeing from the soldier and using several of the trees' branches as cover. The area erupted into a battle zone littered with explosions of pine and wood chips as the soldier ran after Lukas.

"*Stoppen!*" the soldier yelled, and then he was off and running again as Lukas fled. This racket was becoming unbearable, and an operational disaster. Sam joined in the pursuit. As he followed, he saw Lukas sprinting in and out of the trees. Luckily he was fast, because the soldier opened fire again.

A storm of bullets tore through the forest. Each bullet ripped bark, leaves, and branches from the trees above Lukas' head, showering him with debris. At least Sam had found him. The firing ceased again.

Sam could see the soldier struggling to reload. He was fumbling with the gun while trying to keep track of the priest. Sam had a window of opportunity, but it came and went quickly.

The soldier opened fire once more, unloading the entirety of his ammunition into the forest, so Sam cozied up behind another broad tree. *How much ammunition is he carrying?* The forest had grown more dark under the cover of trees. Sam peeked his head out, but he saw no one. He'd lost track of Lukas, and the soldier as well—the hunter had lost his advantage.

For a moment, Sam just watched and listened. He

took in everything—the smells, the sounds, even just the general movements of the forest. The warm breeze returned once more, bristling the pine needles gently and carrying the smell of the salty ocean beyond. All of the liveliness in the forest had been silenced by the rifle. Where one might normally hear the chirp of a bird or the song of a cricket, only the breeze whistled.

He'd entered into a densely populated area, a community of trees that looked ready to form a small democracy. The pines were so abundant that a man could be completely obscured if he positioned himself just right. Sam waited for a few moments before he finally saw Lukas again. The priest had gotten the same idea as Sam: use the cover to his advantage.

Now it was the three of them caught in some dangerous game of hide and seek. When Lukas paused, Sam directed his knife to catch the light so it would glisten. He angled it in such a way that the blade's reflection projected forward, and the glint caught Lukas' eye at just the right moment—Lukas spotted him. Sam pressed a finger to his lips and signaled quiet. Lukas nodded in understanding.

Sam set off again, this time with even more grace in his step. His ballet-like movements were admirable, and quite possibly a weapon even more formidable than the blade in his hand. He listened carefully as he moved around the pine in front of him, then heard the sound of displaced earth crunching under the soldier's feet. His inability to see his target made his approach all that more difficult. This game would be based around sound and sound only.

Lukas nodded once more to Sam as if to signal his own willingness to help, then sprinted forward and out of Sam's sight. Sam heard swift steps clomp through the dirt, and the soldier fired once again through the trees. The aim was sloppy, and he'd given away his position.

Sam tracked the soldier's movements through his mumbling cries. He was right on the other side of the tree and ready for the taking. Just as Sam was preparing to attack, he heard the solider shouting a command at Lukas. Lukas, unarmed, held his hands up for the soldier. The man was barking orders at the priest, commanding he lie face down on the forest floor. Sam's fear that the soldier would fire on Lukas overtook his caution, and he leapt from his place of hiding knife-first.

By the time Sam heard the crackle of gunfire, he'd already plunged the knife through the soldier's neck. The shot rang out with a violent ping, and once Sam saw the life leave the man's eyes, he pulled the blade out and let his body fall limp. When the man hit the floor, Sam kicked his weapon free of his hands.

Sam's ears rang with a shrill, piercing tone as if Hell's bells themselves had sung. The subtleties of forest sounds were gone. The effect of the gunfire was dizzying. Lukas was yelling, and Sam couldn't hear a word coming out of his mouth. It was when he saw that Lukas' eye line was not meeting his own that the full realization of what had happened set in.

Finally, he heard Lukas yell, "Sam!" Sam noticed the panic in the priest's eyes, and then followed Lukas' gaze down to his own hand. Sam felt the pain immediately. He'd been so hopped up in the moment that he hadn't even realized the bullet had hit him. He extended his hand out and was dumbfounded to find the pinky on his left hand missing where it met the palm—it had been torn off completely.

26

The shock set in quickly for the spy. He also felt the dizziness that comes along with flying so high and then coming crashing down. He wobbled slightly, now weak in both limbs. Lukas ran over and gripped his forearm tightly to get ahead of the bleeding. The blood loss was fast—it was coming in spurts that seemed never-ending. The wound hadn't even been clean either. Where the palm began, there was now a shredded mess of bone, muscle, and flesh.

Lukas grabbed a small handkerchief from his pocket, tore it into two thin shreds, then wrapped one around Sam's wrist with as much pressure as possible.

"You alright?" Lukas asked, trying to distract Sam. His hearing was returning slowly. Sam sighed deeply, then nodded. He was doing his best to look away from the injury, but he couldn't help checking it again. "Look at me," Lukas said. He asked again, "Are you alright?

"Yeah," Sam said. He looked to his right hand—his knife was still clutched within it with a vise-like grip.

"You didn't need that one anyway," Lukas said, trying to distract him.

Sam smiled. It had been the closest thing to a moment of calm the two men had shared since they'd left the cover of the truck. Lukas tended to the wound with the other strip of cloth.

"We need to move," Sam said.

"Not like this, you don't."

"We've made far too much noise," Sam argued. He looked down at the dead man beside them. "This one decided to unleash an entire ammo dump on you." He surveyed Lukas for a moment. "Are you hit?"

"No."

"Then let's get going," Sam said again.

"If I don't stop this bleeding, you're not going to be going very far at all." Below Sam, there was a pool of blood formed in a collection of tree roots. Lukas continued tending to the wound, sizing up how serious it was in the fading light. Both men were sweating. Even at dusk, the heat was unwavering.

"Are you a doctor?" Sam asked as Lukas tore a section of his undershirt off.

"No," Lukas replied. "I've got some basic medical training." That was better than nothing. Sam had some himself, but trying to tend to one's own lost finger while it bled profusely was no easy task. "Keep it away from your uniform."

Sam looked to the western end of the forest. "The light is diminishing. When night falls, I can look for Fowler and get the hell out." As the final words left Sam's mouth, Lukas applied some pressure to the wound that almost caused Sam to scream.

"That bad?" Lukas said. "We need supplies. There was a small kit in the truck."

"There's no time to run errands," Sam said. The blood was spilling through the olive-colored fabric Lukas was using to cover the injury.

"Then I'm going to need to cauterize it," Lukas warned. Sam didn't like the idea, but he knew he likely didn't have a choice. "Do you still have your lighter?"

Sam nodded, dug in his pocket with his free hand, then gave it to Lukas.

"And your knife," Lukas said. "Now you hold this." Lukas passed off the duties of keeping pressure on the wound to Sam. The blood loss was slowing, though only a little.

"Do me a favor?" Sam asked.

"What?"

"Reach into my pocket here and get me a smoke, will ya?" Lukas retrieved a cigarette from Sam's pack, then stuck it in Sam's mouth. Sam concentrated on the cigarette, rather than the missing digit. Lukas lit it for him, then Sam suggested they crouch low to the ground to stay concealed.

"You're a dangerous man, Sam Abel," Lukas said as he heated the blade. It was a very slapdash method of cauterization, but there weren't many options available. If Sam was going to make this trek, they needed to make sure he didn't leave a trail of blood behind. "I've got gloves in my pocket, do you?" Sam did, and he directed Lukas to fish them out of his pocket. "Good. You're going to need to put yours on. We can't have you running around with an injury. That's another red flag."

Sam was impressed. Suddenly it seemed as if Lukas was the operational man and Sam was excess baggage.

He thanked God, even though it was Lukas who was functioning as savior, that the priest was here in this moment.

"Ready?" Lukas asked.

"Yeah."

"Here," Lukas said, and he handed Sam one of the gloves.

"I thought you needed to close it first?" Sam asked.

"That's to bite down on," Lukas explained. Sam readied himself as best he could and balled the glove up between his teeth. "When I tell you to remove the material, you do so, okay?" Sam nodded while Lukas continued to get the blade as close to white-hot as he could. "Okay—now."

Sam pulled away the bloodied fabric, and Lukas gripped his wet hand where the knuckles bunched up, then pressed the burning blade firmly down on the wound. Sam bit down on the cloth with all the force he could while a pained grunt emanated from his throat. The site of the injury sizzled. Now Lukas was *really* clamping down on it, and Sam grew more nauseous as the smell of his own burned flesh filled his nose. The pain was becoming unbearable.

"Done," Lukas said, then he fashioned some more fabric around Sam's hand as best he could. For Sam, the pain lingered even in the aftermath. "Put the gloves on." Sam did, and Lukas wiped the blood from his own hands, then washed some off with the water from a small canteen he'd brought along. "Good as new," Lukas joked as he pointed to Sam's fabric tenth finger. Sam laughed, even if only because it was a momentary distraction from the searing pain of the missing finger.

"Thank you," Sam said.

Lukas nodded. "That's not a cure-all. You're still going to need medical attention. It could get infected."

"All the more reason to get moving," Sam said. He surveyed the forest to the west. It was quiet again. Only the breeze was producing noise, and it was doing so in the form of a pine-orchestra symphony. They couldn't remain at the site of the crime any longer.

When Sam turned to Lukas, he saw the priest kneeling at the head of the dead soldier. Lukas surveyed the young man reverently, then brushed his fingers past both of his eyelids to close them. He tilted his head down and closed his own eyes.

"What are you doing?" Sam asked. "We need to leave."

Lukas turned to Sam, annoyed by the interruption. "So does he."

"He'd dead," Sam snapped.

"A dead man is still a *man*," Lukas retorted. "On a different journey than us, no doubt, but in need of a prayer nonetheless."

"Do you pray for all of your enemies?" Sam asked facetiously.

"More so than my friends." Lukas lowered his head, muttering to himself while Sam kept an anxious watch. The prayer was short-lived, maybe because Lukas could sense Sam was trying to get moving, or maybe because Lukas didn't have much to say. Regardless of his lack of oration, Lukas clearly felt the need to say something. The man lying before them was dead by proxy of Lukas' presence, and Sam sensed that Lukas felt some responsibility for it. Lukas rose, then said, "Thank you."

Sam nodded. He might not have understood it, but he accepted it anyway. He wondered whether the dead soldier would have returned the favor. "Go hide," Sam said. "Don't stray too far from the truck. Do you have a watch?"

Lukas did.

"If I'm not there by midnight, get moving. You'll have less trouble traveling at night."

"And leave you?"

"If we're both compromised, then this operation's a bust. I don't want to have lost it in vain. If I don't return, you can assume the worst and report the same. Protect the truck. Act the part. You're looking for the intruders too. Talk your way around if you have to. If anyone comes looking, lead them back here. That will kill some time."

"Should have called it Operation: No Finger," Lukas added.

"Get moving," Sam said with a glare, and the two split apart. Sam headed north toward the farm, and Lukas went west for the truck.

———

Lukas moved swiftly, careful to use any cover he happened upon. He did not move like Sam. He was accustomed to moving and behaving like a normal civilian, not a mercenary. His heart was throbbing, and his head was light and airy. His senses were overworked. He and Sam had sounded every alarm at Peenemünde except the air-raid siren itself.

He was so close to the finish line, *so close* to never seeing this dreaded island again. All the work that he had done had come to fruition, and if he could manage to get back into Switzerland just one time, he would earn a much-deserved respite. It wouldn't be the end—far from it. Just because the Peenemünde Army Research Center had been destroyed did not mean the threat of the Nazi rule was quelled. The only true victory would come with the fall of the Führer and his dreaded cronies—and furthermore, the independence and removal of the *Reich* from Lukas' beloved Austria.

The forest floor ahead of Lukas shuffled, forcing him to pause. He dropped low, using a patch of brush as cover. It sounded as if an entire battalion had arrived. The sounds contradicted that theory, though, because when soldiers venture out looking for enemy combatants, they don't tend to whistle and laugh. He searched ahead, trying his best to gather any information he could.

Soon his assumption was corrected—he did not hear the voices of grown men, but rather the squeaky sounds of pre-pubescent boys. When he finally saw the first one, who was leading the troop on this tour of the woods surrounding the farm, he tucked himself further out of sight and watched. They formed a column, hiking through the pines with only a few steps between each of them. They seemed wholly unaware that a fire fight had just taken place nearby.

As they filed along, Lukas found himself growing sick. None of them could have been older than thirteen. Surely they belonged to the facility, even if they were cleared to leave it for their training. Though none of them were even close to military age, they all seemed to be preparing for duty. They marched as they sang, several carrying the vocals while the others whistled in harmony. Lukas counted: there were ten.

What filled him with the most dread was knowing

that all of these boys, prepared or otherwise, could be among the casualties when Peenemünde's fate finally arrived. They were children, dressed up and miming the behavior of men, very much looking to become like their own *Wehrmacht* heroes, but naïve boys nonetheless. *They're still God's children*, Lukas thought, *enemy or otherwise.*

As they laughed and sang, they remained blissfully unaware of the future. Lukas remembered when he himself had shared in that oblivious state of being, far before the *SS* and *SD* had marched through the streets of Vienna and strong-armed their way to the *Anschluss*. But boys became men, and despite their innocence, should the war linger on these boys too would become enemies; when one of them had a gun pointed at a man's face, they would look anything but innocent.

Still, Lukas' stomach churned. Confronting the consequences of his own actions was not something he had planned to do. The thwarting of the rocket project seemed—from a distance—a necessary task. He had been so far removed from the realities of his actions that seeing the potential result in front of him was a weight he was not prepared to bear. He, protector of God's creatures, was witnessing the possible casualties of the forthcoming destruction on full display. Would these children die in the upcoming assault? Only God knew.

When the kids had finally cleared the path ahead, Lukas continued his trip to the truck. He was fearful more troops were incoming. The sun had finally set. The forest was bathed in the cool coloration of approaching night. He could only pray that Sam would make it to his destination and get a better answer than Lukas had. It would be some time before Lukas knew.

The smoke from the rocket launch still lingered along a low-flying swath of clouds above the river. It gave the landscape a ghoulish shadow, which seemed to foretell the fate of Peenemünde through the heavens themselves. If there was something divine above, it was not visible tonight—there was only the grim hue of approaching death.

27

Udo Ramm had been afforded the luxury of a courtyard in his Bern prison, but he was only granted access to it at scheduled intervals of the day. The first reprieve he'd been given was at roughly one in the afternoon. The woman living in the house flanking the property on the north side would make her daily trip to the market and the neighbor on the southern property was away for work. The second outing generally took place at dusk, when that same woman would be busy tending to her family and the neighbor to the south hadn't arrived home yet. Ramm was also free to roam the courtyard at night because of the high walls, but he was required to use only available light to deter curiosity among the neighbors. The only way to look in the courtyard was from the second floor of an adjacent property, or to poke one's head in along the walls.

Beneath his arm was a large white canvas, and clutched in the other a collapsible wooden easel. Off over the high courtyard wall, the frosted tips of the nearby Alps were peeking above the tendrils of ivy, stark and white against the twilight sky. Birds chirped as they flittered among the large trees that shaded the yard. The foliage obscured the sky, giving the Swiss mountain range an even more picturesque aesthetic—if that were possible.

Great effort had been taken to ensure no one was wise to Ramm's presence. He was a high-value asset, hidden in a sovereign nation by an Allied power. He'd proven his worth, willingly verifying the intelligence gathered by Roger Fowler and Father Jan Lukas, and filling in the gaps where there were any. For a man with few options, his acquiescence to help his American captors in a bid for a good deal on the back end was only wise. He'd treated the negotiations much in the same way he would have attempted to climb the party ladder of his previous allegiances. In fact, even though he was a captive, the Americans treated him far better.

So, as he set out on the calm, agreeable Bern evening, his mind started to fathom the possibilities of what he was capable of doing with his life should the Americans decide to be extra lenient and allow him a go at the American Dream. Dog breeding was something he'd always fancied an interest in. He was particularly knowledgeable about the habits of German Shepherds, but their market value was sure to fall if the Allies won the war. He also didn't see much room for expansion within that type of business. The tastes of Udo Ramm would not be satisfied by small business ownership.

He could manage construction. Though he held no architectural degree, he fancied architectural aesthetics. He could partner with someone who had a better grasp of the physics and logistics of structural engineering.

Maybe he could get his hand in one of those New York firms with their majestic skyscrapers he'd been so impressed with on his last visit—never mind the fact that Sam had almost thrown him out of one.

He had no delusions about his prospects as a front-facing man in any company. That same spy who'd almost killed him from the high floor of a Manhattan hotel had also added another gruesome scar to his face. He'd be perfectly happy working behind the scenes just as he had done in the regime. If he could flatter the men of Nazi High Command, surely he could charm American entrepreneurs. It had been his very intention before he'd been caught attempting to funnel American tungsten out from beneath the country's nose.

But Udo Ramm took pride in his ability to parlay error or misfortune into new opportunity. He never dared say he was loyal to the party, but rather to his own status. Should by chance an event in Ramm's favor present itself, he would naturally oblige the universe and pursue it. His defection, even if incomplete, was made all the more enticing knowing that he could never return to his party—he'd be killed without question. Even if he was telling the truth about his capture, there stood a slim chance he'd be believed; even the most loyal of party men could be executed by a kangaroo court. If he found himself carted off to *Prinz-Albrecht-Straße*, there was no hope whatsoever—men who were brought there were assumed to be as good as dead even *if* they withstood the questioning of Himmler's minions.

He was protected at the Bern home. Under no circumstances did he ever feel as if he was actually an inmate, even though for all intents and purposes he was. If he tried to escape, he probably could, and furthermore, if he wanted to make noise about his incarceration to authorities willing to listen, he could blow the whole operation up in Hank Brandt's face. But that scenario was out of the question as far as Ramm was concerned. For lack of a better word, and to quote one of his American guards, he "had it good" for a Nazi infiltrator who'd planned to undermine the country.

The sun had finally come to rest beyond the Alps. The sky was a magnificent blue and unnaturally cloudless. The peaks of the nearby mountains were known to play with the weather patterns and turn even the most beautiful of climates into ones of fluffy white detail.

Ramm set the easel down, extending the legs without removing his gaze from the vista he'd been planning to paint. He placed the white canvas board on its ledge, then adjusted each of its feet so that it remained level. From a small pouch in his apron, Ramm pulled out several brushes of varying sizes, and from the pocket beside it, some acrylic paints. He'd asked for very little during his stay in Bern, but when his guards had often been sent off to retrieve art supplies to further his work of sketching greater Peenemünde, he'd made some additional requests. Thankfully Brandt and Combe hadn't yet inquired as to why such expensive materials were needed when a pencil and paper would do just fine.

Ramm retrieved a pencil from behind his ear, then set the tip onto the canvas as he squinted into the distance. He started with one broad, diagonal stroke that mimicked the slope of the mountain, then struck another slash of the pencil to finalize the form. His skills with the pencil were as elegant as the handling of his retired knife. He gazed off at the line of peaks once more, then broke into a feverish attack with the pencil, splitting his attention between the mountains ahead and the canvas before him.

He went on like that, violently dragging the pencil against the canvas and sketching the form of his subject as quickly as possible, for to linger in the rough idea of the thing being painted was to never move forward and finish the piece. A brief mistake sent him erasing as feverishly as he'd sketched, and once satisfied that he'd removed an unwanted shape, he set about fixing it before moving on to another peak. He roughly shaded the thin caps of snow still clinging to the range through the summer months. He never tired of seeing snow when the climate around him was so warm and desirable.

The tall, ivy-layered walls always made for a great foreground element, so he started to rough those out too. He was beginning to like the style his work had taken, so much so that he was already beginning to believe today's piece might just be his best yet. He could feel it in his approach, that nagging feeling of inspiration when one couldn't work fast enough to keep up with the vision for the art they currently held. He'd already sketched the scene many times, yet he'd never been fully satisfied with its outcome. The work of an artist was one of constant disappointment and refinement, and Ramm was of the firm belief that no one could ever be truly satisfied with their work; rather, they just continued to needle at it until they'd resigned themselves to move on to something else.

After some time working, Ramm realized how quiet the evening had been. He hadn't seen either of his minders on his exit from the back door to the courtyard.

Normally just a simple nod to signal that he was going out for his deserved break time would do. The wardens were not overly strict with their rules, provided he followed them. Usually he'd spot the silhouette of one of them eying him through the window as he painted, but as he glanced back at the home, he saw no one.

Uncaring about the two men, Ramm discarded the oddity of their absence and went on sketching. Inspiration waits for no man, and it certainly couldn't be bothered with waiting for an audience. Ramm worked from the left to the right end of the canvas. The top portion, the focal point of this particular work, was looking quite well.

Behind him, he heard soft steps on grass as someone approached. Unwilling to break his attention on his work, he called out, "An agreeable evening, wouldn't you say?"

Since his guards were never much for conversation, he wasn't surprised they didn't respond. "I think I've really got something tonight," Ramm continued. "Perhaps I'll get the form of it now, finish up the sketch. Then maybe I'll return tomorrow for some color." Still no response, but the sound of footsteps grew closer. He turned to see which of his two stewards was present, but instead was met with the flash of a blade.

It came down hard in a sweeping motion, plunging into his chest and forcing the brush out of his hand. Before he could register what exactly had happened, the attacker stabbed him several more times. Ramm stumbled, collapsing into the canvas board and sending the easel toppling to the grass behind him. His attacker, now looming above him, was silhouetted by the still-bright sky. The assailant then knelt down toward him and drove the knife into his chest over and over—Ramm lost count how many times in the commotion. Soon he was choking, gurgling on his own blood and writhing as he clutched at the wounds in his torso. He could feel sharp pains all over his body, and the warm flow of blood seeping from them.

His attacker twisted the knife forcefully, causing Ramm to screech before it was removed. Ramm saw his attacker's face—he didn't recognize it, but they seemed to recognize his.

"Aksel Falke sees all," the man said in German. He slapped both sides of the blade against a clean section of Ramm's shirt, then quickly headed for the gate exiting the courtyard.

Ramm's final piece of art left behind was one of a very disturbing nature. The large white canvas was mostly absent of color save for the rough sketch of the Alps he'd begun. Only the broader area of the picture displayed anything of vibrance to speak of—there, scattered across the length of it was a grotesque splatter of blood. After several more struggling gasps of breath, Udo Ramm was dead.

28

Night wasn't far off as Hank Brandt stepped out of the Bern safe house. Far north, the darkness would fall at the same time, and so too the RAF's ordnance. Rare was it that Brandt was in the same time zone as his operation. The demands of a spy chief were so great that he was often pulled away from his current objective, and toward a new, more pressing one. That was the case as he left Combe to deal with the fate of the two operators.

He set off down the front path and toward the gate that separated the high ivy walls from the outside world. He was bemused to find his car and the two New York Boys waiting in a different place than their normal spot, and wedged where they ought to have been was a black sedan of little note. It wasn't running, and it had no occupants. Beside it, Louie and Phil were at a loss as to how the car had gotten there, or who had put it there. In no time the hairs on the back of Brandt's neck were stiff and tingling.

Louie must have felt something strange as well, because he brushed aside his blazer and revealed his firearm. Phil stepped instinctively behind his own car to block half of his body. It was strange how something as unremarkable as a nondescript car could tickle their senses too, but it did. However, before anyone could even discuss what was strange about the car, or the danger it signaled, a gunshot disturbed the coos of evening birds and the melody of summer insects. A bullet ricocheted off the stone wall only inches from Brandt's head. Ivy and debris flew in the aftermath as he retreated back against the plant-draped wall in search of the gunman. It was a struggle since much of the street was covered in shadow.

Then another shot rang out and took a chunk of The New York Boys' car with it. Brandt immediately realized that the second shot had come from another direction than the first, and suddenly felt very exposed in the empty street. Just as he recognized his own fragility, Louie fired a shot across the street at a silhouette that manifested from the tree line overlooking the valley. A handful of shots were exchanged, automatic weapons destroying the tranquility of the serene hilltop retreat. More shots rang near Brandt's ear, peppering his face with dust just as the second rifle-bearing shooter emerged. He was pointing his weapon straight at Brandt, whose only reprieve so far was that the shooter had poor aim.

Brandt, now on all fours, scurried toward the car and reached for the door handle. Glass shattered above him, falling in curtains as the shooting continued. Louie took a bullet to the shoulder that sent him spinning as if it were a jab from a prize-fighter. Brandt swung the driver's-side door open, but was disappointed to find no key in the car's ignition.

Several more shots rang out, and Phil took cover behind the car's fender and narrowly missed being shredded by a hail of bullets. On the wall guarding the Bern station's courtyard, the shadow of the first shooter came into sharp focus when he moved to flank the automobile. Brandt eyed him through the now-glass-free window as he traveled across the length of the windshield. *The balls*, Brandt thought, *attempting an assassination in a neutral country, even if it is filled with dirty spies and dubious men.*

Brandt scrambled for Louie. A pool of blood was gathering next to his shoulder. Brandt spotted the glistening barrel of his gun nearby. The kid had dropped it out of reach, so Brandt moved clumsily to retrieve it. He reached for it, but several more shots came from behind, clanging against the metal gate and spraying wild shrapnel. He was forced to retreat again, and he butted his back up against the car's broad side.

Why Brandt was unarmed himself was forefront in his mind. He knew he was a high-value target, knew he was in a foreign country and away from the safety of DC, and knew that to nab him would be a great victory for any Axis power. But much like the forthcoming raid on Peenemünde, he had less control than he had thought.

There was a small non-verbal exchange between Phil and Brandt as the two gunmen closed in on their position and encircled the car. Phil was telling Brandt to stay put. The second shooter came around the tail end, and without missing a step, Phil grabbed the handle of the rear passenger-side door and threw it open to shield them. A storm of bullets peppered against the door, none of which hit him or Brandt.

As the first shooter rounded the corner of the hood, Phil fired a shot that hit him dead center of his forehead. Every muscle in the man's body seized and the gun fell limp in his grasp. An expression of confusion had manifested on his face, then he fell backwards and onto the road. Beyond the protective car door, the other shooter was reloading. Phil spun the chamber on his gun—then frowned when he found six empty cylinders. He dug in his pocket, fumbling for ammunition as the assassin tried to get a view of their targets.

Phil's fingers were twitching and unreliable as he struggled to get his bullets into the gun. On the courtyard wall, Brandt tracked the shadowy profile closing in on their position. He eyed his options: both of the other firearms were too far away to reach. He'd be tagged in no time. He could hear the steps growing closer, could see the figure's shadow projected on the wall and stepping softly toward his position as if his death was playing on some twisted *camera obscura*. Phil *finally* got a bullet inside the gun, and snapped the chamber shut.

The second shooter flung the door closed and aimed at his two targets, his face silhouetted by the faded light in the sky above. Phil raised his gun to fire, but the attacker kicked it from his hand and sent it skidding across the ground. The shooter aligned the barrel of his gun with Brandt's chest.

Before he could finish the job, a bullet tore through the attacker's temple and sent him flopping against the car. As he collapsed, his body squirmed against a trail of blood oozing from the side of his head. Brandt turned, searching for the shooter, and saw the plump figure of

Ansel Combe, a gun extended in his hand and the barrel smoking.

Combe quickly surveyed the street for any more threats. Apparently satisfied the immediate danger was quelled, he crouched toward Brandt and asked, "Are you alright?"

Brandt, though a man with a strong stomach who had survived far worse situations, struggled to provide an answer—his chest heaved.

"Hank!" Combe demanded again, his fists now full of the lapels on Brandt's coat.

Brandt nodded absentmindedly, then patted his body to ensure he was indeed okay. Combe helped Brandt up, and all three made for Louie. Combe checked the kid's vitals. He was breathing, and slowly he woke from the immediate shock as Combe lightly tapped his cheeks to bring him back to Earth. Phil tore at his own undershirt, quickly fashioned a compress to stop the bleeding, and then helped the other two men guide the injured kid to his feet.

"We've got to go," Phil said while using his body as a shield for his allies. It was one of the rare instances anyone had heard him speak.

Combe turned back to the house as if to give it some abrupt, unceremonious goodbye. "Wait," he said, and he bounded up the front steps just as the last bit of light faded from the sky.

Brandt, his curiosity now piqued, stepped away while Phil helped Louie into the back seat of the bullet-riddled sedan. The spy chief stood over the first of his attackers. Dead center in his forehead was a small black entry wound with a thin trail of blood snaking down the side of it. The assailant's eyes looked up to the sky, shock permanently frozen in them.

He wore no identifying clothing, only black slacks, loafers, and a black shirt under a double-breasted peacoat that was as unremarkable as the car they'd assumedly arrived in. What tipped Brandt off to his origins were his characteristics, which stressed the idealistic Nazi appearance. The hair was thin and well-kept, and it met with a neat part at the right side of the skull. The eyes were a striking blue, glimmering even in death as they caught the pale evening light. His skin was white and unblemished. Sure, he could have been any nationality—his features did not define him—but any man at war with a nation who wanted him dead didn't need a doctorate degree to understand these were Germans.

Combe resurfaced shortly, then hustled around the passenger's side of the car and toward the front seat. Brandt moved quickly to survey his other attacker, and he looked much the same as his partner, both in his physical appearance and in his lifeless eyes. They'd come here to kill. It was only blind luck that the events had played out the way they had. *Sheer chance*, Brandt thought. Say what one will about the skill and preparedness of Brandt's team to react, but now that they were forced to flee their hidden location and leave behind two bodies in their wake, they were the ones who had truly lost on this fateful evening.

"Hank," Combe called out through the missing window. Brandt snapped out of his gaze into the dead man's eyes, recognized the bleeding man in the back seat's need for medical attention, and climbed into the car. The motor roared to life. Brandt was thankful—he'd worried it was damaged by the gunfire.

"What about the intel?" Brandt asked Combe as the car lurched into gear.

"What intel?" Combe asked.

Brandt looked to the house beyond the ivy gate, a place where so much had been accomplished for the Allies and his own personal gain. He recognized the dancing fingers of flames rising in great spurts through the glass windows. Soon, smoke started emanating from unsealed gaps in the home, and the fire began to rise toward the ceiling. The car skidded as Phil hit the gas pedal, then moved beyond the hedge wall and away from the home. Brandt watched through the rear windshield until the home was out of view. Every so often he'd see a plume of smoke through a break in the trees. This Bern station was officially compromised. All that would remain was the husk of a once-great chalet and the bodies of two dead Germans. Hank Brandt hoped Sam and Lukas were far from Peenemünde. The reconnaissance didn't matter anymore.

29

The farmhouse was as ghostly and abandoned as Lukas' intelligence had suggested. Unhindered by any obstacle was the acrid smell of saltwater. When Sam had arrived around twilight, herring gulls were circling above, and with their presence Sam noted the scent of decaying fish wafting up from the shore. They'd come to pick the bones of what was left of the farm, perhaps even the carcass of a missing spy named Roger. Sam considered whether that was the putrid smell he'd detected in the first place.

Sam navigated the property for several hours, eying it from all angles as he moved around the shadows of the perimeter. The moon was high and mighty. Its unobstructed light seemed to etch the house out against the landscape. It had been eerily quiet, something that didn't sit right with him considering how much noise he and Lukas had made.

In the stifling wind, a loose shutter banged on its hinge against the façade. Much of the wheat, unharvested, looked parched and brittle as it swayed under the stress of the breeze. The door in the main entryway had been torn from its jam completely. The farm had been neglected—all signs of an unplanned evacuation.

To the north, a concrete radio beacon was hoisted above a relatively calm sea. There was no visible boat traffic, but who could say for sure? U-boats were so sneaky like that. The tide was low, but the sea seemed volatile in the gusty winds.

The hiss of pine needles dancing in the wind makes a sound that differentiates it from other trees in similar conditions. It was an ethereal tone, a din that suggested something wicked was present, or perhaps approaching. It didn't take a spy to discern the uncanny nature of the phenomenon, but once one heard it, they could never quite compare it to anything else. It was both beautiful and terrifying, because even if the breeze didn't strike a visual distinction, it was frightfully audible nonetheless.

The northern trek from the security of camouflage to the farm house was anything but discreet. There was a wide-open patch of roughly a quarter kilometer in which no man could hide. There were no trees, no walls, and no cover other than the crop fields flanking the northern and eastern plots on the property. Sam took a quick inventory with his binoculars, but it was difficult to see anything. Inside, the home was a pall of shadow.

Sam debated even going inside. It seemed it was business as usual at Peenemünde. The blatant display of the rocket earlier was proof enough of that. Sam saw no military might other than foot patrols by troops. Even if Roger Fowler had been captured, Sam doubted the consequences would affect the forthcoming assault.

Even the SSD's contact at the German Ministry

thought Fowler likely compromised. Sam wondered what might have happened if he had been in Fowler's place. He decided he should come up with something in the way of an answer. It was the right thing to do. Why trek all the way through Germany with death at one's back if he wasn't going to finish the job? He made the trip across the property quickly and silently.

When Sam finally entered the house, all the signs of struggle were present, including, but not limited to, an overturned table at the center of the room, scattered papers and clothing, and the belongings of a man tossed around in no meaningful way. The wind picked up again, howling against the building's exterior in a ghastly, hellish moan. He continued to survey the room, his steps soft and contemplative, while he attempted to recreate the scene with the ghosts of the home's previous occupants.

Whoever had searched the building had left nothing to chance, and every drawer, door, and cabinet present remained open. Sam shuddered. Being in the home reminded him of what was at stake. He expedited his investigation.

Since his eyes had adjusted to the dim light, he continued to search the interior for any confirmation. The disorganized prints of combat boots revealed themselves in scattered ash around the fireplace. He followed their trail, and if the remains of boot marks hadn't been confirmation enough, he also discovered the one clue that made him unequivocally sure of his fear—there was a faint twinkle of light coming from the fireplace. He reached a hand toward the pile of ash, dug into the soot, and retrieved a charred and dismembered magnesium camera. It was destroyed beyond recognition, unless of course one was a spy.

"Sam," a voice bellowed from beyond the house's walls. A cool chill ran down Sam's spine. It was not Lukas' voice, but he recognized something about it. *Few* people knew that name. Certainly nobody from the SSD would use it so freely behind enemy lines.

He found himself unable to move, caught in a whirlwind of surprise and confusion that seemed to make time itself halt. He remained stiff, unwilling—or perhaps unable—to answer. Yes, he knew he remembered something about the inflection. *What exactly?*

"The perimeter is surrounded," the voice said. The words came in German. There it was again: that familiarity. Sam knew it, was *sure* he did—as sure as he was that he was standing here on his own two feet and breathing. "We have this man in custody, and I ask that you come freely and quietly—by order of the Peenemünde *Sicherheitskapitän*. I am not going to ask twice, because we've already done this once before. So either you surrender yourself now, or I put a bullet in this man's head, and one in yours."

After the lengthy proclamation, the realization hit Sam so hard that he grew weak in his knees. His heart rate rose, and his skin grew clammy. He was sure of who the voice belonged to now—so sure that he didn't need to poke his eye through any of the small cracks in the siding to see its source, but did so anyway. Standing in the field, wearing a signature black party coat that flowed ominously in the breeze, was Lothar Eichler. Even in the darkness Sam knew his likeness.

Could he see Sam? It was hard to tell. But Sam felt like he could, felt like the man was staring right through the house's walls and right into his soul. And if someone could see into Sam's soul, what it would reveal was a man who had run out of options. He had no play left but to present himself.

Sam opened the front door and stepped through the threshold. He squinted to better see his enemy. Eichler, painted in the white coloration of lunar light, stood proud amongst a smattering of soldiers—all armed— patiently waiting for their prize. Worse still, Lukas had been captured. He was on his knees, the barrel of a firearm pointed at his head, which hung low in defeat. Sam didn't hold his arms out to yield. He didn't have to. To attempt to fight his way out of this would be suicide.

Sam thought Eichler was smiling, though it was hard to tell. There was something triumphant about the man's expression. Perhaps it was in his posture, his chest pumped out and his body stiff and proud. A moment both men had waited for—and probably never believed would come—had arrived. Here, on this distant island that was so far from their last meeting point, two men who'd sought revenge more than anything were staring face to face.

Eichler waved off the gunman above Lukas. The soldiers, unaware of the history these two men shared, stared on as the silence lingered. It was as if both men wanted to savor the strange moment of chance—or was it fate? Sam wondered how Lukas might have weighed in on the scenario.

"Congratulate yourselves, gentlemen," Eichler called to the men standing by. His eye contact with Sam went unbroken. "You've just successfully discovered the liaison of the spy apprehended recently on this very farm. Furthermore, you've now discovered another of his co-conspirators: a prize more valuable than any old *spy*. This is the man who destroyed Flussrand. That's not just one, but two—no, *three* spies…" He hesitated. "Better yet, we've just brought down an entire network." There were snickers and devious grins all around from the troops.

"On your knees," Eichler commanded Sam. The spy obeyed. Sam squinted in the dim light, searching for anything he could use. The troops' rifles were stark in the moonlight. Lukas was useless. His eyes were tightly closed and he seemed to be mumbling to himself, bowed over the dirt ground in prayer. *A prayer won't save you now—nothing will.*

Eichler ambled casually over to Sam. With every gun pointed at the spy, the *Sicherheitskapitän* clearly had no fear. Sam sensed that his nemesis—like any man whose victory was now ensured—was going to relish in this moment as long as he could. The destruction of Flussrand had taken place in February of the year prior. This moment of anticipation had been a year and a half in the making.

"Now we will know everything," Eichler said as he approached. "We will pry it out of you. We will squeeze it out of you. We will *rip* it out of you. Because I will not make the same mistake I did last time. I will not give you the benefit of the doubt to come clean and salvage any respect you might have left for yourself. There is no respect left—there is only you and I."

Now Eichler was standing over Sam, his face painted in shadow. In the east, the moonlight dissipated in a foreboding gradient above the ocean. A breeze rippled across the land again as the captor loomed above his captive. Sam experienced the feeling of *déjà vu* as if this had all already happened—that was probably because it *had*.

Across the river the trees bent and swayed in the wind like an audience. Sam could almost hear them jeering. Even in the dead of night, the heat did not waver. It seemed to only grow stronger with each gust coming from the east.

Eichler stared at Sam, and the defeated man maintained his gaze as if to display the only effort at bravery he could muster. Sam had been skilled enough—or perhaps just lucky enough—to escape from the man before him not once, but twice now. Could he possibly be lucky enough for a third time?

What do two men who want nothing more than to kill one another say when they are finally face to face? Both might argue that there was so much they wanted to say. Yet, now that they were finally able, neither was saying much at all.

Eichler looked as if he was about to speak, his lips parting slightly, but then they closed again. His jaws clenched firmly, displaying the sharp, hard lines of bone beneath his skin. Sam wasn't prepared for the next statement: Eichler's fist slammed against Sam's cheek. Like a bad memory returning, it was the same cheek Eichler had injured so long ago. Laughter echoed across the farm from the troops beyond.

Sam spewed blood on to the dirt. The strike apparently did nothing to quell Eichler's rage. Both fists were firmly closed and resting at his sides. He let Sam compose himself again. Then, Eichler stooped down to the ground, placing his grinning face right in front of Sam's.

"You never asked how I learned your name," Eichler

said. Sam didn't speak. "She was saying it between gasps of air. When she wasn't choking to death on her own blood, she was calling for you. 'Sam, Sam, Sam…' "

Sam slammed his head forward into his nemesis' nose, sending him tumbling backward. The taunting had become unbearable, and the invocation of Sigrid Lang with such irreverence brought out something primal and vengeful within him. The soldiers charged forward. One delivered a boot to Sam's mouth.

Eichler wiped his face—blood was trickling from his nose. He then instructed the troops to take Sam into custody. Both he and Lukas were frogmarched forcefully toward the back of a truck after being cuffed. During the arrest, they removed Sam's gloves, revealing his injured hand.

Lukas was despondent, his face shameful and defeated. Sam, bewildered by how easily and quickly this operation had fallen apart, considered whether this had been a trap all along. The *SS* perimeter guards had let them pass earlier, and perhaps now he knew why. They'd planned it to play out like this. Sam had planned too—he'd stuck the kill-pill between his molar and gum before he'd stepped out of the house.

30

When Sam arrived at the truck, the two soldiers gripping his arms directed him up the small foot ladder. Just when his feet hit the bed, the soldier behind him struck Sam in the spine with his gun, forcing him onto the floor. Two of the soldiers climbed in the back cargo area with the spies and sat on the two bench seats beside them. Sam lay on the floor for a moment as he caught his breath, and when he rose he found both men pointing guns in his face.

"You move, I'll kill you," one of the men said. Sam sensed hesitation in his voice.

Don't worry, Sam thought. *I'm not going anywhere. I'm right where I want to be.*

The truck set off into the dark forest and down a winding road. Around them the tall, pillar-like evergreens hugging the path rose into the night sky. Sam knew immediately they were heading east by the glitter on the pines facing him. Only a full, bright moon could decorate the forest like that.

Soon the unfinished path gave way to pavement, and though the truck remained in the forest, the trip became far less bumpy. Both soldiers continued to stare at Sam, their guns drawn and unwavering. There was no sense in trying to disarm them. They were seated alongside him in such a way that attacking one would only provoke the other to shoot. Sam was going to have to ride this one out until he was presented with a chance to escape.

He could look for a window of opportunity—after all, these weren't *SS* men, or combat-hardened types. These were patrolmen at best, and they likely hadn't seen much action before being transferred to Peenemünde. Their trigger fingers looked shaky, and their attitudes unsure. In fact, both of them looked pretty young to be in the *Wehrmacht. I'd be surprised if either of them has ever even stepped foot in the field.*

But then again, was escape really his priority? Sure, he'd need to get out *somehow.* Staying in Peenemünde was a death sentence. Yet all Sam could think about was Eichler's face. How long until he saw the man again? Five minutes? Ten? The anticipation felt like it would kill him before anything else.

And what would Sigrid say? How might she react if she knew that Sam came willingly back into harm's way —back to the place she had freed him from only a year and a half before. She'd given her life to let the spy live another day, and here Sam was in the same predicament all over again.

Sam was reminded of the A-4 rocket launch—its mighty propulsion, its massive weapons payload, and its hellish capabilities. If Sigrid had her way, she'd have seen to it another rocket never left the pad. She'd have hoped Sam would do the same.

And so, he felt no regret during his journey, nor any shame. He felt no remorse that he hadn't managed to escape, and no fear that he might never see home again. He was right where he *needed* to be.

Lukas remained silent. Sam hadn't heard him say a word since Eichler had brandished him as a trophy. Sam was capable of handling the delicate nature of the situation, but was the priest? He showed no indication of it. The soldiers exchanged some words in German, and Sam was struck with an idea: he and Lukas possessed a coded language between them the soldiers likely didn't understand—English.

"Are you alright?" Sam asked.

"I'm sorry," Lukas replied through garbled speech.

"Quiet!" one of the soldiers commanded in German. It was Sam's first inkling that he was right—they *didn't* understand English. Sam, never one to play by the rules, continued on.

"There's no need for apologies," Sam advised. "They're going to separate us soon. You may have to make your own way."

"I'm not going to tell you again," the soldier barked. Sam scowled. *I can only say so much before things get violent.*

"I'm prepared for whatever they throw at me," Lukas mumbled. The priest's unclear pronunciation was a clue, but it was the defeat in Lukas' face that told the truth: he had also placed his kill-pill in his mouth.

"That's a last resort, Father," Sam said. It was the first time he'd ever used the priest's title respectfully. "Do you hear me? It's an absolute end-of-game option. Don't—"

The soldier beside Sam slammed the butt of the rifle against Sam's ribs. The strike forced the wind out of him and he was left gasping. However, he'd made his point. They both had a way out. The difference between them was that Lukas was unpredictable. Sam, on the other hand, had no intention of ending his life when Lothar Eichler was so close by.

The truck slowed, then turned left. The trees gave way to a large field. The moon once again provided enough light to see nearby. They were surrounded by water on both sides, and the truck jumped briefly when it cleared the lip of a small bridge connecting to the island. They paused, were cleared for entry, then passed through two high posts that denoted the main entrance to the Peenemünde Army Research Center—they were inside.

They traveled a bit farther, deeper into the bowels of the island, passing homes and offices and *Wehrmacht* barracks' as the truck rattled along the pavement. Sam decided not to speak further. He didn't want to suffer any more than he already had. His hand was throbbing with a ghostly sensation as if the finger that had vanished was still very much there—a phantom digit.

Beside the truck, large smokestacks rose into the night sky from one of the manufacturing facilities, each with tufts of cloud spewing from their mouths. A supply delivery rail line ran alongside the building. Sam considered it might be one of the Experimental Works buildings Ramm had pointed out. Inside, madmen were likely constructing the weapons in mass numbers.

As the truck traveled, the housing facilities and workstations became dull blurs in the distance. Sam had a feeling he was not meant to have seen those buildings. As he'd been warned, the security at Peenemünde had been much more efficient and ready than Flussrand—at least for those trying to break in on foot. A saving grace was that Sam still had not even seen any anti-aircraft defenses, and that meant that though men like him could easily be discovered, the RAF wouldn't meet the same type of resistance he had when they came.

Soon the truck was engulfed in deep forest again. The path was now shrouded in darkness. The trees had done a good job camouflaging Peenemünde. Sam had barely been able to see anything other than the airfield from the east bank of the farm. The same difficulty was true inside the perimeter. After another checkpoint, the truck halted completely, and Sam and Lukas were forced to wait.

————

Lothar Eichler had never been so excited to place a call in his life. He'd radioed his team ahead of his arrival, and Falke was on the line as soon as Eichler arrived at his office. He found it difficult to wipe the grin from his face, and even his subordinates were smiling and saluting when he approached. Congratulations were surely in order, but not until Eichler had confirmed his next steps.

"Herr Falke," Eichler said into the phone. He was beaming—it was evident even in his voice.

"Herr Eichler," Falke replied, and before Eichler could respond, he continued, "I'm told you've needed to speak with me. More developments, I hope."

"I've apprehended the saboteurs, Herr Falke," Eichler proclaimed.

There was a long silence.

"You've taken them into custody?"

Eichler sensed the note of disappointment in his voice. "It was imperative, you see, Herr Falke—"

"You were under strict orders to *not* confront those in question, Herr Eichler."

"I understand," Eichler said. "But under the circumstances—"

"Please, describe those circumstances."

"The man arrived with another, far more valuable operator," Eichler began. "The spy who destroyed Flussrand, the one I requested information about—it is him. He is one of our own and has caused us much strife. It is quite fateful."

"Be that as it may," Falke said, "you've now jeopardized the long-term plans of this operation. If I wanted the man captured, I could have seen to that myself."

"But Herr Falke, perhaps now that these men are in custody your other captive will be more apt to talk—if he knows no one is coming for him and his entire network has been compromised—"

"That man is dead, Herr Eichler," Falke quickly corrected. "He can't talk because he has *been* long dead." Eichler's skin crawled. He'd believed the musings of Vogel involving the fable-like tales of torture and snakes, but now they'd seemed to be confirmed. Eichler grew concerned that now he could be usurped. Could Sam or Dieter or whatever his real name was become the property of *Der Fänger*? "You're to detain both men until I can arrange transport. One I've arrived, you will turn them over to me."

"I took initiative, Herr Falke," Eichler said. He pumped his chest out as if Falke was standing right in front of him. "I have a personal duty to see to it the man is handed over to the proper authorities and that justice is served. To let him escape once more would have been a great tragedy. If you would like to claim your own man, you may. As far as the defector Dieter Stein is concerned, he is my quarry and I am charged with serving him directly to the *Reichsführer*. Good evening, Herr Falke."

Eichler slammed the phone down on the receiver. He felt invigorated, strong, *alive*. No longer would he play these bureaucratic games. He'd done the work, and he'd reap the rewards. Even the legendary Aksel Falke could not convince him otherwise.

His next plan was to seek the audience of the *Reichsführer*, but that was interrupted by the wailing of the air-raid siren. It gave Eichler brief pause, but when it started to wane, he proceeded with the call anyway. He was halted once more by the arrival of Officer Vogel, his trusty adjutant, who seemed on edge standing in the doorway.

"Herr Eichler," he spit out in between gasps for air —he looked as if he'd run a marathon.

"What is it?" Eichler asked.

As Vogel struggled to compose himself, the air-raid siren sounded again. This was a common occurrence in Peenemünde, and rarely cause for concern. Sometimes it was just being tested, and sometimes it was signaling an air raid in a nearby city like Berlin or Hamburg. Never once had it signaled that Peenemünde itself was under attack.

"An—an air raid sir," Vogel choked out. "In fact, multiple."

"And?" Eichler asked. "We've an air raid nearly every night."

"I'm told we're to proceed with full lockdown protocols, sir," Vogel said. "Reports have already come in from an attack on airfields at Stade and Jagel. Fleets were spotted in the general direction of Rügen. Luftwaffe night fighters have already engaged with Allied combatants in Berlin." Once more, the scream of the siren subsided.

"Who issued this order?"

"It has come in from High Command, sir," Vogel said. Eichler returned the phone to the receiver. Now, even though he had Sam in captivity and his glorious prize was within his grasp, Eichler was forced to change hats and don the one belonging to *Sicherheitskapitän*.

———

Inside the truck, Sam was keenly aware of the siren as well. The grunts and maneuvering of troops outside the dark box were easily recognizable. There were tones of concern. Sam looked to Lukas, and the priest seemed to sense something was amiss as well.

The soldier beside Sam commanded his partner to check outside to figure out what exactly was happening. Only one remained. Sam considered his options: stay put, or risk taking this guard out. The spy had no weapons on him, and neither did Lukas. Even if they did manage to subdue the guard, finding the keys to the cuffs could present a problem. They couldn't fire guns from behind their backs. And even if they found the keys, that still left the difficult task of escape. How many people had been alerted to their description, and how much could they possibly blend in? Sam dismissed this idea quickly, but the heightened state of alert that seemed to have manifested outside the truck was making everyone, the guards included, very nervous.

After some time, the other soldier returned. When the door opened, Sam caught a brief glimpse of Eichler staring at him. His face was filled with frustration. Whatever was happening, Eichler was *not* happy about its timing.

The soldier who'd done the reconnaissance spoke in German to his partner: "We're to take the prisoners to Trassenheide."

"Why?" the other asked.

"No further reasoning given," he replied. But before he could elaborate, he simply said, "We're being called in for defensive positions. Something is happening."

That was all Sam needed to hear. That 'something' was very likely something big, a something that he and Lukas were both privy to. Lukas' face was riddled with the fear of a man who knew *exactly* what was coming— and was terrified of it. Sam believed that what Lukas had told him earlier about this predicted RAF raid had been very true. What Sam had not expected was that it would be happening tonight. Sam thought this coincidental, but in the company of Lukas, questioned if fate played a role. As the truck started moving again, traveling south back through the island and past the housing estate, the interior was bathed in the bright luminescence of the full moon. For anyone that had started paying attention to night-time-flying operations, it was the absolute perfect moment to strike at an enemy stronghold.

31

Sam checked his watch in the idling truck. It was nearing one in the morning now. Only one soldier had been left behind in the rear with the two captives, and the other had taken over driving duties. When the doors to the rear of the truck opened, the world outside was in absolute chaos.

They'd arrived at Trassenheide, the work camp; Sam remembered when Ramm had described it. It was surrounded by high fences of razor wire and lookout posts. Inside the fenced areas, there were wooden huts. *Tinderboxes*, Sam thought. *They would go up in flame easily should they be hit.* The gate opened, and Sam and Lukas were ushered out from the rear of the truck and moved to the front entrance at gunpoint. All around the site, soldiers seemed to be in disarray. Sam and Lukas' handcuffs were removed. Just as Sam had finally gotten a sense of the place, he and Lukas were separated and marched to different housing units.

Sam wanted to leave Lukas with some words of

encouragement, but they didn't come. He wanted to tell the priest everything would be alright, that they'd make it out, but he knew that wasn't a guarantee. Whether fate was at work here, Sam hoped there was a chance they'd see another day, even if they were currently imprisoned in the most top-secret Nazi camp on the globe.

Sam was delivered into the housing unit via a boot to the back. He collapsed to the wooden floor below, aware that his entrance had caused quite a stir among the already imprisoned. He looked at the other prisoners in the room—the first thing he gathered was an abundance of battered, bruised, and dirty feet.

The siren cut through the forest once more. It had been going off intermittently now for some time. An old man with a tangled, salt-and-pepper beard stood from the rickety bed he'd been resting on, then slowly approached Sam as if looking to engage in conversation. In a comforting voice, he said in broken German, "Don't pay any mind to the signal. It sounds every night, and every night no one comes. It's hardly a cause for concern."

"It is tonight," Sam said.

"The first time one hears it, they panic," the old man said. "But it typically sounds whenever a city is under threat—Berlin, Hamburg. It's a precautionary tactic."

"It's not for Berlin or Hamburg," Sam replied.

"Then Munich?" the man asked.

Sam didn't continue to thread the yarn of that conversation. Instead, he asked with urgency, "Is there shelter for these men?"

"We've begun to dig trenches recently," the old man replied. "I'd hardly call it proper shelter though. You won't need them. There are few places safer than Peenemünde."

"This is the *most* dangerous place you can be right now," Sam warned.

The old man eyed Sam curiously. He appeared intrigued by the spy. Unlike many of the men inside the shelter, Sam was fresh and inquisitive.

"Friend," the old man said. "You're new here." His accent was a concoction of European dialects. Though he spoke German, everything about the man told Sam he was likely Polish, and the spy even thought he heard a tinge of Yiddish. Thick, weeks-old dirt was caked anywhere his skin was visible, and his eyes were blood-shot. He looked tired—in fact, everyone present looked so damn *tired*. Sam checked his breast pocket for a smoke, then was sorely reminded that they'd been confiscated earlier. What Sam knew that the others didn't was that there'd be plenty of smoke soon enough.

Sam redirected his attention to figuring out how he was going to get out of the hut. He scrutinized a window on the broad side of the shelter. It was barred shut.

The men were packed into the hut nearly shoulder to shoulder. Most were civilians, but Sam thought he spotted a couple tattered British and Russian military uniforms among them. The men were in varying degrees of ruination and decay. Their clothing was ripped and disheveled. Healthy men build muscle when they work, but malnourished and mistreated men only grow weaker. These men were sinewy and pale. Their ghostly white skin only gave way to color in the redness of their calloused hands.

"Many faces come and go from this place," the old

man said. "But I can always tell a new one. Where are you from?"

"Far from home," Sam said, as if there was such a thing as home.

"We are all far from home," the old man replied. "Were you brought here, or captured?" Sam didn't answer—he was too focused on the guard patrolling the field surrounding the shelter. Through the iron bars covering the window, he could see there were many shoddily crafted shelters just like the one he was in scattered around the camp area. Surrounding the field, a tall barbed-wire fence stood as a deterrent for anyone contemplating escape. Several guards paced through the field with rifles slung over their shoulders.

"How many guards are there?" Sam asked.

The old man contemplated the question, then said, "Several at any given time."

"And between here and the housing estates?" Sam asked.

The old man snorted as if Sam had told a joke. "My friend, if you are considering attempting an escape, you would be ill-advised."

"I'm not considering it," Sam replied. "I'm planning it."

"Well," the old man began again with a subdued chuckle, "you'd do well to know that there is a rifleman standing at the front door as well." Sam's attention turned to the wooden door holding all of the men inside the hut. "He's a particularly difficult one. I don't think he cares for his work any more than we do. You'd have to disarm him, and in turn, his friends. Several men have attempted escape. They usually wind up with a bullet in their back before they've even begun to scale the fence."

"You wouldn't happen to have a cigarette, would you?"

"Friend, I have nothing but the clothes on my back," the old man said. He displayed his shredded sleeves. "And even they are of questionable value."

"We need to get out of here," Sam warned the man.

He looked at Sam as if perplexed, like Sam had just made it seem that escape was as simple as waving goodbye to the patrolling officers and stepping through the gate. "I'm not sure you understand where you are. *No* man leaves this place."

Sam looked among the prisoners piled in the room. None looked fit enough to overpower the man outside. Some looked like they hadn't slept in days and others appeared as if they'd been working equally as long. If they were going to get out it was going to have to be a group effort. Sam considered the fact that to try to take the guards by force would result in deaths. It was an inevitability, so if that was what had to be done, Sam would lead the charge.

"What's the closest point of safety?" Sam asked the man.

"This is Peenemünde," the man said. "There is no safety for people like us."

Sam wasn't getting anywhere with his rally call. Perhaps the old man was right and an attempt at storming the fence was foolish. Sam said to the man, "Listen to me. Any minute now, the RAF is going to send a fleet of bombers. They're going to level the manufacturing facilities."

Perhaps that was a poor statement to make, because Sam sensed he'd caused a panic in the room.

"About time," a Brit from the back of the pack

announced. Several other men nodded. Maybe Sam had caused the spark to ignite the men into action after all.

"We can use that attack to our advantage. Can any of you fight?" Sam asked.

The old man stared in confusion at the spy. They both knew he need not motion to the malnourished men nearby to bring Sam back to his senses. Sam pondered his next move. As he watched the guard patrolling outside, a truck rolled up to the gated area of the fence at the far end of the camp. A soldier hopped out of the passenger-side seat and left the truck idling, then sprinted to the pacing guard. Sam could sense the urgency with which the soldier moved—the heightened alertness the spy so often relied upon was triggered as if a pair of antennae had shot straight out of his head.

The soldier slung his rifle over his shoulder, then pointed to the tree line beyond the camp. Sam couldn't hear the conversation over the idling truck, but he was sure the chatter was one of an urgent matter. The old man appeared at the window, then said, "That's the man who oversees the work camp. He doesn't normally show his face this late." Sam turned toward the old man—as if Sam's warning had clicked, the old man's face grew suspicious.

There was a brief argument between the two soldiers. The one who'd arrived by truck barked several orders, and though Sam still couldn't hear the details, the one the man had come to meet pushed back on his instructions. It was a scenario in which the body language of both men said all that Sam needed to hear. The superior said something, then the subordinate gave a rebuttal. After several exchanges, the conversation had devolved into a full-blown argument, then the man who'd arrived by truck pointed once more to the sky, checked his watch, and hustled back over to his vehicle.

The soldier, who obviously resented the orders, tossed his cigarette away. Then, as the truck exited, the soldier ran back over to where the vehicle had entered and relocked the heavy gate behind it. He grabbed his rifle, gripped it in his hands, then confirmed a round was chambered before calling out to his coworkers. Several of the men gathered at the center of the camp. Now that the truck's noise had subsided, Sam listened to their conversation.

"Something's wrong," the old man said to Sam. The spy silenced him with the wave of a hand and a shush. It was dark and difficult to see or hear much. Sam picked up bits of the conversation through fragmented words, though he heard one statement crystal clear: "*Wir müssen her bleiben. Die Anfahrt ist West, Nordwest. Niemand verlässt die Unterkünfte.*" A cool chill ran down the back of Sam's spine—it was *happening*.

The soldiers scattered. Sam thought he could still hear the groan of the truck traveling through the woods, but then the sound took on a depth that suggested something larger. Sam's attention turned to the sky above, but the tall, pointed tips of the pines obscured anything besides the large, pearl-like glow of the full moon. The light it cast on the site was angelic, a contradiction to the madness at the research base.

The groaning grew more massive, and drew closer. It was deep and guttural. It was not one motor—it was the collective battle cry of many: a dull yell as the flying machines charged their enemy. Soon, the men around the shelter became aware of the sound too. Several men rose to their feet and began to speak amongst themselves about just *what* this noise signaled.

A light buzz broke through the rumble as if a kazoo had sprouted wings and joined along for the fun. The flimsily constructed shelter began to rattle. The plane was *low*. Sam looked to the sky once more, and this time he saw something different: one lone plane traveling toward the labor camp. The reflective glow of the moon outlined the ship, revealing its bird-like form.

It was a risky maneuver—bombers did not often fly at such low altitudes for fear of flak fire. This particular plane had made it all the way to the southern body of the island without incident, yet the bombing hadn't started. *Was it a diversion?*

The commotion inside the cabin grew to a fever pitch. A bevy of voices began to yell over each other, a babel of dialects representing different cultures. Many of the men seemed to be arguing about what was about to ensue—and, Sam suspected, if the spy had made a good point when he'd suggested freeing himself. The plane traveled closer, now clearing the tree line completely. It was just about over the camp perimeter.

Sam saw something leave the belly of the plane, a faint little object that traveled with a feather-like grace to the Earth below, then flickered for a moment. The glow grew before it illuminated the forest with a violent bright red light. *No*, Sam thought. *No*.

A flare could only mean one thing: *bomb here*. Now Sam could see the camp in such bright light that it seemed as if the sun had decided to change its schedule. The interior of the cabin lit up, painting the panicked men's faces in a sinister cherry hue. The noise of the aircraft dissipated, and Sam realized it wasn't likely a bomber at all, but instead the master bomber. Tasked with throwing a flare down, the master bomber directed their fleet to attack by marking the target.

No, Sam thought again. *Not here!* He was screaming internally as if trying to convince the pilots en route that they had been wrong. Several of the men banged on the wooden door. They were screaming, "Let us out!" in their various tongues. The commotion grew to a roar, then the men started pounding on the door with such ferocity the lock began to buckle under the stress.

The soldier standing guard barked back, "*Weg von der Tür! Weg von der Tür!*" Sam heard the indistinguishable *crack* of the guard's rifle butt strike the door, but the men only screamed louder. They were pushing the door now, many of the men bunched up next to it and thrusting their weight against the wood with powerful heaves.

Sam could feel the might of the approaching fleet. The arrival was dwarfing the commotion inside of the prison. There were screams from the shelter nearby, and Sam looked once again to the center of the camp, where men from one of the other huts had already managed to pry their door open. Several men funneled out, and their guard took aim. He shot one, sending the frail prisoner tumbling, but the group surged toward him in unison, knocking him and his rifle to the ground before trampling him. Sam tracked the group as they double-timed across the field—most made a break for the fence in the distance.

The men grabbed hold of the fence—some were trying to climb it, and some were attempting to take another section down completely. Inside Sam's shelter, the men were still in a battle with the guard. A *ping* echoed in the doorway. The men had forced the lock off, torn it from its very hinges.

Outside, the rolling thunder of the fleet felt as if it was quaking the Earth. Sam watched the escaped men freeze for a moment, many directing their attention to the sky above. They seemed to be stuck in a state of shock.

Sam, realizing the bombers were about to strike their target, sprang toward the men bunched up at the door. The lanky soldier barring the door outside wouldn't be able to hold it for long. Sam cleared the men of the doorway, wedged himself up front and center, then threw all of his body weight into the door. The door budged slightly, and Sam yelled, "Push!" in German, then in in Yiddish, then in English, and then in every other language he could muster. Ansel Combe had said a man who possessed many languages was many men—he'd been right.

The prisoners pressed their bodies up against Sam's, now forcing their collective weight against the door in unison. Sam yelled louder still—this time it wasn't a request, it was a *command*. The spy growled, the muscles in his arms bulging and screaming from exertion. The men behind him yelled too, and then finally, with a forceful heave, the door swung open and Sam was face to face with the guard. The soldier held his gun in the spy's face, his hands trembling and unsure. Sam grabbed the barrel of the gun and jerked it away from himself. The soldier fired, but the bullet went whizzing through the open air and off toward the forest. Sam cracked the guard in the face and he fell easily. The men Sam had been packed in with dispersed, most heading toward the fence.

The noise above demanded Sam's attention: the armada was gliding across the sky, their engines rumbling like a stampede of mighty animals. It was as if the sky itself had parted to reveal the attackers, and several bombers in a "V" formation passed the tree line —they were heading directly toward the camp. The first several were followed by several more, which made up their own small squadron, and then several *more* beyond that. They spread across the sky in almost every direction, their growth in numbers seemingly exponential.

The metallic bodies of the bombers flickered red from the light of the glowing marker below. Now that Sam could see the forest in its entirety, he recognized two more marking flares that had fallen near the bulked-up wall of trees to the north. A moment later, Sam heard the first whistle emanate from the lead plane.

A small object exited from the belly of the plane and plummeted toward the markers. Its whistle grew more vibrant as it fell. Sam watched its course: between the markers and the moonlight he could see its silhouette very clearly, even in the night. The bomb finally landed between a cluster of trees and exploded on impact. It sent several trees scattering wildly in an explosion of dust and wood and pine. *No*, Sam said to himself once more. *This isn't the target!* His internal voice had seemed so loud in his mind he'd almost thought he'd yelled the words.

His cries were futile. Another whistle sounded, then another—the planes were letting their payloads loose. It was the most haunting harmony Sam had ever heard. Explosives of varying shapes and sizes plummeted right toward the camp. Now the sky was decorated not only with the planes, but small black masses that were falling down like the deadliest raindrops in history.

They landed one by one, ripping the forest to shreds. The ones that didn't destroy things in their wake roared with fire. Those were the incendiary devices, designed to *burn*, and they were the stuff of nightmares. The cries among the men in the camp grew to a crescendo, then the first bomb dropped inside the perimeter. After the blast, a massive hole was left in its place, the explosion spraying dirt, debris, and smoke all around it. The next fell only a handful of feet away from it. The prisoners raged through the camp as if someone had instigated a riot. Screams echoed throughout the forest. Explosions roared in all directions. There was *madness*.

Anyone who'd been freed from their wooden prison ran panicked through the camp. Several bombs struck right near the front gate, but they hadn't damaged it enough to create an exit. The number of men scaling the tall fence had risen into the double digits, and several guards stood strong against the remaining shelters to ensure those prisoners didn't exit.

Another group had the same idea Sam's group had— they forced their shelter door open and toppled over the soldier guarding it. The mob-like exit of the captives flattened the door on top of the man's body, producing a makeshift bridge over his torso.

The bombs fell in indiscriminate patterns across the camp, each exploding with incredible force. The degree of chaos and confusion was like nothing Sam had ever experienced. Around him men who'd been hurt cried for help. The amount of smoke filling the camp made it difficult to see. Sam felt disoriented. The onslaught of firepower made it difficult to gain any sense of direction, and where there wasn't fire or smoke there was a constant, concussive attack on the ears.

Another incendiary bomb fell directly ahead of Sam, igniting the shelter it struck. The dry, wooden structures stood no chance against the fury of the ordnance. The sea of flames ahead stopped Sam in his tracks. The spy, for the first time in his life, felt *true* panic. No amount of skill could protect him here. To get through this was going to be blind chance—or was it fate?

Where is Lukas? Sam searched frantically, but there were so many bodies moving about the camp it was hard to tell anyone apart. He wasn't sure what hut Lukas had been taken to, or whether he'd been freed yet.

He maneuvered around another shelter, passing through a small alley in between two others that hadn't yet been hit by the bombs. The breeze became more forceful, and when there was a gap in the smoke, Sam reoriented himself with the large fence the men were still attempting to scale. Above, the number of bombers only seemed to grow—the stream seemed endless. Every bomber seemed to be dropping their payload on the camp below.

"*Geh wieder rein!*" a guard yelled toward the door of a shelter. The men clamored around the door much in the same way they had among Sam. They pried at the barred window, clawing and pulling and attempting to rip the very walls of the shelter apart, and then a thin whistle sounded through the air. The soldier looked up, and before he could even register what it was he was seeing, the explosive fell right in front of the structure and erupted in a violent blast. The attack killed the soldier instantly, and also tore the entire façade off of the structure. A gaping hole was left where the front wall had once been. Several of the men inside lay burning, many screamed, and the ones who'd been lucky enough to be toward the back of the shelter funneled clumsily out of the building. They stepped right over the bodies of their fallen mates—at that moment, it was kill or be killed.

Another bomb fell nearby, this one completely leveling another structure that, thankfully, had already been emptied. Then another landed near the fence line, this one engulfing everything in a house-sized radius in flame. The fires that had started inside structures began to rage, and soon the light from the combined flames dwarfed the ones from the flares. The entire camp was burning.

Sam heard a shot fired from his rear, then discovered a rifleman aiming at the men scaling the fence. A bullet struck one prisoner in the back, and the man fell from the top where the razor wire was. He had almost made it over. The soldier reloaded, then took aim again, but before he could fire the blast of a small bomb that fell to his rear slammed into him like an out-of-control car.

The level of panic was evidenced by one of the most horrifying images the spy had ever witnessed: several prisoners were pulling away the razor wire rolls from the top of the fence with their bare hands. Sam could see their bloodied limbs frantically yanking at the wire as if they'd become feral animals. Another group of freed prisoners formed a wave of bodies moving toward the fence, poised to storm it, among them two uniformed soldiers who had the same idea. In the chaos, even the jailers had joined in the escape.

There was one priority for every man present in the

nightmare: *get out.* The men grouped together against two of the posts holding the fence in place. They rocked both posts back and forth in unison, trying to pry the fence from its foundation.

Sam searched the camp again for Lukas. Bodies were silhouetted against bright light and smoke. Blasts disoriented anyone attempting to escape. Sam finally spotted the priest—he was the only figure frozen in such a peculiar manner that he stood out from the crowd. He was standing in the middle of the camp, his head tilted to the sky as the armada soared above.

Sam sprinted toward Lukas, swatting smoke from his face. He dodged another group of men heading toward the fence, one of whom knocked Sam with a shoulder so forcefully that the spy was almost toppled off his feet. When he finally reached Lukas, he saw the glazed-over look in his eyes, and the sheer shock of the weight of his actions embedded within them. The priest was witnessing hell on Earth.

"Jan!" Sam yelled, but the priest's hypnotized gaze remained unbroken. Sam grabbed his shoulders, then screamed again into his face, "Jan!"

Lukas turned to face him. He looked as if he'd overdosed on hallucinogenic drugs. His eyes were glassy and far away, but he seemed to recognize Sam standing in front of him.

"We've got to go!" Sam said. "Do you understand me?" Lukas nodded absentmindedly, and Sam all but threw him forward toward the fence.

The prisoners continued to rock the fence, the posts squealing and bending against their force, but the efforts were for naught. Another bomb fell right on top of the group, tearing the fence from its posts with ease and toppling it forward. There was an exit. Sam, Lukas, and many of the men lucky enough to still be alive wasted no time escaping—but avoided looking at the charred and dismembered bodies scattered about. Now they were on the move toward the forests beyond. Those were engulfed in flame and decaying rapidly.

32

Now clear of the camp, the prisoners dispersed into the wooded area north of Trassenheide. The final bombers at the tail end of the group were dropping the last of their payloads, and the frequency at which the bombs fell was dwindling. The forest grew dark as Sam and Lukas traveled north and separated themselves from the burning wreckage.

Lukas paused for a moment to catch his breath, and Sam followed suit. Yells echoed through the forest, both of friend and enemy. When the sky is falling, it is hard to tell the difference between the two.

Sam wiped the tears from his eyes. He had his sight focused in the north toward the blackness of the rest of Peenemünde. Beyond the pines, the siren wailed once more—the attack seemed anything but over.

"You're not leaving, are you?" Lukas asked Sam. Sam turned to face him, then shook his head from side to side. Lukas added, "Because you knew that man, and he knew you."

"Yes," Sam replied.

"Neither am I," Lukas said. Sam looked as if he'd seen a ghost. Why was that so preposterous? Only hours earlier, he *had*.

"Why?" Sam asked.

Lukas fixed his attention back toward the raging fire at the camp below. The images of charred men and screams were at the forefront of his mind—he could still see and hear them. He'd wanted to destroy Peenemünde, but not like *this*. This was not what he had expected when he'd acted to aid the Allies. Seeing it here, now, was far more devastating than the idyllic version he'd dreamt up. Who was dead now? Prisoners? Laborers forced to toil against their will? Why hadn't the bombs fallen on the manufacturing stations, or the test pads?

"This is part of my doing," Lukas said. "Those men back there—I signed their death warrant."

Sam seemed to understand.

"I'm going to head north," Lukas said, "And warn as many as I can."

Sam stepped forward, stuck his hand out, and the two exchanged a firm handshake. One of them needed to head back to Bern, but with Peenemünde in flames, what did it matter? Now they were just two men with recalibrated mission goals—goals that did not in any way involve Hank Brandt's SSD.

"I said you were a dangerous man, Sam," Lukas said. "You are a dangerous man—but also a *good* one."

"You too," Sam said. "You do what you can, then you get as far away as possible. You don't want to be here when the bombs stop falling."

With that, they were both off. Sam set off northwest, and Lukas northeast, both with the knowledge that was likely the last time they would ever see each other.

As Lukas traveled through the clustered pines leading northeast, he did his best to ignore the screams in the distance plaguing his ears. How had the RAF gotten it wrong? They hadn't destroyed *any* production facilities, or any structures with vital secrets hidden inside them. They'd attacked a prison camp, among which were innocent people, slaves forced to do the work the Nazis had forced them to. The target had been wrong, and many had suffered because of it.

Already the fog and confusion had spread upward from the attack on Trassenheide, seeping toward the housing estate and farther north still. How much might the smoke obscure the next target area? And where might that be? The thought of enduring another attack made Lukas tremble.

He felt dirt on his face, and was forced to keep wiping the hair from his view. He was breathing rapidly, his chest rising and falling in overtime. His skin was wet with sweat. The breeze danced through the trees in warm gusts. Lukas ran, then ran harder, until finally the sounds of chaos in the south dissipated and he was met with quiet.

There was not a critter in the forest who dared speak in the intermission. Though the silence was welcome, Lukas knew it was far from over. He was *sure*. If this had been the RAF's entire plan, it had been lackluster.

Thick patches of smoke clouded what the trees didn't of the view ahead, so Lukas squinted to get a better look. He heard the sounds of chatter, but still saw no one. He moved forward, knowing full-well that if he continued his course north he'd stumble across the housing estate.

Even with the uncharacteristically bright moon and the growing fire to the south, this part of Peenemünde remained dark. A blackout had been initiated much in the same way it did in Bern.

But the smoke cleared almost immediately, and it was then that Lukas found himself in a clearing where few trees existed. Not a single bit of ordnance had claimed the territory yet. He cleared the tears from his eyes, scouted the open area, and then witnessed his destination. The scene at the housing estate had not yet reached the state of bedlam Trassenheide had.

There were confusion-riddled faces among those present in the streets, many of whom were in a state of half-dress. Lukas had abandoned any need to try and hide, or to blend in. He was still in the enemy's clothing, the VkN uniform, so that provided the cover he needed. There was far too much commotion for anyone to be concerned with his actions, and furthermore, the smoke still obscured detail. Whether it was the marking flares or the fires, Lukas was unsure, but the thick haze had taken on a hellishly red glow that made the island feel unearthly and fantastical.

The street was wide and long. On each of its sides were neatly spaced rows of houses. Lukas knew that this was where many, if not all, of the project's scientists resided, and judging by the amount of women and children Lukas saw leave their homes, he deduced that families lived here as well. It was surreal to see it all up close for the first time.

Many had gathered on the lawns or in the street to gossip about what was happening south of their homes. Among the women and children were men of varying degrees of party dress. Lukas spotted several *SS* uniforms, a lab coat, and even some *Wehrmacht* officials recognizable by their brass decorations. Some of the men who'd met in the center of the street hadn't even seen fit to put a uniform on. Some were in pajamas. Lukas even saw one man who was currently in only his underwear. Peenemünde was beginning to feel less like a military installation and more like a family community.

A whining began, at first low in pitch and dull, and then as it grew louder, higher and more menacing. It was the air-raid siren, and it heralded yet another attack. Lukas had no idea how many waves of bombers would attempt their assault on the area, but he now knew there was going to be at least one more. He wondered whether he was standing directly in the next of the bomber stream's targets. To survive one attack with the ferocity the bombers had unleashed had been lucky enough— there was no way he'd be so lucky a second time.

No one panicked. *Of course* they didn't. The sirens happened all the time; Lukas had heard them himself on his previous excursions. Hadn't the residents heard what happened in the south, though? Or were they too far separated to be made aware? They were close enough to exploit the labor, but far enough to not know anything else?

The fire raged to the south, now taking with it the tall rows of pines that easily went up in flame. What had started as a targeted attack was now a fire spreading north as if in a race with the smoke preceding it. Lukas still saw no *Luftwaffe* aircraft. Fighters had been late to respond. The scattered effort and diversionary tactics of a combined American and British bombing run had apparently confused the German air defenses and probably sent them in a tailspin. Peenemünde had no worthy defensive response.

The siren screamed again, and yet the residents did not retreat. Lukas wondered why they hadn't sought safety in their bunkers. Anyone with a pair of eyes and a nose could see or smell the approaching fire from the south. Surely they had *some* type of shelter for those present. *It's because they don't think a housing area would ever be attacked*, Lukas thought. That was against the rules of engagement, the rules of *war*.

But as he gazed at the congregating residents, a quick, menacing flash of opportunity was presented to him, and it came in the form of another lone plane soaring low in the sky. The blanket of smoke and sheen of moonlight had morphed it, making it take on a different identity entirely. Rather than a plane, it looked like a demon with wings. As it traveled, the residents watched it let off the next marking flare.

All present gazed with intrigue as the flare burned brightly, then fell into the courtyard at the center of the houses. It was bathing the area in bright white light, different than the prior one that had marked the labor camp in red. There was no time left; Lukas had to do what he'd come here to do.

He stormed toward the congregating people at a brisk pace. It seemed more had arrived while he contemplated his action. As he ran, he started screaming. "Go inside! Seek shelter!"

At first, the residents all seemed to think this very peculiar, but Lukas imagined that as his features came into focus—his sweaty, dirty face and nearly charred clothing—they'd start to heed his words. "Get underground!" he screamed. Now he'd caused a panic, which was exactly what he'd intended. Thank God for the VkN uniform. Had he been in civilian clothing, someone might have just sent a bullet his way and silenced him.

Now people were screaming and fleeing, gathering their children and wives and husbands and collectively making their ways toward shelter. Lukas saw several people retreat back into their houses, and he warned them that it would not be a safe option. Some listened, some didn't. Several people funneled into what appeared to be a basement, and as far as he was concerned, that was acceptable. Anyone who hadn't listened to his warnings just yet soon would; from the northeast, another wave of bombers was fast approaching. Their mighty buzz cut through the sky like the brass orchestra of the devil himself. For all the stories Lukas had read about the strange behavior of people on full moons, tonight seemed to confirm all those fables. If there was ever such a thing as lunacy, it was here and now.

Lukas continued on his mission, now running through the streets like a madman and urging people to take shelter. Anyone who didn't know better might have thought he had lost his mind, but the approaching armada in the sky wiped away any doubt. The fleet was pointing right toward the housing estate, readying itself to loose its payload on all of these people, Lukas included.

Lukas ran in zig-zagging lines, screaming at the top of his lungs and choking through the smoke that was filling the streets. The moon was providing light where the flare did not, and the fires burning to the south were still working their way north. The bombers were nearly at the estate, so Lukas worked to funnel the last of the residents toward a place of protection. He'd done all he could. The fleet above had grown to become a dull roar, and it looked even bigger than the group that had attacked Trassenheide.

Now Lukas was alone. He'd worked so hard to ensure the safety of his enemies, the single most ironic experience he was sure to have had in his life, and now the housing estate was empty and quiet. A scream sounded from beside him—one of the men was holding a door open to a subterranean shelter. He'd barely heard it over the approaching bombers. The man, a scientist of some sort, was waving his hand in wide arches, signaling that Lukas should get in before it was too late.

Lukas sprinted toward the door. He'd been saved by the enemy, and the enemy saved by him. The door slammed shut behind him, and Lukas found himself huddled in darkness with a slew of residents packed into the underground shelter. Lukas closed his eyes, pressed himself against several other bodies, and prayed. Within moments, the bombs thundered again outside.

33

———

In the east, Sam heard the cries of panic. He shuddered to think that Lukas might endure another attack. The onslaught had been every bit as horrifying as he could have ever imagined. As he trekked through the forest at a good clip, he was reminded of Sigrid Lang's fears on the fateful night they'd shared in Karlsruhe.

"I can see the future of my home…" Sigrid had said. "The structures tremble with the screams of a hundred assailants from above. The city shakes at its core, one last unearthly scream before its prolonged silence. A thousand bolts of lightning strike it at once, each bringing with it the roar of thunder. It sounds like the beating of hell's drums. When the storm has stopped, there are only screams and panic. The sky burns with light, but not from the storm—it is from the fires that rage up toward it in protest. Mothers search for children in rubble, and they in turn cry out for their mothers."

He remembered her far-away gaze as she watched this scene play out in her brain as if on some dystopian projector. "There is a tower of bodies—all of which are unidentifiable—and it reaches into the heavens. It parts the sky, penetrating the clouds, but blocks out the sun. The city is cast in darkness, and all that is left is the tower of dead. They are faceless, and charred, and blackened. No one knows who they are… but *I* do. They are my friends, my family, and the people of this city. The bodies on the tower cry tears in such abundance that they overflow into the city. It's *tainted* by the storm that took everything. They are men and women and children alike. Very few make it out alive, and those that do shuffle like specters in the smoke and debris, lost and aimless and confused. They wade through the high waters from the tears that have flooded their city."

He recalled the justification of her sabotage and defection: "That is why I have done what I've done. When boys want to fight, they take the battle to the schoolyard. *Your* people are not innocent in this either. How many must die until there is surrender? The Führer has no intention of that, nor do his compatriots. They will take all of us with them, and what will be left? No man or woman or child should see what I have seen. And I believe that what I am doing is right—perhaps that is why you are here."

And perhaps it *was* why Sam was here. It was why he'd come back, why he'd done the bidding of Brandt, worked from the inside like a fine needle through thread to do what he could to undermine the enemy. Perhaps it was because at one point, even if he hadn't realized it then, *he* was the enemy. And perhaps it was why he was here, enduring the wrath Sigrid had predicted; he was searching like a predator for its prey, and his prey was

Lothar Eichler. His anger was renewed. Sigrid had been right, and now he would do the one thing that would bring him any sense of vengeance, *even* if it meant navigating hell itself.

The fate of the two men had seemed to be intertwined. Sure, their first encounter had been once of chance, but the second had been likely, and now if Sam found him this time, it would have only been inevitable. Where the Nazi secret weapons projects were Sam Abel was, and so too was Lothar Eichler.

Sam worried that he might see another wave of attack himself. There was no form of protection left. The bomber squadron had seemed to unload the ordnance indiscriminately, even if it was against the rules.

But were there any rules? Were there any true guidelines? Sam certainly didn't follow them, nor did Brandt or Ramm or Eichler or Sigrid or Whelan or Lukas or Combe or anyone else who'd been ensnared in the game they'd all been playing. The rockets certainly wouldn't discriminate between enemy or civilian, so why should the bombers? The rules had *changed*.

Sam finally happened upon a *Wehrmacht* barracks. It seemed the best place to find Eichler. Sam took the opportunity to seek cover behind the side of one of the buildings closest to him. Clustered in the center of the station was a grouping of older men. Many had white hair or were bald altogether. One of the men yelled loudly over the others, "Wir müssen mit Flak antworten!" They were a flak battalion. After an exchange of words, the bulk of the men took off in a double time north and, Sam supposed, were likely to man some stations. Sam understood why the location kept few defenses, but having *no* flak whatsoever meant the bombers could come and go freely. That would change if there was another wave.

A truck came careening around the far corner of the street, then sped down the center and dispersed the people. In the rear bed were a handful of armed soldiers. The passenger stuck his head out the window, screaming to the bystanders as the truck barreled down the road, "*Get in deine Schutzhütten! Get zu deinen Häusern!*" *Go into your shelters. Go into your houses.* It was quite the opposite of what the prisoners had been instructed to do. The siren screamed again. Sam sensed a shift in the level of panic in the streets—another warning.

The truck vanished as quickly as it had appeared. With the command, many of the people retreated to their homes, but some took off east. Where were they heading? The only thing east was the beach. Sam thought perhaps they were on to something—the beach wasn't such a terrible idea.

The whine of the siren died down, and the spy was left in quiet. The town had taken on a ghostly calm after those present started to seek shelter. A strong breeze swept through the open street, disheveling Sam's hair further and reminding him that he was drenched in sweat. If he hadn't felt the warm air earlier in the night, he might have thought it was a product of the fires to the south. The spy wondered if there was a hell, and if so, did it too feature the same hot winds?

Sam had no plan. Was he supposed to go knocking on doors and asking for Eichler? And what if the bombers came here—even if in error? Could he knock on a door to change plans and seek shelter? "Hello, my name is Sam, and I'd like to know if I can share your home. Never mind the fact that I'm an American spy." The idea was foolish.

He was still in the VkN fatigues, which gave camouflage. They had been very similar to the ones he'd worn in Pforzhiem. Just the thought of the forested town reminded him of Sigrid again. The imagery in his mind —her bleeding, her dying, the confusion in her eyes— reinvigorated him. How many opportunities would he get to be in Eichler's company again? What were the odds that he'd meet the man face to face, and if he did, would the conditions allow for a confrontation? If Sam was going to die here, he was going to take Eichler with him.

The spy allowed the mission to become personal. Brandt had warned him about that. He'd been warned that to allow the victories and defeats to sink into the soul would poison the well, and the burned man had been right. But what did it matter? Sam hadn't managed a proper escape plan, nor had his ally. The bombs were falling, and the operation had come to fruition in the grander sense. The mission was a success, and he could die content knowing that, but he felt apprehension that Eichler could still live.

Sam set off down the main avenue, searching through the dark windows of the buildings. He was accompanied only by the sound of his feet striking the dirt path. There were no insects chirping, no owls hooting—only the continued pummeling of the housing estate in the east.

The toasty breeze howled against the structures. Few men might ever experience such a sensation. Most often, a breeze was cooling, *refreshing*—the weather that had come to Peenemünde this night was anything but. It was an anomaly, a peculiarity that sort of felt as if it defied the laws of nature. It was as if a supernatural force had come to warn of the bombers' intentions.

When the air shifted, it brought with it tufts of the smoke from the south. Sam lost sight of the road ahead. After a few moments, the smoke cleared—that was when Sam saw the huddled-together men.

Three of the men were *Luftwaffe* officers, Sam could tell by their uniforms, goggles, and helmets. Several others were in civilian clothing, albeit armed. Their well-kept appearances led Sam to conclude that they were soldiers as well. The group was partially obscured by returning smoke, so Sam had to squint to see them. There was a man with a map in his hands, tracing it with his fingers as the other men watched eagerly. He was talking to them, giving instruction, but Sam couldn't hear well. The wind whistled around his ears and became the dominant sound in the environment.

Sam recognized the man's stature immediately. *Could it be?* Perhaps it was the height, maybe the man's build or his stance. Sam was sure there was something familiar about him. The spy continued forward, but now his steps slowed. It was if he'd been hit with an epiphany or some magnificent reckoning, and an internal voice that said *prepare*. Every cell in his body knew it. It was intuition, maybe *fate*.

Several of the soldiers spotted Sam's approach. They watched skeptically. Sam wasn't behaving in the fashion befitting of a soldier. In fact, any man who'd seen him and could recognize the vengeful, furious look in his eyes might be given pause. Sam behaved as if zombified. The man Sam couldn't see turned slightly. It was difficult for Sam to make out the features of any of them, but something about the man's visage told Sam he'd found what he was looking for. The soldiers alerted the man of Sam's arrival. That man said softly to his subordinates, "Go."

The soldiers scattered as the man folded the map up and deposited it into one of the deep pockets of his coat. Sam paused. The man stood there for a moment, his back turned to Sam, his head held high and his shoulders at attention. It was *him. Lothar Eichler.*

He wouldn't be hiding underground. No, he'd have to see it through. What had Eichler called himself? The Peenemünde *Sicherheitskapitän.* He was there to defend the facility until the last man fell.

His coat billowed in the warm breeze. He turned to face his enemy: the man who had had thwarted his plans not once, not twice, but *three* times now. The misty red haze outlined his dark figure in some unholy, spectral light and the cap covering his head cast his face in grim shadow. He removed the cap ceremoniously. Sam saw him, and he saw Sam.

For a moment they both just stared. Eichler didn't move, but rather turned his head slightly and squinted as if to confirm what he was seeing was real.

Sam didn't realize he'd grabbed for his knife until he witnessed Eichler's eyes move toward it. It was as if his brain had silently and sub-consciously directed his hand to his weapon—the assassin's instinct. His eyes now remained fixated on his enemy's.

Eichler stepped forward softly. The closer he got, the more his eyes flared with a reddish intensity reflecting the chaotic and burning environment nearby. Eichler stopped again, and Sam thought he saw a smile in the man's face.

"I knew they'd send you," Eichler said. He crossed his hands and folded them across his waist and stood proudly. His chest jutted forward, and his sharp chin remained elevated with pride. "It seems I have a recurring problem."

"Yeah," Sam said. "*Me.*"

Eichler drew a Walther from his waist and aimed it at Sam. The spy didn't have a firearm of his own. It had been taken from him during his capture.

Eichler lifted his head up toward the horizon behind Sam, scanning the bright night sky with curiosity. The uncharacteristic breeze whipped through the trees once more, then calmed. There was a rumbling sound in the sky.

Sam heard it too. It took him a moment longer than Eichler to recognize it, but the ominous groan of more bombers approaching grew louder.

"Another wave," Eichler said to Sam. "How many, I wonder?"

"Enough," Sam replied.

34

The sky was a bloody-red canvas of smoke and fire, and the landscape glistened with the macabre sheen of a pearlescent moon. Above, another fleet approached—the *third* wave. Standing directly below its path were Sam Abel and Lothar Eichler, both dark silhouettes staring each other down across the haze of battle.

Eichler tossed the gun aside. Sam was caught off guard—he hadn't thought the son-of-a-bitch had the guts.

Sam sheathed his knife. If he was going to kill Eichler, he was going to do it with his own damn hands, and if Eichler killed him, well, he would have to do the same. Another hellish breeze blew through the empty space between them, and with it came the smell of smoke and a stream of sparkling embers carried from the fires raging on the island.

The sound of swarming bombers grew louder still.

"By the looks of it, it's possible neither of us will leave here alive," Eichler called over to him.

Sam didn't know whether to pounce or flee. What does a man do when the thing he most seeks stands in front of him, all while the threat of annihilation approaches? Eichler looked up toward the northwestern sky, squinting to get a view of the approaching fleet. The sky became clouded from the smoke carried on the wind, obscuring many of the craft as they neared the island.

"He's dead, you know? The man you were looking for. Dead just like *her*. You would have done the same thing in my place," Eichler said. He lowered his head again to face Sam. "She was a *defector*. You might have had to do what I did should it have been one of your *own*."

He's right, Sam thought. Had it been one of his SSD allies, Brandt would have moved heaven and earth to capture the traitor. If they were lucky, perhaps they'd be put in front of a tribunal and left to rot behind bars rather than catch a bullet in the way Sigrid had.

"Then again, who are you? Does he know? The man with the burn scars? Does he know who you *really* are?" Sam's ears perked up at the suggestion of Brandt. "Yes…" Eichler began again, "Daddy has made quite a name for himself, hasn't he?" Eichler's eyes wandered to the approaching fleet. "I hear he's next on the *list*."

Sam gritted his teeth. His jaw stiffened. A rage was welling up inside his chest, ready to burst. Despite Brandt's unwillingness to tell Sam the truth, would the chief have unleashed his operator in this moment if he had been there?

Because it was Eichler who'd been the single

common thread. Sure, Brandt had blackmailed Sam into joining in on the action, but that was because Eichler had presented the threat. It was Eichler who'd drawn Sam back to the fight again and again—back to the fatherland. He'd killed Sigrid Lang, and he was standing before Sam right now.

Sam *had* to kill Eichler, not just to get revenge for Sigrid, and perhaps everyone else the mad German had trampled in his path, but also to protect Brandt, even if he'd lied to Sam.

Sam could feel the ground trembling beneath his feet. The vibration of engines buzzing in the approaching fleet was shaking the very Earth itself. Soon they'd let loose their bombs once more, and judging by the armada's direction, it was possible their target was the very spot both he and Eichler were standing on. In the distance, Sam witnessed several families fleeing through the streets and toward the forest. If Sam or Eichler wanted to get out of the path of destruction, it was now or never.

But neither man was going *anywhere*. Both sought revenge. Had the Führer himself been standing there next to them, Sam would have passed him by and gone straight for Eichler.

"It should not be me you blame for her death," Eichler began, "but *yourself*. She was free to leave, wasn't she? You had done your job. You had successfully escorted her from her home and sent her to freedom. But no, she came back for *you*."

The words sent Sam into a blind rage—he felt like a rabid animal. He leapt forward, his feet flinging forest debris in his wake, and Eichler braced for the impact. Sam dropped his shoulder when he neared Eichler, then speared him with all the force he could. The impact knocked Eichler to the ground, and Sam raised a fist and hooked his enemy in the jaw as soon as he had him pinned to the floor—Eichler responded with a fist into Sam's throat.

Sam fell backwards, knocking his head against the forest floor while he choked. He wondered if Eichler had crushed his trachea. But despite the dizzying sensation, he managed to catch his breath. Sam scurried backwards before climbing to his feet once more as Eichler pursued him.

Sam got his first good, close-up look at his enemy. It had been sixteen months since he'd last seen the man, and Eichler looked far healthier than the last time they'd met deep in the dark forests surrounding Pforzheim. Sam dared say he'd put on some muscle—the punch to the throat certainly felt like it. What was most different this time was the burning fury Eichler possessed in his eyes that he hadn't before.

Sam charged Eichler again, this time cracking him square in his nose with a sickening crunch. Eichler, far taller than Sam, delivered a fist straight to Sam's gut. Before the pain even registered, Sam hit Eichler once more in the eye, sending him staggering backward. Eichler pawed at the blood trickling from his nose, then checked the tips of his fingers with a snarl. He returned the favor with a jab that knocked Sam off balance.

It was as if Sam had forgotten all of his technique. He heard Shiner mocking him in his head. He was fighting sloppy, exchanging blows with the tall man in fits of anger that lacked any real skill or training. They were just two men hell-bent on killing each other through brute force. There was none of the resourcefulness Sam had used when he'd fought Eichler's animalistic lackey, Bär, or the ballet-like tactics he'd employed when he'd squared off with Ramm. In those fights, Sam had been trying to survive; in this one, he was trying to *kill*.

Now the whole area was groaning with the arrival of the bombers. They weren't far off. Their ordnance would leave only destruction in their path. The window for escape was closing.

Let them fall where they may, Sam thought. He was so close to Eichler now that if a bomb fell in their path, there was no doubt in his mind it would kill *both* of them. Death was not his aim, but neither was allowing Eichler to leave here alive.

Sam pressed forward again, and this time he threw a jab at Eichler's face with the swiftness of a professional boxer. It was a left shot, something he thought Shiner would have appreciated, and when it connected Sam was reminded of his missing pinky—pain shot through his hand. Eichler followed the attack with his own, hooking Sam near his kidney. In the ring, that was an illegal move, but Shiner had made it clear the rules did not apply in a situation like this.

Eichler had no art to his attack. Every bit of strength he had came from his size. He was much larger than Sam—not the largest man the spy had ever fought, but big nonetheless.

Eichler hit him again—this time with a hook to the eye—which made Sam see nothing but darkness from the left side of his face and screwed with his peripheral vision something fierce. Eichler grabbed Sam's collar with both hands while the spy was dizzied. He delivered a fierce head butt to Sam's skull—payback. Sam collapsed to the ground. Eichler wasted no time delivering a knee to Sam's chin a second later, sending the saboteur backwards to the floor.

As Sam fell, he caught a glimpse of the bombers in the distance. They looked like a community of birds traveling south for the change of the seasons. Their formation was of a "V" pattern, each fighter equidistant from one another and maintaining a collective course toward their destination.

Then Sam was yanked forward by his collar once more, and his face met Eichler's. Eichler retracted his fist, but before he could follow through, Sam delivered a swift kick to Eichler's knee that sent him collapsing to the floor and screaming in agony. Sam thrust a fist downward against the man's face, and the attack sent Eichler to the dirt floor.

Both men were breathing rapidly, gasping for air and panting, but the death match was nowhere near done. "*We're all ugly, all of us men,*" Sam had heard Ramm say. The statement had never been more true. They were just two ugly men, bloodied and dirty and heaving.

Sam saw the gun resting beside Eichler's body, and wondered why he shouldn't just grab it and shoot him through the eyes. Would Shiner have recommended that? Weren't there *no* rules in this scenario?

Sam dismissed the thought. He wanted to feel the life leave Eichler's body when he did the job, wanted to see the man reconcile that his death was approaching and that Sam was the cause.

Eichler rose to his feet once more, then squared up with two bloody fists. Sam did the same. Both men waited for the other to make the first move. They were running out of steam. The bombers were not. Had there been a bell present, it seemed both men would have been waiting for it to ring. There were no officials for this fight, though, and that meant that there was no referee to break it up now that it had gotten ugly.

"*When you're out there, there ain't no ring, no referee, no score cards. All's fair—ya'd best remember that,*" Sam heard Shiner saying in his head.

Above, the sound of the bombers had grown to a steady rumble. The thunderous blanket had covered the sky, each of the aircraft reflecting the silvery sheen of the moon. Sam didn't dare turn his head to look, but he was sure there were hundreds. Hundreds of bombers brought thousands of tons of bombs. The chances of making it out alive were slim. He didn't care.

"The time for escape has gone," Eichler yelled. He wiped a thin streak of blood from the corner of his mouth, then revealed his teeth like an angry hound. His teeth were smeared with a wicked red glare instead of the normal bright white. There was red *everywhere*—the fire was red, the markers the RAF had used were red, the blood dripping from both of the men's faces was red, and in the distance, a red Nazi flag billowed in the warm breeze. *Sam* saw red.

A thin whistle sounded from behind Sam, and against his better judgement, he turned to look. Even in the blackness of night, he could see the projectile falling from the cargo doors of the plane and making its way to the ground below. Then another whistle followed, and another. The third wave had begun.

A concussive blast sounded from behind the spy, and with it a fireball ripped through the forest, completely disregarding everything unlucky enough to be in its path. The fire climbed into the sky, and when it had finally engulfed everything in the vicinity, a pillar of black smoke rose as if a signal to mark its success. Sam turned back to Eichler, who also had focused his attention on the beginning of the raid, then resumed his glower at Sam. Sam rushed forward again, and both men clashed like angry wolves, grunting and growling. It was a ferocious meeting of fierce blows and sloppy grapples.

The fight continued with the same lack of finesse as it had started: bone met bone and blood sprayed into the air as each man did his best to crush the other through sheer force. Sam took a fist to the cheek—the same cheek that had given him trouble all this time. Had it been broken yet again? The attack only served to enrage him further. It made him think of Sigrid, and *Erdschlag*, and Brandt and everything that had been a part of this mess he'd gotten himself into. He blamed Eichler for all of it.

Another whistle followed, but this one was closer than the last. A bomb fell right on to the structure to Sam's side. The home was completely razed in a matter of seconds. Wood and brick collapsed like thin tissue and the impact sprayed earth and debris on Sam and Eichler. Before Sam could even register what happened, another fell just ahead onto a building flanking the avenue. It took with it the entire exterior wall, leaving behind only a gutted cavity of flame and smoke.

Eichler took the offensive this time, slamming a fist into Sam's chest that sent him tumbling backward. Sam felt sloppy. He'd defeated better men than Eichler, but he was still leading with anger instead of technique.

Sam swung a left hook that connected with Eichler's face, and a searing pain traveled through his hand like an electric shock. A red tear welled up at the corner of Eichler's eye. *Maybe I've broken a bone in your face*, Sam thought. *Just like you did to me.*

One more whistle sang, but this one ended in a ball of fire that hit the fountain at the town's center. It was a plume of fire: an incendiary weapon. The warm blast knocked Sam to his feet, and he rolled in the dirt while trying to get away from the heat. Sam raised his head, then spotted Eichler grabbing for the gun.

"This has gone far enough," Eichler replied through desperate pants. Smoke wafted in the breeze. The air quality was quickly becoming unbearable for both men. Eichler aimed the gun at Sam. Sam's enemy was cheating, but as Shiner might have suggested, there *were* no rules in this ring.

Another blast followed. Sam looked to the noise—a cracking sound—and watched as a massive pine began to bend at the root and start to collapse. Eichler saw the action too, and both men scrambled to get clear of the zone of destruction where the mighty tree would fall. It landed with a loud crash right where they had been standing, and Sam rose to find he and Eichler had been separated by it.

Sam searched frantically for his enemy over the flaming pine, but he'd lost sight of the man. Another bomb landed in the street, and Sam ducked for cover behind the hefty pine once more. The explosion tossed debris toward Sam, but the thick trunk shielded the spy from the blast.

Above, the fleet painted the black ocean in the pattern of RAF fighters as if someone had wallpapered the sky. Silvery crimson glows traced the outlines of each of the bombers. The sounds of explosions and roars of fire sounded from every direction. Soon there'd be no buildings left to speak of.

An incendiary bomb smacked the roof of a structure with a violent thud, and out of the home ran a family consisting of a mother, a father, and three children—*all* of them were burning. Flames curled around their bodies, and the fire spoke so loudly they made the screams of the family almost inaudible.

The scene nauseated Sam. Of all of the chaos the spy had seen in his life—all the pain, death, and destruction—few things had been worse. The scene was the visualization of exactly what Sigrid had imagined when she'd told Sam her fears that fateful night before she died.

The whistles had grown to a symphony of haunting tones conducted by the planes above. The hellish landscape only grew redder with every bomb that landed, and soon there was hurricane-like conditions of black soot whirling around the center street and obscuring the landscape. Sam looked for Eichler once more, but he only found flame and smoke.

Sam heard the click of the gun behind him, then turned to face the man holding it. Eichler said, "Nothing will ever undo the difficulties you've caused for me." Sam thought of his next move—he had nothing. Eichler was too far away. The gun would make quick work of the spy. "You've set me back on numerous occasions and derailed me at every angle. Nothing will bring me adequate satisfaction. Vengeance will have to do."

Sam considered rushing him. He was staring down the barrel of Eichler's gun. Would he take a bullet in doing so? Probably. As he stepped back, he bumped against one of the charred trees. An ominous whistle sounded from directly above—this package would land on top of them. There was a divot beneath the trunk and the ground—Sam could slither under it. Sam considered Shiner's advice: "Ya can't just haul off and start sluggin' a man when you've got the fire in ya—you've got to let him beat himself." Rather than move for Eichler, Sam retreated beneath the tree.

Before Eichler could shoot, an incendiary bomb dropped in front of his feet and spewed a blast more massive than any of the others Sam had seen yet. The explosion spread a plume of fire marbled with black tufts of smoke. The impact sent Sam flying beyond the protected side of the pine. Eichler's entire body flared— he'd become a pillar of fire.

Sam felt the heat immediately, and wondered if the damn bomb hadn't melted every single hair on his face. When the fire from the blast cleared, he rose to see the result. Eichler ran flailing from the scene like a phoenix flapping fiery wings. Sam heard him screaming. It was an unearthly cry, the desperate and pleading wail of a man whose body was nothing but flame. Soon Eichler's features couldn't even be seen; he was just a mass of fire and smoke in the shape of a human torso. He reached toward Sam as if to beg, and then collapsed in a pyre onto the dirt.

When the fire subsided, Sam noticed Eichler's skin was charred and burned like an overcooked piece of meat. His uniform had melted to his body completely, leaving behind a blackened mass of melted man and cloth. A large trail of smoke rose from his corpse, and Sam breathed a sigh of relief—even if it was through choking breaths—that his enemy, the man he'd sought revenge on for so long, lay dead in the street opposite him. Sam thought the punishment was fitting.

Sam stood there for a moment as the fire burned through everything it could. His eyes teared in the smoky street, and though he was struggling for air, Sam allowed himself a moment to watch his enemy sizzle. The hellish breeze whipped through the street once more, this time wafting with it the smell of burnt Eichler. The stench was abhorrent. Brandt had once asked Sam, "Have you ever smelled a burned body?" Sam had not. Now he was sure that Brandt hadn't been lying—it was one of the worst odors Sam had ever been subjected to.

What would Sigrid say? Would she be happy the man had died in a way befitting of his transgressions, or would she feel shame it had been in the exact way she'd warned would come? Sam wondered if he'd done her memory proud. It didn't matter anymore; both she and Eichler were gone.

Sam looked above to the sky—the bombers were still coming. Now all that was left was a town of burning structures and the dead bodies that had once inhabited them. Sam could see fire in every direction. The tall pines flanking the village and standing as a barrier to the beach area were going up like tinder.

It was over. Eichler was dead. Sam thought it poetic that the man should die in a city of his own creation, among the weapons he had championed. Eichler had felt the pain he'd intended for others to feel, and Sam was satisfied the man had suffered an agonizing death. Had Eichler lived, how many would have had to endure a similar fate?

Sam may have harbored some resentment toward

Brandt for not clueing him in to his nemesis' presence at Peenemünde, but the smoldering cityscape surrounding the spy made him consider that Brandt had kept Sam's best interests in consideration. Few would survive this night. How the hell Sam would escape this war zone, he still didn't know.

35

S am searched for a route of escape. The mists of death and destruction seemed to populate almost every direction, but ahead and to the north, the coast was still clear. It seemed none of the bombers had yet chosen the upper parts of the island as their target.

He considered the idea of moving toward the airfield and taking a *Luftwaffe* pilot hostage and forcing him to fly at gunpoint. It was desperate, and reckless. It was also preposterous. He wasn't thinking clearly, and now with Eichler dead, escape was foremost in his mind.

The moon was his key. Could he head northwest and make his way into Denmark? What about the land to the north, Rügen? How hard might that trip be? The southern tip of land that would take him to Rügen was only a couple miles north, but he wasn't confident he could swim that distance, especially in the middle of the night. He was also exhausted. Amidst the raging sea of fire rising in almost all directions, he found it difficult to think.

He decided to trek north—the smoke from the south was steadily creeping toward his location. It seeped through the pines, covering the land in large clouds that were still making it difficult to see. The bombing had ceased for the moment, though the spy had no clue how long that would last. He knew no details of the mission or the amount of ordnance the RAF still planned to drop on the community. For all he knew, many bombers were still on their way. Above, he heard the whine of fighters searching the sky for targets —German fighters. They'd been scrambled. Now they were climbing and diving, darting and circling. The rattle of automatic fire came from the planes in battle above.

In the south, the fire only seemed to grow, now spreading across the island rapidly and engulfing anything in its path. Explosive weapons in addition to incendiary types was a smart move; blast what you could and burn the rest. He kept to the forest as he traveled. He might be stuck in Peenemünde and risk being captured once more if he didn't get free of the area. If he remained nearby, he could be spotted when the fires subsided and rounded up with any British survivors and thrown back in the camp—whatever was left of it.

Maybe there'd be a dingy or a rowboat in the north he could use for the rest of the trek. Sam had to be honest with himself: it was a terrible plan. Heading south was a *worse* plan, though, so he double-timed his step toward the airfield. Perhaps the area would be clear now that the fighters had been dispatched. He wasn't worried about encountering enemy soldiers along the way—anyone with half a brain had likely sought shelter at this point.

As Sam sprinted toward the airfield, all he could hope was that the bombers en route were not targeting his location. He didn't dare look just yet. His body ached. His lungs were burning and his eyes stung. His left hand throbbed. Blood was seeping through the wrapped cloth. At this point, escape was a roll of the dice.

He heard the whistle of a bomb falling, then another, and another. The thunderous crashes rumbled against the ground under his feet. The flares from the bombs ahead lit the path. He looked up to the sky, which was still glowing, and recognized the silhouettes of low-flying Lancasters traveling south and right toward him. There was no safe direction to run.

He'd never witnessed a sight quite like it. There were so many aircraft he thought them capable of sinking the whole island into the ocean itself. After another minute or so of running—right *toward* them—the explosions were now in his immediate vicinity. A *boom* ripped through the trees at his side, splintering wood and pine into his face. Another followed from the opposite side, and with it came a violent burst of dirt and bark that obscured his view and smelled of death and earth.

He looked above once more and saw the orange flashes of tracer ammunition tearing across the sky and heading toward the Lancasters—the *Luftwaffe* had found their targets. A buzz above his head grew loud and unbearable, and he looked to the source to see a *Luft-waffe* plane—he wasn't sure what kind—pass *right* above his head. He heard the loud clatter of the plane's guns, and watched as it fired directly into the belly of the British plane above it. The plane was so close it made Sam feel as if he needed to dive for cover.

He wiped the muck from his view, a mixture of sweat and dirt and soot, then squinted to look for his target: the airfield wasn't far. He could see structures through a clearing in the trees, and beyond that the sea. The bombers ahead were still soaring in large numbers. He felt the heat of the flames, and with every breath he inhaled the noxious chemicals of burned materials.

A cough had developed deep within his chest. His pace mixed with burned *everything* in the air was taking its toll on his lungs—though the cigarettes hadn't helped. A blast pummeled the forest floor ahead, tearing several trees directly from their roots and causing them to fly away like bowling pins being struck by a well-placed ball. The fire spit directly toward Sam, forcing the spy to an abrupt stop against a nearby pine. If this got any worse he might come home looking like Brandt.

The weapon had incinerated a large circular patch of forest and left an inferno in its wake. Sam changed his course to one bearing more west—there was no getting around the flaming fence that had formed.

The engines of the bombers above grew louder still, now humming above his head like a colony of gargantuan bees. The better number of them were low in the sky—they couldn't have been higher than roughly six thousand feet—and some were even lower than the majority, maybe even four thousand feet or less. Sam had never witnessed an armada flying so low for an attack. It was uncharacteristic, and probably meant the British meant *business*.

Another Luftwaffe plane—perhaps a Junkers— zoomed above Sam's head from the south heading north. The German fighter was picking off his enemies from below. Sam heard the distant *clang* of a bullet pounding the belly of the British aircraft above, and soon a burst of flame erupted from the engine, followed by a billow of black smoke. The German fighter banked west; he was taking a loop to return for more action. The Lancaster above descended east along the tops of the pines, then Sam lost sight of it.

The whistling became near-infinite, a chorus of tones competing with each other as the weapons descended from the bombers above then echoed across the forest floor in a ghostly symphony. With every landing, each of the bombs exploded like a crescendo to their musical approach. The assault was coming toward the end of the concert. The supply of bombs wasn't infinite.

The horizon flared as the attack continued. Sam likened it to the proper end to a magnificent fireworks show, and unfortunately he had a front-row seat for this particular one. Each bomb that exploded lit the trees with a strobe-like effect bright as a summer day.

Sam sprang from his heels and tore through the trees again. He was going to continue to head straight on against the approaching fleet. No man on two feet would be able to avoid the attack in any intentional way, and so Sam just fixed his eyes on the airplane field ahead and moved with every bit of speed he could muster. He was running faster than he'd ever run in his life.

The spy's estimate of the distance left when he'd initially left for the airfield had either been wholly inaccurate or he'd just moved *that* fast. He thought the frequency of the bombs had slowed. Perhaps he had a chance after all.

A bevy of people materialized from in between the trees, heading straight for Sam. The smoke had obscured their point of origin initially, but a gust of air revealed a large building—and still more people. Sam recognized the uniforms of the men: these were *Wehrmacht* officers. They were disheveled; some were missing boots or shoes and some their pants or shirts. Alongside them were women and children, presumably their wives and kids, and many were still in their nightgowns or sleepwear.

Some took note of Sam. He recognized the curiosity in their eyes, since he was running *toward* the attack. A whistle, louder than the others, emanated from above the building, then pounded it with the force of God's fist. A *boom* rippled through the forest, tackling several of the people still within its range. Sam paid it no mind, but rather continued forward toward the site of the chaos. What were the odds a bomb struck the same place twice?

A second later, Sam was left with no clue what had hit him. He was disoriented and dizzy. He shook his head, and with it a cloud of dirt left his hair. It was then he realized he was on the ground and lying on his side. He couldn't see straight. The world was spinning and tilting and so was his body.

Once he recognized that he was awake, and furthermore, what had just happened, he realized he couldn't hear anything. There was a ringing—not painful, but disorienting. It was thin and slight and seemed to come from within Sam's brain itself. The base tones were still present. Sam could feel the vibration of the ground below him as bombers continued to punish Peenemünde.

He tried to rise, but the concussive force had made his body weak and flimsy. He crawled to his knees, then looked around to gather his whereabouts. What the hell happened to *north*? He was spinning in drunken circles, searching desperately for a landmark to point him in the right direction.

Sam heard screams from nearly every direction. Many people had not been lucky enough to make it to a proper shelter. The spy glimpsed a man, a *Luftwaffe* engineer judging by the color and cut of his uniform, who was missing most of the hair on his head. Much of his uniform had been melted to his body and he walked aimlessly, *zombie-like*, through the forest as if he'd suffered some type of debilitating concussion. He probably had. Smoke was still lingering in his wake as he traveled back south.

Then, a mother pulling two children in each hand ran past his view. She was speaking rapidly in German, and the children were crying, but Sam couldn't make out the finer points of speech over the roar of destruction. The mother had wrapped both children in wet clothing; Sam could see the dark colorations of wet linen and the steam that lifted as they traveled. Tears streamed from each of the children's faces, likely both from the abrasive smoke and fear.

Sam watched the family navigate debris. At first, Sam thought they had likely just dodged some brick or wood that had been blown from the blast. Upon further inspection he recognized a man's torso. Nearby and scattered along the dirt were the rest of the man's limbs: a leg and an arm.

Of all of the damage that had been done, it was the farthest point south, Trassenheide, where the fires seemed to burn the grandest. Dark tufts of smoke billowed into the sky, carrying with them thick ash. The breeze had carried the smoke north for the better part of the last half hour, and Sam wondered whether the RAF had to contend with the elements and if the obscured geography had made their attack any more difficult.

Sam felt pain *everywhere.* He didn't dare look for the sources of his injuries just yet, but did a quick once over when he was on his feet to be sure that he wasn't losing blood. Satisfied that all of his injuries were surface-level and that he wasn't going to bleed out, he steadied himself and attempted to wipe the soot from his eyes. Both eyes teared like leaky faucets, and his nine knuckles were covered with moist, caked ash before he could finally see clearly.

Above, he heard the whine of a plane's motor—it quickly devolved into a scream. At first the spy was concerned more bombers were on the way, but when he raised his head to look, he spotted a British Lancaster spiraling down toward him. The plane dove further, now picking up speed as flames shot from in between both engines on its left wing.

He fell before he'd even made it several steps and found himself with a mouth full of dirt or ash or whatever had covered the floor. The entirety of his body felt like one gigantic bruise. He may have survived the incendiary elements of the assault, but he had still felt the punishing effects of the bombs. He rose to his feet once more, trying his damndest to filter out the pain as he attempted to escape the scene, but no amount of mental conditioning was going to help push him through other than to just endure it.

The plane above screeched, and he took inventory of its location once more to make sure he was on the right path. Above, he saw the black mass crashing through thick smoke—it was right on top of him. The plane slammed into the forest floor behind him with a sickening crunch of metal and glass. The blast followed, an explosive fireball that pushed Sam forward and knocked him face-first to the dirt yet again. He felt the heat at his back. Flames were spewing from the fuselage. The screams of the men inside struggling to get out of the plane came soon after. Some had not gotten the opportunity to ditch the aircraft via parachute.

Sam attempted to lift himself from the ground, but now struggled to do so. A sharp pain snaked through the back of his left leg, and when he attempted to put his weight on it, the pain became unbearable and he fell yet again. A quick glance at his calf reveal a shard of mangled metal protruding from the muscle. Panicked, but sure it had not hit any major arteries, he pulled the jagged piece from his leg with a nauseating squish. Blood poured from the wound, but he ignored it while he continued to flee the wreckage.

Another barrage of heavy gunfire sounded from above—once, twice, then three times. Sam rolled on to his back and saw black smoke trailing from another Lancaster's engine. Following closely behind was a German night fighter riding its tail. The plane stuttered, then banked, then the German fighter gave its enemy one more package of bullets before the Lancaster went into a violent spiral toward the beach. Sam watched as the plane fell, and then after, he heard a distant *thud*. A plume of fire rose behind the column of pines that walled off the beach area.

What was left was only the crackle of burning trees and structures and intermittent gunfire in the distance. Red and green hues from the bombers' markers decorated the landscape where fire had not touched—and there was very little it hadn't. On the horizon, silhouettes of pines that had not been torched were quickly engulfed in smoke.

The bombers turned slightly over the Baltic, and the German night fighters followed in close pursuit. Those bombers unlucky enough to be in the third wave would still have to contend with the pesky German planes as they traveled back home.

A final hellish breeze whipped across the island. In its arms it carried glowing ember and flame. However, the bombing had ceased. Sam was alive.

36

Brandt stood in the courtyard at *Edelweiss* with his eyes set to the north. He'd gnawed his pipe beyond recognition, and where the tip met the wood one could find shredded plastic that had endured the fury of an armada of teeth. There wasn't even any tobacco left in it. Brandt had run out while awaiting the return of his operators and hadn't been able to seek out more. Travel within Bern was—for some time—out of the question.

There were no phones at the safe house. Whether or not the RAF had achieved their mission was still unknown. A lockdown protocol had ensued temporarily for Americans in Bern "in-the-know." Phil was recruited to gather as much information as possible—true or false —from the front. Brandt needed to know. He'd already learned about Ramm's death, as well as the demise of the defector's minders. It was that news which had triggered the shelter-in-place message. Brandt assumed the men who killed Ramm were the same who'd made the attempt on his own life, and now they were dead too.

A table in the sitting room was host to the injured Louie. The bullet he'd taken had shredded his shoulder and torn clean through his clavicle, shattering it in the process. He was conscious, in a lot of pain, and lucky to be alive. Had the bullet traveled a bit lower, it might have punctured his lung.

Hugo had managed the kid's pain with a bottle of his homemade rice liquor. Fittingly, Gale had been the one to tend to the wound—being the meticulous examiner that he was—and it was of his expert opinion that true medical attention should be sought out soon. He'd cleaned the wound, removed the bullet and splintered bone fragments, ensured the injured party was as comfortable as could be, and determined that nothing of vital importance had been damaged. Still, he said a qualified doctor should examine the wound for better accuracy and also formulate a plan of care management. Edelweiss was home to few medical supplies and certainly no antibiotics.

Ansel Combe mourned the loss of his station on a small moss-covered bench resting at the corner of the courtyard. The area was spotted by pinholes of moonlight that trickled through the large tree above. Earth's satellite glowed vibrantly on this cloudless night, outlining the professorial man in silver. Beyond, the Alps towered above the sky like judges sentencing the poor Combe. Brandt was struck by just how grim the whole scene was. The occupants of the home spoke sparingly.

Brandt hadn't moved from the back porch area overlooking the courtyard; the vibrant platform of white stone provided ample light on the bright evening. He'd been out there for hours now, pacing nervously in wide lines from one end of the granite to the other. His feet were cold and wet. There was dew on the grass and the temperature had cooled considerably around the lake. He was in complete discomfort, yet he couldn't bring himself to stop pacing and he didn't have the stomach to look at the poor kid who'd taken a bullet for him. The guilt was still too raw.

The tobacco-starved Brandt witnessed Combe light up a cigarette, and he shuffled over shamefully to take the seat beside his Bern man. He waved a hand to request a cigarette from Combe. Combe, so in his own head and shell-shocked, obliged robotically. After both cigarettes were lit and the two men had taken several puffs each, Brandt cleared the silence.

"We've got more questions now, Ansel," Brandt said.

"Don't we always."

Neither man looked at the other; both just fixed their attention on the bold moon.

"You'll stay," Brandt added. "Both of the shooters are dead. It was me they were after, most likely, so we shouldn't consider you blown. Especially since neither can talk."

"We'll have to build it all up again," Combe said. "Thankfully, nothing of great importance went in the fire. Anything of value was already home."

"That's good," Brandt said, unconvinced. "I won't be back for a while."

"I know."

"I've got to get away from all of this—distance myself in case anyone starts asking questions. But hey, I've got you as an alibi."

Combe managed a soft laugh, then turned to Brandt, his cigarette cherry flaring in the wide lenses of his spectacles. He said, "I think you've got more to worry about back home."

Brandt groaned in agreement. "We'll have to rip this thing up from top to bottom. We've got to know if they were a step ahead of us."

"It's good to clean house from time to time," Combe agreed. "Helps to make the living environment more friendly."

"It's 'friends' I'm worried about."

Neither man was unclear about what was being implied. Someone in the SSD may have flipped, or had never been on the team from the beginning and had slipped through the cracks. Roger Fowler had likely been delivered up. Brandt could smell it. Both men sitting on the bench had probably been caught because the crumb trail had led to them and they'd given themselves away in the process. It made complete sense.

Fowler had been captured and Lukas had been followed, and while the spies were spying they too were being spied on—and they were a step behind their enemies. If Sam and Lukas didn't survive, well, make that two steps. So here they were, two men weeping about something they'd orchestrated gone wrong—two little men with big ideas.

They spent the better part of the night out there. Neither spoke often, and if they did it was to try to figure out where they had gone wrong. Both Brandt and Combe suspected the threat was back home in DC where information for plans was sorted, yet neither could be sure. Inside, the injured party was finally getting some sleep with the aid of a good helping of alcohol.

Late in the night, Gale fetched some food by stealing

eggs from a neighboring chicken coop. Going into town was out of the question. Besides, what good was a spy if he couldn't even pilfer an egg from a chicken? They did have consciences, though, because Gale replaced the value of the eggs in the form of Swiss Francs left outside the coop.

The group was unanimously confident of their safety at *Edelweiss*. Only those individuals present knew of its location, and if they hadn't been followed there, then the safe house was still considered safe. Had another attack been coming, it would have already happened. Brandt and Combe agreed that the first attempt on their lives should be kept entirely under wraps. There was no need to give the enemy the satisfaction of knowing they were right, and the SSD's failure to remain camouflaged while in Bern would only lead to controversy back home.

Phil arrived just as the dark finally went into retreat. The spiked pines decorating the mountainside were silhouetted against the blue morning dawn. He arrived not by car, but sweating and panting on a bicycle. All agreed it was still unsafe to travel in a car possessing flagged plates or familiar faces. When he finally dismounted the bicycle, he tumbled onto the grass in exhaustion, his knees buckling under the stress.

A hand shot up when he finally regained his composure, his back flat against the cold, wet earth. In his grasp was a brown envelope. Brandt double-timed his response and helped him up. The cyclist was breathing, perhaps even grinning, having realized he'd actually made it. Even Gale was in awe at the endeavor when he arrived at the patio, and he was no slouch himself. He quickly offered the courier water and a chair.

Brandt wasted no time decoding the message after

tearing off the top of its container, and as he set about scanning the letter everyone looked on in anticipation. What for, no one was sure. Perhaps just some shred of information that was a distraction from the current situation. Were these men supposed to revel in the achievement that the secret weapons project had been foiled by the RAF, bombed to high hell? Or were they to mourn the two operators who may have been killed in it, and assume that the third was already dead to begin with? It was hard to tell. Every man's face was a picture between the frown of concern and the arched eyes of hope.

As Brandt scanned the letter, his face seemed to almost droop in slow motion to the observers. He seemed to be holding one elongated breath, fearful of exhaling until he'd finally finished reading. His head rose, met every pair of eyes held firmly on him—even Louie was upright and listening in the window—and licked his lips. He owed them as much, this beaten, dejected crew.

"Finding for CE Brandenburg," he read. This was Brandt's Bern operating identity. "Please be advised an undertaking has been executed, confirmed by multiple reports, regarding a certain site "Finger"—Peenemünde's SSD code name—and its surrounding areas. Early reports confirm a success, but verification forthcoming. The following is a preliminary report: heavy casualties likely, successful targeting of crucial industrial elements highly likely, some early targeting error reported that was quickly rectified. Location still obscured by too much smoke for official investigation. Sortie intel forthcoming."

Brandt paused, glanced up again for a moment at the attentive gathered, then bowed his head briefly before resuming the letter. He'd just compromised top-level information to operators who weren't privileged to know, yet he didn't care. He trusted Combe, and he trusted Hugo and Gale, and The New York Boys and Lukas and Sam. He trusted all of them because none of them had goals of wealth or power or advantage. They weren't forced or blackmailed—well, perhaps Sam had been, but he'd become sainted. Rather, they were motivated by ideology, which generally made good operators bulletproof as far as reliability was concerned. Hell, earlier one had taken a bullet for the chief and looked like he'd live to tell the tale.

"Further reports confirm few losses proportionally on the queen's side. Resistance was fairly limited. Went off swimmingly, by early reports. How did it go on your end? All clear? *Tschüss*."

Brandt blushed. He hadn't realized he'd read that last word aloud. *Tschüss*, because that's how Iris signed off, which meant the report had come from one of the most reliable sources within the entire SSD. If Iris said it happened, it happened.

Brandt folded the paper reverently before tucking it back into the breast pocket of his long coat. A moment of silence followed, perhaps to mourn the missing SSD operators within the zone of destruction, and the lack of intel regarding how they had fared within this whole rotten ordeal. If this Bern team had been targeted, the likelihood that Operation God Finger was completely blown, or that its facilitators were *dead*, was high.

Ansel Combe broke the tension with a handshake to Brandt. *Because that's what we were here to do*, Combe seemed to be intoning without actually saying. *We were supposed to grab as much information as we could before the place was blown to high hell, and that's what we did.* The sun began to shine on the men in the courtyard. Then Combe turned to Gale and shook his hand. Brandt thought the scene bittersweet. He took Hugo's hand, which triggered handshakes all around.

In the north, Brandt thought perhaps he could see the glow of a distant fire. He was wise enough to know Peenemünde was too far away, but it hypnotized him anyway. In truth it was just the sun peeking up from the east and slashing a swath of light between two mountain tops.

Though over a year of intelligence had led to this moment, the celebration was short-lived. Brandt and Combe had made good on their promise to Lukas, and the site had hopefully been devastated. Within the next forty-eight hours Brandt could scrounge up a full report on the targets damaged and the outcome. It was a blow to the kidney of the German *Reich*, and all of it had been facilitated by a handful of men dressed as janitors, a farmer, and a priest.

When the news of success had finally been disseminated, there was a small break in the tension. Everyone started going their separate ways. Hugo went about brewing coffee and Gale tended to eggs for all parties. When the time was right, an attempt would be made to get Louie some proper medical attention. There was a doctor in the city proper on standby for occasions just like this. He was discreet and vehemently anti-Nazi, and therefore could be trusted. A house call would have been better so they didn't move Louie, but all agreed bringing the doctor to the home was a step too far.

Combe would put in some calls to his network—who were hopefully in contact with the two Polish janitors that had kicked off this whole escapade—to see if any information could be learned about Lukas or Sam. Given that all parties were under cover, and furthermore that they weren't aware of each other, he wasn't optimistic about a speedy outcome. Combe couldn't be sure the janitors were alive either.

Was Hank Brandt content with how the events had played out? One couldn't have guessed it from his expression, which was pained for the better part of the morning as he remained outside in the courtyard. His shoes had finally dried and the sun was shining, but despite the comforts the burn-scarred man remained stoic and unblinking as he stared at the mighty Alps. His mission had been compromised right under his nose, and this great victory came with the feeling of foolishness. No one dared speak to him until Gale finally offered him some eggs, but he declined with a grunt. It had been quite a long time since he'd slept. Perhaps he was still flying high from the attempt on his life. Events like that could kill appetites.

Once some medical attention was organized for Louie, Brandt would make his return trip home. He should have already had his feet on the ground in DC, but the prior night's events had derailed that plan. Brandt hated the idea that sending the kid out to a doctor would also serve as another piece of bait if anyone was still looking for them, but Combe had assured him they had to do it. Brandt would need to move very carefully until he was back on safe soil. It was agreed that Combe would continue to cultivate the network—albeit now from *Edelweiss*—until a new location could be found and vetted.

At noon, Brandt decided to go for a walk up an old

mountain trail that must have been carved out by the original property's owner. Combe suggested it was unwise, but Brandt refused to listen. He needed to get away from the house for a brief respite, and he figured a walk would do him some good. Gale and Hugo also protested, but who could stop a spy chief from doing what he wanted to do?

When he arrived at the summit of a lesser peak, he stared down at the city below. It was painted in a morning light that made it look as picturesque as the many oil paintings on sale in the city—or, more fittingly, those done by Udo Ramm. It was just another reminder of the great frustration he'd felt. How long had they been watched? It seemed so hard to backtrack now.

When he returned to the safe house, something on the home's grassy lawn grabbed his attention. Had he been blinking he might have missed it. There, peeking out from between a rock formation, was a lone edelweiss flower blooming in the early-afternoon sun. *Fancy that.*

AFTERWORD

Thank you for reading *A Taste of Vengeance*. If you've made it this far, you've probably already been on several adventures with Sam Abel. If you haven't, I'd recommend checking out the three prior stories that feature him: *A Whisper in the Oaks*, *The Shadows of Might*, and *Everywhere and Nowhere*. You can find all of those titles —including an additional novella about Roger Fowler called *Cold-blooded*—in ebook, paperback, or hardcover formats wherever books are sold. This is the sixth of many books I have planned for release. I'll be offering both stand-alone novels for those like me who like contained reads, as well as series for those who like to stick with a longer story. If you're enjoying my books, feel free to leave a review wherever you review them.

Normally this is where I give a bit of background on the story and its creation, but I don't have much to say this time around other than another thank you if you've been keeping up with my books. This was my biggest book by far, both in terms of word count and research.

It took me quite a while to crack this story and it went through many changes before I really felt I'd found it. It is the end to what I consider to be a loose trilogy, but certainly not the end for Sam Abel. Hopefully you want to know what happens to him just as much as I do. I know he'll be back soon.

ABOUT THE AUTHOR

Clarke Mayer is a filmmaker, photographer, and writer from New Jersey. Most of his day is dominated by a Black Mouth Cur named Pam who doesn't ever run out of energy. He likes to write, hike, and run, but most of all he likes to read and watch crime, spy, horror, and thriller stories.

www.ingramcontent.com/pod-product-compliance
Lightning Source LLC
Chambersburg PA
CBHW030918300726
48970CB00001B/223